THE WASHINGTON ADVENTURE

Stephen Michael Moore

Viv
Thank so much
for all your help
and support

SM X

click imagination

The Washington Adventure

Published by Click Imagination

This paperback edition 2015
ISBN: 978-0-9933926-0-3

For more information about this novel and the author,
please visit

www.clickimagination.com

For Mothers

Preface

The story of how Washington fell to the British doesn't begin aboard HMS Marlborough in the smokey, grand cabin of Sir George Cockburn, Admiral of the British Fleet. Nor does it start in Robert Banks Jenkinson's cabinet office at Downing Street. Instead, it begins in the now forgotten Parish of Tornbridge with a young, witless financier named William Peel.

You may ask yourself why it took over two hundred years for William Peel's ineptitude to make it into print or indeed why anyone would dramatise William's exploits at all considering that there are far more deserving, and considerably less ridiculous, historical figures who have vanished into obscurity. The reason is very simple. With the present Lord of Tornbridge's whereabouts unknown, Mayor Parsons, Tornbridge's most prominent figure, decided the time was right to set a few records straight – and in doing so show the world the kind of banality Tornbridge residents have had to put up with since 1729.

★★★

In 1814 Tornbridge was a partially independent autocracy within the British Isles and had been home to the infamous Peel family for almost a hundred years. By the late eighteenth century, the Peels were reputed to be the wealthiest family in the world. With banks, as we understand them today, being scarce, the Peels were a ready source of finance with very few questions asked - subject to favourable terms, of course. Secretly, the Peels funded Emperor Napoleon's campaigns in Europe, the copper cladding of the hulls of Nelson's fleet before Trafalgar, not to mention staking the odd theatre production and romantic novel. The Peels were, as President James Madison put it, the grease that kept the parts moving. Although he did later accuse William Peel of greasing some parts more than others.

Peel influence was never more prominent than in the spring of 1814 when Britain was at war with both America and France. Which side prevailed would be determined by their finances. Napoleon had been backed by the Peels from the start and in the spring of 1814 Sir Charles Peel committed further funds for The Emperor's long planned invasion of Britain. In exchange, the Peels would get almost a fifth of England and secure complete independence for Tornbridge. In truth, Napoleon only wanted Britain as a holiday home and once he had stripped her of her navy, he would give the rest to his brother, Joseph, as compensation for losing Sicily.

There was to be one twist of fate, however. One unforeseeable turn of events that would jeopardise Napoleon's plan. Sir Charles Peel, the adventurer, inventor and philanthropist, died of smoke inhalation on April 20th 1814, on the eve of his son's eighteenth birthday. The great manor house, and almost all of its priceless contents, were ravaged by a blaze that took all night to extinguish. William, Sir Charles' only child, suddenly took the helm of a business empire that determined world politics. Unlike his father, however, who was shrewd, clever, diplomatic and respected, William Peel was vain, pompous, and a constant disappointment to his mother. The thought of William being at the helm of anything bigger than a toy sailboat struck fear into politicians' hearts and caused emperors, kings and queens to rush for the brandy. William Peel may not have had the cunning of Napoleon or the courage of Wellington but what he had made him even more dangerous; he was a buffoon with the largest personal fortune the world had ever known.

William Peel, Lord of Tornbridge

The huge courtyard of Peel Manor had been tented to serve as a venue for William's eighteenth birthday party and was lined with furniture salvaged from the blaze. William was insistent that the party should go ahead despite Mother's strong objection to the fact that the guests would be eating off smouldering tables. It was to be his first decision as the new Lord of Tornbridge and, as far as William's decisions went, it was uncharacteristically sensible. The party would have been impossible to defer. The orchestra had arrived from Florence, the chef and his twenty strong kitchen staff had come from France, and one hundred and fifty pineapples were already being unloaded by the east gate.

The guests would be arriving at noon. Many had travelled days in order to attend and it would have been poor hospitality, not to mention unfeasible, to turn away kings, queens and emperors at the gate. True enough they would see the state of the house and realise for themselves that the bedrooms were likely to be very draughty, but there was nowhere else for them to go.

Despite the obvious practical complications of hosting such a grand party in what was little more than a derelict building, the preparations had run like clockwork. This was, in no small way, due to the months of planning and an element of fear in relation to William's temper. William, as many Peels before him, would happily take a riding boot to any staff whose performance needed improvement. Whatever the motivation, dozens of servants busied about the courtyard like an army of ants, fetching linen, decorating the tables and setting the chairs.

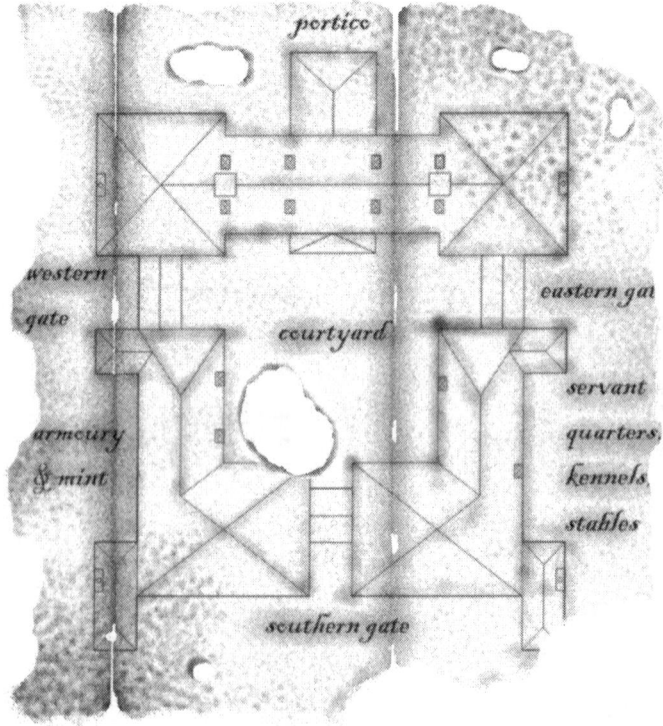

Only one of the two 'L' shaped annexe buildings to the rear of the manor remained intact. Rooms in the west annexe, which housed the mint and armoury, were utilised as kitchens. The east wing, which formed the servant quarters, stables and kennels, had been the source of the fire. The collapsing roof had taken the walls of the upper floor with it and by morning it looked more akin to a derelict abbey than a grand, neoclassical building.

Canvas sheets were supported using taught guide ropes secured to the facades that overlooked the courtyard. These would protect the guests and furniture from the unpredictable spring weather. The staff had moved what clothes and precious belongings they had salvaged of the Peels into the gatehouse which had become the Peels' new home. Although a substantial building in its own right, the gatehouse wasn't a suitable venue for the two hundred or so guests. The courtyard, however surreal it appeared with its half-burnt furniture and singed portraits, was the only practical choice. One stroke of luck was that all the wines and spirits for the party had been safely tucked away in the cellar of the manor and were completely unaffected by the fire. Once the servants had cleared the timbers and rubble leading to the cellar doorway it was a work of moments to bring the crates up to the surface. The other stroke of luck was that the two hundred-piece gold embossed dinner service, specially commissioned for the party by Sir Charles, had been secured in a vault in the west annexe. The silver cutlery and glasses were also intact as they had been locked away in the kitchen's strong room. A few had been affected by the heat but there were still plenty left to service the guests.

By noon, Tornbridge Road was a veritable traffic jam of highly polished carriages, many brandishing royal crests and all jostling to be first through the main gates of Peel Manor. The Bonaparte brothers, Joseph and Napoleon, had locked carriage wheels with King Ferdinand of Sicily. After a period of bickering out of their carriage windows they suddenly caught sight of the great manor house ahead and immediately fell silent. The grandest and most splendid house in all of Europe, if not beyond, had been reduced to charcoal in a single night.

Although most of the invited guests were long and loyal friends of the Peels, many were not so friendly with each other. The Bonapartes were, of course, unpopular with almost everyone. So much so that other guests often refused to attend Peel functions if the two brothers were invited. This was certainly the case for Wellington, the famous Iron Duke, who had declined the last two Christmas invitations for that very reason. His absence had been a particular disappointment to William as he really enjoyed Wellington's battle stories. Wellington had been William's favourite Uncle growing up because he had always made a fuss of him. William especially loved it when they play fought. For many years, Wellington had challenged William to punch him really hard in the stomach just to see if he could hurt him. *"It's iron, my boy,"* Wellington would chuckle, slapping his belly whilst blowing a smoke ring from his cigar. That was until one New Year's Eve when William's aim was a little low and caught Wellington square in his less than iron jewels.

Sir Charles' memorial service was held in the family cemetery, tucked away in the south-east corner of the Peel estate. It was, by all accounts, a somewhat peculiar affair as the illustrious guests had not packed anything remotely suitable for a funeral. Most had, no doubt, intended to out-dress each other in a shameless attempt to endear themselves to Sir Charles. They were all trying to look regal and dignified despite their jewelled heels sinking in the mud.

William Peel stood beside Mother at the graveside as the chaplain conducted the service. She gripped her teenage son's arm tightly throughout. The poet Byron, another guest in attendance, later commented that this wasn't out of affection, or for support, but to stop the dullard accidentally falling into the hole.

Mother, as she was affectionately known, was a matriarchal figure. The Peels had entertained many illustrious guests over the years, both for business and pleasure, and Mother was an equal to them all.

Unlike the average scrawny man of Tornbridge with his soiled leggings, ale stained tunic and wooden teeth, William Peel was a portly six-footer with a smooth, handsome face and an unblemished complexion. He would be described as chubby by today's standards but in the early eighteen hundreds it was a sign of health and wealth to be portly.

The birthday party itself commenced a little after two o'clock and despite the unusual venue, and the fact that the house was still smouldering behind them, the atmosphere amongst the guests was rather jovial. Mother's black mourning dress and veil was a striking contrast to the colour and splendour of the gowns, hats, jackets, and jewelled furs the fashion minded had to show. The place hummed with laughter and conversation. At exactly three o'clock trumpets sounded and the butler, Dobson, requested all of the guests be silent and upstanding.

"Your Royal Highnesses, distinguished guests, Lords, Ladies and Gentlemen," he announced, respectfully. "Lord Peel of Tornbridge."

William entered through the west gate to a fanfare and rapturous applause. He had changed from his bland mourning attire to a specially commissioned tunic and matching britches woven of pure gold thread. Around his shoulders he wore a windcheater trimmed with ermine and encrusted with huge jewels. The shoulders were so wide he couldn't fit through anything but a double doorway. Ahead of him strolled George, William's pet lion, sporting a specially commissioned gold collar and leash that matched William's outfit. The lion roared and the path ahead of William grew wider as the sound reverberated through the crowd. Which was exactly the desired effect. Mother's jaw locked when she caught sight of her son but not even her icy stare could temper the moment for William. He stood, regally soaking in the applause that was echoing about him. Just when his pomposity was it its highest, there was the sound of smashing crockery and shrieks as George broke his leash and bounded off through the screaming crowd at the scent of something edible.

As George vanished through the south gate, William tapped a glass above his head. All eyes turned on him as he took to a small podium. The guests watched expectantly as William then patted his sides in search of his speech. When it was nowhere to be found, he muttered the word "*arse*", then cleared his throat.

"You have brought great gifts to celebrate the occasion of my eighteenth birthday," he eventually began, in his customary dandy drawl. "I have decided, therefore, to share one of my own great gifts. I'm talking, of course, about the gift of song." A plate slipped from someone's grip and shattered somewhere in the crowd. William continued regardless. "It was Cleopatra who said that song is the one thing that distinguishes us from animals." He paused, sensing that wasn't quite right. "There are a few other things, I'm sure," he added, letting out a little laugh. "Hats, for one. And the love of a good cheese. Oh, and riding in hot air balloons!" Mother broke the stem of her wine glass.

William sang for a little over half an hour. Although a few more plates were dropped, presumably due to the reflex action of people covering their ears, no crockery was actually thrown. William Peel was not the most gifted vocalist and, where some accounts of the rendition were sympathetic, Architect John Nash said that he would have preferred to slide naked down a splintered banister rail carrying a vat of boiling tar than listen to more of William's insult to Mozart's work. It was Emperor Kokaku of Japan, though, who had been perhaps most scolding. In pigeon English, and using some inappropriate mime, The Emperor likened the noise to that of a man being violated with a dry Nasu (fruit of the Japanese Eggplant, which is about eight inches long).

After the recital had concluded, Mother backed William into a corner and, with her arms tightly folded, made it clear how displeased she was that he had abandoned the prepared speech. Setting aside the song, which the crowd was still feeling the ill effects of, William hadn't even mentioned his father's passing. William tried to justify his actions by saying he thought the speech needed an injection of tempo. This didn't convince her. Mother also pointed out that George, William's pet lion, had mauled to death Byron's horse, eating everything but its shoes. She was insistent that an apology and replacement horse would be needed. William vehemently objected, noting that two events would need to occur first. One, that he would have to lay a huge egg. Two, that the egg would have to hatch into a creature with the head of a bear but the body of a peacock. The bearcock, as William called it, would likely be flightless and possess an unpredictable temper. None of this made any sense, of course, and only served to raise Mother's blood pressure further.

"Bearcock?" she enquired, studying her son's expression with a mixture of bewilderment and anger. "You do understand the enormous responsibility that accompanies your title and wealth?" Tired of William's idiocy, she sighed and walked away.

"It's the fathead's perfume," said William, calling after her. "I should say Byron's got off lightly. We are in the mating season after all." Mother didn't look back.

Napoleon cornered William by a scorched Welsh dresser and questioned whether he enjoyed the shit that he put for him in a bottle. He meant to say ship, no doubt, but as he had sacked his inept translator earlier in the day, Napoleon had no choice but to conduct his own affairs.

"It takes from me a great deal of patience, oui?" he said, struggling for the right English. "The neck of bouteille is petite. Regardé?" He acted out how he held the bottle. "Un jour, le shit slip from my doigts... er... fingers. Napoleon's shit is delicate, oui?"

The mental image of The Emperor trying to force his poo through a small bottle neck was too much for William's sensitive stomach. "No, Uncle!" he said, fighting his gag reflex. "In Tornbridge we do not make presents of shits in bottles." He paused and decided to qualify the statement. "Well, perhaps the peasants in the village do, I will enquire about that, but certainly we Peels do not." With that, he cocked a snoot and strode away.

Mother, who witnessed her son abandon Napoleon so abruptly, stepped in seamlessly and apologised for William's behaviour stating it had been a stressful day for him on account of being up before eleven o'clock. She then began, with great dignity, to answer his question regarding the fire of the previous evening. The fire, she explained, had been started by Godfrey 'Samuel' Boyle. Samuel was the village idiot who had been employed by Charles as an act of charity.

William had become pretty fed up by hearing "*Yes, he was a good man*," and "*of course, you must come and stay with us at our huge palace.*" Deciding he needed some time alone, he made his excuses.

He was approaching the courtyard's southern gate when the butler, Dobson, intercepted him.

"Mr Parsons is here for his audience, sir," said Dobson. "He is waiting for you in the Chinese garden." William frowned. "The walled garden, sir," Dobson added.

"Ah! By the wine trees," William replied.

"If you mean the vineyard, sir, then yes," said Dobson, numb to William's stupidity.

"Yes, yes," said William. "I didn't know the garden was Chinese though. Just thought it was built badly."

"No, sir. That's the pagoda."

"Extraordinary! Oh well, ready a mount for when I've done, there's a good fellow. A cheroot is needed and enough distance from Mother to enjoy it." Without another word, William made his way through the southern gate and away up the path to his meeting.

It's fair to say that William didn't care for the Chinese garden. The path was too long and there were far too many unnecessary bridges for his liking. But then he didn't care for this man Parsons much either. There was something about the fellow's flat sided head that bothered William. Parsons was the lawyer who handled the family's more *complex* business interests. In theory, William had been well prepared for international affairs. This meeting was William's first without his father's guiding hand or, for that matter, the occasional prod in the ribs if he had dozed off dreaming of Gorgonzola.

As William made his way along the meandering path he caught sight of Mr Parsons up ahead. He was clutching his precious satchel as usual.

"My Lord," said Parsons, with a bow. "Congratulations on your birthday."

"Indeed," William responded, with a heavy sigh. "Not exactly the circumstances one would plan. Still, we Peels are made of stiff stuff."

"I'm sure you are correct, sir."

"Quite so," replied William, staring down his nose at the lawyer. "And see to it I get a direct path from the gate to here will you? It will save all that pointless walking."

Parsons, who didn't have the patience to tell William that paths were someone else's department, chose to ignore the question. "Napoleon has requested additional funds, my lord."

"Has he, indeed?" replied William.

"Yes, sir." Parsons caught William's blank expression and helped him fill in some of the spaces. "You are financing The Emperor's invasion of Britain, sir." The news took a few moments to soak into William's brain. "Sir?" enquired Parsons again.

"Yes?" said William, the information finally processed. "I'm just recalling my knowledge of the matter. Father and I spoke at length about it, of course." William would never admit he had forgotten something. "Tell me this," he continued, "as I've already dealt with many matters of high commerce this morning. Didn't we just give the British a wedge to help Uncle Ferdinand kick Uncle Boney off Sicily?" said William, referring to the King of Sicily, of course, and the fact that Tornbridge lent him money for munitions so he could extricate Napoleon's forces.

"True, sir. British control of the Mediterranean is at present to our advantage. When Napoleon controls the British fleet, however, it will be very different. Sicily will fall to the French once more."

"Ooops! Poor Uncle F. Hope he doesn't have plans to re-gild the fireplaces, what?" William chuckled to himself, reflecting on the irony. "Does Mother know?"

"She had your father's confidence on the matter, yes, but it's important it reaches no one else. The British live in fear of a French invasion and to hear one is being funded by the Peels might cause the Regent to view you in a less than favourable light."

"Strike us off the Christmas party list, you mean?"

"Undoubtedly, sir," Parsons quickly replied.

"Understandable. Tell me, is it a French tradition to bottle one's own dried turds?"

"I... I have no idea, sir," responded Parsons, taken aback. "Shall I make enquiries?"

"No, no. Just a thought. Pray continue."

Parsons took a moment to pick up his thread. "Shall I inform The Emperor that the funding will continue?" he asked, assuming the decision was a mere formality.

William pondered. The easiest thing to do would have been to say yes but, despite his father's enthusiasm for the deal, William had a nagging doubt.

"No!" he said, stiff backed.

"But, sir!" questioned Parsons, with genuine concern. "Victory in the Peninsular is poised on a knife edge if..."

"Then Uncle Boney should have thought of that before he started bottling his dung," said William, cutting him off. "No, it's crockery we seek, damn it, not clay and promises. Why, the man must go through a pair of shoes a day the way he drags his feet." He clapped his hands to indicate the discussion was at an end. "That it? Sparkling! It might take me an hour to find my way out."

William had already taken a few steps away up the path when Parsons coughed. "There is another pressing matter, sir."

"More business you mean?" enquired William, turning back with a sigh.

"Two very important guests, sir." Parsons glanced about to make sure they weren't being overheard. "Who have travelled far and at great personal risk to see your father."

"Should I care how far they've travelled, Parsons?"

"If you'll allow me, sir," Parsons responded, directing William's attention towards Peel Manor. "The subterfuge, as you will soon see, is entirely justified.

The President's Proposition

Parsons led William along the gravel path through the orchard towards the southern facade of Peel Manor. Ahead of them stood the two huge annexe buildings. The east and west annexes, as they were called, were joined by an arched entrance. The entrance, protected by a portcullis, led directly to the courtyard where the party was taking place. The stable block to the east, where the fire had started, was a blackened shell. The west annexe, which contained the armoury and mint, was the only part of the great manor that had remained intact. Parsons led William under the archway and through a small security door outside the portcullis. As they walked along the stone corridor, they could hear the sound of clattering pans in the makeshift kitchens housed in the armoury itself. Heading up the stairs and out onto a landing, they were immediately faced with a row of impenetrable looking oak doors.

The document room was lined with reinforced cabinets from floor to ceiling. The iron window shutters were closed and the room was dimly lit by only a handful of the many oil lamps available. In the middle of the room was a large partner's desk. William had to enter sideways through the doorway due to his ridiculously wide shoulders.

William and Parsons were immediately greeted by a gaunt, middle-aged man sporting the type of large forehead that is usually associated with intelligence. The man had been waiting expectantly and greeted William with an eager smile. He offered William his hand to shake but then lowered it at the last second in favour of a bow. William took an immediate dislike to his thin curly hair, which reminded him of a shabbily constructed bird's nest.

"William Winder, sir," said Parsons, by way of an introduction.

"It's an honour, sir," Winder responded, in a strong American accent. "Our country is indebted to you for your family's past generosity."

William watched as Parsons indicated to another figure in the room who was dressed entirely in black and concealed by shadow.

"And may I present James Madison, sir," Parsons said. Something in his tone suggested William should know who this man was and be impressed.

James Madison was about twenty years Winder's senior. He had a large nose and puckered lips. He bore an intense, austere expression that gave William to believe it must hurt him to smile. His bow was a little more than a nod of recognition. William wasn't impressed and immediately took to a chair.

"I'm sorry for your loss," said Madison, his American accent a little softer than Winder's. "Please forgive the timing of this meeting. I would have rescheduled were it not for the efforts of a great many people just to get me here."

William offered a brief smile then leaned back in his chair. He attempted to cross his legs but found his gold britches too stiff. "The accent?" he enquired. "Dorset?"

"America," replied Madison.

Madison took a large document from his pocket and placed it flat on the desk. It was the plan of a new city. Written across the title box was 'WASHINGTON – District of Columbia'. "Lord Peel," said Madison, proudly. "I present my country's vision."

"Vision?" William glanced briefly at the map.

"Washington is the new capital city of America."

"I'm happy for it," said William, trying again to cross his legs. "Is this leading somewhere, because it is my birthday, and…" He stopped, troubled by the crotch of his trousers. "What in the name of George's ball fluff is going on with these britches!"

"Likely the woven gold," Parsons replied, smugly. "It lacks the flexibility of more traditional fabrics."

"Oh! A tailor as well are you? You sarcastic ass!" snapped William, cocking his nose.

"My country," continued Madison, "is at war with the British. We have no regular army, therefore every able man is enlisted in the militia and…"

"Bit of an oversight that," cut in William.

"Sir?" Madison looked up.

"Starting a war without an army. Surely top of the list when one contemplates engagement. That and smart uniforms and so forth. Muskets too. Those with pointy knives on the end. What are they called, Parsons?"

"Bayonets, sir."

"Quite so."

Silence fell until Madison picked up his thread. "We need slaves to carry on the building work on the capital. It is a matter of national pride that the works be finished."

"If all this is true why doesn't your idiot President simply buy more slaves? Seems a perfectly obvious answer to anyone with more than peas and mash for brains."

Parsons let out a loud and uncomfortable cough before leaning into William's ear. "My lord," he said, privately. "Mr Madison *is* The President of the United States."

"No, no!" William objected, in the strongest terms. "It's Jeffry something. Jefferson!" he said, with a click. "Yes, that's him. Lovely man. Gave me, oh, what was it? Yes, paints, and a book of birds."

"President Madison," said Winder, "is serving his second term."

"Really?" responded William, reflecting a moment on how time flies. "Good lord. How are things going?"

"We're at the brink of financial collapse and at war with the most powerful empire on earth."

"Yes, still, at least you have a house. Look what I have. An inexhaustible supply of charcoal and a singed lion."

"Tell me, Mr President," asked Parsons. "How do you intend to pay for these slaves if America has no bank?"

"Yes," cut in William. "I was about to ask that."

Madison paced the room, his eyes glancing to Winder for reassurance as he contemplated his next words. "I'm authorised to offer you land. Some considerable acreage in exchange for increasing our existing debt obligation and providing additional slaves."

William let out a laugh and slapped his palm on the table with excitement. "Mr Mandleson," he said, oblivious to the fact he had got his name wrong. "You think me an ill prepared fool? Need I remind you of the great Yaboo affair?"

"Yazoo, sir," Parsons corrected.

"One of the biggest frauds ever witnessed," continued William, not missing a beat. "The Peel fingers still feel the burn."

Madison let out a sigh. It was a fact he could not deny. The legislature had sold twenty-million acres of land in Georgia only to later dispute the ownership. Investors, including the Peels, lost a fortune.

"You have my word," said Madison, proudly, "corruption will never again happen in the United States."

"I couldn't give a monkey's ears!" said William, with a chuckle. "We Peels have no issue with corruption. Providing, of course, we're not on the smelly end of it."

"And when we succeed against the British," said Madison, with conviction, "land values will rocket."

"And you think your playtime militia stand a chance against Uncle Wellington?" asked William. "I should say a very harsh lesson awaits you all."

"Our militiamen are defending their homes. They will fight with all they have."

"Rot!"

"With all due respect," Winder interrupted, fervently.

"Our enemy is distracted in Europe. The British focus is on Napoleon. They cannot fight two wars at once. They underestimate us."

"I think it is you who underestimates," said William, standing. He turned to Parsons and thumbed his gold waistband. "Perhaps Dobson could open a window? Get some air through the place. The Peel plums are practically steaming."

Madison took a step forward. His eyes steeled. "My Lord, you stand to make, what, six percent on our current loans? The land we are offering will net you at least one hundred percent. More than enough to rebuild your house."

"Maybe enough to rebuild a President's house," said William, nose upturned, "but not Peel Manor."

Parsons sensed the discussions had come to an end and, with as much tact as he could muster, he directed Madison's and Winder's attention to the door. "If you will excuse his lordship, his lion has just eaten a footman."

Madison bit his tongue. His nostrils flared and fists clenched. After offering the same slight bow he showed at the beginning, he left.

"A footman, you say, Parsons?" William asked.

"Not a particularly capable footman, sir," replied Parsons, with a reassuring smile.

Winder hadn't followed Madison out of the room; instead, he had waited until he caught William's eye. "Gentlemen, The President thanks you for your time." He took a nervous step forwards. "He is under a great deal of pressure. As he said, we had dissolved our national bank before the war and… well, I can't overstate the financial peril we are in. If, at any point, you wish to reconsider, I, we, America, extends to you an invitation." And with that, followed by another nervous bow, he was gone.

A Peculiar Turn of Events

Thinking it best to leave Mother to her grief, William kept as far away from the house as possible during the weeks after his party. On April 20th, he was busy fishing on the shore of Lake Winston with Franny, his eighteen year old, buxom French Governess, who was reading aloud at his side. Although, technically William was a little old for a Governess, Mother had hoped Franny would encourage her teenage son to develop interests other than fine clothes and cheeses. William, of course, missed the point entirely.

Technically, William didn't do the fishing either. He assumed an overseeing role and the business of holding the rods, baiting, casting and so forth was taken care of by four of Peel Manor's stable hands. William had never exchanged more than a disapproving snoot in their direction prior to his birthday but following the fire, Mother had engaged all the regular servants in cleaning items recovered from the blaze.

The stable hands immediately became William's personal staff, although, without any formal training they were completely ill suited for the role of domestic servants. William noted in his journal that he had given up all efforts of recalling their names. As such, any reference to them individually was simply made by the tall one, the short one, the gaunt one and the lazy eyed one. In an attempt to try and make them look the part at least, William kitted them out with matching britches, tunics and waistcoats. Unfortunately, the new overcoats had not yet arrived and William was not prepared to allow them to continue wearing their old ones, as this would completely spoil the look. This, despite it being spring and a cold one at that.

It was a fresh, calm day with barely a ripple on the water of the great lake. William was wrapped up snug on a recliner in a large fur coat. In spite of the cold, Franny was wearing a low cut summer gown. Her teeth chattered as she read Pride and Prejudice aloud in William's direction. Her pigeon English caused her to stumble over unfamiliar words. She was busy grappling with one such unfamiliar word when William lifted his chin out of his coat.

"Of course, one sympathises with this Darcy fellow," he said, drawing the fur in tight around his neck and gesturing Franny's attention to the stable hands who were trying to hook some bait. "I mean look. This is exactly the idiot behaviour one observes in your average peasant."

"Their hands, they are cold you think, yes?" suggested Franny, lowering her book.

"Rot!" replied William, dismissively. "You don't see me shivering. It's a weakness in the marrow." He could put up with their incompetence no longer and shouted, "You do know the idea is to use the little worm-thingy to catch the fish!" This caused the stable hands to jump and drop the bait pot. William sighed before turning back to Franny. "It's a good job I hadn't favoured falconry today. These idiots would have had their eyes pecked out by the impatient bird."

William's lecture was cut short by the arrival of the butler, Dobson, who presented him with an envelope. "A correspondence of some urgency I believe, sir."

"Curious," said William, as he studied the handwriting on the envelope. He slipped out the letter and issued Dobson a nod to send him on his way. His eyes had not gotten half way down the page when they suddenly closed tight in shock. A moment later, he was on his feet and shouting at Dobson to return.

"What is it?" asked Franny, concerned.

"A large helping of cowpat pie," William replied, handing her the letter. "Which, if you didn't know, is the worst kind of filling and the worst portion size."

"Sir?" enquired Dobson, approaching.

"Summon Parsons quickly and not a word to Mother. Oh, and get some fresh britches. These are creased at the knees from sitting cross legged."

As Dobson headed off, Franny's eyes scanned the page.

"This cannot be," she said, reading it again. "A clever forgery by someone who wishes distress. Oh my poor lord I..." She took to her feet and gripped his arm tenderly. As she squeezed him, her breasts pressed into him. "If there is anything I can for you do. Anything to palm away your stress."

"You mean 'calm away', surely?" he corrected, oblivious to her offer and the fact that, for once, her English had been spot on. "Sadly, I fear it is anything but a forgery. It's Uncle Boney alright. I'd recognise the buffoon's daub anywhere." He then blushed as he caught sight of her goose pimpled cleavage.

William arrived at the gates of the ornamental garden to find the path still annoyingly meandering. He could see Parsons waiting by the pagoda, clutching his trusty satchel. William spent a moment attempting to squeeze between two raised planters, to effect a short cut, then gave up with a flounce when he spotted a small soil stain on his britches. "Bastard!" he cried, brushing it clean with his handkerchief whilst cursing the Chinese and their silly gardens.

"What of my instructions for this blasted path, Parsons!" enquired William, sternly, as he approached. "Am I not lord and master?"

"Of course, my lord," Parsons replied, bowing. "Except, Mother has forbidden the work."

"And you take her wishes over mine?" said William, offended.

"She was most passionate on the matter. The house, in her view, should take priority."

"Well, clearly her mind is not her own," said William, handing Parsons the note from Napoleon.

"The handwriting?" questioned Parsons, examining the page. "You are sure it's his?"

"One only has to look at it. It's Uncle Boney alright. It's

the writing of an idiot."

> Dear my William,
>
> Without your additional funds needed for the prolong my campaign of war I have no choice but abdicated.
>
> Needless in saying I won't be able invade to the Britain after all and claim extensive lands for Tornbridge. I trust this is too much at your inconvenience and I hoping to see you soon.
>
> Yours full of me
>
> Uncle N
>
> P.S if you find la translator thrash s'il vous plait

"The translator, sir, is now assistant to the blacksmith," said Parsons, playfully, as he offered back the note. "His English, so I'm told, has very much improved."

"Well isn't that wonderful," said William, sarcastically.

"Perhaps," Parsons sighed, "if we had continued to finance Napoleon's efforts as I advised then…"

"Oh, no, no," replied William, with a dismissive waft of his hand. "This is no time for falling on one's sword. You must not blame yourself. I'm no headhunter. Besides, we can't all be schooled in diplomacy and high finance."

"Most gracious," said Parsons, with an uncomfortable bow.

"So, how far up the trouble tree are we stuck?"

"Well," said Parsons, composing himself. "The terms of Napoleon's abdication will need to be agreed. The treaty, which will establish the distribution of his assets, title's and so on, will then be signed by the coalition and The Emperor himself."

"Oh, I can propose a few titles," said William, with a sneer. "Question is how do I get my blasted gold back?"

"Oh, it is unlikely that the coalition would honour any such claim even if the paperwork were present, which it's not, sir. Your father trusted Napoleon completely and wanted nothing written down that could possibly fall into British hands."

"But the idiot lent Napoleon thousands, surely?"

"A little under three and a half million, to be precise." His expression was emotionless. "Francs, of course."

Turning away, William screwed his fists up then bit them with his bared teeth. His face contorted with frustration and rage. This lasted a good minute before he took a breath, and composed himself. He smoothed his jacket then turned back to Parsons. "Excuse me a moment," he said, before vanishing into the pagoda. Parsons waited as a whirlwind of destruction and swearing came from inside. Pottery smashed, timber banged and crashed. Moments passed. Silence fell. William then reappeared, shooting his cuffs, his anger satisfied. "Well?" he enquired, getting his breath. "What was it Shakespeare said about fearless minds?"

Parsons didn't know but he did go on to explain that with the Napoleon deal scuppered and the house gutted there was a considerable hole in the Peel budget. In his view, William had no option but to accept President Madison's land deal.

"Oh, very well," agreed William, with a sigh. "I'll leave the details in your capable, if rather spindly, hands. I'm going for a long brandy and an even longer lie down."

"Ah," sighed Parsons, resistant to the idea.

"Ah?" repeated William, inquisitively.

"Such negotiations are traditionally kept with his lordship. It's the family way, sir."

"*Traditionally?*" queried William.

"I fear so, sir. Besides, such a delicate matter is best handled by someone *'schooled in diplomacy and high finance'.*" Parsons was taking some pleasure in William's predicament.

William took a gulp. "Yes, well... As you put it that way."

William wasn't exactly enamoured by the prospect of going to America and showing up at the Madison's with a customary olive branch. That was until Parsons suggested that any potential frost in The President's reception would no doubt be melted when William presented him with the three hundred slaves needed to realise his country's vision of a gleaming new capital. There was the small matter of getting three hundred slaves, however.

William could also see that it made sense to leave Mother to the tedious reconstruction of the great manor. Although, he didn't fancy telling her that they would be skimping on the furniture because he had pulled the plug on Uncle Boney and cost them three million pounds.

"So much deal mongering," William sighed. "I feel like that animal… Oh, what's it called? Franny would know… Has lots of little birds living on it, or something, feeding off tiny bits at a time. It carries on like that apparently until there's just the poor animal's head left. Anyway, the point is, when it dies, all the bird things die too. Just like France and America. Do you see my point?"

"No, sir."

"Well, probably clearer if you saw a pop-up picture. Anyhoo…" William racked his brain as to how to broach the subject with Mother.

"Perhaps, I should simply ask if you can go, sir?" he said, a wry smile playing about his lips.

"No, no," said William, straightening. "Mother will simply have to accept that I'm going to America. She has already expressed faith in my professionalism and attentiveness. At least I think she did. I had been distracted by a wonderfully aromatic stilton. So as far as she is concerned, you keep your lips buttoned."

"*The Pride of Emily* will be made ready to sail," said Parsons. He bowed once more then paused, remembering a matter of some political delicacy. "But ensure you sail home before August. I hear Admiral Cochrane has cooked something up in America and the fact that he had not been to your father to chip in for naval costs means he is keeping the details very much to himself."

The courtyard of Peel Manor was filled with mannequins, which were draped in all manner of exotic fabrics and cloths. Tailors from across Britain had received word that Lord Peel would be travelling and wished to refresh his wardrobe. They had descended on Tornbridge in their droves.

George, William's pet male lion, was sprawled out in the corner devouring a sheep's leg. He licked the blood off his whiskers and watched William as he thumbed the samples.

William was just remarking on the poor button quality of one particular jacket when a familiar cry shattered his enjoyment.

"I'm not happy, William!" declared Mother, entering the courtyard with purpose. As Mother was frequently 'not happy', William generally thought it best to remain silent until he could figure out exactly what she wasn't happy about. On this occasion, many reasons sprang to his mind. It could have been his scuppering of the Napoleon deal, the loss of millions, or the fact that he had commissioned a highly ornate commode when the house didn't even have a roof. "You are to sail to Africa?" she asked.

"Of course," he replied, casually. "It's where one purchases slaves."

"Leave us!" Mother barked suddenly at the dressmakers, causing William to let out a nervous gulp.

The dressmakers hurried to pack their things and were ushered out by the stable hands.

"This will not do, William," Mother snapped. "Your place is here in Tornbridge. Send someone else."

"Parsons, you mean? I believe his head to be too narrow for the voyage. It would whistle in high winds and cause unrest."

"Oh, don't be absurd!"

George, not liking raised voices after a meal, got up and stretched his legs before plodding off through the south gate.

"Absurd or not, dear Mother," Continued William, "we can't have The President's slaves driven to distraction on their Atlantic voyage. They would wilt."

"You have some qualities, William," said Mother, stern faced, "but your wit is not amongst them. You are simply not ready for the real world."

"Rot! All I need do is sail to Africa to purchase a few hundred slaves then pop across the Atlantic to America and broker a deal with their idiot President for oodles of land. What could possibly go wrong?" He drew himself up. "Anyway, it is not a woman's place to dictate the world of commerce."

"William, you are aware that the British have outlawed the slave trade?"

William was surprised that she knew such things. "Seeing as you press me, I am aware. Of course, I am." (He wasn't aware and noted so in his journal).

"Slave traders are outlaws no different to pirates or smugglers. A grave fate awaits you if you're caught."

"More rot!" William replied, determined. "If Walter Raleigh's mother had been of such a view, the fellow would have never discovered America. So too, if some indigenous child of the arctic region hadn't pestered his mother into letting him play with the pile of snow with a nose then we would never have known about the polar bear."

Mother closed her eyes in despair.

The inquest into the blaze at Peel Manor lasted an entire week with the Magistrate presiding making sure it was a full and thorough affair. Why it needed to last more than a day, William couldn't fathom and told Mr Cuming, the magistrate, over a double brandy in his chambers. Mr Cuming was an elderly man made frail by a heart condition and plagued with arthritis of the ankles.

"Arson isn't about fire, of course," said William, savouring his brandy, "it's about power. It's well documented that arsonists do it for control. It's all about degrading people."

"You mean rape, surely?" replied Mr Cuming.

"I'm pretty sure it is arson but either way it's a dark business."

"Oh, it is, it is," Mr Cuming agreed, eagerly.

"So, justice demands you throw the book at the filthy beggar responsible. You do have a suitably heavy book? One with sharp corners too, perhaps?"

A more cut and dried case had never been heard as far as William was concerned. None of the testimony given over the course of the week changed anything at all. The blaze had been started by that idiot, Samuel Boyle, who had inadvertently set fire to the backside of his trousers whilst sleeping under a faulty oil lamp in the hayloft. Being the village idiot, son of the previous village idiot, and brother to a regular runner up, this all appeared thoroughly plausible. The court later heard separate testimony from William's four stable hands who stated that Samuel had been told to fix the lamp but neglected to do so.

Samuel was eventually charged with arson and convicted on the evidence of his own singed buttocks. When asked if he had anything to say in his defence, Samuel simply apologised and offered to pay for the repairs. When pressed on how he expected to come up with the half a million in building works and lost art, he simply shrugged, gormlessly, and said he would gladly work weekends until he had paid it off.

William put Samuel at the same age as himself. He wasn't ugly or carrying any disfiguring marks just very dirty, spotty, and sporting a smell somewhere between damp dog and incontinent, elderly peasant. His expression was a combination of a smile and a toothy grin. He had a rather dull sheen to his crossed eyes. It was as if his mind was absent of thought yet strangely happy at the same time.

Tornbridge's partial independence from Britain afforded the Peels some latitude where the punishment of poor people was concerned. Fortunately for Samuel, the punishment for arson had been downgraded since it was established by Winston the Bastard, William's grandfather, in 1799. It was no longer the case that the guilty party would be kicked near to death then tied to a horse by the neck and dragged through the streets until their head fell off. Being a more enlightened age, the penance was for the guilty party to be dragged around the streets, alive, then stuffed into a barrel and kicked down Gout Hill. Gout Hill being a rather steep, bracken covered incline infamous for being as unpleasant to walk up as it was to look at.

This was the punishment that awaited Samuel Boyle.

The following day, William took up position on the old ducking stool jetty next to the River Torn and watched from his horse as the barrel bounced and rolled its way down the hill. For a good few minutes it tumbled on with a life all its own.

"The fellow's brains must be shaken loose," observed William to Able, his burly bodyguard, who was watching alongside him on his own horse. "Like a badly bruised vegetable."

"That they will, sir," replied Able, cool as ever.

The barrel arrived in the river with such force that the wake shot twenty feet into the air and drenched the huge crowd of villagers gathered along the opposite bank. They all cheered regardless. William and Able cantered over and arrived just as the barrel was being fished out by two broad-shouldered locals. All eyes fixed on it as the lid was smashed open. By the speed of the descent, and the number of knocks along the way, everyone expected Samuel to be poured out of the barrel like a few gallons of bloody clothes. Instead, his grubby face popped out sporting a huge smile. His eyes were crossed but then they often were.

"Again! Again!" he demanded, with customary, dim-witted enthusiasm.

The crowd groaned in disappointment and quickly dispersed.

"Well, what are we to do with him?" William asked Able.

"They'll kill him, sir, the villagers will, for what he did," he responded. "Your father wouldn't want that."

"What reason my father had for employing him in the first place, I cannot fathom."

"If you are going far away, sir, maybe it's best he goes far away with you. Be the kindest thing to leave him where no harm can come to him nor others."

"Yes, I see your point. Good God! Is he drooling?"

"He does that when he's excited, sir. And quite a lot when he's not."

A Peel at Sea

May 31, 1814. The port of Dover was like no other place. The dockside itself was busier than a Saturday market. It reeked of excrement, foul fish, sweat, and dead flesh from the nearby tanneries. Sailors, traders, pickpockets and prostitutes all jostled about their business in the shimmering haze of an unpleasant warm day. In the midst of it all, four polished black carriages pressed on heedless to the impoverished masses shoved aside by the horses. The impeccably dressed driver of the lead carriage drew on the reins then swung down to open the carriage door. The door was embellished with the Peel Crest.

Moored at the dockside was the most beautiful ship William had ever seen. Although, in actual fact, he had not seen very many. Compared to the tatty, floating mass of driftwood crammed in and about her, she looked as if she were built for a divine purpose. A topsail schooner with triple masts and gleaming white sails; her polished copper hull panels glinted in the sunlight and made it look as if she was floating on gold. Unlike some of the other vessels about her, that were blackened with pitch or shabbily painted, *The Emily* was immaculately finished in nimbus blue. Below her stern windows were large, gold plated letters '*The Pride of Emily*' and above them 'Tornbridge'. She was the flagship of the Peel fleet and looked every inch the part.

"She's lightning fast in the water, sir," came an eager voice from her gangway. "And she has more than a few tricks up her sleeve should we find ourselves in a tight spot."

William turned to see a fresh faced lad, walking to greet him. He was well built but rather less well dressed. His look was complimented by an assortment of throwing knives sheathed along his belt. However, it was the twinkle in his eye that William took immediate exception to. That and the fact that every word he uttered appeared tinged with sarcasm.

"Daniel Penny at your service, sir," said the lad, gesturing William should board. "We're at the mercy of the sea I'm afraid, sir. Do you need a hand with your bags?"

"You are not the captain?" enquired William.

"No, sir. The bo'sun, sir."

"Is the gold aboard?" asked William, tugging his beautiful gloves off by the fingers.

"Aye, sir. May I ask how you want it guarded?"

George, William's pet lion, then emerged from the carriage, shook his massive mane, and flashed his enormous teeth to the world. Screams of panic rippled across the dockside as George walked to the foot of the gangway.

"A most effective deterrent," gulped Daniel, stepping aside nervously as George plodded past up the gangway. "Does he bite?"

"A few gardeners, yes, and recently a footman. He once mauled a chef too but then if you play with a lion whilst your hands smell of raw venison what do you expect?"

Daniel, somewhat apprehensive about sharing a confined space with a large lion then caught sight of the stable hands struggling up the gangway with the huge, leather and gilt travel cases. They were specially commissioned for the journey, William was keen to point out.

"Are you sure I can't lend a hand, sir?" offered Daniel, as he watched the stable hands puff and pant. "They look awful red from exertion."

"They make it look more effort than it is. A peasant trick," responded William, batting away a fly with his glove. "I should know, I watched the cases being packed. There's little more than a sock in each. Where is the captain did you say?"

"Readying for launch, sir," said Daniel, puzzled by the scene unfolding on the dock below. Coachmen were unloading all manner of objects from the rear of the carriages. There were guilt framed family portraits, a heavy mirror, William's new pearl trimmed commode, and even his ornate harpsichord. "This your first voyage, sir?"

William raised an eyebrow in contempt. "My dear fellow, my family has sailed the seas since before Poseidon was potty trained. Salt water runs in our veins. Rigging, and... and..." he faltered but kept going regardless, "whatever that stuff there is tied to the mast, is woven into the very fabric of my being. It will be like my return to the womb."

William began vomiting, violently, as soon as they were clear of the moorings. He saw little else but the last day's meal spilled out onto the deck in front of him for almost two weeks.

"The trick is to fix on the horizon, sir," remarked Daniel, playfully, as he swilled William's partly digested chicken pie off the deck.

"It's not sea sickness," barked William, a green tint to his complexion. "It's the blasted food." He gripped the main mast for support. "Are you quite sure this Southgate fellow is a trained chef?" At which point, he doubled up again and presented the carrots. William was ill for a fortnight; then, without explanation, he simply awoke one day without nausea.

The great cabin was just as its name suggested. It was twenty-six feet square and lined with finely carved gilt panelling. All of which was fitted to meet the Peels exacting standards. To the stern, there were four gently arching leaded windows on the bulkhead that overhung the rudder. Except for the tiller, and the ropes that connected it to the wheel on the quarterdeck above, there was enough headroom for William to move about without stooping.

The cabin was crammed with William's especially commissioned travel cases which, in simple terms, were a complete set of transportable bedroom furniture. A large wardrobe that hinged down the middle, a chest of drawers and even a dresser complete with mirror. They were all beautifully finished. The large oak dining table that once served the senior staff was pushed to the side and piled high with crates of fine wines and cheeses. William's ornate commode was placed in the port side corner nearest the bow. He also had the paintings of heroic naval battles removed from the panels and replaced with various scorched ancestral portraits salvaged from Peel Manor.

With his sea legs firmly established, William was keen to explore his lovely ship and had only a two-hour breakfast before setting about trying on several tunics to find the desired look.

"Ah, yes," he said to George, as he admired himself in the mirror. "Most seaworthy. Perfect for inspecting my pretty little craft." As a finishing touch, he attached the diamond and ruby brooch that was given to him as an eighteenth birthday present from his Uncle Ferdinand. As William adjusted his cuffs, the fat stable hand appeared and sprayed him with a light mist of scent.

"What the?" snapped William, wafting it away. "Smells like fox pizzle!" He snatched the bottle and inspected the hand-written label. It read Wild Scabbard and was one of Lord Byron's custom-made scents. It was a present for the voyage although William had thought he had thrown it away. After a moment adjusting to the fragrance, it occurred to William that the smell wasn't actually that bad. He passed the bottle back and was immediately distracted by his pleasing, plump profile in the mirror.

"George, stay!" he said, stroking the lion's mane. He

then turned to the stable hands, "He'll probably do his business in an hour. Remember what I told you. Don't look at him when he's doing it. If you do he won't go. And the last thing this crew needs is a cranky, constipated lion brooding below decks. And don't move in to clean it up until he's lost all interest or he'll have your throats. Good lads!"

As William ascended to the deck, he was struck by the blistering heat of the midday sun which felt magnified by the vast, calm sea about them. He shielded his eyes and cast a gaze at the clear blue sky as far as he could see. A far cry from Tornbridge, he thought. Wind fluttered in the sails above him. Ropes creaked and timbers groaned to the gentle heave of the sea. Waves broke across the ship's bows sending a light spray of salty mist across her deck. The smell of sun baked oak, resin, and cooking smoke was punctuated by the occasional waft of sweat and farts. It was then that William noticed the great hive of activity about him.

Tatty looking seamen engaged in some nautical purpose or other. Some were scrubbing the deck whilst others knotted ropes. They all offered a mystified glance in William's direction. They were barefoot, wiry, and tanned. Most of them were longhaired although one or two were short cropped or shaved. A striking fact was that most were lame in some way either by a lost finger or a scar to the body or face. One sailor, who was busy installing a new cleat to the rail, had only one eye and the cheekbone below it was misshapen from being smashed and badly re-set. William watched as the fellow suddenly held up a sucked finger to check the wind direction then dropped his breaches. Much to

William's disgust, the fellow proceeded to sit on the rail and empty his bowels over the side with a grimace. William shuddered at the sight of it and turned away, muttering words of indignation.

William scanned the calm, sparkling sea littered with far-away ships. In the distance he saw a vague shoreline overlooked by the famous Rock of Gibraltar itself. William pondered for a moment as to whether he was the furthest from Tornbridge he had ever been. He let out a sigh. He still did not much fancy the idea of turning up on President Madison's doorstep but he did like the idea of returning home with land in the Americas and enough profit from the deal to re-roof Peel Manor. Although, it would be the pleasure of finally proving Mother wrong and offering a two-fingered salute to Parsons behind her back that had William most enthusiastic about the adventure ahead.

William's quiet contemplation was shattered by a series of musket shots fired in rapid succession. He turned to see a man taking aim over the stern rail with an ornate musket that was sophisticated in its design. Much to William's surprise, the man fired another series of shots without the need for reloading the weapon. As William approached, he could see a bunch of turnips bobbing about in the ship's wash some hundred yards to stern.

"The Strait of Gibraltar," said the man, sensing William behind him. Before turning, he took aim at a turnip and peppered it with four quick shots. He was a middle-aged man, dressed about as impeccably as one could on a sailor's budget. His tunic, his britches, and leather boots were all pristine. From his belt hung a Japanese sword with a black lacquered scabbard. It's fittings glistened in the sunlight. The man was good looking, save for an inch scar on his left cheek which William surmised was likely from duelling. The man lowered his musket and offered a hand for William to shake.

"And you are?" asked William, disregarding the man's outstretched hand.

"John Carr," he replied, annoyed by the snub. "Care to try?" He offered William the musket. "It's your father's design."

"Are they following us with murderous intentions?" enquired William, nodding towards the turnips. He then directed Carr's attention to a nearby ship. "Are they friendly, do you think?"

"Merchant ships, fortunately," said Carr. "But when we leave port in two days time it will be different. The most dangerous waters on earth await us. Packed with pirates, Barbary raiders, and savages," he added, slinging the musket over his shoulder. "The quicker we exchange our gold for a belly full of Bowman's slaves the sounder I'll sleep."

"The captain, I assume, should always sleep soundly."

Carr smiled at the veiled insult. "I'm not the captain. I'm the first mate." He turned to the helmsman. "Bare away, if you please," he cried.

"Aye, aye, sir," came the response.

"Stay clear of the skipper," said Carr, stepping to William's shoulder. "Your taking over the great cabin has left him mighty prickly. He is very fond of his ship and not a man to see vexed."

As Carr strode away, William took a step. "You forget yourself. Surely, he would not begrudge a Peel adequate quartering?"

Carr stopped in his tracks and glanced back over his shoulder. "Harmony on board ship is key. For the sake of all our lives." He turned to fix on William's gaze. "One bad day and we're all guests of Davy Jones, or worse, captured by raiders."

"Perhaps you would have me swinging in a hammock and breathing the farts of your crew?"

"Of course not," said Carr, as he departed. "A man has to earn a hammock!"

Carr vanished below deck before William could muster a satisfactory retort. Instead, he spied Samuel, the village idiot responsible for burning down Peel Manor, on all fours scrubbing the deck. Whilst muttering words of frustration, William kicked Samuel hard in the backside and sent him flying over his bucket.

The Emily departed Gibraltar on June 16, 1814, and began the Mediterranean leg of her voyage. During his shore leave, William had collected new menu ideas and the ingredients to implement them. Southgate, *The Emily*'s peg-legged cook, was less than impressed. According to the ship's log, Southgate took exception to the predominantly French dishes and had to be restrained from sticking his peg leg up William's pompous backside. This caused great tensions at the dinner table.

After departing Gibraltar, William temporarily gave up his quarters, the great cabin, to host an evening meal with Daniel, Carr, and the surgeon, Barker. Barker was a gaunt, morose figure with wispy, copper sideburns and a freckled bald head. The captain was notable by his absence and so too Jennings, the slave master, who had boarded at Gibraltar and remained in his cabin ever since. He was reported to be a very private man who passed the time drinking, smoking, and sketching a twelve year old Indian boy.

To avoid Southgate putting spurious ingredients in William's serving, the cook was never told which plate was his lordship's and he was kept out of the great cabin for the duration of the meals. Most meals played out the same way. William would enquire about past adventures and Carr, the first mate, would respond with modesty. The subject would then move onto a technical question William had about sailing.

Barker, who felt the effects of drink quicker than most, would go into some detail about how he loved his younger days as the captain of a cutter. As a surgeon, however, he loathed the futility and brutality of war. He would then become animated and sob over the meaningless repetition of his life and how he missed his wife with a young man's passion. Daniel would then steer the conversation back to the lighter side with an impressive back-catalogue of inappropriate jokes and humorous anecdotes. As the wine and port flowed, William would go into great depths about subjects he knew very little about. He would also pause regularly to remind everyone not to feed George from the table.

"For one thing, it just encourages him," William would note. "Secondly, he's a meat eater and anything else gives him terrible trots."

Daniel ignored such advice and fed George secretly at every opportunity. He did it out of mischief, of course, taking pleasure in the knowledge that William's night would be disturbed by a flatulent lion. It also meant that George struck up a friendship with Daniel that the others didn't share.

Mealtimes came and went perfectly harmoniously until the evening of June 25th when Southgate attempted steamed mussels in Vermouth. The incident occurred when William, who had been caught out by a strong sherry on an empty stomach, was heading back to the great cabin after a breath of fresh air. He had drunkenly made a wrong turn in the fore companionway and found himself in the galley as Southgate was attempting to prepare a white wine sauce for the dish. Much to William's horror, Southgate had left the skillet on the heat. A frank exchange of views ensued with William lecturing him, in the strongest possible terms, that the flavour of the mussels would be lost if the one legged 'dung flap' took his eye off them. Southgate replied by advising William that he would have no choice but to take his eye off them as he would be busy jamming the skillet up William's fat arse.

"Again, more bottom insertion threats," slurred William,

squinting to focus. "Why are you so obsessed with backsides anyway? Is it because you resemble one yourself?"

Southgate flew into a blind rage which involved him waving a cleaver, wildly, and shouting strong maritime vernacular. The exchanged ended with Southgate losing purchase with his wooden leg and inadvertently chopping off two of his own fingers as he fell to the floor.

William spent the rest of the evening dining alone. He drank copious amounts of fine wine and fatted himself with large helpings from the cheese platter.

"This captain must be a sour fellow indeed," he said, drunkenly to George, who was making light work of a pig's trotter. "To not even greet his employer on arrival. Not even a wave. Where is he? The boat sails well without him. Why do I need him?"

"It's just rude," said one of the stable hands from the shadows.

"Don't speak to me, damn you!" shouted William angrily, slamming his palm on the table then pushing back his chair. "Jesus, in a tree house!" he exclaimed, staggering to his feet. "What next? Am I to suffer a chattering chair? An improving lecture from the commode? Perhaps I have a harpsichord with views on owl farming?" He braced himself against the panelling, drunkenly. "Damn life on the waves! Where is the sophistication? Tell me that, George? Not a single man aboard with a passion for poetry or culture. Do you know what I saw this morning? Do you? Two men proudly breaking wind in unison as they emptied their bowels over the rail. This rail here," he added, pointing up out of the window. "This is what greets William E. Peel, Lord of Tornbridge, as he takes his view of God's new morning. Bastard peasants!"

The Emily cut her way through the waves of the Mediterranean in silence and darkness. A mild wind flapped the sails and there was nothing on deck but the faint shadows from the oil lamps. The crew were gently swaying in their hammocks on the lower deck. It was Samuel's watch and he was high up in the crow's nest on his own. Commonly considered the worst job on ship, William intended it as a penance for Samuel's buttocks having caused him such personal tragedy. But instead of scanning the horizon intently with a spyglass for signs of danger, Samuel was seated, knees under his chin, tongue poking out the corner of his mouth, drawing little pictures in his notebook. All was peaceful. All was quiet but suddenly, there was the sound of a harpsichord followed by a high, falsetto voice attempting an operatic piece in Italian. It was coming from the great cabin.

The peace of the lower deck was shattered as the once sleeping crew opened their eyes and struggled to comprehend such a rasping growl.

Carr too was in his bunk when the sound of music, singing and growling drifted under his door. It was William warbling and his damn lion was joining in. Carr lowered his book and narrowed his eyes in anger.

Carr burst into William's quarters to find the young lord seated at his harpsichord. William was following the sheet music in front of him with great passion and vigour. George was seated by his side, mouth open, head upturned, meowing. Carr glanced to the side-lines where the four stable hands stood to attention with fresh fruits and wine poised. Sensing Carr, William stopped singing but continued playing the instrument.

"Isn't it heart breaking?" he asked, drunkenly hammering the keys. "*Le nozze di Figaro*. The marriage of Figaro. This is the second act, of course. The countess laments her husband's infidelity." William began singing again and attempted a few very high notes. He was playing one handed, while his other hand stroked George's neck. The lion meowed again.

Carr took a step forward, his teeth locked. "My lord, it's four in the morning!"

"The man that hath no music in himself," replied William, "nor is moved with the concord of such sweet whatnots, Mozart in this instance, is fit for, well, pretty much nothing but fetching and carrying."

Carr stepped forward and, with great purpose, shut the harpsichord lid. William had to snatch back his hands to avoid them being trapped.

"Steady on!" exclaimed William, counting his fingers. "A delicate instrument. And so too the harpsichord," he added, letting out a drunken chortle. "A rendition of *To Anacreon in Heaven* perhaps? I believe it's popular with you common men. I have the sheet music but shush!" he whispered. "Mother believes such music weakens character."

"My lord?" said Carr, at the end of his patience. "I

know my Mozart and my Shakespeare but I fear the men care for neither."

William moved with purpose from his seat taking his wine with him. He spilled a little on the oak as he gesticulated. "Then we must educate them, damn it man! Music hath charms to soothe the savage beast. Or is it breast? Anyway, at the very least stop them shitting past my window."

"Perhaps so, but not so late on the eve of sailing the most dangerous waters in the world." At which point Carr withdrew, closing the door with purpose behind him.

William downed the last of his wine then moved across to his hammock. He threw his leg over the peculiar swinging bed but misjudged his balance and ended up crashing to the floor in a mangled heap. "Don't just stand there, damn you!" he shouted to the stable hands. "Fetch the potty." At which point, he passed out.

William awoke the next morning to find his world spinning and not just with the red wine revenge. His cases, belongings, and even his lion were taking to the air and crashing down about him.

"What the buggering hell?" he blustered as he watched George get purchase on the oak with his claws only to slide off in another direction as the boat lurched. His father's portrait suddenly leapt from the wall and smashed in its frame. William ordered the stable hands be quick with his boots and he scurried out of the quarters.

As soon as his head cleared the deck hatch, he was bombarded with a wave of shouts and sea spray. He flinched as a musket cracked beside him and he followed the shot's direction to find another ship alongside *The Emily*. The two vessels were crashing, rail against rail, as if they were a pair of steeplechasers charging, neck to neck, over fences. A musket ball splintered the boom above his head and William leapt for cover. He slid towards the capstan as *The Emily* dived forwards over a wave and a shower of foam drenched the deck. William was hurled amidships as the bows crashed through another huge white horse. He slid again, this time gaining purchase on the iron grate of the main hatch.

"Christ on a pit pony!" he cried out, as the crest of a wave drenched the deck about him.

Clearing the sodden hair from his eyes, he studied the attacking ship and its crew. A band of pirate devils from all corners of the earth. With tatty clothes and sun baked faces, they were screaming and whooping like savages. Lashed up high in their rigging, they scrambled to load their muskets in the heave of the chase. Another volley of shots had William burying his head in prayer as the sodden deck about him was peppered with gunshot. As if by answer to William's plea, the deck suddenly reverberated to the growl of an adult, male lion. William opened his eyes to see George, mouth wide, teeth glistening in the direction of the pirates. It was an intimidating display but unfortunately one that wasn't to last long. Another wave suddenly broke across *The Emily*'s bows and George was soaked from mane to paws.

The sight that followed churned William's guts and caused a curse or two to slip from his mouth. A dozen savages had jumped across onto *The Emily*'s deck with their swords raised. Without a pause, William found Peel strength in his legs and bolted forwards towards the glisten of a sword blade drifting in the wash ahead. He snatched it up and turned to find a battle waging about him as *The Emily*'s crew dropped from the rigging and met the pirates sword to sword. William parried, slashed, and stabbed through four pirates without a pause. Fortunately for him, he was still a proficient swordsman in spite of the many lessons he had slept through and the handicap of a buggering hangover.

One of the pirates kept George away by slashing at him with his scimitar. Although George took a deep cut to his shoulder, he retaliated, claws bared, with such a powerful strike that it tore the ribs from the pirate's chest and sent the villain flying in pieces over the rail.

High above the carnage, Samuel was fast asleep in the crow's nest. He was cuddling the alarm bell and completely oblivious to the carnage below him.

It was a mass brawl on the deck with not just swords hacking at limbs but elbows were going into noses.

"Dirty blighters!" shouted William, as he watched a pirate sling one of the crew over the side by his hair, as another stabbed his opponent's crotch with a concealed knife. With William's quarry beaten, he and the crew took a moment to appreciate their work. In all the excitement one happy-with-himself sailor quite forgot his manners and tried to pat William's back. William quickly slapped the fellow across the face and offered some home truths about the man's mother having unnatural relations with a horse.

William turned to see another man, a huge man, six-foot-eight at least, running towards the stern. In his hand he had a rope with a hook on the end which he began swinging with increasing speed. With perfect timing, he let the hook fly and it shot up high into the rigging of the other ship. Then, without a pause, he took the slack with a tug and leapt over the stern rail of *The Emily*. William watched in amazement as this heroic figure swung, one handed, up high over the other ship. Drawing his sword with his free hand, the fellow let go of the rope and brought his blade full to bear on the pirate helmsman's head. The power of the cut split the helmsman to his belly.

"Who is this fellow, George?" William shouted above the carnage. "A display almost worthy of a Peel."

"Volker!" replied a nearby crewman, with a knowing smile. "The Cap'n, sir."

Volker threw the helm hard to port and the pirate ship lurched sideways and veered away from *The Emily*. William gazed on as Volker was hacked and slashed at by a wave of pirates descending on him. He was done for, for sure, and seemingly without even a thought for his own life. *The Emily* was far from safe, however. As the pirate ship keeled violently to port, a long gun fired and the cannon ball clipped *The Emily*'s main mast. Samuel woke with a start as the mast began cracking and splintering below him. As it toppled, Samuel grabbed the rigging in a mad panic.

"What the hell are you doing!" shouted Carr, suddenly appearing at William's elbow. The Japanese sword in his hand was dripping with blood. "This is a hunting party, damn it! You're not safe here!"

William was about to lecture him on talking to his betters when the mast gave way and began to topple like a felled tree above them. The crew dived for cover as the rigging snapped and the sails folded. Distracted by the looming shadow of the mast as it fell, William completely missed the lone figure of Samuel swinging towards him at the end of a rope. Before William knew anything about it, Samuel's buttocks were in his face with a smack and William toppled over the ships' starboard rail and splashed into *The Emily*'s wash. In an instant, William was engulfed by the foaming sea.

The last he saw of *The Emily* was her rigging in tatters in the water as she dragged her main mast towards a rising wall of water. All his wealth and influence could do nothing for him as the deck of his beautiful ship, his lion, and his crew, were suddenly consumed in a massive explosion of water. He had little time to let out a cry of, 'oh, sparkling' when the same wave engulfed him and turned his world into a silent darkness.

The Notorious Captain Bowman

A bright white emptiness engulfed William's senses and with it came a feeling of serenity and inner calm. His clothes were the finest he had ever seen. He was stood, yet could feel no ground beneath his feet, nor see scenery about him. He had no sense of up or down. He was the only thing in a vast expanse of nothingness. He had been contemplating the predicament for a moment when suddenly he felt a presence, a faceless interruption in this blank oblivion. He glanced quickly in all directions to seek its origin.

"Don't drown you ass-brained idiot!" came a celestial voice. "Cough, damn it!" it shouted.

William felt the world rush back at him in an explosion of colours, sounds, and smells.

William came to on a sun baked shoreline coughing and spluttering the sea from his lungs. The hot sand cooled as the sea gently lapped about him. He raised his head and realised very quickly that he wasn't on the deck of *The Emily*. His memory came flooding back like the sea about him. He remembered the chase with the pirates, the battle that waged about him on *The Emily*'s deck. He replayed in his mind the sight of the huge white horses rising like mountains before her bows then exploding across her bow rail.

It all seemed like a dream to him as he gazed across the calm and empty sea. The only thing between his feet and the horizon was miles of sun struck waves that flickered and sparkled. As his gaze broadened, his eyes caught sight of a figure some distance away along the shore. One of the crew, William thought, as he slowly took to his feet. He checked the shoreline as he limped over but there was nothing but palm trees and a few stucco buildings that shimmered in the heat. They were all too far away to be of concern.

It was like no place William had ever seen. There were parts of Tornbridge that William had often considered bland but nothing like the place he now found himself in. The beach and land were one for as far as the eye could see. Even the mountains in the distance looked like huge piles of sand.

"This must be Spain," he uttered, recalling a pop-up book of beaches Franny had once shown him. He also remembered stories of such places from his Uncle Wellington. Tales of dark-skinned savages and exotic creatures.

As he neared the figure in the water that was bobbing about in the ebb and flow, his mind filled with anticipation. Was it Carr? William thought. Such a fellow would know a way out for sure. Daniel, maybe? William concluded that it was likely some weathered and wise old sailor who would know in a flash how to get dry clothes, some decent lodgings, and a plentiful cheese platter. However, when William eventually rolled the unconscious figure over onto his back, his worst fear was realised. It was Samuel Boyle. The simpleton who had torched his ancestral home and burned his father to a cinder. To add to that, the utter ape's ass had also managed to knock William over the side of his own ship.

"Oh, blasted well sparkling!" William shouted, giving the unconscious Samuel a swift kick in his ribs. "Well if that's not just the business end of one great meaty shaft!" Samuel regained consciousness and spluttered as he coughed up water. Much to William's annoyance, Samuel then tried kissing William's feet as if the kick was some form of correctly administered first aid.

Just as William was discouraging Samuel's affection by repeatedly slapping his face, he heard a bell behind him in the distance and the growl of an unusual beast. He turned to see a figure clad head to toe in black with a camel in reins at his side.

"A lumpy horse," said Samuel, straining his eyes.

"Indeed," noted William, with customary disdain. "Or a perfectly normal looking camel."

"Friendly?" asked Samuel.

As if on cue, the figure slowly raised a glinting scimitar from beneath his Bedouin gown and shouted enthusiastically a word or phrase in his native tongue that William would later understand to mean "Christian scum dog! You will soon learn the agony of a thousands lashes."

"Sounds like just a lot of A's, L's" and Q's," William

said to Samuel, oblivious to the truth. "Damn funny carry on!" Unsure of the etiquette, William favoured a direct appeal to the stranger. "Any chance you could tell us where we are?" He got only silence in reply. "No? Well, is there a trusted couturier nearby?" he added. "These britches have shrunk so much it feels like they're trying to eat my crotch."

Without warning, dozens of figures sprang up from beneath sheets covered with sand. An army appeared in seconds. All brandished scimitars and all were wailing the same chant of A's L's and Q's.

"Is that a no?" enquired William, timidly, before whispering to Samuel. "Cannibals most likely. You can tell by their sunken eyes, ridged finger nails, and the fact that the bigger, hungry looking fellow keeps licking his lips." William began circling his hips like an athlete warming up. "Are the Boyle's capable runners?"

"Er, no," responded Samuel, confused. "Our legs are bendy."

"Excellent, because we Peels are second only to a startled cheater. So, last one to bolt themselves inside one of those dung houses is an al fresco starter." With that, he gave Samuel one last slap on the face and ran off up the beach as far as his chubby Peel legs could carry him. Which wasn't far. A little under twenty steps later, he was shot with a rock from a sling and spilled forwards into the blisteringly hot sand. William Peel was unconscious once more.

William had never been lashed by the wrists to a camel before let alone dragged through a desert whilst staring up into the backside of one. He remarked as much to Samuel who was being dragged along side him. That was after twenty minutes of William explaining to Samuel why he should sacrifice his own life if need asked of it. The only decent thing to do considering it was Samuel, his buttocks, and the common man in general that were to blame for William's unpleasant predicament.

As the first miles literally dragged on, William had time to study Samuel up close. He wasn't bad looking, William thought, as he focused closely on the shape of his nose. It was slightly hooked. A profile not too dissimilar from William's own.

Samuel was Tornbridge's official village idiot and it was well known, he was descended from a long line of equally bereft of wit dullards. That wasn't to say he was a sure fire winner though, as there was stiff competition for the title. To win, the successful candidate had to demonstrate a complete inability to possess even the most basic of common sense. Although Samuel's stupidity was well known, and equally well documented, he had never previously put his name forward for selection. It was only by accident, in fact, that he was awarded the title at all as technically it was his brother, Nobby Boyle, who had actually been shortlisted. According to the Tornbridge Chronicle, Nobby had suffered from tooth ache and demonstrated his eligibility for the competition by suggesting that Samuel act as dentist to remove his bad teeth. The plan, according to reports, was stupidly simple. Samuel's father was to get Nobby horribly drunk, by way of an anaesthetic, and return him home at lunchtime so Samuel could carry out the procedure in bright sunlight. Samuel was to be waiting with a hammer and the blacksmith's pliers in the back yard.

What actually happened was that brother and father both got so horrendously drunk that they arrived home a day late and at night. In the darkness, Samuel mistook his father for his brother and began his dental career operating on the wrong patient. Samuel didn't realise the error until twenty minutes into the procedure but by which time he had already removed eight of this father's front teeth. Had the story ended there then, without doubt, Samuel's brother would have won the prize. Tragically for everyone, however, it didn't.

After realising his error, Samuel set about removing his brother's teeth too, all of them in fact, as he had got into a horrible fluster. To cover up the gross professional misconduct on his father, Samuel then forced the teeth back into his father's bleeding gums and banged them home with the hammer. An hour later, his father awoke to find what he assumed to be nothing worse than a typical hangover. He spotted his unconscious son in the yard, bloodied and toothless, and surmised that everything had gone true to plan. It wasn't until a later examination of his own teeth, in the bar mirror of the Dog and Gun Tavern, that the true horror was revealed. Samuel had filled his father's mouth with a collection of teeth with little care if they were the right way around or the wrong way up. He had even used some of his brother's teeth. By all accounts it was a truly horrific sight. The Tornbridge Chronicle reported that, although Samuel had only removed eight of his father's teeth, he had hammered thirteen back in. He was duly crowned village idiot without challenge but forbidden to practice dentistry again.

The desert journey continued in silence until William hit his shoulder on a rock which caused him to plunge face first into the desert.

"Oh, this is preposterous!" he snapped, spitting sand. "Have these peasants no respect for their betters?" He looked up to the rider. "You, sir? You there?" he repeated, with no reply. "Can we at least stop for some tea, damn you! It is that time, surely?"

At some point, presumably when William was unconscious, their party had been joined by other horsemen. They totalled about two hundred from what William could make out from those ahead and behind them. They had formed a great caravan through the arid and featureless desert. It was still impossible for William to get his bearings let alone see where they were heading. All he could hear were the bells of the camels and the chatter of the horseman in a language that baffled William.

"Sounds like Welsh," he noted, straining to hear. "Highly unlikely, of course, the Welsh are a characteristically moist race and unlikely to set up home in such an arid climate. Unless the proximity to the sea is..." he was suddenly silenced, spotting a buzzard circling above them. "That's not a good sign," he said, remembering Franny's pop-up book of birds. To his right he then spotted a half-naked figure laying in the sand. It was the dead body of a man with his face burnt from the sun. His hands were bound together like William's and Samuel's. Looking closer, William noticed the tattoos on his shoulders.

"Oh God!" he gasped out loud. "Isn't that one of those filthy pirates?"

Straining his neck, William arched up to see the front of the caravan. They had veered right and he could see the horseman from the side. Each of them were dragging at least two men behind them.

"They must be Barbary raiders," explained William, his heart sinking. "A race of merciless warriors whose barbarism and code of honour is... Hang on!" paused William, as he glanced at his chest with a realisation. "The filthy bastards have stolen Uncle Ferdinand's brooch!"

There was a commotion ahead up the line. Craning his head again, William could see lots of people. They were approaching a settlement with high walls the colour of the desert sand. The caravan slowed to a stop and the raiders dismounted. They kicked their captives whilst laughing amongst themselves.

Without warning, a whip cracked beside William and a one-eyed raider, with a complexion of saddle leather, yanked him up by the hair and shoved him into a line with other unfortunates. Each man looked equally terrified and confused. They were all lashed together and marched, to the sound of whips cracking in their ears, towards an arched entrance in the high stucco wall.

Once inside, they found themselves in a narrow passage with hardly room to breathe. The place heaved with traders jostling for business. There were stalls with sweet smelling and colourful spices in pots. Fabrics of every colour imaginable were draped across the pathway and seemed to glide over the faces of the terrified human caravan as it was marched onwards.

The city was heaving with traders dressed in traditional thobes, a long, lose fitting gown. Some punters were browsing and some haggling. Some were vocal as they gesticulated whilst others bartered with a quiet, relaxed confidence. They were all, however, busy in their conversations and paused only to waft away a fly or two with a casual flick of horsehair. Whether it was a sword slung on a strap or a dagger in the belt, all were armed. It wasn't the sort of place you dared enter otherwise.

The man in front of William fell from exhaustion and, although the caravan initially dragged him a few feet through the dust, it eventually ground to a halt. The raider next to William stepped forward and raised his scimitar. He shouted something that William imagined to mean *'get up you filthy scum dog'* or some other such degrading words lacking in originality. The raider was shorter than the others with broad shoulders and with a thick, dark beard the style of which William didn't think suited his round face.

"But then what does suit a round face," William whispered to Samuel. "Not a huge moustache at any rate. The fellow's face looks like a button."

When the fallen man refused to rise, the raider hacked

at his bindings. This caused a great sigh of relief along the line as everyone thought he was done for. The man was then dragged to the edge of the street and, in plain sight of everyone, the raider cleaved the man's head clean off his shoulders. Everyone's eyes fixed forwards in a universal silence as the head bounced off a good ten feet down the street.

"What a place," William uttered under his breath, with a shudder. "It's littering at its most grotesque!"

Suddenly, a group of young boys, no more than ten years old, grabbed the head with great excitement and ran off with it into the crowd like it was a new toy.

Everyone found a fresh pair of legs after that and the line soon found themselves rushing into a large, private courtyard. A pair of sturdy wooden gates were swung shut behind them and secured with a timber brace that was dropped into iron cleats. The courtyard was white-washed and bounded by a smooth rendered wall. It was too high to climb but wide enough for the savage guards to patrol along. The place was like a fort. To one side there was a small door with a residence above it. Across the courtyard were cages with bars flush with the wall. Faces of all nationalities peered out from the shadows.

William's line of captives was marched into the middle of the courtyard and brought to a stop. A dozen savages, wearing nothing but loin cloths and sandals, appeared about them. They were sour-faced men with jet black hair and eyes to match. In a great wave of objection, they began to strip everyone in William's party. Those who refused soon found the hilt of a raider's scimitar in their ear which brought an abrupt end to their protests.

"Filthy welt!" exclaimed William, in objection as a savage pulled roughly on the hem of his finely embroidered jacket. "Is it not enough that I gaze at a camel's arse for hours, I now have to suffer your filthy paws!"

William was about to backhand the peasant when a raider's scimitar point pressed between his shoulder blades. It was enough to steady his further outburst and William proceeded to strip with the rest. He carefully folded his jacket muttering strong words of indignation. The bearded raider approached him and grabbed his clothes. As he searched the pockets, the raider suddenly stopped and smiled. He had found something. A gold guinea. He grinned at William as he kissed the coin then he slipped it into his own pocket. He then threw the clothes into a heap at William's feet, spat on them, and kicked up some sand.

They all stood naked as the day they were born. A rag-bag collection of bodies. From the pale white of William's soft skin to the blackest black. From scrawny sailors to lean and muscular farmers. Many were tattooed and most were scarred. Except for William, of course, whose unblemished skin was as white as cream.

All captives were doing their best to cover their modesty; all except Samuel who couldn't hide his even if he had wanted to. Not that it entered his innocent mind to even try. Everyone, even the savages, sneaked a curious glance at his manhood. It was like a baguette, noted William in his journal.

The distraction of Samuel's gigantic privates was soon to end, however, as other raiders appeared in the courtyard and examined each captive from head to toe. They carefully inspected their hair, their teeth, and their ears. They were all searched with a blatant disregard for dignity or privacy. They were all stripped of rings or piercings. William watched as the other savages milled about showing off their booty to one another. From what he could make out by the grunts, the one eyed raider's name was Hassan and he assumed some seniority. William presumed it was because he was uglier and scarier looking than the rest.

Suddenly, one fellow down the line attracted a great deal of interest and discussion amongst the raiders who proceeded to prod and poke an infected wound on his thigh. He was ordered to jump up and down and it was slapped as he did so. It was obvious, even to William's untrained eye, that the poor fellow was lame but they were making as sure as they could. After a good five minutes, the chap was unceremoniously clubbed to the ground and dragged away by his hair. His legs kicked up a cloud of dust as he vanished through a small gateway in the courtyard wall.

To William's left, a raider then grabbed a pile of clothes and shoved them into the owner's stomach with a grunt that indicated he should dress. Everyone followed suit as savages appeared and attached leg irons to their ankles which were in turn chained to canon balls.

The captives were only allowed a moment's pause before a whip cracked and they were ushered through one of the gates and into a cage. Once the last poor soul was shoved inside, the gate shut with a metallic rattle and the dark, sun baked face of the guard peered in through the bars. He laughed like a devil as he turned the key.

For the next hour, the huddled mass went from strangers staring blankly at each other's confused and terrified faces, to comrades who formed groups segregated only by language. It was all about finding out facts. Some, like William, didn't even know where they were. Others had been in the cell before and paid their way out before. One thing was clear, they were in the hands of a slaver whose reputation took the strength from the legs of many in the cell. Captain Bowman, William discovered, was British and formally of the East India Trading Co. He had since set up on his own and carved out quite a slaving career trading with the British, Spanish, and Americans.

William stood with the English speakers. Four sorry excuses for men that repulsed him so much he kept a scented handkerchief under his nose as they leaned into him to tell their tales.

"We're brothers now," said Tilly, a tatty man whose face was blotchy from sun and drink. "Those who can pay their way, speak up. I knows how to make a deal." Everyone remained silent, glancing from one to another. It was obvious by the rags they were barely wearing that they didn't have a pot to piss in let alone enough money for Bowman's ransom. William remained silent. He was not about to reveal that not only did he have such a pot but it was embellished with gold and emptied by his own personal staff. "Then who's with me?" continued Tilly. "I say we rush them as one." By his tatty hair, he could have been any age from twenty to sixty but his black teeth put him middle aged. William surmised he was probably a beggar; a repulsive beggar at that.

"Clever plan!" said William, wafting his handkerchief in front of his nose. "I doubt they would have seen anything to match its brilliance. Best of luck!"

"And who might you be?" growled Tilly. "With your clever clothes and fancy words."

"My clothes are indeed clever!" said William, playing his cards close. "Clever enough to think it's best not to rush a locked gate in a guarded courtyard. Are you a lecturer on military tactics?"

"A p-p-point w-w-well m-m-made," said Potter, a young man who shivered constantly, from nerves, William presumed. If it had been disease, William was sure the raiders would have dragged him away by the hair to save him infecting the herd.

"Really?" growled Tilly, taking against Potter's comment. "You question my experience, do you? Me a fighting man all my life and he a pale-skinned lady."

William glanced away for a moment and spotted Samuel sleeping like a baby in the corner. William was about to call his name when he felt a finger prod his ribs. It belonged to Corbett, a sailor from his garb.

"He looks like a man used more to thinkin' up plans than puttin' 'em to works, I reckon," he said, pointing to William's well kempt hair. "His pretty forelock might just find 'im safe passage too if I remembers Bowman."

William's puzzled eyes stared deep into Corbett's for a

clue as to what the hell he was on about but he was suddenly snapped into the present by the ringing of a bell in the courtyard.

"This is a business is it not?" asked William, as they all moved to the bars to see what was happening. "I'm sure we can simply agree some financial terms."

"Then we shall talk," said Tilly through his rotten toothed smile. "I'll do the negotiating on your behalf. Represent your interests, so to speak."

"Sparkling!" William replied with a splash of acidity. "If you leave me your card I will be sure to book an appointment through your office?"

The huddled mass of captives was awash with rumour as the cage next to theirs opened and out of it marched a band of captives looking similar to themselves. They were formed into a line in the courtyard and forced to kneel by the raider, Hassan.

As William moved closer to the bars, Potter extended a shivering finger to an iron grate being removed from the courtyard wall by two burly savages. Behind the grate were the glowing embers of a small furnace. One of the savages stoked as the other fanned. It was all disturbingly well rehearsed. Savages appeared from every direction carrying all manner of items. Before a moment had passed there was a table covered by cloth in front of a grand, carved chair. A place was set for a meal complete with goblet and wine bottle. The last item placed on the desk was a quill and a pile of papers held against the breeze by a rock.

"M-m-marking t-the r-r-right-l-less," whispered Potter,

as a branding iron was forced deep into the furnace embers and primed. "N-n-no l-long-err f-free m-m-m-men."

Order fell among the savages as a slim, western figure entered the courtyard from the residence doorway. He was kept in shade by palm leaves held aloft by two serf boys who traced his every step. He was dressed in white linen trousers and a cream tunic. Very dapper, thought William, as the figure approached the table. Once the stranger knew all eyes were on him, he made a protracted announcement in the native tongue about everyone being his property and them forfeiting rights etc. etc. The abridged version being that the poor blighters kneeling in the sand were no longer master of their own destinies and doomed to be sold for whatever unpleasant purpose their new owners saw fit.

"Hence forth you are mine," the calm voice then announced in English, such perfect English it made William raise an eyebrow. "My property. My goods. My trade. Your very life is my possession and believe me, I will benefit from you. My name is Captain Bowman. See to it you remember. Hence forth you are no longer free men. You are simply stock."

To add injury to insult the one eyed raider, Hassan, then grabbed the branding iron from the furnace and approached the first man in the line. The steaming, business end of the iron crackled and spat as it neared him. Two savages then braced the fellow expertly by the head and shoulders as the iron was plunged into the captive's bare chest. The sound of sizzling flesh was lost in an instant by the fellow's screams. It was all in a day's work for Bowman who ate quartered fruit in a nonchalant and camp manner. A demeanour not unlike Byron, William noted.

William gripped his own plump chest in apprehension as the raider and the savages repeated the process down the line pausing only to refresh branding irons. Only three captives were left to brand when a voice cried out for mercy.

"I beg you, sir!" blabbed a man in English. "I can get gold. Lots of it. My master has riches beyond the dreams of Solomon. If I could just contact my ship."

"Bastard!" muttered William, under his breath. "That was to be my fiendish ploy."

Hassan readied a new iron.

"Wait," said Bowman, barely looking up from his fruit bowl. "Were I open to offers of such riches, I issue fair warning. You say false and it won't be the arms of slavery that welcomes you it will be the jaws of death."

"My ship is real, sir," added the captive, wetting his lips. "Crammed with gold and weaponry like you wouldn't believe."

"The name!" barked Bowman, "before my patience falters."

"The Pride of Emily, sir."

William's heart skipped a beat as he grabbed the bars of the cage. He didn't know what to make of it. Was the filthy beast really one of *The Emily*'s crew or just some tricky blighter trying his darndest to avoid a life of fetching and carrying?

Bowman studied the papers on his table without a word. He was meticulous as his finger scanned his list of ships. The only sound to be heard was that of the creaking leaves of the palms as they were fanned above him. When his searching was complete, he leaned back in his grand chair.

"Oh, dear," he said, calmly. "It appears there is no such ship in port. Nor is it along the coast weighing anchor. Believe me it is my business to know."

The captive became desperate. "She was taken off guard, sir. Pirates! A sleeping watch so rumour be. Her main mast was struck but she wasn't done for. She will have docked to make repair. If you look tomorrow I…"

"If she lost her mast as you say, she'll be plundered already in these waters." Bowman nodded to Hassan who drew his scimitar. "Claims like this waste so much time. I'm sure you agree that I must make an example. Such is commerce. Hassan?" he said, casually leaning back again and taking a grape. "Bring me his ears. With the head attached, of course."

It had been the second beheading the captives had witnessed and they weren't getting easier to watch. The mood amongst the captives darkened over the hours that followed. Desperate schemes were discussed. Many talked of rushing the raiders and scaling the walls. None of the plans, William believed, had any merit. By the time the evening food arrived, most captives had become resolved to their fate.

By night time, William was pacing the cell dragging his heavy ball amongst the sleeping masses. The only light was that from the flickering torches about the courtyard. It wasn't the rat-meat pie that had kept him awake nor was it the fact that everyone else appeared to thoroughly enjoy it. It was actually the horror of his predicament that kept his feet walking and palms sweating. With *The Emily* gone so too was his lifeline. His bare pockets couldn't buy his way out nor was it worth suggesting a letter home to Mother for a few gold coins in case Bowman demanded his ears for just thinking it. William very much liked his ears and it soon became clear that he was going to have to survive by his own wits.

William was, as ever, supremely confident in the ability of his wits despite their track record for landing him neck-deep in potty water. There was something else that niggled William as he paced. According to Tilly, who it had to be said William found unable to shake, Bowman had a tendency towards 'the late night company of good looking men' and not to discuss the finer points of branding. William feared his Peel looks and portly physique would turn Bowman's head.

"I say you take your chances where you finds 'em," said Tilly, from the shadows.

"Agr!" William cried, jumping with surprise.

"He's granted freedom before for the willing," said Tilly.

"And for the not so willing?" replied William, regaining his composure.

"He'll be along the bars soon enough. His eyes peering for what he likes."

"Well, he'll find this harbour closed," William replied, picking up his iron ball.

"Then your only way out is in chains with the rest. With Bowman's mark upon you," responded Tilly, his tone turning menacing.

"Tell me, Mr Tilly, do you have any suggestions as to where I can stick this?" replied William, holding up the iron ball.

Samuel was awoken by the crack of William's hand across his ear. He sat up with a start and rubbed his eyes.

"Shush and Listen," said William, checking Tilly wasn't ear wigging. "It appears an opportunity has presented itself. A way for you to make some recompense for falling asleep at your post and costing me my pretty boat. Not to mention my gold." William checked over his shoulder again. "I'd also include costing me the loss of *The Emily*'s crew except I don't think they warmed to me. So, no love loss there. Blaggards!"

"Ship," said Samuel, picking his nose. "Not boat."

"Oh, thank you for the lecture in nautical vernacular," replied William, prickled by the correction. "A great comfort I'm sure when my flesh sizzles under the branding iron," he added. "Anyway, let me finish. In older times, a Knight would fall on his sword for the disaster you have left in your wake. But in this more enlightened age it will be sufficient that you need only..." he checked over his shoulder again and chose his words. "Fall onto the sword of another man." Samuel's eyes widened indicating he understood. "Now, I really don't want to discuss the detail," said William, recoiling. "I find the whole thing too upsetting." He slipped off his jacket. "I'm told the Italians rather enjoy it," he said, offering the jacket to

Samuel. "Come on! He's unlikely to feel amorous with a peasant who smells like a stable floor." William looked into Samuel's brainless eyes as he slipped on the new jacket. "You do understand, don't you?"

Samuel nodded in his dim way then admired himself in the fine, fresh smelling jacket. "I pretend to be you and go to the slaver man."

"That's it!" exclaimed William, rubbing his hands eagerly. "Then when, 'William Peel'..." he winked before continuing, "gets his pass to the gate, you bring it here to me."

"Britches," said Samuel, pointing.

"Britches? Yes, of course," responded William, slipping them off. "Can't have Bowman believing the lord of Tornbridge would have soiled pants." William noticed Samuel looking puzzled at his own very warn boots. "Very well," sighed William, reluctantly. Keen to see the plan work at all costs, he slipped off his fine, hand crafted footwear. Although he did doubt the plan for a moment as he saw Samuel's filthy and cheesy foot pop out of his own tatty boots.

William stood back to admire his own clothes. They looked a little baggy on Samuel but it was dark enough for people not to notice. William smiled to himself that the crazy plan might just work.

"Good fellow!" said William, slapping Samuel's arm. "Take one for Tornbridge."

William suddenly became aware of his new stinking clothes. As he moved to cover his nose, his hand brushed his side and felt something in the pocket of Samuel's old tunic. It was a small, leather bound notebook. Samuel's eyes widened and he reached to take it back but William clutched it suspicious that the village idiot would need, or could use, such a thing.

"Where did you get this? Was it in the house?" William queried, flicking the pages quickly but finding they were mostly blank save for a few messy pencil scribbles. After another scan, just to be sure he hadn't missed some important reference, William's excitement turned to regret. Well, as much as any Peel ever had.

"Quite right," said William, handing it back. "Not my business."

William let out a little growl of excitement as Samuel shuffled off towards the gate. There was an exchange of words between Samuel and the guard and, although William couldn't hear what was said, the opening gate meant the plan had worked. William had a stomach of knots as he watched Samuel walk gormlessly across the courtyard. After another moment of discussion with the guard at Bowman's door, Samuel stepped into the hall and the door was closed behind him.

Minutes passed. Then hours. William, who had initially been pacing the cell with nervous apprehension, suddenly found his eyelids becoming heavy. He thought it best to conserve his energy for the impending journey as a free man so he took a seat. He was reassured that whatever Samuel was doing, God help him, Bowman was certainly making the most of it.

Sometime later, William woke with a start as a distant scream hit him like a bucket of ice water. His heart was pounding like a drum as he rushed to the bars. The screams were followed by what could only be described as the sound of the death throes of an impaled animal. It was an agonising sound. "Oh my God!" William gasped. "That buffoon, Samuel, has killed him." He began to play the scenario through in his mind. Samuel must have fought for his honour and bashed the amorous fool's head in. William bit his fist expecting the savage guards to rush into the courtyard at any moment and bring Samuel out in pieces. "Oh, what's to become of my clothes?" he gasped. "Blast his eyes!"

Moments of waiting stretched into agonising minutes. Suddenly, the door across the courtyard opened up and light poured onto the scorched sand.

What William saw next was one of the most peculiar sights of his entire life. Samuel emerged from the doorway with his arm around Bowman like some love struck couple. They were clearly drunk as lords as they staggered out into the moonlight. They raised their bottles aloft in a raucous toast before downing long gulps.

William squinted in disbelief as the pair made their way to the main courtyard gates and kissed in such a passionate embrace that it caused Bowman to drop his bottle with limp delight. Once recovered, he wiped Samuel's slobber off his mouth and the pair clinked bottles. Bowman then threw the large wooden brace off the gates and yanked them open. The last William saw of Samuel was Bowman waving him off to the words "You have your freedom, William my love."

William banged his head onto the bars as the realisation hit him. The idiot Samuel had gotten so drunk he had forgotten to go back to the cell so they could exchange places. William banged his head again when he also realised he would be stuck in the clothes of a peasant and stinking to high heaven in another man's filth. Adding to which in a few short hours he would be branded and shipped off to God knows where. He would be forced to live out his remaining days chained to an oar in some vermin infested pirate ship or worked to an early death picking cotton in some American plantation. He pictured steam coming out of Mother's ears when she heard the news.

"Elephants arses!" he cried, startling a few captives about him.

With the dawn came the distant cry of Adhan, the Islamic call to prayer. It echoed in every corner and intensified with the rising of the sun. Shadows of the high wall creeped across the courtyard. A new day had come. Half an hour later, the clatter of the bell and the same hive of activity in the courtyard as William had witnessed the day before. Except this time, William wouldn't be a spectator he would be the main event. The table was set and the furnace stoked. The cell occupants swelled back as the guard's key hit the iron lock and in he stepped with his whip cracking. William backed to the wall with the rest and found Tilly's eyes peering at him.

"Any pretty words now?" Tilly chuckled.

"Just a few," replied William, through his most condescending of smiles. "Something to do with you boiling your fat head!" The whip cracked and the captives were ushered towards the cell gate in an orderly line. William took his place and flashed Tilly a look of contempt. "Despite all your scheming, you scrotum-faced worm, the same fate awaits us now."

"You think?" said Tilly, who threw back a knowing smile.

William felt a grip at his shoulder but before he could decipher Tilly's expression, he was shoved into daylight.

Just as William had witnessed the day before, the captives were lined up in the courtyard and forced to kneel. Light glistened off the scimitar that hung at Hassan's side as he angered the embers in the furnace with an iron. Glancing briefly at the terrified faces all fixed in his direction, Hassan pulled open the draught to make the flames glow hotter. He enjoyed the fear in their eyes. It all seemed so inevitable. William was cursing Samuel under his breath as the door to Bowman's quarters opened. Out stepped Bowman under the shade of the palms held above him. As he made his way to the table, William noted a distinct limp. Although Bowman did his best to conceal it, it was obvious that every slow step was agony. He arrived at his chair which was pulled back in readiness. Yet, unlike the previous occasion, William noticed a large silk cushion on the seat. Bowman tried to sit with as much dignity as he could muster but as soon as his backside touched the silk he stood again quickly with a flash of agony in his eyes. He tried to sit again but again the pain was too much to bear. He ordered the chair be removed and he stood to make his usual speech about ownership.

William closed his eyes as Hassan brought out the branding iron and two savages tore the shirt from the first man's chest and braced him in readiness. It was Corbett and, much to everyone's surprise, his chest already bore a long healed brand mark.

"I'm back!" he shouted, winking at Hassan. "Come for another coat, ya desert dog!"

Hassan glanced to Bowman for guidance.

After a moment's consideration, Bowman nodded. "Refresh his memory!"

Hassan plunged the iron onto Corbett's chest over the old scar. Corbett grimaced but to his credit he didn't scream.

Potter was next in line with William after him.

"F—f—heck," he stuttered, shuddering as the iron approached his flesh. As it thrust towards him, he let out a scream that made everyone's ears hurt.

As Hassan left to re-charge his iron, William cleared his throat. He knew time was running out.

"A moment if I may," he said, adding a loud cough for good measure. "A terrible error has been made and a worse one is here and now."

Bowman's eyes narrowed with curiosity, "How so?"

"I am none other than William Peel of Tornbridge," said William, expecting gasps of astonishment. There was only silence. Bowman let out a brief laugh and waited to hear the explanation. "Hard to believe it may be," continued William, "but I assure you it's as true as baby is to breast."

"Tall tales are rarely so tall," said Bowman, doing his best to hide his pain as he approached William. "I see you have fallen on hard times, my lord," he added, and those who understood English laughed.

"I have been wronged and tricked into peasant clothes. Less said about that the better. Suffice it to say, the man beneath them is quite genuine. I am one hundred percent Peel."

"Your father's name?" enquired Bowman, sternly.

"Charles Mortimer after his great grandfather."

Bowman grabbed William's hair, roughly, and studied his features closely. "You look nothing like him. Which, it has to be said, is a credit to you. As you see, I have met your father," he added, tearing the tatty tunic from William's chest. He studied his bare, pale white flesh. It was skin too pale to be a commoner and Bowman knew it.

"I get my nose from Winston," said William, proudly, "my grandfather. My jaw is from Oliver so I'm told. Fortunately I don't suffer his affliction. He was prone to testicular inflammation, you see," William whispered. "Ugly business."

"I can imagine," replied Bowman, somewhat puzzled.

"Oh, yes. He found it agonising to wear cricket pads and was often observed riding side-saddle."

"Funny thing is," said Bowman, beckoning Hassan to pass his scimitar. "Only last night I met someone else who claimed to be William Peel. Seems like a popular pastime.

You see my predicament?"

William gulped as Bowman jabbed the point of the scimitar into his breast. A trickle of blood ran down over his chubby stomach. "Ouch!" exclaimed William, recoiling. "And no, I don't see your predicament you blasted donkey's dangler. I am William Peel. Even an idiot with a moderately disabling hangover and a bruised liver can surely see I'm not a bloody sailor." He glanced at Corbett, adding a quick. "Well, it is true," before resuming discussions with Bowman. "The man last night was simply wearing my clothes. Badly, I might add. As part of a clever *ruse de guaree* by myself in order to win over your affections and get me out of this God-awful midden. The idiot, Samuel Boyle, has since vanished. Heaven only knows what's become of my clothes."

"Well, the world can live with one less Peel impersonator," said Bowman, gripping the handle of the scimitar tighter and readying to make a killer strike.

"Wait!" said William, urging for a moment. "You kill me and I will see to it no one will deal with you from Tornbridge to Timbuktu." Both William and Bowman paused, sensing at the same time there was a flaw in the logic. "No! Hang on," William back-pedalled. "Scrap that. If you kill me that's clearly not going to happen." He paused a moment, racking his brain for another idea. "It's always the bloody same. I feel like the Indian Tree Mouse. Do you know the creature? It collects nuts and things. Anyway, when it gets attacked by a hawk, it quickly eats all its nuts in one go. It doesn't even chew. The idea being that when the hawk tries to fly off with the little creature it's too heavy. The hawk, which is caught out by the weight of the tiny mouse, crashes to the ground and breaks its neck."

Bowman studied William for a moment, somewhat mystified. "I don't understand?"

"You were just about to untie me, I think," said William, flashing his pearly white smile.

Suddenly, there was a solitary bang on the gates. So loud that it shook the sand from the joints. All eyes fell on it. A moment later there was another bang. The huge gates shuddered in their frame and the hinge-pins rattled.

Bowman withdrew from William and nodded to a savage to open the gates. As the man did as ordered, other savages rushed into the courtyard with their scimitars unsheathed.

The savage at the gate gripped the timber brace and shouted something. William surmised it was likely a request for name and business. Silence was the reply. Suddenly a sword tip skewered through the savage's back and blood poured over his loin cloth. In an eerie moment, he began to rise off the ground. Three feet up, the sword reached the brace and lifted it up clear of its cleats. In a flash, the savage fell as the blade was withdrawn. He crashed to the sand at the same time as the brace.

Bowman's eyes were locked with expectation and he raised his scimitar readying himself for what was to come through the gateway. At that moment a smoke bomb landed with a thud in the middle of the courtyard and fizzed into life. Everyone was consumed in a plume of grey cloud. Intense musket fire then rattled off in all directions.

As the smoke cleared, the savages all lay dead and Volker, *The Pride of Emily*'s captain, stepped in through the gateway. It was the first time William had really seen him up close and he was taken aback by the sheer size of the man. He was a mountain with shoulders that bulged out the sides of a well worn leather waistcoat. His jaw looked like it had been set square by a stone mason and gave the impression that his skull was unbreakable. Fixing his gaze on Bowman, he spat with defiance into the sand.

Glancing up to the wall of the courtyard, Bowman could see Carr with his one-of-a-kind repeating musket poised in his direction; its barrel was still smoking. Next to Carr, Daniel was putting an unused throwing knife into one of the sheaths across his chest.

"Now just wait!" said Bowman, trying to bluff it out. "You know me, Volker. I'm a business man. This is business."

Volker stepped in and glanced at Hassan who gripped his scimitar, motionless. Their eyes met in recognition and both took a step to face the other down. Hassan hunched and growled at Volker through bared teeth. In a flash, Hassan lunged forward and chanced a strike. Without time to move, Volker snatched the incoming arm from the air and punched Hassan with such force that it dislocated his jaw. As Hassan dropped to one knee in agony, Volker grabbed the scimitar from his grip and, without a pause, he cocked his arm and cut. A flash of light danced along the edge of the blade as it sliced the top off Hassan's head at the ear. He dropped like a puppet with its strings cut.

Volker and Bowman had known each other for a long time. Not just from the slave trade but before when Bowman was in the East India Trading Company and Volker a privateer. But it was Volker's reputation built during the Tyrolean Rebellion of 1809 that made him infamous. The peasants, Volker's family, rose up against French and Bavarian occupation. His unflinching heroism during those engagements cast fear into Napoleon's mind and cost him his first defeat at the Battle of Aspern-Essling. Bowman knew that Volker was capable of great barbarism if need called for it and it was that thought that had Bowman's guts twisted.

"You should have told me you captained a new ship," said Bowman, tossing his scimitar into the sand.

"You vill untie him!" ordered Volker, in his rasping German voice, "and za rest," he added, spitting again with contempt.

Bowman weighed up his options but was smart enough to realise he didn't really have any. He slipped a key from his pocket with a sigh and released William's chain from his ankle.

William stood and dusted down his britches. "Well, I have to say," he said, inspecting his torn tunic. "I have never witnessed such poor hospitality. Well, except perhaps from the Bulgarian royal family." To which he picked up a scimitar, and after a moment of judging its weight, he jabbed the tip into Bowman's chest. Bowman stepped away in pain, clutching his wound. "You deserve worse for last night's stew alone," William added. "Not to mention the absence of a cheese course. These are savage lands, indeed."

Suddenly, a whistle came from the parapet. It was Daniel,

"We need to move!" he shouted, pointing into the distance. "Company!"

Without a pause, Volker grabbed William's arm and ushered him to the gates.

"Wait!" exclaimed William, slipping free of the grip and rushing back to Hassan's body. He turned him over and searched him quickly but found nothing.

"My lovely brooch!" exclaimed William.

"No Time," growled Volker, as he hurried William away.

Volker and William ran like the wind through the gateway and out into the busy street. No one gave them a second glance as they ducked fabrics and leapt spice pots. After a few moments they were joined by Carr and Daniel who ran alongside.

"Dare I take it there is a plan?" gasped William.

"There's a harbour," responded Carr, breathless, "about an hour away."

Suddenly, a knife whooshed passed William's head and stuck into the door ahead of them. Glancing over his shoulder, he could see a dozen raiders. They were all dressed in black like Hassan and they cut their way through the screaming crowd with their scimitars.

"Oh Sparkling!" shouted William. "Some plan!"

"We're not dead yet," responded Carr, as another knife stuck in a stall they passed.

Daniel drew a pair of short-swords from sheaths on his

back. "Don't wait for me," he shouted to Carr. In a flash he turned on his heels and charged at the raiders with his swords whirling like a thresher. His blades clattered against the scimitars as he engaged half the raiders at once.

"Don't worry," said Carr, seeing the surprise in William's eyes. "There's only six."

"I was actually more worried about the brutes still chasing us," replied William, nodding in the direction of the half dozen raiders still chasing them.

Ahead they could see the outer wall of the city and the entrance. They pressed on faster, lungs burning, legs aching. The moment they reached the entrance, the shade of the walls vanished and sunlight hit their eyes like an explosion of white. But instead of open desert ahead of them, they were met by the barrels of two dozen muskets. William's heart sank. He closed his eyes tight as a volley of shots rang out.

It took a moment for William to realise that he wasn't dead. He had his eyes closed so long that, when he finally opened them, they took a moment to adjust to the bleaching sunlight. Blurs became shapes. Shapes became people. Finally, he recognised the men ahead of him as some of the crew of *The Emily*. Their musket barrels were still smoking. He turned to see the raiders dead in the sand.

Moments later, Daniel appeared, exhausted, at the entrance. He and Carr exchanged a nod.

"You're slowing, young Daniel," said Carr, as he quickly loaded cartridges of powder and shot into the butt of his repeating musket.

"It's been a long day," smiled Daniel, slipping his swords away into the sheaths down his back.

"Well, it's not over yet," said Carr, sliding the empty cartridges into loops on his belt. "Take off their outer clothes!" he shouted to the men. "We dress as locals!"

William watched as the men stripped the long thobes off the raiders and dressed in them. It was obvious to him by the ease in which they wrapped their heads that this wasn't the first time they had worn such garb.

Volker scanned the horizon with his huge spyglass. "Raiderz to za south and wezt but zhey don't appear interezted."

"Let's not wait to find out," said Carr, turning to the crew and barking, "LET'S GO!"

William turned to see Volker sliding closed his glass. Volker was just staring at him. Staring through him. Neither angry nor inquisitive. A moment passed between them. Volker slung his musket over his shoulder and, after a customary spit, he turned away.

Daniel handed William the reins of a huge, white Arabian stallion.

"Can you ride, sir?" he asked.

Without a pause William snatched the reins, slipped his foot into the stirrup, and swung expertly up into the saddle. The horse reared onto its haunches as William drew on the reins. It was an impressive display.

"Like returning to the womb, eh sir?" asked Daniel, playfully.

"All beasts know their master," responded William,

digging in his heels and galloping off. Sadly, he spilled from the saddle only ten yards away. "I'm alright!" he shouted, pained. "It's the blasted sand. I can't blame the beast for stumbling."

Bowman gazed about the empty courtyard at the bodies of the shot savages. He tapped an empty leg-iron with the toe of his sandal and contemplated the money he had just lost in stock.

"It would have been wise of you to run," said Bowman, seeing Tilly out of the corner of his eye. "For a man whose job it was to seek out those willing to buy freedom or those with value in ransom, you managed to monumentally fail in this instance. Letting slip William Peel himself."

"I confesses, sirs," said Tilly, approaching like the slithering snake he was, "my edge was blunted by his snooty beak and the easy way he looked along it."

"So it would seem." Bowman sighed and limped off towards his quarters, despondent.

"But as that other fella said," added Tilly, trying to appease. "His ship was disabled anyways and most likely plundered."

Bowman got another yard then stopped. "*The Pride of Emily*?" he questioned, struck by a thought. "She must be docked for repair and somehow missed."

"Aye, Lampedusa? Malta, maybe."

Bowman turned quickly, his eyes bright. "No, no.

Volker could limp a ship to safer waters."

"Sicily?" questioned Tilly, doubting it could be done.

"Tell Captain Banda, I want use of his ships and all the men he can muster. Tell him *The Emily*'s gold is his. That should get the greedy bastard motivated."

"That it will, sir," said Tilly, excited.

"The ship and its crew are mine."

"Very generous, sir. And what of the huge captain?"

"Kill him," said Bowman, casually. "Carr and Daniel too. William Peel we keep for ransom." His eyes flashed with a playful thought. "Or, maybe I'll find some other use for the lord of Tornbridge."

As Bowman limped off towards his quarters, Tilly spotted something gleaming in the sand by Hassan's body. It was William's brooch.

The desert winds howled angrily and made the sky and ground appear as one. William and *The Emily*'s crew galloped on as best they could in the vague direction of the coast with nothing but the baking sun to guide them.

William rode alongside Carr with Volker, Daniel, and the crew following. All had their heads wrapped in shrouds to keep out the sand of the desert that whistled about them. The coastal buildings had finally fallen within sight and there was nothing but a few palm trees between the party and them.

A few miles on, the wind died down completely and

the party reduced speed to drink and catch their breath. Carr watched as William sipped from his canteen with his little finger pointing aloft like he was taking tea at the palace.

"If you don't mind me asking?" Carr enquired, curious. "Why did you come on this trip? Seems to me you have all you could ask for back in Tornbridge."

"The burden of position," replied William, taking another drink. The pair continued in silence for a hundred or so yards, swaying in their saddles with the motion of their mounts. "But I tell you this," William suddenly continued. "My father always had stories. He would perch on my bed and, quite animated, tell me of his adventures. Like how he and a band of fellows had helped out Uncle Gustav of Sweden by dressing as Russians and faking an attack. Only, as it turned out," he began laughing, "Denmark, who were good friends of the Russians, then declared war on Sweden. It all got a bit messy apparently. Anywhoo, I always thought such tall tales were just nursery fiction."

"But you don't now?"

"I met some insufferable bore at a party in London a few months back. Percival something or something Percival. British Prime Minister at any rate. He recanted the same exact tale by way of explaining the dangers of international affairs. Prig! As if I, a Peel, need such lessons. Well, of course, I knew then it was a true account."

Carr just stared at William. He wasn't really sure how to follow such a comment.

"He was shot, of course. Percival, I mean," said William. "I'm sure you read of his murder. Can you read?"

Carr nodded. "Good show. Anyway, what was I saying?"

"Bedtime stories," said Carr, trying not to smile.

"Well, I craved such adventures. To besiege a great city or... or storm a what-not with my sabre aloft. Plus Mother had stopped me smoking in the house."

As they neared the coastal settlement, the desert sand beneath their hooves was replaced by earth and patches of scrub. The buildings ahead were simple. Hut's mostly with wooden roofs and stucco walls. Scattered about them were brightly coloured tents. There was the distant sound of people. The clattering of pans, children's voices, and laughter. The smell of fresh bread carried on the wind and, for the first time in days, *The Emily*'s crew could smell the fresh sea air in the distance. Inside the tents, they could see the tribesmen sprawled on cushions; they were chatting as they drew deeply on their hookahs. About the tents ran packs of children, playing, as their mothers prepared food in a group and chattered in their native tongue.

As William's party approached the buildings beyond the camp, Carr slipped his musket off his shoulder and laid it ready across his lap. William turned to see the others do the same.

"You expect to find trouble?" asked William.

"This is raider territory," replied Carr. "You don't have to look hard for trouble here."

Once amongst the buildings, the crew filtered down to single file. The locals carried on about their business as the party trotted on past the stalls and houses. Peering in through the windows, William could see cooking pots steaming on the stoves and piles of washing. It was similar to peasant life he had observed, from a safe distance, of course, in Tornbridge village.

When they were clear of the settlement buildings, the party found themselves at the coastline itself. The beautiful Mediterranean Sea glistened below them and shimmered like a tray of diamonds under the midday sun. It was a welcome sight for the crew and they all took a deep breath as if picking up the scent of a loved one. They were a good two hundred feet above sea level at the top of a steep incline of rocks and scrub that led down to a rocky outcrop and the beach below. William's eyes scanned the various bright blue and white launches tethered to a long jetty just off to their right. He could make out a handful of people loading a boat with provisions. Beyond the jetty, the coast was littered with at least forty craft of all shapes and sizes. Some were making sail and some floating, crewless, without a sign of life on board. It was impossible for William to determine which were friendly and which were hostile. He then remembered Carr's words the first time they met. They were probably all pirates.

"Keep your wits about you men!" called Carr, leading the way. He steered the reins as his mount's hooves found purchase on the scrub track that wound its way down to the beach.

After a moment of considering each craft, William turned to Daniel who was close to his flank.

"Where is *The Emily*?" he asked, in a concerned tone. "Where is my boat?"

"Sicily," responded Daniel.

"Sicily?" questioned William, "But that's…" he paused, attempting to recall his geography tuition. "How far is that exactly?"

"Just over three hundred, sir."

"Yards, I do hope?"

"Miles, sir."

"Preposterous!" scoffed William. "Why, this plan is no plan at all."

Ahead, Carr pulled on his reins and stopped dead. Turning in the saddle, he steeled his eyes on William. "Sir!" he said, in as loud a voice as he dare. "We are about to enter a pirate nest. That is to say, everyone you see is a pirate and any one of them will take a knife to our throats if they think for one breath we're Christian. I beg you now to save your questions until we have this place to our backs. Our very lives depend on it."

William looked away, pointing his nose skyward. "Fine!" he said with a huff.

An uneasy silence fell about the group. Carr paused for a moment as William refused him eye contact. He was about to trot on when William's voice stopped him in his tracks.

"I was merely enquiring as to the whereabouts of my vessel," said William, determined to be in the right. "Not unreasonable."

"Under normal circumstances, no," said Carr, glancing towards the jetty. "But with raiders likely hiding behind every rock we…"

Childishly, William suddenly began singing some operatic ditty just as he would do to silence Mother. Avoiding all eye contact as if completely blocking out Carr's words. "La la la laaa la la lalala laaa lala," he sang.

Carr couldn't believe his ears and neither could the rest of the crew who quickly raised in their saddles with muskets poised. Their eyes scanned the savages below as they prepared for the attention that this was likely to attract.

"Sir?" repeated Daniel, urging for William's silence.

Eventually William stopped singing and tilted his nose skyward. "I trust I have made myself clear?" he said. When no one challenged him, he dug his heels and galloped off past Carr. Carr threw Volker a glance of frustration and disbelief before facing forwards and cracking his own reins.

The track met the shore on a rock shelf where the sea broke and swelled across it. Carr ordered everyone to dismount and he slapped the flank of his beast to send it racing off up the beach. Everyone followed suit and ran for a group of rocks where they could hide to avoid being seen from the savages only fifty or so feet away on the jetty. Overseeing the savages work was a raider. His hand rested on the handle of his huge scimitar as he barked at the fellows for slacking.

Carr glanced over the rocks for a moment then ducked down out of sight. "We're the fourth launch along," whispered Carr, and all leaned in close to hear the plan. "Daniel, you take four men and charge the group loading the boat. Volker and I will handle the raider."

They all ducked down sharply as a raider spied the

horses and his eyes traced along the shore. A moment later, the brute returned to the business of berating the savages for their laziness.

Carr stuck his head up again as far as he dare. He then ducked back down a second later and thumbed in the direction of the jetty. "Sixth boat along on the right. See it?" Everyone chanced a quick glance. "Five pirates with muskets," Carr continued. "They look to be sleeping. We must be quiet."

"Where is Lord Peel?" asked Daniel, suddenly.

The crew glanced amongst themselves but William was nowhere to be seen. Carr and Volker exchanged a look as they realised at the same instant what the likely answer was. They peered over the rocks. Sure enough, William was casually strolling across the rock shelf in the direction of the jetty.

William was far from happy. Not only was *The Emily* nowhere to be seen but he was desperate for his potty and all of Carr's tactical scheming was causing an uncomfortable delay. William had managed to walk within feet of the raider, undetected, before the brute caught sight of him and took a step to block his path.

"Good morning," William said, cheerfully. "Very close today, don't you think?" he said, fanning his face and blowing. It was plain that the raider understood very little English and certainly nothing that William said. He replied curtly in his native tongue. William continued. "Are you aware of Shakespeare's Antony and Cleopatra?" William enquired. "Beautiful story. It's a love affair really. On the one hand you have the handsomely heroic Antony, here in his boat." William held up the index finger of his left hand to represent Antony. "On the other hand we have the exotically complex Cleopatra, she too in a boat," he said, holding up his right hand index finger as well. "Now, picture a sea battle that goes horribly wrong and these two lovebirds," he said, flexing each finger, "decided to split and make off across the sea at great speed." The raider didn't follow but was intrigued. As he focused on the fingers, William suddenly thrust them forward into his eyes. "Well, they soon reached land, of course, as you can see. Or rather you can't see." The raider fell to his knees, clasping his eyes, screaming. Conscious that the noise would alert the savages loading the boat, William kneed the raider so hard under the chin that he collapsed backwards unconscious.

William gulped as the savages in the boat spotted him and quickly snatched up their swords. They were preparing to charge when Daniel and Carr appeared out of nowhere and leapt upon them. In less than a breath, the savages were all clutching their bleeding guts.

"Was my plan boring you?" asked Carr, stepping onto the jetty and flicking the blood from his sword.

"We Peels are free thinkers."

"Really?" said Carr, sheathing his sword and indicating the 'all clear' to Volker. "It's my job to keep you alive."

"Quite so," said William, casually rocking on his heels. "It appeared a very thorough plan, Mr Carr, I was just conscious of the tide," he added, with a sarcastic tone.

Volker led the crew from behind the rocks as Daniel

ran off, silent footed, up the jetty.

"Hiz eyez za bleeding," said Volker as he arrived, indicating to the raider still unconscious on the ground.

"Shakespeare's work can do that to the uninitiated," William said, nonchalantly.

Daniel checked that the savages sleeping in the launch hadn't stirred then signalled so to Carr and the rest.

Moments later, *The Emily*'s crew were all running up the jetty as silent as the creaking timbers would allow. As they neared their launch, Daniel kept guard, watching the opposite boat, intently, with his swords drawn. The armed occupants were snoring, dead to the world, clutching their muskets like comfort blankets. Behind Daniel, *The Emily*'s crew were silently climbing into the launch and taking their places at the oars. Daniel's heart leapt into his mouth as one of the sleeping savages stirred; the man batted a fly from his nose and farted loudly. Once he had settled again, Daniel urged Carr to get everyone seated quicker. It all ran like clockwork. The crew were readying the oars in the rowlocks as Daniel climbed on board and untied the bowline from the jetty. William took to his seat silently. He was oblivious of the danger. Volker and Carr were exchanging a nod in recognition of a smooth operation when suddenly there was an almighty shout.

"You bastard!" cried William, as he stood bolt upright and pointed into the boat at Samuel who was seated at the bow. "You left me for dead whilst you drank and round mouthed your way to freedom."

"Move it!" barked Carr at the oarsman as the woken

savages scrambled to their feet and found their bearings. The launch lurched forwards sending William toppling back into his seat.

"Typical," added William, bracing himself whilst continuing to berate Samuel. "You think nothing of others."

Every member of the crew not rowing was readying a musket as the savages let off a barrage of shots from the jetty that splashed the water, splintered the timbers, and clipped an arm or two. There were cries and crewmen clutched their injuries. Carr moved to the stern and eyed in a shot – BANG! One savage was hit in the chest and flew back across the jetty. William watched as Carr aimed again – BANG! Another savage was hit in the eye as he sighted a shot himself. The remaining savages let off another volley and everyone except Carr ducked. Shots whizzed passed but Carr, unflinching, took aim and – BANG! He took out another savage. With his quarry needing to re-load, Carr had time to steady each shot and hit the remaining three in as many breaths with his repeating musket.

As Daniel tended to the wounded, Carr twisted open an ornate end cap on the butt of the musket, his eyes still scanning the dock for danger. He pulled out a long, thin, polished metal cartridge from the musket butt and replaced it with one of many he had secured in loops on his belt. He then replaced a similar oval cartridge of powder and twisted the end cap of the butt closed. As quick as he could he took aim again on the jetty. He waited and watched. When he was happy the launch had rowed out of range, he sighed and passed the musket to one of the crew.

"You're a brave chap," said William, to a man with a chunk missing from his shoulder. "Don't think it has gone unnoticed. It's times like this that define us, don't you find?" At which the injured fellow passed out and slumped forward.

Samuel was huddled at the bows with his head buried under his arms. It was pretty clear by the way he peeped at William then cowered again that he knew William's anger was justified.

"Samuel sorry," said Samuel, lifting his head for a moment.

It was actually only by chance that he had been picked up at all. He had been found by one of Carr's scouting parties as his appearance matched the description of the clothes that William had been wearing when he fell overboard.

"You're a daft little arse!" said William, unable to think of anything more befitting. He had considered stripping the little idiot of his fine garments but as they were splashed with blood, he didn't really fancy touching them. Instead, William turned his attentions to Daniel who was kneeling beside a bare-chested sailor and attempting to pull some shot from his stomach with pliers. The sailor bit hard on a rope and grimaced as Daniel rummaged about his insides. "Looks tender," commented William, peering over Daniel's shoulder. "I guess you have to know what you're doing."

Daniel let out a frustrated sigh and withdrew the pliers; he was unable to fish out the shot. He wiped his sweating brow. "It's not really the best conditions, sir."

"Quite so," continued William, "Funny to think

something so small can mean the difference between life and... well... you know... the other thing." William went on to explain the importance of sterilising surgical equipment but stopped when he saw the look of hatred in the injured sailor's eyes.

Daniel plunged in again and this time found purchase on the bullet. "I have it! Thank God!" When he pulled out the pliers a jet of blood came with it. Daniel scrambled to keep pressure on the hole. "Powder someone, quickly!"

Carr rushed forward and handed Daniel an oval cartridge from his belt. Daniel snatched it with his blood-soaked hand and poured a measure of charge inside the wound. Working perfectly as a team, Carr grabbed a flint from his pocket and struck it above the wound. There was a blinding flash, a stench of singed flesh, and the sailor passed out from shock. Daniel sat back safe in the knowledge that the wound was cauterised.

"Will he make it?" asked Carr.

"We'll know soon enough," responded Daniel, breathless with exhaustion.

William leaned into Carr's ear. "I can't help but feel I'm in some way responsible for this," he said, causing Carr to frown in disbelief. "Oh, I know not directly," he continued, "as this was your mission but as owner and spiritual leader to the crew I..."

"Sir!" snapped Carr, cutting in. "Why don't you go and f..." He stopped himself from voicing the frank opinion he had poised in his throat. "Why don't you find yourself somewhere quiet to sit. For now. It's been a long day."

William, nodded. "Quite so. You're a good man, Mr Carr." Suddenly, his eye caught sight of what lay ahead of them. They were rowing directly towards a triple-masted pirate galleon with at least a hundred negro faces staring at them from the rail. "What in the name of Satan's potty?" William asked, his jaw hanging.

"Your new ship, sir," smiled Carr. "The crew in much need of spiritual leadership."

The French Twins

The deck of *La Senora Se Levanto*, The Lady Rose, was a world away from the quality and cleanliness of *The Pride of Emily*. She was a split-level galleon, triple-masted, with the foredeck and quarterdeck a dozen steps higher than the main deck itself. Amidships had about twenty oars with benches to take three oarsmen each oar. She stank with years of sweat and God knows what else soaked into the timbers. It was no place for a Peel. No place for anyone with sense and certainly no one with a sense of smell. The slaves, utilised for rowing the craft, were a mixture of African, Spanish, and French. All were chained at the ankles.

"That's how they caught *The Emily*," said Carr, indicating to the slaves. "Combined with the sail she has an impressive turn of speed," he added, climbing down the steps to the main deck.

"This is the pirate boat that chased alongside *The Emily*?" asked William, following. "When the idiot Samuel knocked me over her blasted rail?"

Carr headed off towards the steps leading to the quarterdeck which were central to the ship. All the slaves watched in silence as Carr, William and Daniel walked past and climbed up onto the quarterdeck.

"*The Emily* is in dock at Sicily," said Carr, searching his pockets. "It will take a few days more to make her seaworthy. The rest we'll tend to on route to the Americas."

"How long to get us there?" asked William, sweeping his hand along the rail then inspecting the resulting stain on his fingers.

"If the wind stays with us we'll be there in a day, maybe less," replied Carr, taking out a cheroot.

"You expect me to protest?" asked William

"I do," said Carr, unguarded in his response. "She's not as pretty as you're used to and below deck is worse but she's solid, armed, and fit for what we might find ahead of us."

William smiled and rocked on his heels. "Mr Carr, you think me too demanding?"

Daniel and Carr exchanged a look, a smile which William missed.

"I think you have high expectations," responded Carr, lighting his smoke.

"Too high?" questioned William.

"Life at sea doesn't suit all."

"True," responded William, pacing. "One has been accustomed to better things, of course. Food without flies on it, palatable wines, and clothes that don't cause a rash. I hope, however, you have now judged for yourself that I'm not made of China."

"Oh no, sir," said Daniel, with his usual sarcasm. "Not China, sir."

"Good show. Now if you will excuse me," William said. "I assume a cabin has been prepared?"

"Daniel?" said Carr, putting on an air of formality. "Will you show our guest to his quarters? I'm sure he will find the fittings to his liking."

Daniel led William to the captain's quarters; the cabin directly below the quarterdeck. It was the full width of the ship and had leaded windows to the stern. It was empty, except for a tin bath, a bed, a table and chairs. By the various silhouettes of once placed furniture and pictures, the place had been cleared, disinfected, and probably fumigated. Hanging up to the right of the door was a set of gleaming clean clothes. William's heart raced when he saw the splendour of the gold stitching to the tunic and polished buttons of the jacket. He had only been in the room for a moment when the stable hands rushed in about him and set the table with fruit and a bottle of wine.

"Well, this is most agreeable," said William, as a glass was charged and offered to him on a silver tray. "The captain's cellar or mine?" he enquired.

"Yours, sir, beggin' your pardon," replied the fat stable hand.

"No, no. It's all fine," he said, raising his hands above his head thus desiring his tunic be removed. "Mother would disapprove of the last few days, of course, which is excellent. And how is George?"

The stable hands began to lift the tunic off William but stopped when it was half way past his head. At that moment William heard the sound of hurried feet and the door creak closed. He then felt the tunic slowly lift once more.

"Not eaten anyone, has he?" William asked, as his britches were slipped down his legs. "Hang on!" he said, peering below the hem of the tunic as it was suddenly snatched free from his arms.

Much to William's surprise, the stable hands had vanished and two handsome young women were standing before him. They were naked as the day they were born. Twins, he determined, from their matching curly red hair and piercing blue eyes. In a flash, William clutched his modesty and was about to protest when a velvet French accent cut him off.

"We are to bathe you, if sir wishes it," said one.

"Really?" asked William, taking a nervous gulp. "But your... your... your clothes are missing," he added, his voice raising to a high pitch.

"We can be very messy when we wash," said the other, with a giggle.

"Makes sense to be naked, yes?" added the first, looking up at him as she tugged his britches off completely.

William found himself gazing down at her swaying breasts and, as a gentleman should, he quickly averted his eyes. He also found a sudden urge to change the subject.

"I... I... I am quite surprised by the climate of the Mediterranean," he said, staring intently at a dowel in the ship's timbers.

"One must be careful of the sun," said one, approaching with a jug and sponge, "and have plenty of fluids."

"Why, sir, you are quite shivering," said the other as she placed a hand on his inner thigh.

"It's… it's ex-exhaustion… it's… it's been rather an eventful we—eeee—ek," he shrieked, as the wet soapy sponge touched his stomach.

Carr and Daniel were at the stern rail watching the wake when they heard William's operatic singing ring out through the window of the cabin below them. They exchanged a knowing glance and the glimmer of a smile.

Nine hours later, William strode up on deck sporting his new clothes and with a decided spring to his gate. It was dusk and there wasn't another ship to be seen for miles. Far ahead was the dark outline of Sicily with a scattering of tiny lights along the shoreline. Towering over them in the background was the eerie silhouette of Mount Etna.

Daniel was leaning against the stern rail talking with Carr who was loading musket shot into custom-made cylindrical cartridges.

"Gentlemen," said William, slapping his stomach with contentment. "Making good time are we?"

"Good bathe, sir?" asked Daniel, nudging Carr.

"Most invigorating, yes. I have to say I've never felt anything quite like it. Extraordinary."

"A new you?" asked Carr, turning to fix on the horizon, fighting a giggle.

"I should say so," responded William, approaching the rail. "Took three washes to get the stink of Bowman's fort off me."

Daniel doubled up with laughter, which he hid by

pretending to cough.

"Are you alright?" William enquired.

"Excuse me, sir," he said, backing away with haste. "Tickly cough, sir." He turned and laughed his way down the steps.

"Nothing untoward, Mr Carr? Everything ship-shape?" asked William, trying out a newly learnt expression.

"We're not out of the woods, if that's what you're asking," said Carr, his eyes fixed on to the lead shot he had tipped out into his hand.

"No? Well, I feel in safe enough hands," said William, choosing his next words carefully. "Mr Carr? Those two young ladies?"

"Young ladies?" responded Carr, playfully acting ignorant.

"The two who joined this leg of our voyage."

"Ah, Amelie and Aimee," acknowledged Carr, smiling as William offered him a cheroot. "Charming company so I'm told."

"Quite so. Are they, by any chance, staying on with us to the Americas?" probed William.

"Women are bad luck."

"Surely not such little ones?" said William, hopefully.

They both took a light from a match which Carr then tossed into the wash.

"Whether you believe it or not, it's superstition," added Carr, turning to lean against the rail. "It angers the sea."

"Then why are they aboard?"

"Volker thought you might benefit from, how shall we

say, a good 'scrub-up' following your ordeal."

"SHIPS TO STERN!" Came the cry from the watch above them and a chill blew across the deck.

Carr turned in a flash and focused on the horizon. There was nothing he could see. "GLASS!" he shouted and one was duly dropped down to him by the watch. He had it fixed on the horizon when Volker and Daniel rushed to his side.

"What is it?" asked Daniel, as he raised his own spyglass to see.

"Pirates!" said Carr. "My God they've gained some water if they've followed us."

"Not vone! Zere are three," piped up Volker, sighting them with his huge spyglass which was twice the length of Carr's.

"Hiding their numbers?" queried Daniel.

"Hunting something, za dogs!" stated Volker, before spitting an oyster over the side.

William was curling his lip with revulsion at the sight of Volker's spit vanishing into the wash when all eyes fell on him at the same instant. It was obvious to everyone that the pirates were hunting William.

"Rot!" exclaimed William, his nose tilting up. "Hunting a Peel indeed. Would a mouse hunt a hawk? Would a wildebeest stalk a tuna? Err, I meant Puma."

"ALL ZTATIONS!" shouted Volker at the crew. "FULL ZPEED!"

Carr turned to William. "You better get below."

"But they can't catch us, surely?" William enquired.

"Zhey mean to try," said Volker, his voice filled with determination and enthusiasm. He jumped the steps and rushed amidships amongst the chained slaves rowing at a steady pace. "VOR YOR LIVEZ!" he barked, taking a place at the end of an oar. He pulled so hard he took the slack off the three slaves next to him. Shocked at his power they all doubled their efforts.

"How long?" William asked Daniel, who still had the glass to his eye, judging the speed.

"It will be close, sir, very close."

"Time for me to bathe again, perhaps?"

Ahead of *La Senora Se Levanto* was the coast of Sicily and the harbour of Marina di Ragusa; a small fishing village south of Vittoria. It was home to white and blue fishing boats and large pleasure launches. They were all tethered to a single timber jetty that jutted out a good hundred yards from a harbour road. Boats gently swayed to the rhythm of the evening tide as a scattering of fisherman packed up after a day's hard work. Beyond the harbour road was a row of shops and painted cottages. Between a few of the buildings were narrow, steep streets bounded by more cottages. It was a sleepy little place that lived and breathed by the success of the fisherman's nets.

Between the harbour road and the sea was a narrow stretch of beach strewn with rowing boats, nets and lobster pots; all were ready for the early morning's work. Directly opposite the jetty, a small tavern was open for business. Drunken revelry and music poured through its small, crooked doorway. A few Sicilian fishermen jostled and joked on the pavement outside as they gulped their liqueur and smoked their pipes. It was a beautiful evening for sharing tall tales.

A mile from shore, and closing fast, was *La Senora Se Levanto*. She was ripping through the gentle waves as fast as the wind and oarsmen could muster. Volker joined Carr and Daniel at the stern rail. All spyglasses were fixed on the enemy who was then only a thousand yards behind. Carr watched, unflinching, as a flash on the deck of the lead ship was followed by a familiar crack in the still air. The pirates were in range and using their deck cannon.

"INCOMING!" shouted Carr, as a cannon ball whistled alongside them. It missed them only by yards. "The next will be closer," he said to Daniel, looking towards the distant harbour. "They'll be alongside us before we reach safety."

Daniel snapped closed his spyglass with frustration then watched as there were two more flashes behind them.

"INCOMING!" shouted Carr again.

A cannon ball rattled through the rigging above them but was too high to cause much damage.

They were putting their minds to the problem when William arrived casually on deck. He was sipping a glass of sherry as if taking in the evening air back at Peel Manor.

"Good lord, they're close at our heels," he said, seeing

the ships behind them. "Shouldn't we try and out run them?"

"What an excellent idea, sir," responded Daniel, rolling his eyes. "Perhaps though it would be safer if you returned to your cabin. In case we fail, sir. They'll be along side in ten minutes or less depending how we slow."

"Slow?" questioned William, savouring a drink. "Why would we slow?"

Daniel sighed, he was not really in the mood to explain. "We're approaching land, sir. We slow because the sea below us is about to run out!"

William took the spyglass in one hand and glanced back at the enemy ships. He nearly spat out his sherry when his gaze landed on none other than Tilly himself. "The wretched sewer trout!" Tilly, as it happened, also had a glass on William and casually nodded a greeting across the expanse of water. "Dirty bastard!" William turned the glass towards the harbour. "Seems to me the only course of action is to hit the harbour full speed. Use the advantage to make our escape on land."

Daniel responded with disbelief, "Perhaps if we had *The Emily*'s sea brake, yes, but…"

Volker smiled, he could see some merit, crazy as the plan was.

"Yes, we aim for the line of fishing boats," continued William, with confidence. "They will act as a damper and break our progress. There will be damage to the boats, of course, but Ferdinand, The King, is my Uncle. I'm sure he won't mind when I explain the urgency." He passed back the spyglass, adding, "I'm schooled in the sciences. Providing we brace ourselves casualties will be unlikely."

"Your Uncle?" asked Carr, impressed.

"Well, not my proper Uncle," replied William, downing his sherry. "You know what it's like when you're growing up and your parents have friends around for afternoon croquet. It seems too formal to call him King, your highness, or what not. Truth is, I don't have any proper uncles," he sighed, "just oodles of improper ones."

The crew were apprehensive about the idea of crashing into the jetty and cries of "Land ahoy!" were issued with increasing fervour. Volker dismissed them all with a spit over the side and barked orders regardless. As expected, Tilly's ships slowed as they approached shore and *La Senora Se Levanto* fell out of range of their cannon. Daniel slapped Volker's shoulder at the sight of Tilly's ship lowering her sails.

"Normally, I would cheer at such a sight," said Daniel, "but there is the matter of us hitting land at full speed."

La Senora Se Levanto was a minute from the shore and couldn't stop even if the crew had wanted her to. Volker gave the order to brace and, after lowering her sails, everyone rushed about to find a suitably sturdy part of the ship to cling on to.

Carr, who had tied himself to the mizzenmast, rang the deck bell with great vigour to give the villager's what warning he could. Ahead, he could see the locals gazing upon the huge approaching bows with shock and horror. Those people on the boats or the jetty jumped clear for their lives as the bows of *La Senora Se Levanto* carved through the side of the first fishing boat like a knife through toast. The little boat's mast and rigging shattered and ripped as the huge hull sliced it in half. Quite against William's plan, *La Senora Se Levanto* showed no signs of slowing and made light work of the second boat then the third. Wood splinted and shattered in all directions as the bows became speared with timbers and adorned with snagged fishing nets and pieces of sail. All with little or no affect on speed.

On the deck, Daniel and the rest of the crew buried their heads as wreckage and spray showered about them. One crash after another shuddered through the hull timbers.

The pursuing ships had long since stopped and weighed anchor. Tilly stood at the bow watching as *La Senora Se Levanto* decimated the last few boats and skimmed up the beach towards the harbour road. Tilly barked at everyone to man the launches and the pirate crew, quick to follow his orders, lowered the small boats over the sides of the three ships. A minute later, a hundred men were jumping into them bearing muskets and scimitars.

La Senora Se Levanto carved a path across the beach and slammed into the jagged rocks. The whole ship reared up with an explosion that tore her keel to pieces. Fortunately, the screams from the fishermen outside the tavern were enough to effect a prompt evacuation and the street quickly filled with locals running for their very lives.

Lurching onto her side with a dull thud, *La Senora Se Levanto* ground her way across the road and smashed straight through the tavern wall. A shower of stone and slate gradually became nothing but rubble and dust. The ship came to rest with a loud groan from her hull. When the last of the dust had settled, the extent of the devastation was clear. Not only had the ship destroyed the boats, the jetty, the road, and the tavern but she had also caused extensive damage to the adjoining buildings whose insides were on show for all to see. An old woman in the cottage next door timidly approached the edge of what used to be her bedroom and peered with disbelief at the ship which had her rug and some of her clothes littered over its bows.

Slowly, the crew emerged from the wreckage covered in dust, coughing. They limped across the rubble and out onto the harbour road where they formed themselves into groups and tended to their wounds.

Carr, Volker, and Daniel were picking bits of timber from their clothes and hair and patting the dust away when an impeccably well dressed William eventually emerged. He was arm in arm with the two French twins who were still naked and careless of the fact. William had avoided injury by bracing himself to a bulkhead and he had used the fat stable hand to cushion the impact. He instructed the gaunt and cross-eyed stable hands to do the same for his naked, French companions. They didn't object.

The locals gathered about them with raised voices whilst pointing to the buildings, their boats, and the mangled jetty. The crew were somewhat shell-shocked and couldn't find a word of response. Even though no one spoke Sicilian, it was pretty obvious that the locals were furious that their livelihoods, nay their very lives, were ruined. It was only when Carr was grabbed by an old fisherman, and pointed out to sea towards the wreckage of the old man's boat, did the reason for their state of affairs suddenly leap back to his mind.

Tilly's men had almost reached the beach. Some were already over the side of their launches and wading through the water with their muskets aloft.

Carr snapped back into reality. He grabbed his musket and let out a shot into the night sky. Everyone froze and their gaze fell on him.

"R-U-N!" he shouted, pointing in the opposite direction to Tilly.

It was apparent as William and the crew ran for their lives that many were too injured from the crash to make good an escape. They managed to get only a quarter mile through the pretty town, as far as the square, where they were suddenly faced with a battalion of Sicilian soldiers. Hundreds of muskets were pointed in their direction. They were surrounded.

So used to parties of raiders, the Sicilians had become well versed in dealing with an attack and had encircled not only William's party but Tilly's as well. In a perfectly orchestrated operation, the Sicilian Army had closed off the side streets behind them and penned them in. For the second time in as many days, William was captured. Only this time it was by a recognised authority who charged them all with piracy. Such a charge only carried one punishment. A very public execution awaited them all.

The Sicilian Misunderstanding

William Peel hadn't seen a basement in his entire life. He was forbidden to go into them by his parents. A cellar was for wines, cold meats, and for the house staff to go about their numerous duties such as polishing coal and ironing cushions. The air would disagree with his delicate chest, noted his childhood nanny, Mrs Forbes, in her strict Scottish brogue.

So, for William to find himself behind bars in the damp bowels of some ancient Sicilian fort was a matter of grave concern and he soon understood why they were not the sorts of places one should frequent. The low vaulted ceiling created a rank humidity he could taste with every breath. There was also the obligatory dripping noise. The mouldy, stained walls oozed with a hundred years of angst from tortured souls. Prisoners were kept in iron-barred cells with ten or so men per cell. The only light came from a flickering oil lamp by the door. It was a miserable place. The only saving grace was that those who shared the cells were those who had been captured together so William shared with Volker, Carr, Samuel, Daniel, plus the stable hands.

A few of the slaves who had been tethered to the oars

of *La Senora Se Levanto* smiled at William through the bars of the next cell. They were enjoying the fact that he too knew what it felt like to be caged like a beast.

William paced. Which was highly annoying for Daniel who was sitting against the wall unable to do anything else but watch him. Volker was stretched out on a bed, snoozing, whilst Carr tested the bars hoping to find a weakness.

"We somewhat overshot your calculations, Lord Peel," said Daniel, unable to contain his sarcasm any longer.

"I believe the error came, not with my calculation, thank you Daniel," responded William, with typical resolve, "but in the inferior hull strength of the average Sicilian fishing boat."

"And the wall strength of the average Sicilian Tavern?" Daniel replied, resting his head back against the wall.

"We can sit about criticising local boat builders and stone masons all day," said William, sharply. "But our attention must surely be to our immediate predicament. This damp will be the death of my stitching!" he added, closely inspecting the hem of his beautiful tunic. "Perhaps someone from *The Emily* will realise we are late returning and send another party?"

"Unlikely," said Carr. "Once *The Emily* is seaworthy, Barker will set sail. That was the deal. There's no rescue party for this rescue party."

William sighed. He was desperate to sit but there was nowhere clean. Even the bars weren't clean enough to lean against. "Oh, this is just intolerable! What is our crime? What cause do they have to keep us like this? Without food or water. And why is there no response to my note?"

"William thirsty?" asked Samuel, pointing to William then his own mouth.

"Yes, of course," snapped William, with a flash of contempt, "and no need to point to your mouth, I know where the blasted water goes. It's the lack of it that's the problem."

Samuel indicated that William should watch him as he approached the wall and pointed to a trickle of damp.

"Oh God!" exclaimed William, curling his lip. "Tell me you're not suggesting we..." He watched as Samuel lapped away at the damp wall as a kitten would a saucer of milk. "Yes, you are suggesting that," said William, cringing. "That's lovely. Problem solved. Everyone find a dribble!"

"Don't you have some diplomatic powers, sir?" asked Daniel. "Surely they can't tie up a head of state, or whatever Tornbridge is, and you are, and keep you like this?"

"It's complicated," sighed William. "But when Uncle Ferdinand receives my note, well, his doe leather gloves will be across the faces of many a Sicilian jailer. Have no fear."

Next morning William found himself sitting at a sturdy desk and staring across at the balding head of some Sicilian official as the fellow hunched over his notes. Next to him was a bookcase containing important looking books. The walls were littered with poorly executed paintings of great sea battles. Presumably successful campaigns, William noted to himself as he listened to the man's quill scratch at the paper. Next to the desk stood two serious looking Sicilian soldiers with muskets at their sides.

The man behind the desk leaned back in silence to

review his papers. He was in his late forties with a hook nose and unusually large ear lobes, which William found strangely fascinating. It was then William noticed it. Attached to the breast of this stranger's tunic, and gleaming bright as day, was William's brooch. William fought the urge to snatch it from the blaggard whilst, at the same time, grabbing his huge ear lobes and using them to bang his head repeatedly on the desk.

"My name is Jose Escobar," came a quiet voice in adequate English, as the man put the paper back on his desk. "I have many forms to complete. Your name?"

"William Ernest Peel of Tornbridge."

"A long name," replied Jose with a laugh, and he wrote what William had just told him.

"No, no!" said William, seeing the misunderstanding. "The 'of Tornbridge' is where I'm from."

"Oh, I see," replied Jose, correcting his form. "And 'of Tornbridge' is England, yes?"

William let out a sigh and gave the whole thing up as a bad job. He really could not be bothered with trying to explain that Tornbridge had partial independence therefore was not wholly under British rule. He might, of course, then have to explain that it only got said independence to 'hush up' the fact that old Mortimer Peel, William's great-great grandfather, had bedded The King of England's wife whilst drunk at a party. The independence meant Tornbridge had its own flag, its own currency, and was pretty much left alone until someone needed Peel money.

"Did you, per chance," enquired William, "pass on my

note?"

Jose wrote for a moment longer then looked up. "Oh, I see. The letter to The King. That was you? Well, it's unusual to say the least but yes, I did."

"And?"

"And I send message to The King as you ask."

"And?"

"And he respond."

"And his response was?" William pressed.

Jose sighed and picked up a piece of paper. He read it to himself and laughed about it to himself. He then put it down. "It appears The King will not help you."

"What! He's my Uncle."

"Really? A proper Uncle or just someone who was friends with your parents?"

"Never mind that! I only saw him a few weeks ago. He gave me a brooch for my birthday." His eyes burned into the glistening jewels on Jose's chest.

"Do you have it?" asked Jose, his nose pricking up at the scent of a pay day.

"Not on me, no. It was stolen. Filthy bastards! Still, I expect it will turn up one day on the lapel of some greasy spillage. Such things are the currency of kings and whores."

"Shame," said Jose, smiling. "It would have helped your predicament."

"So I believe," responded William, with a sarcastic sigh. "And may I say it's refreshing to hear an official so openly celebrating corruption."

"Of course! As they say in England, it's the squeaky

weasel that gets the grease, yes?"

"Almost but I actually think 'greasing the wheels of commerce' is what you were clumsily stumbling for. Anyway, forgetting for the moment that what you actually described was the lubrication of a small mammal, can you please just get on with the business of the note's content."

Jose picked up The King's note again. "He writes that he now knows you sided with Napoleon," at which point Jose paused to shake his head at William and offered a few tut's before he continued reading, "a fact I discovered at your party. A fact I pro... protes..." Jose stopped reading and squinted at the page. "Please, his writing is very bad."

"Protested?" suggested William, rolling his eyes.

"Oh yes," responded Jose, before continuing. "A fact I protested with some animation in your def... defence. Only to have received a kick in my gusset from that French ass for such trouble." Jose passed William the note. "The Bonapartes are not very popular here. They invaded. Did you know this?"

"Kicked in the gusset?" queried William, reading the note. "I don't recall mention of this. What's the old fool talking about?" On hearing which the guards took a step forward and presented the points of their bayonets at William's head. "All I'm saying," said William, in his defence. "Is that I'm eighteen. I haven't had time to side with anyone. Besides, he's got a nerve. It's not so long since you were all closer than bread and pâté. Oh, which reminds me," he paused, recalling a very important point. "It was my family who financed the operation to kick Napoleon off your blasted island. Surely that gives me some prestige?"

Jose dismissed the guards back to their corner and reclined in his chair. "Lord Peel, my job is to supervise your execution. It's not a job I relish you understand but if I do not do it someone else will. Such is my wife's view. Piracy is big problem here. When we land such a prize as your party it's our duty to set example. Nothing says we officials are working hard like a few public killings."

"What? – Death? - Over a couple of cheap boats and a public house. That's hardly civilised!"

"Some of the marked slaves who rowed your boat were known to me. They were taken by pirates and raiders of your gang. One was my neighbour, Enzu. He has borrowed many things over the years without returning them so I would not mourn his loss but... The other is Nello, my tailor. I happen to like Nello very much. He is very cheap."

"Evidently," replied William, glancing him up and down.

"Well, you will excuse me," replied Jose, somewhat prickled by the insult. "Your execution means much preparation."

Jose leaned forward to pick up his quill. Before William could raise a word of protest or explanation, he was picked up by the elbows and bundled from the room.

William returned to captivity to find a bowl of some kind of food that looked like potatoes floating in urine. Glancing to the next cell, he noticed that the slaves had all been removed. Only three other cells were still full of pirates.

"Have you negotiated our release?" asked Daniel, with

more sarcasm than hope in his voice.

"Release of a sort," replied William, curling his nose up at the food. "We are to be executed." A thought hit him and in a flash William rushed to the bars. His eyes traced the sorry lot in each cell. "Tilly?" he called. "Tilly, you blaggard! Show yourself, damn you!" But there was no reply. The pirates just stared back in silence.

Carr took to his feet. "What is it?" he asked, with genuine concern.

"He was on the boat. I saw his little rat eyes. The blaggard has bought his freedom, I know it. The little Bowman-rat bought the key to his cage with my brooch."

"What?" Carr questioned, not following William's point.

"It was Bowman's damn hunting party after me. Tilly hasn't the wit to act alone," he searched Carr's eyes but Carr still didn't get William's theory. "Bowman is after *The Emily*! My gold. And probably me. Now he knows we're on Sicily!"

Daniel stood up. "You don't know that, sir. Coincidence is all."

"No," said Carr, weighing it up. "Lord Peel is right. We limped *The Emily* here knowing she would be easier to hide than on Malta or Lampedusa."

"And now Tilly's scurrying back to tell Bowman," said William, with urgency.

Carr paced, rubbing his neck. "Then we need a plan."

"I have one," said William, eagerly. "There must be one of you with a guinea about them?"

They all glanced at each other blankly then Carr caved in. "Here," he said, reluctantly before turning to the wall. He unscrewed one of the caps from a button and tipped out a shiny gold coin. Out of the corner of his eye, he saw Volker peeping. "And don't you get ideas," he said, to his old friend. "They're not for betting on Mah-jong or whoring." Volker smiled and rolled to the wall.

William took the coin, tipped out the food from his tray, and banged it on the bars to get a guard's attention.

A day passed after William had paid the guard with Carr's guinea to deliver a note. It was early morning and dawn light poured through the iron grill in the ceiling. William was lost in thought as he paced.

Carr was seated with Daniel and Volker. They were all getting agitated by William's restlessness.

"I did say that you should have split the coin," said Carr, "only given him the other half once you knew it was delivered."

"Balderdash! He gave me his word," responded William. "Besides, there was no effort in the task. No reason for him to not complete it."

"Sir is there something you've missed?" probed Daniel. "Perhaps an instruction you relayed in error. A lack of urgency?"

"There was no error," said William. "Damn it! A British gentleman should sense the importance of a hurried note delivered by a prison guard. Such a note should go straight to the top of the Consulate's pile. Not be put to one side on the 'I'll get to that in a few days' pile with the blasted bills."

They suddenly became aware of a commotion above their heads. Through the grate, they could see movement and hear men at work with hammers against wood and metal. For two hours it lasted. The sound then changed to that of a gathering crowd and the jeers of a rowdy mob. Whatever was going on, the crowd sounded enthusiastic and excited about it.

The pirates in the cell next to William could sense something was happening too. A cold chill drifted about the cellar. Hope, it seemed, was slipping into despair.

William watched as one pirate, one of the biggest, leaned with his head against the bars of the cell opposite. The man was muttering to himself with a look of terror in his eyes. Suddenly, the front of his britches began to darken with a lengthening shadow that became a trickle of urine over his sandal.

William shuddered at the sight of it then his eyes fixed on the main door as the rusty iron bolt clunked back and the hinges groaned under the weight as it swung open. In rushed half a dozen Sicilian soldiers with Muskets levelled through the bars. In a well-rehearsed operation, they took positions at the furthest cell. Muskets were poised at the figures huddled beyond the bars. The pirates backed away into the shadows as a prison guard unlocked their cell door. He barked at the pirates to leave the cell and held out a stack of cloth sacks for their heads. When his calls were met with reluctance, a solider fired his musket indiscriminately into the shadows. A pirate fell clutching his chest. The victim had barely hit the ground when the others were forming an orderly line. With the sacks placed over their heads, and their wrists bound tightly behind their backs, they were marched out double time. The main door was swung shut again and the bolt shot.

Volker, Carr, William, Samuel and Daniel moved to the edge of the cell to try and look up through the grate above. A moment passed then they heard the crowd roar with excitement. It was followed by an announcement in Sicilian, which Carr translated as the death sentence. There was a bold statement from Jose about how the authorities will not stand by and see their loved ones and tailors be taken in the night by cowardly dogs.

There was silence.

Suddenly, there was a mechanical thud and the crowd erupted with applause.

"Guillotine!" announced Daniel. "No way for a sailor to die."

There was another thud. Then another cheer.

"Jesus!" said Carr, gripping the bars. "There's hardly a pause between them."

"Look," said Volker, pointing across to the far wall where there was a trickle of blood running down through the ceiling grate. "I vas not born to die like zis," he said, stepping back.

"Then we have to fight!" whispered Carr. "If we don't get away it will be an end to us and the rest of *The Emily*'s crew."

In that instant the door creaked open and the Soldiers rushed in to take aim at the pirates in the next cell. As before, the guard quickly followed them in with sacks for each prisoner. This time though, the pirates knew what fate awaited them. As soon as the cell door was opened, they rushed it and surged forwards with gritted teeth and balled fists. They hit nothing. Having only travelled a yard, the front few were met with musket shots and fell dead. When the smoke cleared, the rest were subdued and dragged out. Once again, the door was pulled shut behind them.

"If the route out is the same as we took coming in," said Carr, "there is a narrow corridor where we were forced into single file. That's where we'll leave." He silenced when he heard the familiar thud above them and the cheering that followed. "Anyone spots a chance, take it. We all follow."

The door swung open and the soldiers marched in with muskets raised. It was their turn. If the timing of the last group was anything to go by, they would all be dead in less than five minutes. William gulped as he contemplated the guillotine blade slicing his beautiful collar. As the muskets were poised, each man was handed a sack for their heads.

As they were led from the cell, William could see the faint outline of shapes through the weave of the sack. He could make out the courtyard doorway ahead of them from the daylight that poured through it. He could hear the distant cheers as the guillotine fell and could smell air tainted with sweat and fresh blood. Suddenly, there was a commotion behind him. He could hear the sound of crashing furniture and a growl of power. It was one last scream of a man making a break for his life. He turned to see Volker's massive shoulders crushing soldiers against the wall as he ran. William took up the pace. He had to or he too would be crushed in Volker's wake. Ahead, William could see that the corridor was clear. Suddenly, a lone figure appeared through the doorway ahead of him. By the silhouette, it was a soldier of some size. William lowered his head and charged. With all he had, he charged. It was like being a boy again back on the summer lawns of Peel Manor. He remembered charging at Able, his trusty bodyguard, with a cushion under his arm. It was a game they played often. That was until William complained of a stitch and had to go inside for some restorative chocolate. This was no game though and William had gone no further than a couple of yards when it felt like he had hit a wall. His world instantly turned to black in one painful crack as a musket butt struck his head. With the sound draining from his ears, he felt his face hit the cold stone floor.

William opened his eyes. Not to see the inside of a wicker basket and a fading sky but the office he had been in the day before. His hands were untied and, except for a pain in his head and a ringing in his ears, he was very much alive and well. Seated across the table was a well presented man in his thirties. His face was youthful, flushed and, judging by his stocky shoulders, he was a sporting type kept young by clean living and physical exertion. Neither of which William put any store by. William was just about to utter his first pained words when he suddenly realised he was not sitting with Volker, Carr, Daniel or Samuel. Nor the stable hands either for that matter. Not that their safety was the first thought that entered his head.

"There were two young women in my party?" enquired William, his head throbbing. "French girls. Very small."

"You needn't worry," said the stranger, who was an Englishman. "They have been taken to safety."

"You're British?" William enquired.

"I most certainly am. A fellow William. William Bentinck. You are Lord Peel? Although I have to say, I'd never heard of Tornbridge. Independent lands within the British Isles, indeed. Who would believe it?"

"My note came to you?" asked William.

"Note? I have seen nothing of a note. Field Marshal Wellesley..." he was about to finish when William interrupted.

"Tut! Don't talk to me about that puffed up ass!" he snapped. "The fellow's a side plate short of a full service."

At which point, Bentinck coughed and darted his eyes in the direction of the doorway. William turned to see Field Marshal Arthur Wellesley, the Iron Duke of Wellington, leaning against the frame. His broad shoulders almost blocking the doorway.

"Uncle Arthur!" exclaimed William, with a smile which soon slipped. "Why weren't you at my party you big log?"

Wellington stepped in and, after patting William on the shoulder affectionately, he perched on the desk in front of him. "War as always, young William. War as always. How is Mother?"

"Still widowed if that's what you mean."

"I am sorry, William. I wanted to be there, really I did."

"Rot! Uncle Boney made it."

"The Emperor of Elba you mean?" Wellington smiled, winking to Bentinck. "And how is Able? Keeping well I hope?"

"Never mind the blasted staff," said William, impatiently. "So my note came to you?"

"What is this note?" questioned Wellington, wearily.

"I paid a guinea for a prison ape to get a note to the British consulate. I was forced to. Uncle Ferdinand is in a flounce over something."

Wellington let out a laugh. "Your prison guard would have made straight for the nearest Tavern, William. Except that, in this case, he would have found a slave galleon in it. You only give half up front, my boy."

"Anyway," said William, desiring to change the subject. "If you didn't get my note. And he didn't," he said, pointing to Bentinck. "Why are you here and where are my crew?"

"Your Uncle Ferdinand and I were dining together," said Wellington. "He's very distressed. His young mistress went missing on route to Naples. He's enlisted the help of the British Navy."

"This is all very well, Uncle, but I was nearly beheaded. Which I'm told is very painful and difficult to reverse."

"He's not happy with you, William," continued Wellington, "and neither am I. Financing the French, indeed. You do know that Napoleon kicked Ferdinand out of his palace not long back? Crowned his brother, Joseph, as King."

"Uncle, I refuse to discuss business. Whatever deals made, or not made, by my father are no concern of yours. Unless they are a direct concern of yours. If you follow?"

"Not really," said Wellington. "Your crew are next door, by the way. All safe. As for your Uncle Ferdinand, I think he just wanted you to sweat a little."

"So I may go?"

On hearing this, Wellington nodded to his colleague behind the desk to take over.

"It's not that simple, my lord," said Bentinck. "There is the matter of the harbour repairs."

"Balderdash! Uncle, you're not going to sit there and let this buttock tap me up for a few rotten boats."

"The repair estimates are considerable," said Bentinck. "It's not just the boats, it's the tavern, the cottages, the road, the loss of earnings etc. Not to mention dismantling the pirate ship you wrecked. To top it all," Bentinck added, leaning in, "you injured the local prostitute and the tavern landlord. Apparently, he was seeing to his business in the tavern cellar when you sailed into his bar."

William sighed, sensing what was coming. "And the prostitute was presumably seeing to her business, which was seeing to the landlord? My God, it's like some awful music hall farce."

"So you see," said Bentinck, leaning back. "It's an ugly business that won't be cheap to fix."

Seated in the next room was Volker, Daniel, Carr, the stable hands and Samuel. All were under the watchful eye of nine British Army Red Coats who were stood with muskets ready by their sides. Suddenly, all eyes fixed on the adjoining door as a crash came from the other side. It was followed by William's raised voice exclaiming "How Much? Not whilst I have a hole in my backside".

The commotion continued for a while then silence fell. This was followed by a burst of William's operatic la-la-la's for almost a minute.

Silence fell.

William backed away from Bentinck and Wellington who were approaching him, palms forward, urging for calm. The sturdy desk was upturned and the floor was strewn with papers.

"This is robbery as sure as a musket through my carriage window!" shouted William. "You should have a tricorn hat you juicy swine! That money! That sum you mentioned, which still sours my ears, is all I have aboard *The Emily*," William paused, sensing he had dropped a boob in mentioning it. "Not that I probably should have said that but it is and it will leave me with nothing. Not so much as a copper button for the conclusion of my business in the Americas. I will be forced to return home and face Mother's best 'I told you so' stare. You've seen that stare, Uncle. You know it cuts deeper than any blade."

"It's the best and only offer, William," said Wellington. "I know, believe me I know, what it will cost in face back in Tornbridge but anything less will cost you your head here and now."

"The British are soon to leave Sicily, William," said Bentinck. "Negotiations are underway. Our weight diminishes daily."

"That's why I'm here, William," added Wellington. "To discuss the detail."

"Ok, Ok!" said William, calming. He thought for a moment then tried a different tack. "What say we put this on account?" He flashed his most convincing smile. "Uncle, you can vouch for me, surely? I'll chuck in a few crates of brandy as expenses and maybe a new dress for the prostitute. Yes? All is well?"

"Ah, no," Bentinck frowned. "Regrettably not. It's the gold or your execution I'm afraid."

"Bastard arses!" shouted William.

It was a sixty-mile carriage journey across Sicily from Vittoria to the coastal village of Syracuse where *The Emily* was in dock. Which, for William, meant a four-hour drive with the bureaucrat Bentinck. Not that William had a choice. Bentinck had insisted on accompanying him and personally taking possession of the gold. William had resolved his mind to the fact that the payment was unavoidable and derived some pleasure in blurting out "cock" just as Bentinck was dozing off and then blaming the noise on a pothole when he woke with a start.

Bentinck was a duller companion awake than he was asleep. He tried, without success, to engage William in political discussion but was met each time with a snub. As the scenery rolled by there was little to pass the time and, as only four carriages and six carts had been provided for the crew, William was glad that he didn't have to share with Samuel. Especially considering the heat.

"You have actually met Captain Bowman, I understand?" enquired Bentinck, as he watched William manicure his nails. "A house guest, I'm led to believe."

"As you consider capture, imprisonment, and the theft of one's worldly goods the correct way to treat one's 'guests', then yes. Similar, one could say, to Sicilian hospitality."

Bentinck watched William for a while not desiring to rise to the comment. After a short period of glancing at his own, rather tatty nails, he found a smile and continued. "He's an intriguing fellow, this Bowman, oh yes. Very clever. He has the local raiders eating out of his hand. Never takes too much and never get's greedy. He has watched others get richer. Those who have started their own fleets and exported their own stock. And he has watched others lose the lot to the British or French. He learnt the importance of intelligence in the East India Company and has the coast full of paid spies. He keeps detailed records of all ships that pass."

William raised his eyes and frowned, puzzled. "To what end? I've made the trip from his grubby hovel to the harbour and can tell you that any ship that passed would be long gone by the time word reached him."

"Looking for patterns. These waters are more predictable than you would imagine. Once a name or rumour of some shipment reaches his ear, you can bet it stays locked in his mind."

"So he's wealthy?" asked William, taking an interest.

"The story goes that the city is his. The raiders are not of his employ, they simply trade with him. Three hundred or more horseman round up the stock he needs."

William leaned back, pondering. "The pirate boats seized off shore, what will happen to them?" he asked, blowing the nail dust off his fingertips.

"Stripped of anything useful then booby-trapped. Jose does like to make an example."

William was suddenly aware of the smell of fresh bread on the breeze. They were passing a small bakery with loaves stacked up by the doorway and smoke billowing from its crooked chimney.

As William peered out of the carriage window, he was faced with a sight that immediately listed his spirits. In the distance, he could see *The Pride of Emily* moored by a jetty. She towered over the fishing boats and launches tethered about her. She was as beautiful as William had remembered and an involuntary smile sprang to his face.

The small convoy of carriages and carts made its way through the village square. It was packed with people milling about whilst enjoying the setting sun. Children played in the square's fountain as their parent's talked amongst themselves outside their pretty little painted houses. With the working day ended, everyone was readying for food.

William watched from the window as his carriage headed along the narrow cobbled street that led to the harbour. Street sellers moved aside to let them pass then offered their goods for sale.

Bentinck flicked a coin at a flat bread seller and took what was offered. "It's very good," he said to William, taking a bite. "The olives are lovely here. Care to try?"

"Greasy little specimen," said William, curling his nose up.

"Oh, no. They're quite lovely, I assure you," said Bentinck as the carriage drew to a stop by *The Emily*'s gangway.

"I wasn't referring to the olives," noted William with a snoot.

William Peel's Infamous Escape

The two days *The Emily* spent in dock at Syracuse were the closest Daniel, Carr and Volker had to a holiday for some time. With nothing to do, they occupied their days sitting on the dock consuming flagons of ale delivered by a buxom tavern wench named Lucia. She was a plump lass with an enthusiastic nature who took a shine to Volker and, of course, Volker reciprocated. Most of the time though, the group sat watching the harbour under the shade of *The Emily*. They puzzled over the stable hands constant errands for William and watched as the three of them fetched and carried a whole manner of secret supplies back on board ship.

As for the rest of the crew, they either played Mahjong on the deck or took the opportunity for a tattoo or two from Barker, who apparently picked up the skill in Japan. He proved to have quite a flair for art, however, with a somewhat limited range. For example, he excelled at dolphins, sharks and cannon but struggled with birds of prey, human hands and women. Which was evident in his work on Coleman, the cook's mate, who asked for a spread eagle over his back but ended up with, what could best be described as, a trampled chicken.

The locals of Syracuse mostly kept their distance. Maybe it was the drunken revelry amongst the crew, the bar fights in the taverns, or the sight of George tucking into cuts of beef on the gangway. Although George very rarely left William's side, and certainly never allowed anyone else very close, he did, according to the ship's log, allow Daniel the occasional stroke. This was because Daniel had been delegated the job of feeding him in William's absence. George attracted a great deal of attention from the local children who would gather at the end of the jetty to marvel at a creature they had only ever heard about in stories. They would dare each other to step closer and got braver with each visit.

One morning, two plucky young boys edged a few feet onto the creaking boards whilst clutching each other in fear and excitement. Volker, Carr and Daniel were all snoring away, oblivious, at the opposite end of the jetty. George, however, suddenly caught the boys scent on the wind and, as if to impress, he stood as tall as he could and roared at them with teeth bared. They ran off screaming. The roar was so loud it echoed about the town and had Daniel, Volker, and Carr on their feet in an instant with their hands fumbling for the weapons that they had actually left on board ship.

"George!" called William, from the deck. "Come!" George slowly closed his mouth, licked his lips, and then plodded up the gangway to William who greeted him with a ruffle of his mane. "Don't eat the peasants," he said, tickling him under the chin. George let out a faint meow and licked

William's hand.

"Zhat woz not goodt for me," said Volker clutching his racing heart.

"I think I soiled myself," said Daniel, doubling over to catch his breath. "Seriously, I have an uneasy feeling."

Volker and Carr burst into hysterics immediately. Daniel, who was a little slower in seeing the funny side, eventually joined in laughing.

"Only a Peel," said Daniel, "would make having a thirty-five stone lion seem like a perfectly normal pet."

The next day, William summoned the gang to *The Emily*'s great cabin. They arrived to find he had constructed a scaled model of Bowman's fort and the surrounding city. It was complete with savages, palm trees, and little raiders dressed in black with tiny scimitars. The fort was crudely made from kindling wood which William had taken the trouble to paint, albeit rather quickly. He had used real earth for the pathways and small inkwells as the spice pots for the market stalls. The Captain's Log for *The Emily* (always dictated to Carr by Volker) described it as like the effort of a child or the therapeutic project of someone recuperating from a serious head injury.

"Gather around," indicated William, enthusiastically. "I bet you've all been excited to know why I delayed our voyage? Well here is the reason." He stood back with a *Tada*.

"Is it going to be the Taj Mahal, sir?" asked Daniel, peering at it.

"Vhere is za dome? Za ozer towers?" quizzed Volker.

"It's very impressive," said Carr, with a hint of sarcasm. "Bowman's fort unless I'm mistaken." For which he received the type of glance from Daniel and Volker that is generally reserved for the class suck-up's.

"Thank you Mr Carr, I knew you would appreciate the artistic merit," William smiled. "William Blake was a tutor of mine for a while. As you can imagine, he instilled in me a great passion for art. It's technically accurate. Taken from memory. Which, I have to say, is keen on scale and so forth. See the little branding iron?"

"The main gate was in the west wall though, surely?" said Carr.

"No, no. North," responded William, with conviction.

"It vas za vest I zink also," said Volker, folding his big arms.

"I'd have to say west too, sir. Definitely," added Daniel. "And there were four guard turrets, not just two."

William coughed. "Well, except for a few technical disagreements, I think we can say…"

"And the city has two entrances," said Carr, cutting in.

"Ok! Ok!" William snapped, getting ruffled. "You are rather missing the point. Which is that I have made this lovely, and mostly technically accurate model, for a good reason."

"Posterity?" asked Daniel.

"We're not going to America just yet," said William, expecting a reaction of surprise that didn't come, "nor are we going home." Still no reaction. "That's right, we're going to raid Bowman's fort, steal his slaves, and then tear out faster than a stupid footman with a stolen beef sandwich tucked into his britches who found himself in a gatehouse with a hungry lion."

The cabin fell silent.

"Maybe I'm missing something," said Carr, after a moment pondering. "Why don't you just go home and get more gold. Why put yourself into one of the most dangerous places on earth. A place you only narrowly escaped from before."

"It's really a question of commerce," said William, taking a step back and pacing in a bid to look intelligent. "It's all pretty complex stuff but my Uncle…"

"Which one, sir?" asked Daniel, cutting in.

"It doesn't matter!" said William, with a glare. "Look, what matters is that I get to America and conclude this land deal and it's much quicker this way."

"Only marginally, sir," said Daniel, "if…"

William cut him off. "Look here! I'm not going back home to Mother with empty pockets and no slaves to show for my troubles. Nor too will I tell that pigmy, Parsons, that you fellows were just too scared to clinch this deal. Uncle Arthur's bound to dine out on the tale of how Volker here sailed into a public house and we had to be rescued from a beheading. I am not going to give Mother the satisfaction of uttering something condescending like 'Well dear at least you had a good go at it'. Is that clear?" Everyone either nodded or shrugged in agreement. "Sure, it might be a suicide mission. One of you might not make it back. But wouldn't you rather give your life in the service of a better man than take the easy course?"

Everyone stared speechless and glanced at the others for a reaction.

"No, sir," said Daniel, finally. "If it's all the same, I'll take that easy course."

Carr and Volker began chuckling and nodding in agreement.

"Za eazy courze iz goot," said Volker.

"People underestimate the easy course, sir," said Daniel.

"All due respect to a better man," said Carr, "which you indeed are by birth. Volker and I intend to retire on our return to Dover and spend the modest prize monies we've amassed. My friend here..." he said, slapping Volker's big shoulder, "has some acreage in Spain and plans on taking an old whore as a wife. As for myself, I have a tailors shop in . London with rooms above."

"And you and Mrs Carr, I'm sure, will be happy but..."

"Just myself," said Carr, correcting.

A cold silence hung and for the first time William noted a vulnerable side to Carr.

"Trouble has a way of finding us, sir, true enough," said Daniel, changing the subject. "But we don't look for it."

"Rot! It's a walk in one of my lovely parks for heroic fellows such as yourselves. We shall have surprise on our side. The fort is wide open." He beckoned them closer and picked up a pointing stick. "Here's the plan. I will present myself at the gate, here, on my own. Well, with just one other person who will carry with him, not a weapon, oh no, but a drum. When Bowman answers and sees it's me, his nemesis... Well, he will be so taken aback by the Peel bravery that he will let me in immediately. Seeing nothing but a drum about my person, he will immediately assume he has the upper hand."

"Which he will, sir," said Daniel, "as he'll have you locked in his fort surrounded by armed savages with nothing but a percussion instrument for your protection."

"Ha!" blurted William, with great enthusiasm. "You've fallen into the trap. The same false sense of security that Bowman will feel. What he won't know is that your men will be preparing to work with hammer and chisel to break through the outer wall and into the cell, here," he pointed with his stick.

Carr could hardly believe his ears. "Won't that be noisy?"

"That's where the drum comes in," William replied. "I intend to distract them through the medium of dance."

"You vill danze for zhem?" asked Volker, with a mixture of confusion and disbelief.

Daniel locked his fingers together on his head and blew. "Oh, God! We're going to die. We're all going to die."

"Have no fear, Daniel," said William, "this is no ordinary dance. It was taught to me by Vsevolod Adamiana, a Russian Shaman my father invited to stay with us during the conclusion of a land deal. Unable to communicate through a common language, he taught us dance as a way of building trust. It's more intuitive than strict in form but the result is mesmerising. I performed such a dance to the

German royal family only six months ago and I can assure you they were quite spellbound. The King was so overcome with emotion that he was forced to leave the room."

"What was the Shaman's view?" asked Carr.

"Oh, no idea. We all got fed up with his piety. Parsons took his land by some loophole and father stuck him on a boat to God knows where."

"Ok! Well, that's something to talk about," said Carr, lost for words. "I think though it would be good to move on from there to other, weaker areas of the plan."

"Of course, of course," replied William, "these are very broad strokes. Pray continue."

"Our problem isn't the fort," said Carr, "it's the harbour. It's getting in and then getting out. Bowman's going to hear of *The Emily* before we dock. She's not a ship that's easy to hide."

William remained silent and flashed a knowing smile. His excitement was hard to contain. "You really think this handsome model and a drum is the extent of my plan?"

"Yes," responded Daniel, with a sigh.

"When you all were enjoying the cross-country trip, I was putting my mind to this very problem. Tilly, the foul smelling crevice, came after me with three ships. He took one back with him, his freedom exchanged for my lovely brooch. Bastard! Anyway, that left two ships. Ships that were supposed to be booby-trapped. Gentlemen can you guess what I'm about to say?"

"You used the wood from the ships to make the model?" Daniel answered.

"I won't dignify that comment, Daniel, and will simply note your continued impudence," said William, with a snoot. "The plan is this: we shall use the boats like the famous Trojan horse of Roman myth." He said, proudly, oblivious to the inaccuracy. "You shall disguise yourselves as pirates and return to the Barberry Coast with myself as a captive. Under this pretence, you shall then march me straight through the harbour. No one will suspect. It's brilliance lay in its simplicity."

"Simple like Rio?" Carr asked Volker, remembering a similar plan.

"I hope notz," said Volker, and the pair started chuckling.

"You remember?" said Carr, recalling. "Disguising King Pedro as a peasant," he laughed, "to sneak him out of his own capital to avoid... to avoid... Oh, what was his name? The guy? The crazy French guy who Charles had the duel with?"

"Junot!" said Daniel, "and your father won, I might add," he said, winking at William.

"Jean-Andoche Junot," said Carr, with a click of his fingers, "that's it! He was a good swordsman."

"Yes, well," said William, annoyed by the distraction, "if we can return to my great plan."

Carr tapped his fingers on the handle of his Japanese sword, unconvinced. "You do realise this plan will hinge on everyone believing you truly are a captive."

"Of course."

"It will be rough on you. We..." he said, indicating to

the others, "all of us will have to be very strict with you to make it real. It's hard to act."

William loosened his body like an actor limbering up. He then gripped his lapels and, putting a foot up onto a chair, he began delivering a Shakespearian speech. "When valour plays on reason…" he boomed, in an actor's voice. " It eats the very sword it fights with." He cleared his throat and affected a different voice. "We must have bloody noses and cracked crowns and make them current." He waited for the applause. Which eventually came from Daniel, limp handed with his usual tinge of sarcasm. William lowered his leg and shot his cuffs. "I played the lead in various Shakespearean productions. Spent many a summer learning lines on the lower lawns. Some reviewers were kind enough to remark that they had seen nothing like it. I witnessed one elderly man in the audience actually sobbing. Well, I shall merely use the craft honed as a thespian and channel it inwards to distance myself from the smarting. You may not fear to treat me as the raiders would. Like I said, Mr Carr, I'm not made of china."

Carr glanced about the faces of the others. All returned devilish smiles that just shouted 'count me in'.

"Well, gentlemen," asked William, "do I have your musket, swords, and brute force?"

"Although it goes against the grain to raise a hand to a better man," said Carr. "I'm pretty confident I could even make it look like I was enjoying it."

"Me too," added Volker.

"It would be a pleasure to do my duty, sir," noted

Daniel, giving a salute.

"Although," added Carr, "with your permission, I'm going to tweak the plan here and there."

"Of course, of course," said William, rubbing his hands together with excitement. "You have my full permission to tweak away."

As *The Emily* sailed her way around the Sicilian coast, William spent the morning in his quarters inspecting his clothes and berating the three stable hands for their failure in not getting the right lustre to his many pairs of shoes and boots.

"Again!" William demanded, inspecting a pair. "There is a distinct cloud. There. See? You really must excel yourself. How can I possibly surpass my father's reputation if my boot leather is cloudy?"

William inspected himself in the mirror. He smoothed the front of his pale blue tunic before offering out his arms in order that the stable hands could slip on his dark blue jacket. The diamond encrusted jacket buttons glistened and sparkled. He was pleased with the look and positively purred at his own reflection. Suddenly, a stable hand appeared at William's shoulder and began vigorously brushing.

"Yes, yes," said William, wafting him away as one would a fly. "My God, it's so hard to know how to dress," he said, to his own reflection. "On the one hand, adventuring is an informal affair but as I intend to have a sword fight with this Bowman fellow, metal to metal, then I need to look good doing it. Which reminds me, I will need a sword." He glanced to the stable hands who dropped their gaze and buffed a boot with increased vigour. "You did pack a sword?" asked William, suspicious. Their silence proved its own answer. William's eyes narrowed and he approached them with nostrils flared. "You really are as thick as dung!" he shouted, snatching one of the boots.

The sight of an angry Peel, boot in hand, put the fear of God into the stable hands. Like everyone, they were raised on stories of William's grandfather, Winston the Bastard, prowling the streets of Tornbridge, cheeks crimson with drink, hunting some unsuspecting commoner with a riding boot. Sensing William's blood was up, they took to their heels and sprinted side-by-side for the exit. Each of them jostled for pole-position with none of them letting the other ahead. Consequently one made it neatly through the doorway as the other two ran headfirst into the oak frame and knocked themselves unconscious. They had just collapsed backward on the floor when Daniel entered. He was confused by the sight of the unconscious stable hands and William brandishing a boot.

"Sorry to interrupt your private time, sir, but the skipper wished you to know we're coming up on the pirate vessels."

William arrived on the deck to find George asleep on his back under the burning sun and the crew stepping about him whilst busy lashing *The Emily* to the rail of one of the pirate ships. All three ships were tethered side by side with *The Emily* outermost. Carr and Volker leapt across onto the nearest pirate ship as the crafts crashed against each other sending a spray of water between them. To avoid getting his cream britches marked, William got a leg up over the rail from one of the crew and then strolled off after Carr and Volker.

William followed their lamps down into the hull and the dankness of the empty gun deck. Not the hi-tech space of *The Emily*'s deck but a sweat-ridden stench-hole that was stained and scared from battles. All her cannon had been stripped and the her gun-ports had been nailed open. Ahead, William could see Volker and Carr staring, lamps aloft, at a dozen large barrels that had been stacked in the middle of the deck.

"What is it?" enquired William, his eyes adjusting to the lamplight.

"A stroke of luck, sir," said Daniel, appearing behind him.

"Gun powder," said Carr, over his shoulder.

"But why leave it?" asked William. "Surely it has a value?"

Carr reached above his head and plucked a fine wire, almost invisible to the naked eye, that ran through a series of little hoops screwed into the timbers.

"There's a spring-loaded flint trigger in that rear barrel," he said, pointing. "It's attached by this wire to the hatch."

"BOOM!" shouted Volker, causing William to jump.

"Booby trap," said Carr, his eyes scanning the space as an idea formed in his mind. "And it means, my lord, I have another slight change to your plan."

"You're thinking of a repeat of Lisbon?" asked Daniel catching Carr's enthusiastic gaze. "Mr Simons' infamous escape."

"We will need Barker," said Carr. "Someone has to stay with *The Emily*. The speed and timing have to be perfect."

"Vell," replied Volker with a sigh, "I zapose zomeone haz to tell him za goodt newz." And with that, he left.

"Is this in code?" asked William, somewhat baffled by the discussion.

"You had this in your mind when you saw that model?" asked Daniel, eagerly at Carr's shoulder.

"I considered it, yes," Carr replied, with a devious smile. "Now, if you will excuse me," he said to William, "this will take much preparation." Without another word, he was gone.

When Carr's footsteps had faded, Daniel turned to William and raised his lamp. "It's a fine line to sail between bravery and stupidity."

"Who is this Simons?"

"Skipper of the Fighting Spirit. Volker's skipper on the forerunner of *The Emily*, sir. He was the craziest man who ever found himself at the helm of a ship. What's worse is Mr Carr thinks he can pull it off too."

"Pull what off, exactly?"

"In his attempt to escape Lisbon, Mr Simons cost your father the pride of his fleet and lost his own arm and then his life in the process."

"What?" demanded William. "Oh, my sweet, flatulent lion!" he cried before running full pelt for the exit.

William arrived up on deck to find *The Emily* drifting away and George staring at him from the quarterdeck. Her skeleton crew were raising her sails as Volker shouted last-minute instructions across the water to Barker who was standing by the helm.

"Vatch for za flare!" Volker bellowed. "You vill need tventy knotz."

The rest of the crew, over half, were wrapping sword belts around their waists and loading muskets on the decks of the two pirate ships. They were all dressing to look like a pirate crew complete with coloured cotton woven into their hair. Even Samuel was joining in although he couldn't understand how to put on a sword belt. William moved through the crew to Carr who was sitting on the windlass whilst running a sharpening stone down the edge of his Japanese sword.

"I really think we need to talk," William demanded, breathless. "I know what I said before might have sounded like enthusiasm for your changes but I really think we need to go back to my original plan."

"I don't," said Carr, eyeing along his blade. After a moment of checking the light dance along the perfect, razor-sharp edge, he slipped it into its scabbard and nodded to two convincing looking pirates who approached and grabbed William's arms. A third man then tethered William's wrists so tightly he yelped.

"From now on you are our prisoner," said Carr, with

great conviction.

Across the deck, Samuel spotted that William was being restrained and moved in for a closer look. His sword dragged behind him along the deck. He crept behind the main mast and waited for a moment to protect his master.

"Have you lost yourself?" William barked at Carr, his eyes on fire. "Have you forgotten who I am, blast it!"

"We are doing exactly what you told us. In front of witnesses, I might add. We are going to get your slaves."

"And what makes you think you can do what Simons could not?"

William turned to see Volker stuffing as many pistols as would fit into his waistband. Daniel stepped forwards to where his two short-swords were sticking into the deck. He grabbed them and began twirling them independently by circling his wrists and arms. He was so precise and fast that they quickly became a blur. When he caught sight of William looking, jaw hanging, Daniel stopped and slipped them over his head into the leather sheaths fixed down his back.

"I'll guess we'll soon know," said Carr, offering William a smile.

Volker's eyes met Carr's and they exchanged a nod. It was time. Carr slipped his musket strap over his shoulder and took centre stage to rally the troops.

"Ok, my friends, listen up!" He shouted, to the gathering crew. "We all know what we're doing. Most of us will remember that we have done this before. And we're still alive. That was a rehearsal. This is the opening night. Are you ready to make your skipper proud?"

"YEAH!" cheered the crew, clattering swords above their heads.

"Ready to take your share of the prize?", shouted Carr.

"YEAH!" came the cry.

"Ready to feast on ale and fine whores all your live-long-days?"

"YEAH!" came a louder cry.

"Then let's put some foot to ass!"

The atmosphere was electric. Volker winked at Carr as the crew went wild with enthusiasm and disappeared up into the rigging to ready the two ships.

"My God!" said William to himself. "It's like some terrible, nautical nightmare."

"Don't worry," said Samuel, appearing at his elbow and sporting his usual gormless expression. "Samuel will save you."

"Oh, sparkling!" replied William, spotting that Samuel had his sword belt on inside out and the wrong way around.

With tethers removed from the rails, the two pirate ships floated freely apart. Volker at the helm of one and Carr at the other. The two old friends exchanged a competitive smile.

"It would seem a unique opportunity has presented itself," shouted Carr.

"You zink zo?" replied Volker.

"First one there?"

"I vill look out vor you ozer my shoulder."

And with that, the trim of both ships was adjusted and

wind snapped the sails tight as drums. They were off.

Less than half an hour into the voyage, Daniel escorted William to the quarterdeck where Carr was at the helm.

"Mr Carr?" enquired Daniel, with uncustomary professionalism. "The prisoner has a request…"

"This is preposterous," said William, turning to show Carr his bound wrists. "This is fraying the cuffs! See?" Daniel moved into take a closer look at William's sleeves and nodded to Carr that William was right. "It's a day's voyage!" continued William. "Am I to be bound like this for the entire trip? Why, by God! Surely it's too early? Who can see us?"

"Anyone with a spyglass," said Carr, his jaw tensing. "Bo'sun, take this man below and bind his ankles. He should be fed and watered every three hours. It shall be solitary. Is that clear?"

"Aye, sir," responded Daniel, standing to attention.

"I want my objection recorded," said William. "In very large letters."

"It will, sir" responded Carr, "along with my reason for disregarding it."

"Bastard!" cried William. "And I want *that* recording too," he added, as he was grabbed by the elbows by two sailor-cum-pirates. "Wait! Wait," he protested. "If this is to look real then shouldn't Samuel be flogged or something? For the sake of appearances? After all, we were originally captured together."

Carr thought it through and smiled his agreement to Daniel. "No flogging but take them both down. It's a chance for them to get to know one another."

According to *The Emily*'s log, which was supplemented by separate notes from Volker and Carr on board their own ships, the day and a half voyage back to the Barbary Coast was mostly uneventful. They crossed the path of a Royal Navy frigate at four in the morning which was either on urgent business elsewhere or the captain was too lazy to come about and take pursuit. It didn't stop Carr spending an hour with bated breath by the starboard rail poised behind his spyglass.

Much to Carr's frustration, Volker had the lead all the way and steadily increased it over the hours that followed. Volker noted in his ship's log that he had initially kept pace with Carr's ship for his protection but after coming across the frigate he had decided to increase his lead and stretch out any potential attackers to improve their odds. Any pirate he came upon would have another unknown ship to contend with soon enough. Two ships travelling hip to hip were as good as one target, better in fact, to a clever captain. One ship alongside another hampers the return of fire and creates a shield. Volker was also aware that neither ship had a fitted gun deck and was therefore useless in a fight.

By dawn the next day, they were passing the coast of Malta which was a half-mile to their port side. Daniel watched through his spyglass as the first of the islander's fishing craft were heading out of the harbour; their bright white sails reflecting the dawn light.

Carr calculated that, based on their present speed, they would reach the pirate port by dawn the next morning. At the very least their enemy would be sluggish from the sudden awakening or better still drunk from the night's rations. Although they were Muslim lands, Carr knew the pirates were mostly of Christian birth. Not that religion played much part in their daily lives. It was the raiders though that Carr and Daniel discussed in depth the next morning over breakfast. They were strong and capable warriors. As harsh as the lands they were born in and, since the crusades, they didn't take to infidels.

Carr's crew took turns in their bunks sleeping in a four-hour rotation. Daniel and Carr, however, stayed awake together preparing for the mission ahead. In turns, they worked on interweaving a slipknot into every two feet of a hefty length of rope. By the time Carr's ship came in sight of the Barbary harbour, they had sewn in over three hundred such loops. Carr had also concocted a leather contraption that appeared like a short version of a standard leather belt with a hefty leather tube sewn into it. Daniel watched with great interest as Carr then constructed a flare out of layered paper packed with gunpowder and powdered calcium from the galley. He then fitted a fuse and sealed the ends with wax.

It was literally the darkness before the dawn as Carr ordered all deck lights to be extinguished. He stood at the bow rail as the sailors behind him rallied to backwind the headsail and slow the ship. They were in sight of the coast and about to sail amongst dozens of pirate ships. Ahead, Carr could make out Volker signalling with a lantern by his port rail. He had a smug look on his chiselled, stubbly face that Carr could spot from a hundred yards away.

"How the hell does he do it? Tell me that?" Carr asked Daniel, who had appeared at his elbow. "He made nearly an hour on us."

"Take solace in one fact," responded Daniel, with a smile. "He's ungainly on land."

"Drop the headsails, if you will!" shouted Carr, over his shoulder.

William and Samuel were brought up on deck as Carr's ship came alongside Volker's and both crews readied their kit for shore.

Carr expected a protest from William but was greeted with only cold indifference. William, who had been tied to Samuel for over a day, was in no mood for conversation. According to William's private journal, Samuel never shut up the entire time they were together. As well as Samuel's entire life story, William learned about his diet, his favourite shelf, and why he liked his right foot better than his left. Samuel had also explained how the vicar of Tornbridge once hammered a nail into Samuel's head in an attempt to cure his fear of spoons. It was not a day William cared to recall.

The faint dawn light cracked over the black horizon. "Ve need to move!" Volker shouted at Carr, across the twenty yards of sea between them.

The crews busied to get the two ships underway then paused when they heard the reason for Volker's urgency. It was the distant but unmistakable call of the Adhan. The call to prayer. It meant only one thing to them all. The raiders were awake. The ships were off sailing again within minutes. Volker took the lead and approached a group of three galleons anchored a few hundred yards from shore. As Volker slowed his ship to a stop, Carr's ship slipped past and silently approached a pair of Brigantines. When it came to the escape, Carr knew it was the fast and manoeuvrable Brigantines that posed the biggest threat. Carr's immediate problem, however, was that in order to sink them when the time was right, he had to get his ship in close. Carr's pirate galleon had more draught, a little over ten feet below the water, almost twice as much as the shallow-draughted Brigantines. This presented a major problem the closer they neared the shore.

Carr steered the ship in slowly and silently. It was a walking pace powered only by the top sail. Cautious, as they could run aground at any moment, Daniel cast a line off the bow to check the water depth.

"By the line, six fathoms!" he called, then gathered the line back up before casting again. The only sound was the faint splash of the line's lead weight as it hit the water.

All the crew could do was watch in silence as Carr threw over the wheel as fast as he could.

"By the mark, four fathoms!" called Daniel.

At forty yards off, they were closing on the ships fast but also fast losing depth of water. Whatever happened they couldn't afford to run aground and render the ship useless.

"By the mark, three fathoms!" called Daniel.

An old crewman threw Carr a nervous glance and kissed the wooden crucifix that hung on a string around his neck. It was going to be close. How close would be up to Carr's nerve and skill.

"By the deep, twain!" called Daniel, casting the next line as quickly as he could, as 'by the deep' meant it was between knots on the rope and the water could be three feet shallower than they had thought.

"Drop the topsail!" shouted Carr.

The ship drifted on another twenty yards as the crew hurried to drop the sails.

"By the mark, twain!" called Daniel as eventually the ship came to a stop only fifteen yards from the Brigantines. It was a fine bit of sailing and the crew tugged their forelocks in Carr's direction.

"The cap'n could do no better," said one crewman in passing. This caused an involuntary smile to flash across Carr's lips.

The night watchman in the bird's nest of the nearest Brigantine fixed his spyglass on Carr's crew as they readied three launches and cast the rope ladders over the side. Daniel caught sight of him and walked calmly to the helm to warn Carr.

"I see him," said Carr, his eyes flicking down to his repeating musket propped up by the wheel. Daniel smiled. Carr was, as ever, one step ahead.

Carr waited on deck until William, Samuel, and the crew were all in the launches. Only he and Daniel remained. "Mr Barker knows his part," said Carr, sensing young

Daniel's apprehension.

"And if he misses the flare?" asked Daniel.

"He won't," replied Carr, slapping Daniel on the shoulder, reassuringly. "Now, set the charge and have faith."

A moment later, Carr and Daniel were seated in the launch and four of the crew were slipping oars into the rowlocks. Volker's launches approached behind them in the faint dawn light with their oars lightly slapping the water as they rowed.

A couple of Carr's crew pushed off against the hull of the galleon and they all rowed their way, in silence, towards the jetty.

It was then that William looked to his left and realised he was sitting next to Samuel. Samuel, rather worryingly, was staring down the barrel of a flint lock pistol and blowing into it.

"I got some sand in it," whispered Samuel, his crossed eyes looking to William for help. "Will the ball get stuck?"

"Where did you get that?" quizzed William, quietly.

"Escape plan," responded Samuel, with a wink. "Samuel knows what to do."

William watched him for a moment trying to figure out what the idiot was talking about. It suddenly dawned on him that Samuel must believe that William's detention was real and in his simple way, he had formulated a pea-brained plan to get him to safety. Which was, in itself, likely to be even more dangerous than the peril that awaited them at Bowman's fort. William was about to object when the pistol slipped from Samuel's grip and landed with a thud in the boat. They both watched as the shot rolled from the muzzle and across the timbers like a marble. It eventually stopped at Carr's boot. Carr leaned forward and, picking up the pistol, he shushed them with a finger to his lips. As they neared the shore, Carr slipped his musket from his shoulder and rested it on his lap.

Ahead, the jetty was deserted. A few nets and crates were strewn about next to the many launches and boats tethered to the moorings. No sign of any savages, pirates, or raiders.

They rowed towards the very end of the jetty where lanterns hung on poles at each corner stanchion. Not that the light was needed. By the time the first of the crew were jumping off onto the timbers, the grey light of the early dawn had been replaced with the faint yellow of the morning sun. It brought the heat with it.

The convincing looking pirate crew were quickly out of the boats and walking briskly, but not too briskly, along the timbers towards the shore. William, who had been tied up with Samuel, was frequently jabbed in the back with the butt of Carr's musket to quicken his pace.

Volker took point as they ran across the narrow beach and onto the rock shelf. It wasn't long before they were approaching the foot of the scrub path which in turn led up to the settlement. To their left, in the far distance, they could see a group of twenty figures walking along the beach towards the jetty. They were too far off to make out faces but the light catching off their hips meant they were armed with scimitars and most likely pirates returning to their ship.

Fortunately, as William and the rest were shielded by the large rocks, the pirates were oblivious to their presence.

Volker suddenly raised his hand and signalled for everyone to stop and get low. At the top of the hill were the silhouettes of a dozen or more horsemen. They appeared black against the rising sun. As they made their way down the hill and into shade, their details became visible. They were raiders. Volker beckoned Carr over for a conference. His dilemma was obvious. Do they press on and take their chances with the raiders on the path or try and hide amongst the rocks and risk being spotted by the pirates approaching along the beach.

With his head low, Carr slung his musket over his shoulder and made his way around the rocks to his friend. William and Samuel were left tied together, hiding, with their backs against a boulder.

"Zis iz lucky for uz. Horsez," said Volker, taking a glance in the raider's direction.

"Personally, I'd take my chances with the pirates first," said Carr, glancing back down the beach at the approaching party.

"Nein," said Volker. "Ve has advantage onst za hill."

William was sneaking a look at the pirates when his gaze fell on Samuel whose gormless expression suddenly flashed with purpose. Without a word, Samuel jumped up, grabbed William by the shoulders, and pushed him away up the beach.

"We must be quick," said Samuel, ushering William with such urgency and force that he was powerless to stop him.

"Steady on!" cried William, as he noticed Samuel's grip was crumpling his sleeve. "That's silk!"

In that instant, the pirates caught sight of William's jewelled buttons glistening in the dawn sunlight. After a brief pause for discussion, they charged with their swords drawn.

"Christ on a sack cart!" shouted William, when he spotted the charging pirates.

Carr and Volker were still at the foot of the path debating tactics when they heard the rallying screams of the charging pirates. At the same moment, they also heard the raiders calls of 'yah' as they geed their horses down the track. Wondering what exactly was going on, Carr and Volker then turned to see Samuel and William running full pelt into certain death.

Meanwhile, William, who had realised that the idiot Samuel was pushing him straight towards twenty flailing scimitars, changed direction and led Samuel towards the sea. As he glanced over his shoulder, William could see *The Emily*'s crew, swords drawn, making their frantic charge across a hundred yards of beach to his aid. The pirates, realising that they were in for a tough fight, took evasive action themselves and turned to head back along the shore. William charged into the sea up to knee height then toppled taking Samuel down with him.

Behind him, William could hear the clatter of steel on steel as Carr and the rest of the crew clashed with the fleeing pirates. Daniel sliced and parried with such skill with his two swords that he took out half the pirates single-handedly. Carr made light work of three whilst Volker and the crew handled the rest. A pirate charged at Volker with a jumping kick but he simply bounced off his chest. Volker picked the man up by the scruff of his neck and pulled him into a powerful head-butt. The pirate was immediately rendered unconscious and duly discarded like a rag doll. As William stood and shook the sea from his hair, he watched the water about him darken with pirate blood. In less than two minutes, all the pirates lay dead and bleeding onto the sand. William had a moment's pause to catch his breath but he was far from safe.

Carr turned as he heard a raider's horse rear back on its haunches behind him and kick at him with its forelegs. Carr dived off to the side and rolled to his feet as Volker grabbed the horse's reins and pulled them back with such power that the horse and raider rolled to the ground. As other raiders came about them, scimitars raised, it became a standoff as *The Emily*'s crew fixed on the raiders down the barrels of their muskets.

The bearded raider and his horse climbed to their feet and shook off the sand. Before he could pick up his scimitar though, Carr's Japanese blade was poised under the raider's chin. William recognised him at once as the raider who had beheaded that chap in the city when William was first captured; the round faced raider that still didn't suit a beard. The raider spoke sharply and spat at the sand in defiance. Carr kept his poise and, when the raider had settled to his predicament, Carr spoke to him in his own tongue.

All watched as the pair exchanged heated words with

occasional glances in William's direction. There was a moment of silence, an agreement reached, and Carr slipped his sword into its scabbard with a customary smooth action. He then kicked through the water in William's direction. He grabbed William by his lapel with one hand and slipped a knife from his belt. Without a pause, Carr sliced a jewel encrusted button from William's jacket. He threw it to the raider who snatched it from the air and inspected it closely. William protested but Carr's grip was too tight.

"Silence, scum dog!" Carr shouted at William, giving his best pirate-like growl.

"Scum dog?" puzzled William, curling his lip at the thought of it. "I don't know what the devil's come over you?" he added, before suddenly realising Carr was acting. "Ah, yes... Well," he continued, playing up for the raider's benefit. "Two can play at that game, you, you hairy, cock-faced-mouse!" William wasn't quite sure what a hairy, cock-faced-mouse was or why it suddenly popped into his head but he was pretty happy it sounded tough and insulting.

The raider's eyes lifted from the jewelled button and beckoned Carr cut one more.

"Cock-faced-mouse?" Carr questioned privately at William's shoulder, as he sliced off another button.

"Hairy too, don't forget," replied William, with a wink.

Carr threw the raider the other button and, after a moment inspecting it, the raider nodded his acceptance. The deal was cast. As Carr marched William and Samuel out of the water, the raiders all dismounted and handed their reins to the nearest member of *The Emily*'s crew. There was excitement amongst raiders as they went to inspect the jewels.

"Zay vill get twenty horses vor vhat you paid," said Volker approaching Carr.

"You prefer we walk?" said Carr, pushing William into Volker's grip. "He asked if we were selling him at Bowman's auction. I didn't answer. It sounds like we might have some luck on our side." Carr swung up into the horse's saddle.

The rest of the crew were forced to pair up two men to a horse. Volker lifted Samuel up into a saddle then pushed William up onto the back behind him. A slap on the beast's flank sent William and Samuel galloping off up the beach. Volker then mounted a horse himself and followed.

As they headed back across the beach to the rock shelf, the raiders were already dragging the pirates bodies from the water. The last thing William saw of the raider who didn't suit a beard was him stripping one of the corpses naked and smashing out his gold teeth with the butt of his scimitar.

As the crew formed an orderly line to canter up the path, Carr pulled his horse around and galloped back to William.

"You should tell Samuel the plan," he said. "Make sure he understands."

"And what, pray tell, is the plan now?" William enquired, curtly. "I'm losing track."

"The raider said that Bowman is having an auction today which means he will have a busy courtyard and hopefully an open gate. So we're going to go in and ask him for the slaves. Nicely, of course."

"Rot! It's nowhere near as good as my drum proposal."

"Oh, you underestimate how persuasive we can ask." Carr flashed a wry smile before giving the reins a crack and galloping off up the path.

Carr took the lead as the group rode through the settlement. The locals were more interested in preparing their breakfasts than the party of fake pirates riding two to a horse passing their doorways. Once clear of the settlement, the party trotted through the Bedouin camp. Inside the tents, the men were lying on cushions and tucking into flatbread. Outside, women tended to the washing of the long white or blue thobes, which flapped on washing lines in the light breeze. Next to them on the lines were the brown aba, the overcoats. They filled with a sudden gust of wind that snapped them taught like a sail. The Bedouin were so used to people passing their homes, they were oblivious to their presence.

Carr turned in his saddle to look back at Volker then tipped his head casually towards the thobes on the washing line. It was all that was needed to convey his idea. An idea to improve the plan. He then turned to William.

"I have a job for the prisoner," he said with a smile.

It was noon when the group, dressed in stolen thobes, reached the outer walls of the city. They slipped from their mounts and concealed their weapons beneath their outer clothes. It was baking hot and a veritable traffic jam of horses and camels. Busier than before, remarked William, as visitors jostled to pass through the entrance. The auction was obviously a high point in the social calendar. It was noisier than before too and not just from the grunting beasts and their bells but from the traditional music and singing that drifted about them. The sound of pipes and drums caught on the breeze. A breeze that also carried the sand with it. After a few nods of reassurance amongst the party, they set about the task. Carr covered his face with his hattah and bowed his head. He nodded to William to do the same.

"Keep your head down," said Carr, as they followed Volker though the city entrance. "Don't take your eyes off the floor until I say so."

The city had the feel of a street carnival with entertainment and conjuring tricks replacing most of the stalls William had seen before. Cooking smells drifted about the group as they passed huge, steaming vats. It was as busy as Dover docks with people jostling about them from all directions. William's gaze was limited but he recognised the slow incline to Bowman's fort. Ahead, he could see Volker's sword, the tip momentarily visible below the hem of his thobe. Daniel was the rear guard. His eyes scanned for any danger that would instantly have his hands reaching for his two trusty short-swords.

Bowman's fort was just as William had represented it in his model, except that its wall was a lot higher and the gate was on the west side and not the east.

"Ready?" said Volker, quietly over his shoulder. "Vhen it happenz it vill happen quick."

They had arrived at Bowman's gates. Suddenly, William saw Volker stop and two savages approach him from either side. There were two muffled screams followed by simultaneous cracks. The two guards collapsed to the ground, their heads at unnatural angles to their bodies.

"Now!" shouted Carr, and the pack rushed forwards into the busy courtyard. As William raised his head, he saw for the first time what they were up against. In the middle of the packed courtyard was a small stage where two savages stood by a young woman. She was no more than twenty years old and completely naked. It was obvious by her shivering that she was terrified. She was beautiful, thought William, olive skinned and dark haired, although desperately in need of a good wash. The crowd were from every recognisable corner of the world and dressed accordingly. From immaculately dressed English noblemen to Ottoman princes in silk coats and coloured turbans. About the crowd were at least twenty savages going by a quick head count.

Bowman was seated and conducting the auction from his ornate chair. He was taking bids on the woman and calling them out as he pointed to the various bidder's hands as they raised in the air about the courtyard. As William followed Volker and Carr to the front of the crowd, he was aware of the many swords that tapped against his legs as they pushed through.

They reached the front just as Bowman banged his gavel on the table and pointed to a fat looking westerner wearing an unflattering thobe and dabbing his sweating face with a cloth.

"Sold!" Bowman cried, then repeated it in French, Spanish and Arabic.

The winning bidder stepped forward and slapped the naked girl's backside as he wiped the spittle from the corners of his lascivious smile. He was a repulsive creature and the fate that awaited the poor girl was clear for all to see.

Carr broke through the front line of bidders into the middle and, without a pause, he slipped his repeating musket from under his thobe. In one smooth action he levelled it and shot the winning bidder between the eyes. The fellows brains sprayed a fine, red mist across the crowd about him as he collapsed to the ground in a heap. Everyone swelled back as Carr turned his sights on Bowman and cocked his musket.

Bowman was as cool as a cucumber and casually indicated to his savage guards that they should attack. It was Volker's turn for business and he stepped forward, ripped off his thobe, and drew his sword. Two savages ran at him with their scimitar's flailing. He parried their blades away and punched the men to the ground with his massive fist.

Meanwhile, William and Samuel were back to back and being gradually surrounded by savages. William was weaponless and Samuel was trying desperately to draw his sword but it was the wrong way around in the scabbard and had jammed. The savages were a sword length away from William when suddenly Samuel dived at one of them, teeth bared and bit him on the shoulder, growling like a beast. As they tumbled to the floor, William snatched the savage's dropped sword and swung it madly, clattering away three outstretched blades in one go.

It became a wild fight with William moving expertly

from one savage to the next, deflecting each blade as it swung for him. One savage received a slash across his chest then the other got a stab in the guts. As they hobbled away, clutching their wounds, William put his full attention on the last brute. He moved in at the fellow, knocking away each of the man's weakening strikes. The savage backed as far as he could and came up against a wall. William knocked the outstretched sword from his grip. As it landed in the dirt, the beaten fellow dropped to his knees and begged for his life.

After a moment of reflection, William dismissed him with a waft of his hand and turned to see Samuel jumping up and down on the chest of his foe and flailing his arms like a wild gibbon. William was about to comment that the fellow not only looked dead but also considerably thinner when there was a crack of musket fire which whizzed over his head. William turned to see the savage he had let go dropping to his knees only feet away. He had been shot in the heart. In his raised hand was a knife poised and aimed in William's direction. William glanced up to the wall where he spotted one of *The Emily*'s crew lowering his smoking musket.

Daniel was set upon by three savages coming at him from left and right. He drew two knives and threw them both at once. In a flash, one savage got a knife in the chest and the other got one in the neck. As the third sliced at him with his blade, Daniel drew his short-swords and set upon him in a whirlwind of steel that clattered repeatedly against the savage's advancing blade. Daniel chose his moment and sliced the man's hand clean off at the wrist. The sword dropped to the sand complete with the fellow's hand still attached.

Carr took his sights off Bowman for a flash and, without compunction, shot dead each of the two savages who were shading him with palm leaves. The shots were so quick in succession that the savages hit the ground at the same time. Carr then turned his musket on the crowd. He scanned from face to face then froze. Suddenly, the eyes in the back of his head had seen something.

"I wouldn't do that if I were you!" shouted Carr, over his shoulder as he lowered his musket and turned slowly. Behind him was a tall American, sporting a feathered cap, a huge moustache, and two dandy flint lock pistols which he had pointed at Carr's back. Sensing he was in trouble, the American looked up to the fort wall to where ten of *The Emily*'s crew were aiming muskets towards him. The American gulped and slowly lowered his pistols.

"LISTEN TO ME!" shouted Carr. "Everyone who doesn't want to die should leave now. Anyone who has made a purchase and is aggrieved that they are about to lose their stock can stick around. But all I'm going to do about it is kill you. It's that simple. Oh, and I'm going to start shooting people in ten seconds." The crowd stood their ground. Carr glanced at Volker, "Remember Lisbon? Why don't we learn?"

"Ve are getting old," replied Volker, with a shrug.

Carr raised his repeating musket and shot off two rounds into the walls. Panic spread and the crowd pushed with such force as people fled through the gate that a few were crushed against the walls and then trampled underfoot.

The courtyard was soon empty except for Bowman, a couple of savages with their hands in the air, and the American with the moustache; who looked as desperate as he did terrified.

"I gotta say," he said, stepping to William, palms outstretched. "I'm pretty screwed if I don't go home with those slaves."

"So?" responded William, as he slipped off his thobe and took it to the woman on the stage who was shivering with fear. "It all builds character!" he added, wrapping his thobe around the girl and leading her down.

"I paid for 'em is all," the American continued, wetting his lips. "Fair and square. A deal's a deal where I come from. Plus there's a girl back home. I'm trying to kinda impress her with all this."

"American, is she?" enquired William, "this filly?"

"Yes, sir. Smile brighter than a Virginia sun rise."

"Well, best take some flowers to soften the blow. If she's anything like your idiot President you should thank me for saving you from a lifetime of drivel."

Suddenly, a shot echoed out and dirt sprayed up an inch from the American's feet. He froze again and threw his hands higher into the air.

"This is a robbery!" said Carr, levelling his musket at him. "No fair. No square. Just you with your hands in the air." He smiled, pleased with his little rhyme.

The Emily's crew moved about the courtyard, some

keeping muskets aimed into the shadows, others collecting discarded weapons. Suddenly, the arms of the captives appeared through the cage bars with cries to be freed.

The American lingered, torn between an instinct to run and a desire to conclude the deal for the sake of his girl back home.

"He's quite serious," said Bowman, to the American, whilst picking a grape.

The American gulped. Finally realising he had no choice, he backed to the gate with his arms still in the air. As Carr turned away and aimed the musket back on Bowman, the American ran full pelt out of the gate.

"We're here for your stock!" said Carr.

"Really?" replied Bowman, placing his feet up on the table but wincing with discomfort as he did so. His backside was obviously still paining him. "Have the Peel coffers got so depleted?"

William stepped forward to air his views but was immediately silenced by a whistle from the wall.

"Raiders!" came the cry.

"Numbers?" replied Carr.

"Twenty near abouts."

"Oh dear," said Bowman with a smile. "Tut, tut."

Carr nodded to his men to take out the slaves from the cages. Opening a cage at a time, the crew marched out the fifty men from each, all chained at the ankle. Suddenly, everyone turned to the entrance where a party of half a dozen raiders came into view. Their horses paced as they drew their scimitars and contemplated the force that awaited them inside the fort. Some of *The Emily*'s crew took action and formed a defensive line facing the gate. Worthy of Wellington's invincibles, they aimed their muskets at the raiders.

"You can't possibly expect to succeed," gloated Bowman.

With many of the cages cleared, Daniel took stock as the slaves were hurried into lines into the courtyard. He counted three hundred and four and noted down the numbers of men, women, and children. They were careful to pick the Negros and not those European looking as they were disliked by many of the American plantation owners who preferred a clear delineation of colour. Daniel was checking the numbers again when another whistle came from the parapet.

Carr cast his shipmate a glance and waited for the latest figure. This time the sailor just shrugged, his mouth a little dry.

"I'd say all of 'em, sir," came the chilling cry.

Moments later, the street outside the gates was crammed with raiders. Too many to fit. The men forming the defensive line steadied their aim and wiped the sweat from their brows. All it needed was one man to lose his cool and squeeze off a shot and it would be pandemonium. William watched as Daniel took to his heels and scaled the iron bars of a cage and then up onto the wall. Running along the parapet, he signalled to Carr, indicating that they were surrounded. As he ran along the wall, he signalled numbers where he could. From what William could determine there were upwards of a hundred and seventy horsemen surrounding them.

"Send men for your takings," said Carr, sighting his musket back on Bowman.

"There is little point, really," Bowman responded with typical camp defiance. "To carry it down only to carry it back up again."

"You prefer I kill you first and then search for your gold myself?" responded Carr, stepping closer whilst gripping the trigger. "Shame for you to die a rich man?"

Bowman sighed, "Such desperate violence for someone usually so professional," he said, then stood. He barked an order to a couple of savages who ran to his quarters with obedience. "You'll never get to spend it, Lord Peel," said Bowman, sipping some water. "You are surrounded. There's no way out. Even if you did manage to escape here, you could never leave the harbour."

William suddenly realised that Bowman knew about their ships.

"Oh, that's right, Lord Peel," gloated Bowman. "Your little pretend pirate ships are currently under guard. I control this coast. I had a force assembled the moment you were sighted. So as you see, I am well prepared."

It was a good long minute before Bowman's savages ran back into the courtyard with a foot square, iron reinforced chest, which they dropped at Carr's feet. Carr kicked the latch open and flipped the lid. Inside was a fortune. It was full to the top of gold coins, jewellery and precious gems; all of which sparkled in the sunlight.

"You've been busy," said Carr, as he signalled to his men to close the gates.

"And that's the closest you'll get to it," goaded Bowman, "You'll soon be in the cages, *The Emily* will be mine and the Lord of Tornbridge will be sold to the highest bidder."

William approached Bowman and, without a break in stride, struck him across the face with the back of his hand. "I will have satisfaction you blaggard!"

"My Lord!" demanded Carr, stepping towards William. "We must stick to the plan."

"Honour demands that I show this pig's pecker what happens when you set yourself against a Peel."

"Honour can wait!" protested Carr.

Bowman gazed into William's eyes as he took a moment to decide on a choice of weapon. "I choose Sword," he responded, before enthusiastically drawing his blade.

"Ha!" laughed William, matching Bowman's confidence. "You shall soon feel the pain of a Peel inside you," He snatched a stray sword up from the dirt then felt the need to correct his statement. "I am talking about my sword steel, of course, not my doodah," he added, indicating to his own crotch.

The pair held up their points. William declared "En guard" and they sliced the air together. For a moment neither engaged then suddenly, Bowman took a lunge and William had to be quick to clatter it away. The pair chopped and sliced as they moved about the courtyard amongst the captives making grunted insults to each other whenever they had caught a breath.

Volker and Carr kept their eyes on the walls and the surrounding buildings. They both knew an attack could come at any moment.

William sliced and took a lump out of Bowman's shoulder who retaliated with renewed spirit. He forced William back towards the cages with a series of powerful slashes. As soon as William's back hit the bars, Bowman lunged. At the last instant William stepped clear and Bowman's sword skewered a captive in the chest through the bars. As Bowman's blade was momentarily occupied, William turned and kicked him with all his might in his backside. Bowman dropped like a stone and screamed in agony.

"You dare threaten a Peel!" shouted William, kicking Bowman's backside again. "Steal my property!" he added with another kick. Bowman yelped. "You strip search a gentleman and have the brass gullet to serve a meal with no appetiser or cheese platter."

He raised his sword and, without another word, brought it down on Bowman's head. William's blade instantly shattered into pieces the moment it appeared to touch Bowman's skull. Looking down with confusion, William turned to see Carr at his side his Japanese sword outstretched to protect Bowman's head.

"It's not a fair fight," said Carr, drawing himself up and sheathing his sword. "Besides, we need him. For now."

William dropped what was left of his own sword and grasped the bars to catch his breath. "Quite so," he said, regaining his composure. Suddenly, something in the darkness energised him.

"Oh, Mr Tilly?" he enquired, enjoying the drama. "Would you please step into the light."

Carr levelled his musket and shot the lock off the cage door. A spark flashed as the mechanism shattered. Tilly appeared, stepping out of the shadows. He held himself with fake nerves and squinted his eyes in the sunlight.

"Captive again so soon?" asked William, as he walked to Carr and indicated he wanted the musket.

"He'll have a blade," Carr warned.

"Mr Tilly?" said William, turning and eying down the musket. "You are a scrabbling little rat. If I were to let you live, you would undoubtedly spread some horrible disease. Would you not?"

"Oh no, sir. Please, sir," Tilly weaselled. "I won't be no trouble. If you're taking Mr Bowman with you sir, then I'm free from his service, sir."

"Service!" shouted Bowman, clutching his backside in pain. "You're here of your own free will, you lying dog."

"Twisted words so they are," continued Tilly, "the truth distorted by a desperate man," he added, edging forward towards William and Carr. All his theatrics were hiding the fact that he was secretly taking a weapon from inside his jacket.

William leaned into Carr's shoulder, "Is he any part of the escape plan?"

"No," responded Carr, smiling. "He's what you might call, superfluous."

On hearing which, William turned to see Tilly lunging for him with a knife drawn. In a flash, William raised the musket and shot Tilly through the shoulder from less than a yard away. Tilly stumbled a few steps and dropped to his knees. He clutched at William's britches and coughed his foul breath up at him. William clasped his own nose and mouth in horror to stop him convulsing.

"I'll sees you in hell!" spluttered Tilly.

"I doubt the very devil himself would live with your breath," responded William, as Tilly collapsed face first into the sand. "Besides it's nothing but a flesh wound, you idiot peasant. If murder was my plan, I would have aimed for your ugly, bulbous head."

William shook Tilly off his leg then handed Carr his musket. "This plan?" he asked Carr, "you are sure of it?"

"Oh, yes." Carr smiled, as he took back his musket.

"Sparkling! As it does rather look as though we're up to our plums in trouble!"

Carr took out the leather strap contraption he made on the voyage from Sicily and walked up to Bowman. He slipped the thing over Bowman's head and tied the strap tightly around his forehead. He tied it so tightly that Bowman grunted. Carr then took one of Volker's pistols from his friend's waistband and slipped it into the leather tube protruding from the back of Bowman's head. He then applied a length of string with a pin in the end to the pistol trigger which he cocked. With the pin in place, he released the trigged from its lock. Bowman flinched.

"This is called a dead-man's failsafe," said Carr, at

Bowman's ear. "I fail to remain safe and you get shot in the head. Neat huh?" He pulled Bowman up by his lapels and stared into his eyes. "You asked me how we expected to get out of here. You're going to walk us out." He reached inside his thobe and pulled out the flare. Lighting the touch paper he threw the flare high into the air where it screeched skywards leaving a trail of bright red sparks a mile behind it.

The crew then suddenly rallied with urgency. A ticking clock had begun. Carr indicated to Volker that it was time to move things up a gear. Volker approached the treasure chest and set about scattering the jewels and treasure about the courtyard until the chest was empty and the sand sparkled and glinted everywhere they looked.

"Are you mad!" protested Bowman, struggling against Carr's grip. Suddenly, his eyes fixed on Samuel in his thobe. "You? This is how you repay my tenderness?"

"Oh for heaven sake," sighed William, as he kicked Bowman in the arse again. "Take a grip of yourself man."

"LISTEN!" shouted Carr to the captives in English, he then repeated it in French and Arabic. "Be slaves in America or be slaves here. Your choice. But make it now. If you want to stay you will be led to the gate and handed to the raiders. If you come with us and try and escape, you will be shot. Raise a hand if you want to stay." He waited to see if there were any show of hands. There were none. "Thank God for that," he whispered to Bowman then signalled for the gates to be opened.

Outside was a sight to make any stomach rise. The exit was completely blocked by armed raiders on horseback.

Men and beasts champed at the bit for a fight.

Carr pushed Bowman to Volker then approached the gates, confidently, shouting something in Arabic. After a moment, a voice called back.

"English, pig! Do not insult our tongue." The raider who responded stepped up to the gap in the gate. He was formidable looking warrior. His once black hair had long turned grey with age and the lines on his face had deepened with at least fifty years of sun. His name was Fakhira.

"Trade?" said Carr.

Fakhira looked into the courtyard at Bowman with the pistol strapped to his head. "For Englishman?" he asked.

"For your horses, yes. In return we will set Bowman free at the coast. Along with your horses."

Fakhira peered inside the courtyard and looked about. He then glanced down and spotted a gold bracelet in the sand, which he turned over with his sandal. He looked up again and spied the empty chest and the other jewels scattered in the sand. He knew it was all part of some clever plan.

"You and your men can occupy your time picking it up and getting rich," said Carr, "or chase us and leave the treasure for the locals."

Fakhira rubbed his chin and smiled, "You are cunning like the scorpion."

"The treasure is yours," said Carr, immune to flattery. "We only want the slaves. The Englishman is collateral."

Fakhira rubbed his chin again, trying to read Carr's expression. After a further moment of consideration, he nodded and held out his arm. Carr gripped it at the forearm and they squeezed to seal the deal.

Fakhira called back to his men and one by one, they dismounted and led their horses in through the gateway.

Volker hurried the captives onto their mounts. There were two for each horse. When the courtyard started to fill, Volker took a horse for himself. After a nod in Carr's direction, Volker started leading the captives out into the city. They were all under the guard of *The Emily*'s crew.

About them, the raiders were already on their hands and knees sifting the sand for jewels.

"The girl will ride with me," said William, as Carr handed him the reins to his mount.

"Of course," responded Carr, before pulling William in close. "There's no telling how long the jewels will keep the raiders distracted. Ride fast!"

William nodded and helped the girl up onto the front of the saddle. He then took to the saddle himself and reached around her to hold the reins.

Carr lashed Bowman's hands tight behind his back and pushed him up into the saddle. As he mounted the saddle himself behind Bowman, Fakhira approached.

"Two men will follow," said Fakhira, slipping his hand through a bracelet. "To take horses. My word they will not be problem."

Carr nodded to show he understood then wound the failsafe string around his hand to take up the slack. He reached around Bowman to take the reins.

"This is far from over," said Bowman.

"Oh, I have no doubt," replied Carr.

About them, the last of the captives were leaving the fort under the watchful eye of the crew who were all mounting up. Carr cantered alongside the group and they all made haste through the gateway and out into the streets. Locals cleared a path as they galloped by.

Upwards of three hundred and fifty men made the long ride across the desert to the harbour. None of them had any idea of the fate that awaited them.

"My name is William Peel of Tornbridge," said William, over the shoulder of the woman as they pounded across the desert sands towards the coast. "Perhaps you have heard of Tornbridge?" he asked, spitting her flowing dark hair from his mouth.

"Kyra," she responded timidly, not knowing anything of English.

"Kyra? Kyra?" William repeated, baffled for a moment. "Oh, I see. Your name is Kyra?" As they rode on, William was desperate to come up with some small talk. "So is this the first time you've been sold into slavery?"

She remained silent for the rest of the journey.

The group rode on hard through the Bedouin camp where some of the men were still arguing with their wives about their missing thobes.

A path cleared through the village as the group galloped through the narrow street with purpose. As they all reached the cliff overlooking the Mediterranean, Volker signalled for everyone to stop. His men took up positions around the perimeter of the captives as Carr, Volker and

William trotted to the edge. Below them they could see the harbour and the jetty.

"My godt!" said Volker, as he gazed upon the sight below them. The beach was full of pirates readying for battle. So too the jetty, which was strewn with pirates checking their weapons. They were all obviously experienced fighting men who were busy checking their muskets and sharpening their swords.

"I told you," mocked Bowman.

"Am I to assume," said William, over Kyra's shoulder, "that the plan consists of sneaking past those fellows to the launches?"

"No," responded Carr, turning his horse away.

"Good. Because unless my eyes deceive, those are our launches over there," William pointed, "and they appear to be burning."

"That's right," said Carr, slipping from his saddle and pulling Bowman after him.

At that moment, Volker signalled to his crew they were moving out. Like cowboys steering cattle, they corralled the captives into a line as they ushered them along a path that traversed the top of the cliff in the opposite direction to the jetty. As the last of the crew had galloped away, Volker smiled at his old friend, Carr, before digging in his heels and galloping after the group.

"I thought you'd like to see this," said Carr, as he slipped his musket strap off his shoulder and marched Bowman to the edge of the cliff. "Simons, an old skipper of ours, had a really simple way of dealing with being outnumbered."

"Carr?" enquired William, with trepidation. "How is shooting the idiot going to help us escape?"

In a flash, Carr levelled his musket out to sea at the pirate ship they arrived on. The one that was anchored next to the pair of Brigantines. "I'm levelling the odds," he said, and - CRACK - went his shot. Carr immediately sighted in the other pirate ship, the one Volker captained. CRACK - went a second shot. The shots had to travel so far that everyone had a moment to puzzle on their purpose. They, of course, couldn't see the target, which was a train of powder on the ship's deck that led to the booby-traps below.

"I must confess," noted William, "I'm a little lost as to your stratagem."

Suddenly, the first ship exploded into a thousand pieces. The timber hull and mast splintered and shredded inside an ever-growing ball of fire and smoke that consumed the Brigantines beside it. What wasn't itself disintegrated by the blast was set alight. Suddenly, the other ship exploded and destroyed the three galleons next to it. Both fireballs grew and grew as the shockwave reached the shore and knocked the pirates off their feet. Some pirates were set alight immediately whist others were injured by shrapnel. It was a scene of immediate confusion and horror.

Carr pulled the pistol from Bowman's headgear and kicked him face down into the dirt. He then swung a leg up onto his horse. "Consider yourself very lucky, Mr Bowman, that I am a man of my word."

As he pulled his horse around by the reins, he nodded

William's attention out to sea and a ship travelling at full speed along the shoreline. It was *The Emily* and she was making twenty knots. "We have to move!" he said to William as he dug in his heels.

Carr pointed the way and they galloped with great speed along the scrub path that led down to another beach past the rocky outcrop to the left of the harbour. Ahead, William could see the captives being ushered into a line on the beach but he could see no transports on the shore. There were no boats at all except for a small launch drifting abandoned out to sea some hundred yards away. William and Carr whipped their mounts to drive them on harder towards the beach. Soon the path became sand and they galloped to the crew. The hooves of the horses threw up plumes of sand in their wake. Carr slipped from his horse before it had stopped and slapped its flank to dismiss it. He grabbed William's reins and urged his beast to stop.

"We must be quick," he said, offering a hand to Kyra.

As they both slipped from the horse, William spied pirates on the horizon behind them. Bowman was taking point and charging with a sabre aloft.

Carr led William to the end of the line of captives and picked up a rope that was lying in the sand. It was the rope with the loops every two feet along its length that Carr and Daniel had made during the voyage from Sicily. Carr slipped William's wrist into one of the loops, then did the same to Kyra's.

"They're coming!" called a voice down the line and William turned to see pirates taking to the path that led to the beach.

"It will be close," said Carr, slipping his own hand into a loop just as *The Emily* appeared around the outcrop. Barker was at the stern with a small anchor. He saluted to Volker then tossed the anchor into the sea by the drifting boat. In an instant the anchor line tightened as it snagged on something. As William spotted the rope they were tethered to floating on the water, he suddenly realised the plan. He glanced over his shoulder where he could see the pirates had reached the beach.

"Tell me, Mr Carr?" asked William. "Is this how Simons lost his arm?"

He never got an answer. The rope snapped taught and shed a faint spray of water along its length. With a barrage of screams, the whole group were suddenly, and violently, yanked forwards into the air. One by one, everyone felt their legs take to the air and they crashed into the sea. In an instant, William found himself being pulled, coughing and spluttering through the foaming sea. He lost all bearing of up or down as the sea engulfed him one second then seemed to spit him out the next. The hell felt like it would never end until, eventually, he felt himself hoisted from the water. His arm felt close to tearing free and his wrist felt like it was on fire from the rope. His head banged against the rail and he felt hands grip his clothes to pull him on board. A moment later, he felt his body gently touch the deck. He could sense figures about him. He could hear voices and feel the warmth of the sun prickling on his face. Then there was blackness. Suddenly, he came to. There were smelling salts under his nose. He was on the deck of *The Emily* looking up the huge, white sails that were tight as drums. Watching over him were Carr, Volker and Daniel. George, William's faithful pet lion, nuzzled his master's side and licked his hand. They had made it and the crew let out a cheer as they offered insults to Bowman and the pirates on the beach.

They had escaped against all the odds. William drew himself up onto his elbows and, after catching sight of his soaked and ruined clothes, he felt faint once more.

"Oh sparkling!" he uttered, before passing out.

The Abominable Mr Jennings

Since the early days of the Atlantic crossing, William had become increasingly fascinated by the science of navigation and all things nautical. *The Pride of Emily* was, despite being the flagship of the Peel fleet, a pretty dull place to be if you're not mucking in with sailing it. Which, of course, William Peel was not. He soon learned that there was only so much dressing up and petting one's lion he wanted to do in a day.

Desperate to occupy his time, his mind wandered to how pleased President Madison would be to see him. He pictured The President waving at him from his front step as William, and three hundred half-naked Negros, waved back from the drive. The President would then invite William in, minus the Negros, and after a beautifully cooked meal with a cheese-board to follow, William would receive deeds to a large chunk of America which he planned to name Williamsville, after himself.

As far as William was concerned there was absolutely nothing that could go wrong. He had, after all, single-handedly escaped from Bowman's fort not to mention liberating the captives and landing himself a naked concubine in the process. The fact that William didn't actually do any of those things of his own volition, and that the captives were liberated into slavery, never entered his Peel brain. In his mind, he would be across the Atlantic in a matter of days and then back in Tornbridge in time to catch the tail end of the badger baiting season. As was typical where Peel plans were concerned, however, it didn't take long for the whole plot to dangerously unravel.

This particular morning, William was peering out to sea through his spyglass with the hopes of spotting something of interest. George, William's pet lion, was sitting at his master's side. To their right, young Daniel was busy doing an inspection of the deck equipment.

"So the whole Atlantic is like this?" William asked Daniel, as he focused his spyglass on a cutter a mile to starboard. "Full of boats and what-not?"

"This is a coastal trade route, sir," responded Daniel, checking the helm. "We're heading south as far as Cape Verde then, after a short stop in Dakar for provisions, we'll be setting out west across the Atlantic. Most of the ships you can see will be continuing south. They're trade ships destined for the African Ports." He turned to leave but was hit with another question.

"So we don't just simply, well, go straight across?" asked William, stroking George's mane.

"Sir?" questioned Daniel, with a weary tone.

"Well, looking at the charts it appears as though we're sort of, you know, going downhill a bit. Doesn't it? Not that the sea is sloping, of course, it's just a figure of speech."

George rested his chin on his paws and yawned. He was smart enough to recognise that lunch was likely a long way off.

"Like I said, sir," replied Daniel, "it's a trade route." William just stared, waiting for a better explanation. After a moment's pause, Daniel decided to humour him. "Think of it like your estate, sir. Now, imagine you want to get from the manor house to the village. You use the path, yes? It's shorter across the fields but they are vast and you could easily lose your way or suddenly find yourself in some mud or... or in heavy wind."

"Unlikely," William replied, with a snoot. "I know those lands like I know the tops of my own feet." He then glanced at his feet just to check they were where he left them.

"True enough, sir, but it's just an example. Same as trade routes, parish paths are well trodden. The wind and the currents of the trade routes are all charted. Plus you know the times of the crossings."

"All very interesting. And how long?"

"To cross? Thirty, maybe thirty-five days. We'll know better when we get the latest reports."

"A month!" exclaimed William. "Why that's a tenth of a year. Isn't it?" he paused for a moment, counting the months in his head.

"It's vast, sir," replied Daniel, with his usual sarcasm. "That's why they call it an ocean."

"Rot! They call it an ocean, young Daniel, after Oceanus, the Greek God of rivers or... or something."

"I didn't know that, sir," said Daniel, genuinely

impressed.

"Quite so. I only remember that, of course, because the last four letters spell 'anus'. A very funny thing when you're eight years old and have no friends to play with." William then noticed Samuel in the rigging. He was laughing with the sailors. It brought about an unfamiliar jealous flush to William's cheeks and caused him to take a step towards Daniel to continue the conversation. "Knots?" he enquired, determined, "you promised to tell me about knots."

"I'm sorry, sir," said Daniel, letting out a weary sigh. "I really must continue my inventory." Much to William's frustration, Daniel walked away. As soon as he was out of sight, William suddenly became aware of the silenced glares of the crew about him. As he glanced back, they dropped their gazes and continued with their work.

William approached the aft hatch with designs of catching up with young Daniel and probing him about anchors. His hand had reached for the handle when the hatch suddenly burst open in front of him and out of the darkness emerged a terrified negro. Jennings, the slave master, had the man shackled with an iron ring around his neck and his wrists were tightly bound with rope behind his back. Jennings was bare-chested and clad in an old butcher's apron. His filthy body glistened with sweat. Apart from a momentary glance when he came aboard at Gibraltar, William had not seen Jennings since. He had heard stories about him, of course, including the crew's whisperings in corridors. William had heard nothing pleasant. Once in daylight, the slave resisted his shackles and Jennings' huge arms pulled him to heel. It was then William noticed the negro's leg. It was flexing below the knee and obviously broken. Jennings steered the man like a harnessed beast across the deck and shoved him to the rail. It was at that moment that William observed the crew look away. Whatever was going to happen, they had seen it all before and didn't care to see it again. Jennings had the slave backed up to the rail and without a change in his expression, he produced a thin blade from below his apron and sliced the man's throat from ear to ear. William watched with revulsion as the slave's eyes filled with panic as the blood poured down his chest in a torrent. With his hands bound behind his back, the slave was powerless to save himself. Jennings casually slipped off the shackle from his neck and pushed him backwards overboard as if he were disposing of a roll of old carpet into a canal. A moment later, Jennings was back at the hatch and wiping the knife on his apron. It was all in a day's work. As he turned to close the hatch doors behind him, he caught sight of William with George sitting at his side. For an instant, he locked eyes with George who immediately stood up and made it perfectly clear who was alpha-male. A moment later, the hatch doors slammed shut and Jennings was gone.

"Yes, well," said William, his mouth dry from what he had witnessed. As the eyes of the crew fell on him, he relied on the first thing that came into his head. "I'm late for a hair appointment. Good day gentlemen."

William was in the great cabin distracting his mind from the morning's unpleasantness by trying on some lovely clothes. The stable hands brushed him down and picked loose threads off his tunic. About him, the furniture was strewn with fine foods, wines and spirits. George was sharpening his teeth on a bone in the corner. Kyra, the young woman William had single-handedly saved from Captain Bowman's evil clutches, was sleeping naked on a makeshift bed.

"I really find the whole thing bewildering, George," said William, as he checked his profile in the mirror. "Volker has vanished again. Carr has taken to avoiding my gaze and the crew in general appear to give me the same look as they would a Frenchman who has beaten them at cards. Oh, I don't know." he sighed, indicating to a stable hand that his wineglass needed refilling. "What do they want from me? Tell me? And why should it bother me what the smelly peasants think? Can't they see this whole voyage has been horrendous for me too."

At which point Kyra rolled over and muttered something sensual in Spanish from her dream. She pulled a cushion into an embrace and drifted off to sleep again. The stable hands, who had cast a lingering look in her direction, suddenly found William's glare on them.

"I am still in need of defluffing!" he snapped, holding out his arms. "But she's another point, George," he continued. "How long has it been now? Days? And she still insists on speaking nothing but Spanish. True enough she is Spanish but some effort in English wouldn't hurt. Especially as I can't speak a word of her native tongue. And the peculiar creature will not dress. All out of some duty that her existence is now purely to serve me." He let out a lingering sigh then smiled at his reflection. "That's very nice. Yes, I like the back. A flattering profile." He turned this way and that. Suddenly, a knock at the door broke his concentration. "Entrée," he called, practicing his French. Daniel's face appeared around the door. "Oh, it's you," said William with displeasure, before suddenly getting distracted by the sight of his own shoes. "Look!" He gestured to the stable hands. "No! No! They won't do."

"You sent for me, sir?" asked Daniel.

"I sent for the captain."

"He's engaged in duties, sir."

"And Mr Carr? Busy too I suppose? Both too busy for their employer?"

"I believe so, sir, but I will help in any way I can."

William approached him for a discrete word. "That 'incident' earlier with Jennings? Not the sort of thing one wants to see. Wouldn't you agree?"

"The slave in question had started a fight, sir. He had injured two others."

"I have decided, Daniel, that I shall oversee improvements in slave conditions. We Peels are famous for championing good causes. Mine shall be slave welfare."

"Mr Jennings is very temperamental, sir," replied Daniel, apprehensive. "If we're going to get the stock successfully across land to Washington, let alone across the Atlantic, we'll need his full cooperation."

"Rot!" William interrupted. "I will simply study the

business thoroughly and advise where improvements can be made. Just as I have done with the menu. Surely the fellow wouldn't spit out his dummy over constructive criticism from his betters. Besides, we need at least a few of the stock to reach America and at this rate we'll be lucky if we deliver a dozen."

"Beggin' your pardon, sir, but if I recollect correctly, Mr Southgate, the cook, had to be restrained when he received your 'constructive criticisms' and vowed that if he was ever asked to cook for you again, he would put his head in a cannon."

"I do confess his reaction was disappointing. And, of course, utterly theatrical. The oaf could never fit his fat head down the barrel. I told him so."

"You did, sir, yes. I remember the unpleasantries that followed. However, I fear Jennings is likely to stick your head in the cannon and make sure it fits."

"He would be ill advised would he not?" noted William, with a confident smile.

Daniel nodded, feigning agreement. "Will that be all, sir?"

"It will."

Daniel made for the door but was stopped by a thought. "Sir?" he enquired, gingerly. "Just a suggestion but if you don't want to see slaves mistreated and brutalised at the hands of Jennings and his peers..."

"Yes?" enquired William, eager to hear an idea.

"Then perhaps slaving is not the business for you, sir."

William spent the remainder of the voyage making a

detailed account of the slaves behaviour and treatment. His journal, in his own opinion, is a rich source of facts on the subject.

William's Journal, July 11 1814: Jennings appears reluctant to share the intimacies of his trade. I have to confess I find it impossible to stay anywhere near the hold in order to pursue my enquiries. The stench is worse than Mother had portrayed. It is somewhere between the Thames and the aroma one gets near public houses at summer closing times. By which I mean fresh peasant urine, stale peasant food, and peasants in general.

The root cause of said stench would appear to be thus:

The vast hold is divided into a series of platforms with a central staircase. Each platform has approximately five-feet of headroom. Each slave is chained at the ankle at all times.

The hold appears to have only three commodes to serve the 176 adult males. The commodes are lidless and emptied only twice a day by Samuel (at my insistence by way of a penance. Although, much to my frustration, he seems to enjoy the task).

Most of the stock find the commodes difficult or alien to use and rather than suffer the indignity of disturbing the fellow whom they are chained next to, they soil themselves where they lie then attempt to throw said business at the commode. They meet with little success. Understandably, disagreement ensues and fights follow.

The intense heat produced by the confined space results in a perpetual state of perspiration and condensation, which, in itself, produces a rank humidity and feeling of claustrophobia which can bring about vomiting. Similar, one imagines, to the variety productions held in Tornbridge's town hall.

To aid my endeavours, and shield my true purpose from the oaf Jennings, I have enlisted the idiot Samuel to make errands below decks when required. To some degree, I had hoped it would be a punishment for Samuel, however, I had forgotten that his family's principal source of income in Tornbridge was the manual unblocking of the bathhouse sewer. In fact, the first time he reported back from the hold, it made my eyes water to get a waft of the odour from him second-hand. When I enquired how he was able to cope with the smell he simply replied, "What smell?" and continued devouring his lard sandwich. He even took a moment to lick the juice from his fingers. One shudders to recall the sight.

Jennings' inventory shows three hundred and four slaves comprising of one hundred and seventy-six men, believed to be eighteen or younger, and fifty-five women of the same age. There are thirty-four men over eighteen and fourteen women of the same age. There are twenty-five children whose ages vary from ten upwards. Unlike the mixed bag of mostly European origin I shared quarters with courtesy of the bastard Bowman, these are all negro and

Jennings has removed all individuality or identity. All are branded on the shoulder with an identifying number and details taken for the inventory. This wasn't, as I expected, a record for prosperity but a means by which Jennings can keep check on relationships. Some of the slaves were snatched from the same village and in order to keep them from plotting with family and friends, they are kept apart. The stock has also been segregated by gender with the women and children kept at the front and separated from the males by means of a canvas curtain.

William's Journal, July 12: The slaves were exercised today for the first time. Still shackled, they were taken in groups of twenty from the hold and ordered to make a circle of the deck. The surgeon, Barker, made an inspection of each slave as they passed. One of the men, No.47, threw himself overboard in what I thought to be a bold attempt at freedom. I remarked on his bravery to Daniel noting that the fellow would find it dashed hard work swimming back to Africa with chained hands and feet. Daniel's view was that the fellow had actually committed suicide.

William's Journal, July 13: Jennings and I spoke at length today for the first time. Not that he appeared happy about it. I can't imagine him being at ease with any company unless it was chained, malnourished, and he was prodding it into compliance with a stick. Hard to picture him chipping in with a maritime joke or some amusing story at the captain's table like Daniel. With that said, his views are not what I expected either. He sees his role as that of a farmer with the slaves as his cattle. He sees no barbarism in what he does and justifies his actions as necessary for the safety of the herd. The conversation ended as quickly as it began with him advising me to keep an eye on No.19 an older, muscular male with grey streaks still visible in his freshly cropped hair.

William's Journal, July 14: One of the young girls, No.157, died in the night. Barker records the death as an unknown disease. Jennings tipped her body over the side. There was no service. She was No.19's daughter. There will be trouble Jennings remarked.

William's Journal, July 15: We docked at Cape Verde for supplies. Eighty tierces of beans, five thousand oranges, and several cases of lard amongst other things. Being on land is a welcome change and an opportunity to shop. The past two nights have been restless. Kyra wakes frequently and paces the quarters muttering God knows what. It's most annoying. George has become flatulent of late and unpredictably loose bowelled. This isn't conducive to Kyra's late night, barefooted, sleep walking.

William's Journal, July 16: The transatlantic voyage has begun and it's the First time I have seen Mr Carr for several days. He had been checking our course on deck and only acknowledged my presence because I was coming out from the hatch as he was heading below. There is some tension, I can feel it. We Peels are well known for our understanding of the peasant mind. He purchased a new tunic at Cape Verde. A nice style but the overall appearance sadly lessened by the quality of cloth and finish to the buttons. If only the ignorant fellow wasn't avoiding me, I could advise him on how best to improve himself.

William's Journal, July 18: Samuel has stopped his food allowance of hard tack bread biscuit, meat and vegetables in favour of the boiled beans with a quantity of Muscovy lard served to the slaves. I'm led to believe this is against the rules but as Samuel has paid Southgate his daily pint ration of wine for the privilege, I imagine no one will comment. Why anyone would choose that foul slop over the already inedible regular rations is anyone's guess.

Additional note: Do not forget that Samuel is Tornbridge's village idiot and, as such, has the brain power of a fruit loaf.

William's Journal, July 20: Foul weather for the last two days has prevented the stock being exercised. Nos. 17 and 18 were involved in a fight. One died by the other's hand and one by Jennings' blade. Jennings has told me to pray for the weather to break. The cries from the hold are louder than the wind. Three hundred souls in torment. The only peace is to yield to Kyra's advances and then drink oneself unconscious.

Additional note: must seek spiritual guidance from the Archbishop about the morality of one or two things that Kyra has suggested we try on a night.

William's Journal, July 21: Weather worse. Storm force winds. Whatever that really means. All I know is the boat lurches so much that George slides about the cabin as if it were a frozen lake. Not the type of thing that suits a morning's hangover. Kyra has finally dressed and taken to wearing sandals at night. It looks unnatural to see her in clothes. Daniel has warned me that the stench of the hold will carry and I'm advised to remain in my quarters. Rainwater is apparently leaking inside the hold and washing the mess everywhere.

William's Journal, July 23: The weather has broken but left us with another problem. We are becalmed. Which, as I've learned from Carr, means there is no wind for the sails so the boat doesn't move. There's not even enough wind to cause a ripple on the water. The sea, as far as the eye can gaze, is eerily like a mirror. Jennings has used the time to wash down the stock and the hold. He also carried out a detailed search of the hold and found three nails and a knife. Word has spread through the crew with unease following. Jennings believes we were close to having a slave uprising. He suspects No.19 to be the leader. I learned a great deal from this discussion. It's the older stock the crew fear not the younger, fitter types. The older ones are prone to desperation. They are more likely to commit suicide and more likely to rally the younger and impressionable males. Jennings says that's why traders, such as Bowman, closely crop the stock's hair as Negros are difficult to age if hairless.

William's Journal, July 26: We have been lucky that the wind has picked up and brought rain with it. This is a welcome relief to the men as I had rationed water in order that I can wash my handkerchiefs. Some men are drinking their own urine. I can't imagine that ever becoming the aperitif of society banquets. Although I wouldn't put anything past the deviant, Byron.

Many of the older stock have taken to refusing food, out of protest, which greatly concerns Barker. Although everything greatly concerns Barker.

William's Journal, July 28: Barker announces the first two cases of dysentery or 'flux' as he calls it. It's affected two young children No's 198 and 221. Jennings has thrown them overboard in a bid to stem the spread. Considerate of him. Given their young age, I expected more objections from the senior staff but all fear an outbreak spreading to the crew.

William's Journal, August 1: A Monday. One loses track of the days of the week at sea as every day looks the same.

I confess that the constant blanking of the crew has begun to wear me. Still no sign of Volker and his obligatory spitting. Little sight of Carr except when it is by accident.

I have begun to imagine Carr in his retirement. A life in rooms above a tailor's shop appears rather unfulfilling for such an adventurer. He is unmarried, according to Barker, although I hear he was once very much in love but the union was an impossible one. Having spent a great deal of unpleasant time in the company of the cocksman, Lord Byron, my interpretation of 'impossible' is that the lady in question is either married or at least betrothed.

As Daniel appears to have honed his sarcastic tongue to a fine edge, I really only have Jennings and Barker to talk to. Jennings, surprisingly, has an interest in art and spends his spare time painting in his quarters. During one of the long days, I made the mistake of accepting an invitation to his cabin where he showed me some of his latest efforts. They are mostly images of naked negro ladies. Nudes picking fruit or nudes picking wheat, that sort of thing. There was even a nude being branded, which I found most bizarre. His latest piece, entitled 'nude boundaries', depicted a slave girl, naked of course, hammering a fence panel into place. I remarked that she reminded me of one of the slave girls on board and that his style was reminiscent of some early works. That pleased him. By 'early', of course, I meant cavemen-esq. I could easily picture Jennings whiling away a few hours after a hard day's bullying by drawing on the wall of his cave with a stiff turd. It did, however, give me the idea to rekindle my childhood passion for oils and, in exchange for a couple of silver coins, Jennings parted with his easel and paints for a few days.

Kyra and I dined with Barker although I knew after the first five minutes that it was a huge mistake. What started as a sensible discussion about poetry soon darkened. Oiled by my wine, Barker spent the proceeding hour describing the conditions of smallpox, cottonpox, milkpox, and whitepox. I'm sure there were more 'poxes' but my mind had drifted to picturing the fool being so infected by the silly pustules that we had to throw him over the side. My fantasy was rudely ended, however, by his mentioning that they had a case that morning. Needless to say I didn't try and translate anything to Kyra as she was enjoying a soft cheese course. I brought the evening to a quick conclusion by telling Barker that I had tired of his company and desired the use of my commode.

William's Journal, August 3: If I had never seen a man force-fed, I would have pictured my old nanny, Mrs Forbes, plying me with tonic by the devilishly cunning ruse of pinching my nose whilst sticking a spoon into my open mouth. I can now say that this is far from how it's done. The fellow in question was dragged up onto the deck and tethered to the main mast by his waist and his head. He struggled desperately against his bindings. Once prostration had set in, Barker inserted a speculum down his throat, which he then widened using a thread. The effect being that the man's gullet was completely open. Mashed up food was then forced in using a ram. The fellow writhed and blew with eyes bloodshot and nostrils engorged. The whole process, including pauses for water, took a little over twenty minutes, after which the man's hands were tied behind his back and he was taken down to the hold.

Kyra has been restless and taken to delivering passionate monologues. Becoming increasingly animated, she even beats her bare breast whilst prattling on about something or God knows who. In some ways it's strangely reminiscent of Mother when she delivers one of her lectures intended for my improvement. Minus the bare breast, of course. I have to say I'm getting pretty fed up with listening to her blabber on. Today, I tried to lighten things up by accompanying her soliloquy on the harpsichord. She wasn't impressed. I can't speak a word of Spanish but every musician knows that when someone throws a banana in your direction and spits it is time to lower the lid and take refuge behind one's lion.

William's Journal, August 6: A dozen more cases of the flux reported. I am aware of a feeling of panic in the hold. Men and women tethered next to shivering wretches with no control of themselves. I hear reports that the air is so rank and humid that it's difficult to breathe. I sent Samuel in to make a detailed study and he says the numbers are worse than Jennings is reporting. Two slaves jumped over the side whilst being exercised on deck. One was recovered but the other not.

Kyra is in a foul mood over something. She's a hot blooded creature and I guess not used to being cooped up. I narrowly missed an unprovoked sandal to the temple during breakfast.

William's Journal, August 8: The flux has spread to the crew with two able seamen and a top man confined to the sickbay. Amongst the stock, it's worse. A dozen, at least, according to Samuel although, as I have just realised he cannot count, my previous figures should be disregarded. Based on his description, I should say the actual figure of those infected is thirty-five. Samuel also described what I recognised immediately to be pox symptoms. I have decided, therefore, to remain in my quarters until the whole thing blows over.

Kyra calmed last night and brought fruit to bed. What she can do with a handful of grapes and a banana defies explanation.

William's Journal, August 13: The slave known as No.19 incited insurrection. He and a few men made it past Jennings and out onto the deck. Several of the crew were injured. I'm led to believe the slave's intention was in taking control of my boat. Beasts! What provokes men to such rudeness? From my cabin there sounded to be a great deal of unpleasantness. Less than twenty minutes later, however, it was over. No.19 and the ten-strong force behind him were overpowered. In customary fashion, Jennings wanted to throw No.19 over the side. Volker, thankfully, objected noting that the man was healthy enough to sell and should just be gagged and chained at all times.

I'm led to believe that the flux is under control and no other cases have been reported since Barker began medicating everyone on board. I'm also led to believe the symptom Samuel described as smallpox was quite simply someone who had spilled some beans onto their chest whilst eating. I have decided it is a pointless exercise to send Samuel into the hold anymore on account of him being a pea-brained idiot. I would have better luck employing a halibut.

William's Journal, August 15: Mr Carr is displeased with me and has told me such in a manner that I do not care for. He entered my quarters in order to view a sea chart and found me capturing Kyra's beautiful nudeness with oils. Although initially speechless by my natural ability, he suddenly, and in my view unprofessionally, raised his temper. All because I had used the back of some old sea chart as a canvas. Some of what he said I couldn't forgive and some I couldn't understand. Kyra was shocked by his tone but at least she had the decency to put down her banana and cover her ears. The conversation ended with my stating, in very clear English, that we wouldn't need a map to navigate home as we could simply follow the bobbing slave corpses. Mr Carr left the doors of the great cabin rattling in their frame. Blast him!

William's Journal, August 16: I was woken in the early hours of the morning by Samuel who thrust a lantern into my face and beckoned me to join him on deck. After taking a moment to freshen my face and add some perfume, we headed into the aft companionway. As quietly as the creaking timber treads would allow, we climbed the steps and stopped at the aft hatch. Samuel then hushed me and closed his lantern. Taking care to open the hatch quietly, we found ourselves in moonlight.

Keeping low, he led me to the quarterdeck where we hid behind the wheel. What I then witnessed had my blood boiling in an instant. Jennings had a negro woman ripped bare of clothes and was submitting her to his vile advances against the stern rail of my lovely boat. I recognised her immediately as the slave-girl from Jennings' latest, hideous daub. Except, of course, that in this composition, she wasn't fixing a fence. In a flash, I grabbed the lantern from Samuel and flipped it open. Jennings cursed at the sight of me and scrambled to pull up his britches.

As the girl rushed to Samuel for protection, Jennings and I circled each other like two animals sizing up their quarry. Well, make that one sweaty pig and the Lord of Tornbridge. He proceeded to make some disparaging remarks at my expense and I responded with some home truths of my own that he wasn't grown-up enough to hear. Next thing I knew he was at me with his blade drawn and I felt it cut into my shoulder. With a glint of steel, he was at me again. This time he grabbed me by my injured shoulder and shoved me hard against the rail. It took all I had to keep his knife from my throat. I eventually pushed the stinking blaggard back and was about to backhand him when without warning, he vanished from my grip. I turned to see his body flying through the air and his head crack open against the mizzenmast. His body collapsed on the deck behind the wheel. It was then I saw George lowering his paw. He let out such a proud roar that it must have been heard back at Tornbridge.

Many of the crew, including Carr and Volker, arrived quickly up on deck. Without even thinking, I grabbed Jennings by the scruff and, turning to summon Samuel for help, we moved Jennings' body to the rail. Without skipping a beat, I pushed the sweaty blob over the side and watched as he vanished into the wash. A fitting end. The way he would have wanted it. Not that I really care, of course.

Barker later reviewed Jennings' notes and discovered that the girl was in fact No.19's wife. As he dressed the wound on my shoulder, he postulated that No.19 probably mounted the insurrection in reaction to Jennings' liberties with her and probably other females as well. Whatever the reason, Jennings' departure appears to have settled the cargo.

The Pride of Emily was making good time across the Atlantic on route to the coast of America. William was on a sun lounger on the quarterdeck dressed in his finest garments. George was beside him asleep, snoring on his back. To the side, Samuel stood holding a parasol, sporting his usual gormless expression. William sipped his tea and read aloud some Byron. He was repeating a phrase aloud, in order to get the delivery right, when Daniel approached.

"You've had a busy night, sir, so I hear," said Daniel, smiling.

"Sometimes I think the idiot Byron writes any twaddle just to make the reader feel like they are stupid," William replied, lowering his book.

"More Carr or Barker's thing than mine, sir," replied Daniel, his attention caught by George. "Looks like someone is enjoying the summer sun." He approached George with the intention of tickling his stomach.

"I wouldn't," urged William, as Daniel's hand neared George's soft belly. "Imagine if you woke to find a stranger's hand beneath your blanket. There would be disapprobation, I'm sure. Unless, of course, you have Mr Bowman's proclivities."

"Looks like he's not suffered during your absence," added Daniel, changing the subject.

"Quite so, but that's the advantage of a 500lb lion over say, a Spaniel. The common lap dog would simply yap away if you skipped a meal or two in error. You so much as forget George's breakfast and you'll end up a crewman short and with no trace of foul play except for a pair of feet in his basket." There was a moment of silence. "My father was a popular man was he not?" asked William, putting down his book.

"He was, sir."

"With the crew I mean?"

"Very much so."

"Humm," William pondered, his eyes narrowing to slits. "It might just be my imagination, Daniel, but I get the distinct impression the crew have developed an Arctic chill where yours truly is concerned. They have dispensed with even a veiled attempt at courtesy. I thought they would see things in a different light after the events of last night but sadly not. Have you a hypothesis of your own?"

Daniel took a moment to consider his words. "I'm sure it's not my place, sir," he replied, his back straightening.

"Come, come!" exclaimed William, with disappointment. "Have we not fought side by side as comrades in arms? Have we not been shoulder to shoulder in the heat of battle?"

Daniel didn't exactly see it that way but he wasn't stupid enough to correct a Peel. Instead, he offered as tactful a response as he could. "Perhaps it's because the men see you reading poetry on the quarterdeck in shade as they toil in the baking sun, sir."

William took a minute to think it through. "Unlikely," he said, with conviction. "I own the blasted boat why should my reclining be an issue?"

"Then possibly it's because you fed George all the fresh meats and left them with the biscuits!"

"Are they not nice biscuits?"

"Maybe it was because they had to drink their own piss for a week to ensure there was enough fresh water left to wash your handkerchiefs."

William stood with purpose and dismissed Samuel with a waft of his hand. "You can't feed a lion biscuits, Daniel. Anything but meat disagrees with his digestion, you know that. As for the piss business, they surely didn't expect a Peel to have urine smelling handkerchiefs?" He took Daniel's elbow and led him to the rail with an air of genuine mystery. "Daniel, there is less than a day left on the voyage, is there not?" he enquired with a lowered voice.

"Sir," confirmed Daniel

"I don't want to be just a spiritual leader to the men. Nor for that matter do I want to be an unapproachable statue whom they see as beyond the reach of their intellect. I want their respect given freely. Do you follow me?"

"Not exactly, sir."

"I could resort to floggings, of course, but these fellow's aren't gardeners or scullery maids. They are accustomed to pain and suffering." William stared into Daniel's blank eyes. "You're not being much use, Daniel! It's like talking to the blasted mast."

"It's a delicate matter," said Daniel, with a sigh.

"Delicate? How so?" quizzed William, sensing Daniel had more to tell.

Daniel quickly checked there were no crew in earshot. "Normally, sir, the men would get a prize for their efforts at Bowman's fort. They'd get a reward for their courage."

"Really?" replied William, agog. "Surely their glacial demeanour isn't over something as vulgar as money?"

"Yes."

"And how much to, how shall we say, bring about a

thaw?"

"A considerable sum, sir."

"A considerable sum, indeed. I see," said William, with a tone of mistrust. "And what exactly is a 'considerable sum' these days?"

"That's for your discretion, sir."

"This will not do!" flounced William, raising his voice. George yawned and rolled over. "Are we talking drinks all night with enough left over for a whore and lodgings or are we talking a villa on Elba?"

"I should say somewhere between the two, sir," Daniel replied.

"And this will improve my popularity?"

"They snub you, sir, because they think you denied them their prize. That's all."

After some initial fidgeting, William warmed to the idea. "Yes, well, we can't have unrest. Not as we are so close to clinching this deal with the idiot President, Muddyson, and returning home to Mother with a smug smile and pockets full of land." He was struck by a thought. "And this money, should I choose to pay it, may it also discourage the men from crapping past my window in a morning?"

"It might just do that," responded Daniel with a wry smile.

"Very well. If grease for the paws is what's needed, you see to it the men get double wages for the year. Is that good enough?"

"Very generous."

"Yes, I am," William added, proudly, then leaned in for

a quiet word. "Not a bean for Samuel though, you hear? There's a lot more forts to storm before that oaf sees more than board and lodgings."

It's fair to say William Peel of Tornbridge felt justifiably smug. As he watched Daniel headed off up the deck, William's face filled with a pompous look reserved only for those rare occasions when Mother was wrong and he was right. He was smug because, of course, he had survived the odds and was shortly to arrive in America with enough slaves to ensure Madison would greet him with open arms and beckon him lovingly towards his satinwood negotiating table. William gripped the aft rail and let out a little contented sigh. The glistening sea, carved up by the wash, stretched out behind them as far as the eye could see. There wasn't a single ship in sight.

"Sparkling!" William whispered for his own pleasure. He was content in the knowledge that there was nothing and no one to stand in his way…

As usual, of course, he was monumentally wrong.

Sir George Cockburn, Rear Admiral of the British Fleet

It was Wednesday, August 17 when William Peel first caught sight of America. *The Pride of Emily* sailed north-east into the mouth of the Chesapeake, a fourteen mile wide stretch of water bound by sounds, peninsulas, and smaller bays stretching up through Maryland. For a moment, William's mind recalled the violent events that had very nearly ended his adventure. The Sicilian fiasco that could have cost him his head, the pirate attack that could have cost him his life, not to mention the slave trader, Bowman, who could have easily cost him his chastity.

As William strolled towards *The Emily*'s stern, crewmen tugged their forelocks by way of a salute. William confessed to his journal of a somewhat warm feeling at the change in the men. He disregarded any reference of having to pay for it, of course. He arrived at the stern rail to find Carr and Daniel tracing the shoreline with their spyglasses.

"Ah, Mr Carr," William said, warmly with a clap. "All is well I trust?"

"For now," Carr responded, typically cautious.

"If you consider, Mr Carr," said William, "that in life

there are two types of people. Those with a drinking glass half-empty and those with a drinking glass half-full. Do you follow?"

Carr didn't follow him and neither did Daniel. Both lowered their spyglasses to hear more wisdom.

"It's an idiom, you see," William continued, hands gripping his lapels. "If you were to see half a glass of water and say 'that's half-full' then you're an optimist. If, on the other hand, you were to say 'that's half-empty' well, then you're a pessimist."

"What if you don't know how much water there is?" asked Daniel. "It could be an unusually shaped glass. Then you couldn't rightly say whether it's half at all."

"Yes, I... I think you're missing the point," said William, back footed by Daniel's interpretation.

"If it's say, half a pint?" continued Daniel, "well, then I'd say I had half a pint, sir."

"Let me stop you there," cut in William. "You must forget about the quantity. It's a proportional example. The question is, if you had half a glass of water, would you say it was half-full or half-empty."

"Half-full," said Daniel

"Half-empty," said Carr.

They both waited expectantly for William's interpretation.

"Good!" responded William, wishing the subject would change. "I hope you learned something?"

"There might be men who are both, sir," said Daniel, with a playful smile to his lips. "I reckons they would have two half pints."

"Really?" questioned William, with a weary tone.

"Aye, sir. See, the optimist side of him will be looking forward to his pint, sir, however, the negative side of his nature will be expecting one of those glasses to smash."

"Isn't that an optimist?" asked Carr, after much consideration. "He's travelling hopeful that he will have at least half a pint if not a full one. That seems a most positive attitude towards the balancing of probability rather than simply blind reliance on the unlikely and negative event that will cause him to spill his full pint."

"Anyhoo," said William, rubbing his hands. "If we can return to the original question of how are we going?"

"Cannon locked and loaded," said Carr. "We have a British Frigate a mile to the south-east and a Privateer coming down the coast from the north. Neither concern me."

"Just look at it," said William, arms welcoming towards the lush lands ahead. "An incredible sight, is it not?"

It was the shore of Hampton with Cape Charles to the right and Lynnhaven Bay to the left. They were scattered with settlements. William took a spyglass and scanned the shore. He could see figures tending to their daily business of loading boats and preparing for a day's fishing. The scene appeared normal until his spyglass sighted a family loading a cart with their belongings. They were leaving in a hurry and the husband was armed with a musket over his shoulder and a pistol in his belt. As his wife loaded their young girl into the cart, the husband picked up a spyglass of his own and eyed in *The Emily*.

"That's rigging," said Carr, sighting his own glass onto something in the water on their port side.

"A discussion for the quarters," said William, "over a meal perhaps. Mr Volker too, of course, and Barker."

It was all very pleasant and civilised as the senior staff, William and Kyra dined that evening. William was colour coordinated with the stable hands' waistcoats. Carr was sporting another new jacket and Barker had managed a trim of what little hair he had. Even Volker had gone to some effort to shave and run a cloth over his leather waistcoat. Kyra wore a corseted, satin red dress and the sight of her perfectly presented cleavage turned Barker's cheeks crimson and caused beads of sweat to pop on his brow. Daniel, who had taken on some of Jennings' duties, was the last to arrive.

"All fed and watered," he noted, as he pulled up his chair.

"I must say, I'm impressed how you fellows have rallied," said William, indicating to a stable hand to charge everyone's glass. When all glasses were full, they stood to raise a toast. "To a splendid crew," said William, and Kyra said something similar in Spanish. William's genuine sentiment seemed to catch everyone off guard. They expected it to be followed by a note of criticism or a claim for all the glory himself. It never came.

"Here, here," responded Carr, being the first in raising his glass towards the middle of the table. The rest followed suit and glasses clinked.

"In a few days," said William, as they resumed their

seats, "we'll be waving goodbye to our chained guests and heading home."

"This Washington business?" asked Daniel. "If you don't mind, sir, is it important?"

Carr and Volker cast a stern gaze in Daniel's direction as if he was wrong to ask.

"No, no," responded William, gauging their reaction. "It's a healthy enough enquiry. I have put my mind to that very question in recent days. I'll tell you this, I don't think it would be an exaggeration to say it would have a profound impact on the future of Tornbridge if this business was not concluded," he paused for a moment as the stable hands entered with the food. "Not to mention the fact that all the belittling comments Mother will currently be rehearsing will be useless."

Everyone tucked into their meals and, apart from the occasional words of praise for the stable hands' efforts, it was an unusually quiet affair. In spite of the fact that Kyra spoke nothing but Spanish, and therefore everyone was free to speak as if she wasn't at the table, they remained on their best behaviour. Such reservation only lasted into the cheese course, however, as everyone, including Kyra, tucked into William's impressive selection of wines and spirits. Daniel was soon reeling out a string of filthy jokes that made William blush. Kyra was laughing behind her fan at the sight of Volker's big red cheeks and the tears of laughter rolling down them. Only Barker wasn't enjoying himself as, despite knocking back the port a full glass at a time, he looked distant and morose. At ten o'clock the stable hands served a fruit course and Barker took that as his cue. He cleared his throat with purpose and attempted to put on his glasses. Sadly, he was a little too drunk to find his ears. With everyone's attention, he removed a crumpled piece of paper from his pocket.

"Mr Barker!" exclaimed Carr, sternly, sensing what was coming. "This is not the time."

"It will do," responded Barker, flattening the paper on the table.

"If you will excuse me gentlemen, my lady," said Carr, pushing back his chair and standing. "I must check the watch."

"Mzr Barker," said Volker. "Zis can vait. Vinish your food."

"Seventy-seven," said Barker, quickly, glancing over his crooked glasses to Volker, then Daniel, then Carr. "Forty-seven men, twenty-two women, and eight children." The temperature in the room fell instantly as Barker removed his glasses and slipped them away. The only sound in the cabin was that of Kyra's fan.

"You shouldn't drink, you old fool," said Daniel, leaning back.

"This is a slave voyage," said Carr, pushing his chair under the table. "In case you're still confused about our business."

"That's excluding the crew, of course," added Barker, as if he was taunting. "Another eight there. Plus Jennings. Although I'm not sure what I note as cause of death."

"Za vone's left vill haz a new life."

"So we're liberators?" chuckled Barker, playing with the stem of his port glass.

"I won't miss these discussions, Mr Barker," said Carr. "You take the pay when you're sober then regret it when you're drunk. This is just rude. If you didn't like the business you should have stayed sailing ferries. This is our last voyage together and we will finish what we were paid to start. Goodnight." He bowed his head to William and Kyra then made his way to the door.

Suddenly, William's voice stopped him in his tracks. "I too am a slave, Mr Barker," said William, beckoning his glass be charged. He then paused as he tasted the fine wine. All eyes fixed on him as they waited for some qualification to his claim. "Sure, I do not have shackles of iron but I am bound nevertheless by duty and responsibility. For life, I might add. Tornbridge must endure and it is my burden as to how the ends are met." The comment hung and then William stood. "I wish you all to leave now. I will take my fruit course with Kyra."

Barker took to his feet although somewhat uneasily. Daniel and Volker stood and tugged their forelocks in a genuine show of respect.

"I will take on Jennings' role," William continued. "I have studied his methods and learned the ways. Tell the men that I shall lead the slaves when we land. I'm sure they will rest easier knowing this."

August 18, 1814. *The Emily* was making good up the Chesapeake and William was once more enjoying the sun on the quarterdeck. As with any typical day, George was soaking up the rays next to him and Samuel was paying his penance with the parasol. It was approximately 2pm when Daniel approached William with urgency and shattered his peace.

"The skipper wants to see you, sir."

As soon as William got to his feet, he knew something was wrong. Every man on board was either at the rail or motionless in the rigging. Following their gaze, William could see why. Ahead of *The Emily* was Tangier Island and what appeared at first glance to be the entire British Navy anchored about it. William made out at least four ships of the line, twenty frigates, numerous sloops of war, and well over twenty troop transports. Together, they were affectively blockading Tangier Sound.

William walked with purpose to the bow rail where Volker and Carr were poised with spyglasses to their eyes. It was then William noticed the burning boats along Chesapeake Beach to the west. Suddenly, the broadside guns of a distant British warship blasted out in unison. William grabbed Carr's spyglass and traced their direction to a settlement on the west shore. The buildings were obliterated in an instant and engulfed in flame. To the east, he observed British Army Red Coats setting light to farms and outbuildings as far inland as his glass would stretch.

"They're kicking up some blasted fuss over something," said William.

Carr stepped towards Volker. He wracked his brain for an idea. "Can you turn us?" he asked his old friend. Volker shook his head.

At which point Daniel's face illuminated with an idea. "We chance it through!" He pointed. "There between those sloops."

"Even if ve could. Zere is novhere to go."

"One way in. One way out," Carr said, turning to Daniel. "The waters further north are much too shallow to rush."

"Too late," said Volker, pointing towards a warship that was turning to head them off. He ordered *The Emily*'s sails be lowered and the anchor dropped. "Getz uz ready Mr Carr," he said, then took the glass and studied the approaching ship.

"This is more than the usual meddling," said Daniel, gripping the rail.

"Invasion!" said Volker, causing all eyes to fall on him. "Zay vill be soon boarding," he added.

William's mind was reeling when suddenly a thought hit him. He remembered the last words Parsons said to him at Peel Manor 'be away from the Potomac before August' *he muttered,* before uncontrollably blurting out. "Cochrane!"

"Isn't he some politician?" questioned Daniel.

"The Admiral," Carr corrected.

"Oh, poo, yes. Do you know Parsons?" William stared for a moment at their blank expressions. "He has a narrow head? It looks sort of squashed a bit. It makes him look like a pouting haddock? Well, never mind. He said be clear of here before August which we would have been if I hadn't listened to Mother and stayed for that pointless inquest into the manor blaze."

"Perhaps a good time to name drop," suggested Carr, hopeful. "This Cochrane's not your Uncle by any chance?"

"Ah, well, it might be a bit awkward where the British are concerned," replied William, cringing. "A slight awkwardness over Uncle Boney's jaunt around Europe."

William was astonishingly ignorant to the precariousness of his situation. If, during the process of agreeing terms of his abdication with the coalition, Napoleon had let slip about the Peels stuffing millions into his pockets to finance his war then it's likely William would be shot on sight or, at the very least, strung up by his Peel giblets.

"I think we have a more immediate problem," said Daniel, realising another complication. "The slave ledger has The President as the client, yes?" Everyone nodded in acknowledgement. "Well then technically aren't we an enemy supply ship?"

They all looked at the approaching warship, only a few minutes away. She was the *HMS Marlborough* a seventy-four gun, ship of the line, third class, and she had seen recent action by the scars in her foot thick oak hull. The gentle waves of the Chesapeake were breaking across her bows. The crew of *The Emily* could see the Blue Coats clutching their muskets as they filed into ranks on her huge deck. In unison, two rows of starboard gun-ports raised with a clunk and cannon were presented.

"Eazy now!" Volker shouted to his crew. He cast the

approaching ship a defiant glance then spat with venom over the rail.

William watched as the massive *HMS Marlborough* drifted along side. She was an impressive ship and towered above *The Emily*. As the sailors tethered the ships together, a concealed door suddenly opened in the *Marlborough*'s hull and out slipped a gangway that dropped menacingly onto *The Emily*'s deck. The precision of the operation was astonishing and it wasn't long before Blue Coats were pouring onto *The Emily* and levelling their muskets at her crew.

Rear Admiral Sir George Cockburn boarded *The Emily* under the cover of at least two-hundred naval muskets. He was a tall, slightly built man with the presence and arrogance of royalty. He was, after all, the 10th Baronet and it was visible in every considered word and action. At his side was Lieutenant Scott, an impeccably presented flashing blade whose back was unnaturally straight to maximise his short stature and William found his manner immediately annoying.

William demanded to know by what right the British had to board his lovely boat in such a manner. He was immediately cut short by Cockburn who dismissed the complaint with a casual hand gesture as he ordered his men to search the ship.

"Consider us security," said Cockburn, in his high-pitched voice. "A ship could fall foul in these waters."

"Ass!" snapped William, and was immediately presented with cocked muskets. "I am Lord Peel of Tornbridge and by the flag any idiot can see I am neither

British nor American. By what right do you have for this piracy?"

"Just who do you think you're addressing!" barked Lieutenant Scott.

Admiral Cockburn indicated to his men to lower their weapons. "I know of your family, my lord."

"Then you'll also know of our part in the War of Impudence," replied William.

Cockburn smiled. "War of Impudence, I like that."

William meant to say 'independence' but seeing as though it made Cockburn smile, he carried on. "Yes, if you care to read your history books you will see that we supplied arms and munitions to the British sympathisers."

"Indeed you did," said Cockburn, removing his hat and smoothing his greying hair.

Thankfully, those history books didn't record that the Peel fleet had returned home with its belly stuffed with stray slaves that had become masterless when the cotton plantations were looted and torched by the British.

"Tell me, Lord Peel," Cockburn enquired, "what brings you to the Americas?"

"Sightseeing, that sort of thing," responded William, quickly trying to think of a sight to see. "The trees!" he added with a click of his fingers. "Yes! The trees are known to be very nice around here. Like that one there. Do you see it? The one next to that burning house."

At which point, a naval officer returned from searching the ship and whispered in Cockburn's ear. Cockburn smiled as he listened then raised his gaze to William.

"Sightseeing, indeed," said Cockburn, unconvinced. He placed his hands behind his back and stepped forward. Carr and Volker exchanged a look reserved for when they can feel things are about to turn ugly. "You look agitated, Lord Peel," said Cockburn, pausing to read William's reactions. "Perhaps it's your cargo. You are aware that the British have outlawed the slave trade?"

William's brain became a hive of activity, none of it useful, and instead of taking a moment to gather his thoughts into a single, plausible argument, he blurted out the first thing he thought of.

"You mean my staff?" he enquired, inspecting his nails.

"Staff?" questioned Scott, sternly.

"Quite so," replied William, immediately wishing he had said something else. "We're all on holiday here." William had dug a huge hole for himself and knew it. He was never the quickest of thinkers when in a tight spot but this was a dangerously stupid comment even by his standards.

"But they're chained!" replied Scott, not believing his ears.

"Yes, I know," said William, with a gulp. "For their safety. Some fell over the side, you see." It was automatic, William wasn't really sure why he kept on talking but it had something to do with Cockburn's poker face. "They had been looking at the fish, you see, and sort of fell overboard."

"Good God!" replied Scott, getting increasingly annoyed. "Are you seriously suggesting that those men, women and children huddled in the hold are on some sort of cruise?"

"Travel broadens the mind as the saying goes," said William, flashing his most convincing smile. "What good is a gardener without a broad mind? Besides, a bit of sun does them the world of good."

"They're niggers!" Scott growled.

"Doesn't mean they don't like the sun. Quite the opposite, in fact."

Cockburn could see the conversation was getting nowhere and casually cut in. "I admired your great-great grandfather, Mortimer. Very gifted man. As a child I was told stories of his adventures. Some of them were quite incredible."

"Indeed," William replied, "however, if he were alive today to witness your interruption of my afternoon tea, he would likely turn in his grave."

Everyone was suddenly aware of a commotion breaking out below decks followed by a swell of troops stumbling back in panic out of the main hatch. As the last soldier burst out onto the deck, he did so clutching his bleeding and lacerated face. His tunic had been slashed with four diagonal claw marks across this breast. Moments later, George's roar echoed from the belly of the ship and shook the very timbers they were stood on. The injured man ran in terror from the deck and across on to the *Marlborough*.

"That's George," said William, nonchalantly, "he is a little constipated."

Although Cockburn was surprised by the turn of events he was from a family who rarely showed emotion. He had taken a breath to continue when Kyra strolled up onto the deck. She was wrapped in a silk sheet that left nothing to the imagination. Scott blushed as the gentle breeze caused the silk to flutter against her breasts. Cockburn bowed his head as if faced with royalty. "Mi señora."

What followed was somewhat confusing to everyone, William especially. Cockburn and Kyra had a protracted discussion, in Spanish, which ended with Cockburn rubbing his chin in contemplation and glancing awkwardly in William's direction. "I will detain you no longer, Lord Peel," he said, and signalled his men back to the *Marlborough*. A moment later, he too was making for the gangway.

Kyra approached William and kissed him tenderly on the cheek. She then delivered another one of her emotionally charged soliloquies.

"You would think," William said to Carr, as she prattled on, "she would twig that if she can't understand me then I can't understand her. Such is the very cornerstone of verbal communication," to which Carr just shrugged. "Oh, dear! She's even crying now," William continued. "One must assume it's bad news." She took William's hand and pressed it to her tear soaked cheek. After a deep sigh, she pulled away and ran barefoot across the gangway. William, Carr, Daniel and Volker all watched on mystified. "Probably for the best," said William, finally, "we are running out of fruit anyway."

"Mortimer Peel," Cockburn shouted down from the rail of the *Marlborough*, "secured home rule and some independence for Tornbridge. Technically that means British law does not apply to you. Smart Man." He watched as the gangway was withdrawn below him and the ships slowly drifted apart. "I said I wouldn't detain you any longer by force but I wonder if I could do so as my guest tonight?"

"I am afraid I'm rather particular about my food, Admiral," William shouted, with his usual air of pomposity.

"As I am about my company," replied Cockburn, with a wry smile. "Shall we say seven-thirty sharp?"

It was nine-thirty in the evening when William eventually boarded the *HMS Marlborough* for dinner. He had lost track of time whilst supervising the polishing of his solid gold jacket buttons. Scott wasted little time in escorting him to the ship's great cabin where an assortment of blue-coated naval officers and red-coated army officers were busy in conversation around the large dining table. The room fell silent as William entered. It was far from a welcoming reception as no one had a clue who William was or why he was invited. Cockburn strode from a crowd in the corner.

"Lord Peel," he said, warmly, "so glad you accepted."

"Hellooo," replied William, with a brief wave. "I'm not early am I?"

"Gentleman!" said Cockburn, sensing the apprehension in the room. "May I introduce, Lord Peel of Tornbridge." No one appeared to care. "Owner of *The Pride of Emily*. The vessel you've all been so admiring." To which there was an immediate recognition, hearty acceptance, and the conversations resumed.

An hour or so later, everyone was eating and the wine had loosened tongues.

"They must come to heel," noted Bradley, a red faced army officer.

"Who, the niggers or the Americans?", replied Lieutenant Scott. The cabin erupted in laughter and everyone banged their palms on the table in excitement.

"Problem is," added Bradley, "it's hard to see when one stops and the others start. Slavery is so prevalent here, they account for almost a quarter of the population."

William remained quiet. He let the conversation ebb and flow about him as he grimaced at the poor quality meal in front of him. Suddenly, an Irish voice cut across everyone bringing silence in its wake. It came from Major General Robert Ross, his Irish accent as broad as his shoulders.

"And your view, Lord Peel?" he asked, mopping up his gravy. "What's your take of it?"

"About the pork you mean?" replied William, tapping at a piece of it with his fork. "It's certainly testing my teeth," he added, with a chuckle. "More wine is there?" he asked, holding up his glass.

"It's actually chicken," stated Bradley.

"Extraordinary," replied William, as his glass was filled to the brim. "Must have been a very old Chicken?"

"Well, it won't be getting any older," said Scott, with a condescending tone.

"I meant your view on the war, my lord?" asked Ross, with a smile for William's eccentricity. "It can't be good for your business."

Before William could get a word in, Scott went red at the gills. "It's you and your kind who make their damnable profits from suffering," he said, with a snarl in William's direction.

William pondered for a moment. "But you're a professional soldier, surely?" he questioned, picking some meat from his teeth. "So that would apply equally to your own line of work, would it not?" He paused for a moment to take a drink. "Or perhaps, Mr Scott, you simply bore your enemy unconscious?" Everyone jeered at the comment, believing it was good spirited, verbal jousting. Which it wasn't.

"Law is law!" replied Scott, determined to have his say above the laughter. "Our business here serves the greater good."

"Well, good for you," replied William, bored with the discussion and not really wanting to open up the whole can of worms about which side he was on. "Is there a cheese board?"

"It's such a hollow gesture anyway," said Bradley, "to ban trade but not ownership. Despite what William Wilberforce, the Quakers, and those damned Evangelical English Protestants think. They've achieved very little."

"Mark this," said Scott with vigour. "As long as I'm serving in the Atlantic, they won't find mine an easy passage."

William let out a childish giggle at the thought of Scott's easy passage but no one else seemed to share his wit.

"Fancy words," replied Bradley, lighting a cigar. "But how exactly do we enforce such a law? It's meaningless. It's alright harping on about immorality and duty but it won't be effective if it just relies on luck to come upon such ships. We're only just coming out of an economic depression for heaven's sake and have neither the vessels nor other resources to commit. Mark me, Mr Scott, the only ones to benefit from this law will be privateers."

"Here, here!" cheered everyone in unison as they lit their fat cigars.

"And the slaves, of course," said Cockburn, and the room fell silent.

In a somewhat extraordinary twist, Cockburn then dismissed the ordinary seamen and took William into his confidence. He began by explaining that since Admiral Sir Alexander Cochrane had taken over, he had been keen to sort out the old colony once and for all.

"I'm here for a chat with Jemmy." He offered a wry smile and the officers chuckled at his modesty.

"We anticipate a heated discussion in Baltimore," croaked Ross, tearing bread with his lean hands.

"Well, best of luck," replied William, feigning enthusiasm. "I hope it keeps fine for you."

"To The King," Cockburn toasted suddenly, and everyone, including William, stood to raise their glass. "And to persuasive discourse," he added, and there was much cheering. William faked a laugh along with the rest and even managed a half enthusiastic cheer. Secretly, of course, he wished they would all just drop dead from their own pomposity. "Right now though we face a graver challenge," explained Cockburn, sitting. "We need greater numbers to protect us from the militia. I've been recruiting hereabouts, of course, but we can always use more."

William's blood chilled. He spotted what was coming as sure as if there were a dancing bear on the table spelling it out with semaphore flags. The old goat, Cockburn, had designs on William's slaves.

"Do you have any suggestions, Lord Peel?" he asked, through a devious smile. "A way to increase our ranks by say two or three hundred men?"

All eyes were on William as he desperately wracked his brain to come up with a ruse that could save his herd from being killed by American musket fire. "Err, not really," responded William, unable to come up with a cleverer line. "These chaps are builders, tradesman, carpenters and so forth. It's a shame but they have no experience of war. It frustrates me. *Labore et honour.*"

"Please save yourself any unpleasant frustration," smiled Cockburn. "I assure you, we can always find use for any able man." He leaned back with customary confidence. "You really think Jemmy had them pegged for scaffolding and fitting doors? *Ruses de guerre,* my dear. He tricked you. So we take advantage of such trickery. Whether or not they hit what they shoot, I'd still feel much happier if they were pointing their guns at the Americans rather than us."

It was checkmate. William knew that whatever the British had planned, Cockburn didn't give two tossed coins about the fortunes of a slaving ship with a belly full of Negros. For all the Admiral had been smiles and pleasantries, he obviously had a job to do. William was new to the world of high commerce, not that he would have admitted it, but he suspected that that if Madison were to see the slaves charging towards his militia with the devil in their eyes, it was likely any deal would vanish quicker than a sailor's wages in a whore house.

Later that night, Cockburn and William lit up cigars on deck of *HMS Marlborough* as they looked out across the river to the inland fires. Farm buildings, shacks, anything that would hold a flame was lighting up the midnight sky. Both William and Cockburn were a little worse for drink. William thought it surreal to see the horizon ablaze, especially through the gentle swaying of his poorly focusing eyes.

"Truth is," said Cockburn, "these waters are too shallow for the navy. Joshua Barney and his damnable band of gunboats are running rings about us. Ross' troops have been cramped up on the transports for too long so he burns what he can on land to stretch his legs."

"I don't suppose anyone thought to pack a cricket bat?" said William with a chuckle.

"Kyra," said Cockburn, remembering, "is Kyra Mori." He handed William a miniature portrait of her. "Mistress to King Ferdinand of Sicily. She was snatched by pirates on her way to Naples."

William studied the portrait. "Oh, monkey turds!" he exclaimed, drunkenly. "Uncle Ferdinand? That means she's practically my aunt." He gripped the rail so as to control the need to wretch. "Well if this isn't the leafiest bits of the trouble tree."

"She has told me of your heroic rescue. You are a great man, so she says, with a love of art and fresh fruit."

"Christmas will be awkward."

"Such ladies are nothing if not discrete, Lord Peel."

"And your officers?" William enquired, "I wager word will spread faster than a fart in a gale."

Cockburn didn't argue and instead produced a hip flask from his breast pocket. "Perhaps so but if I recall the Peel adventurers of old, your ancestors were renowned for greasing the wives of commerce."

"You mean 'wheels' surely?" William took up Cockburn's offer of a snifter from his flask. "You do or do you not you?" He paused, realising, an error somewhere in the sentence. He eventually took another drunken run at it. "Do you intend to take my stock?"

"Purchase," replied Cockburn, moistening a cigar. "Surely, for the King?"

"Not for any of them," William replied, with a giggle. "I thank you for a truly bland evening and I'll take up no more of your personality. Please pass on my condolences to Mr Scott for being himself all evening." William took a few uncomfortable steps towards the gangway, his hand bracing the rail for support.

"Lord Peel?" Cockburn called after him. "You are aware that the Treaty of Fontainebleau grants those so named by Napoleon immediate settlement of all outstanding debts?" William stopped, thinking it through. He had heard mention of the Treaty of Fontainebleau but couldn't recall where? It suddenly hit him. It was the treaty Parsons mentioned. "The list had your name on it," continued Cockburn. "Quite extraordinary. France being enemy to the coalition and all."

"Is it?" William queried, gingerly, trying desperately to sober. "Well, he is my Uncle after all."

"Lord Castereagh and I correspond. He is handling the whole affair."

"This list?" William asked, desperate to appear like he didn't care, "was there a figure mentioned?"

"Not quite. He has bequeathed your family his extensive collection of hand carved ships in bottles. They are something of a novelty, I understand."

"Oh sparkling!" exclaimed William, with a seethe. "I shall, of course, write to him to explain what I would like to do with them."

"My Lord?" replied Cockburn, sternly. "You are rather missing the point." Cockburn wasn't convinced William understood the gravity of the situation. "Well?" he enquired, gingerly. "Are you reading between the lines of what I'm saying?"

William gazed blankly for a moment then blinked his blurry eyes. "Care to make the lines a little further apart?" he slurred. "And it would help if you could make the writing between the lines a teeny bit bigger."

"If you agree to sell me the slaves, I'll see to it Lord Castereagh removes your name from the treaty before it is sent to King George."

"But won't it be immoral to tamper with such a document?"

"No sport otherwise," replied Cockburn, unashamedly.

William gripped the rail and gave the matter one last consideration. If he was to arrive at Madison's house without the slaves to grease the weasels, as Jose would say, then it's likely he would be about as welcome as Napoleon at King George's Christmas party. William also shuddered at the thought of the awkward silences at Christmas from his Uncle Ferdinand over William's rattling of his beloved mistress. With Napoleon exiled to Elba, and destined to live out his days enjoying long walks and water colours, Tornbridge's future may lie with the blossoming America and its President. No, William sighed, resolved to his plight. Whatever William thought of Cockburn's cheek, it wasn't time to go home. He had to salvage something. "Fine," he finally replied, "collect them in the morning. Not too early though, I think your horrible meal will give me a restless night."

The next morning, William did rise early, well, at ten o'clock. He was being dressed by the stable hands when Volker, Carr and Daniel entered *The Emily*'s great cabin. They had all been summoned. William's mood was light. He sung a little ditty as the stable hands brushed his britches and the outstretched arms of his jacket. He was admiring his reflection in the mirror when his eye caught sight of the gang.

"Gentlemen, gentlemen," he said, greeting them eagerly. "Welcome ye all. It is a lovely American day, is it not?" Daniel glanced at Carr and Volker unsure how to react to William's enthusiasm. "I have been riddled with contemplation all night," continued William.

"We're sorry to hear it," said Carr, "I trust it has passed?"

"Quite so," said William, before screaming, "Ouch!" as the gaunt stable hand, who was knelt brushing his britches, got a little too close to William's crotch. "You ass!" barked William, angrily, and kneed him in the jaw. Volker and the rest watched on as the gaunt stable hand shuffled backwards out of harms way and the cross-eyed stable hand moved in to continue the brushing. William, sensing his visitors were a little surprised, quickly clarified. "The brush," he indicated, "caught my penis. Anyway, I didn't get you in here to witness my morning dangers. Major Ross, the British Army chap, will be taking our slaves to Benedict. Which is a place, in case you didn't know." Carr, Volker, and Daniel were confused to say the least.

"I don't follow," said Carr, hesitantly. "Are we to receive armed escort?"

"Not entirely," William chuckled, trying to pass the whole thing off as comical. "My slaves are to become Colonial Marines. I bet they didn't see that coming?"

"In exchange for what?" asked Carr, concerned.

"I think it's what you nautical fellows call 'the shaft!'" replied William. "Suffice it to say my hand was forced so far up my back that I was able to scratch my own ear."

"Za English dogs!" said Volker, angrily.

"Quite so. Anyway, we Peels are nothing if not adaptable. We are to head up the Patuxent with Cockburn and the supplies. Ross will march his men across land as his transports cannot navigate the shallow waters. Cockburn will rendezvous with Ross at Upper Marlboro and as they head north to Baltimore, we shall head west to Washington and President Mandleson."

"Madison," Daniel corrected.

"Yes, yes. I said that," responded William, not happy about being interrupted.

"What's changed?" enquired Carr, suspicious of William's motives. "Without the slaves, the deal is over, surely? You said that yourself before we raided Bowman's fort."

"Did I?" said William, unable to lie convincingly.

William, like all Peels, played his cards close to his chest. He knew it never served to share family business with anyone let alone the staff. In truth, William had concocted a rather wonderful plan. At least that's how he described it in his journal. It had come to him the previous evening when he returned from Cockburn's dinner to find Samuel urinating over the side of *The Emily* and into a strong, prevailing wind. William proceeded to chase Samuel around the deck and managed to land a few firm kicks to his arse. It was whilst taking a breather from such kicking that the idea suddenly struck him.

The President had visited William before Napoleon had abdicated and there was a chance, albeit a slim one, that Madison had no concept of the British's real intentions in America. After all Cockburn and Madison had not actually met. If William could arrive at Washington just as the British arrived in Baltimore, he was sure to find a worried President amenable to any ready cash at less than reasonable rates. William wouldn't actually need the slaves. He couldn't have planned the whole thing better. He was elated. He would have one-up on the slim-headed weasel, Parsons, and Mother would also have to acknowledge his financial brilliance. Samuel was also elated as it meant William stopped trying to kick him in the buttocks. All William had to do was get to Washington.

William could tell that Carr was not convinced. "The British will serve as protection against this Barney fellow and any local militia we should encounter on the journey," William said with confidence. "Mandydidleson, or whatever his silly name is, is expecting his slaves to arrive at the capital with hammers and chisels not marching with muskets." William suddenly stopped, conscious that Volker and Carr had exchanged a look. "What?" he asked, hesitantly.

"Zis Barney wouldn't be Joshua Barney?" asked Volker, with fervour.

"It would," replied William, watching Carr casually touch the scar on his cheek. "I see there is some history Mr Carr? A duel perhaps? A sword fight atop a snowy mountain? Perhaps one day you will recount the tale and we shall plot the bloodiest of revenges?"

"I don't think so," said Carr, with all seriousness. The room fell silent as William took a moment to process Carr's snub.

"Sparkling!" said William, with a clap of his hands. "Well, cheerful as this is, shall we get back to the plan? Daniel, I want you here on *The Emily* to manage the crew and make sure no one pinches the sails. Mr Volker and Mr Carr, do you still have some adventure left in you?"

"On what terms?" Carr enquired.

"Very well, say a year's wages for each of you."

"Daniel az vell?" asked Volker.

"Of course, of course," William confirmed, "equal shares to you all." Daniel was far from happy and about to protest. "Now, Daniel," William cut in, "I know what you're going to ask but I have made my wishes clear. The Peel mind is steadfast."

Daniel didn't take the news well and straightened his back in a sudden desire to work to rule. "May I be excused, Cap'n?" he said, his gaze avoiding William's.

Volker's eyes flicked to William hoping he would change his mind. He didn't. "I vill come vith you," he said to Daniel, indicating he could leave. "Zere is much to do." Daniel left saying nothing. Volker offered a brief bow in William's direction then left the cabin himself.

"Leaving Daniel is a mistake," Carr quietly advised. "We are a team. Daniel is an expert tracker and able field physician."

"So I understand," said William, "but we have no foreseeable use of either and I need someone who can command the men should *The Emily* fall into harm's way."

"Barker is more than capable."

"Barker is an emotional cabbage!" William replied, sternly. "True enough he can handle the ship, Mr Carr, but he cannot lead the crew. He is wetter than a fish's yawn. I wouldn't trust him to lead his own shadow!"

Carr knew William was right, although he also suspected William's motives were more likely to do with protecting his precious harpsichord and clothes rather than for the overall safety of the crew.

The anticipation of the adventure ahead had necessitated William to make an assessment of his wardrobe and a careful consideration of his shoe collection. After he had selected the desired look, William added a dab of some of Byron's' own Wild Scabbard fragrance behind his ears and checked himself over one last time in the mirror.

An hour or so later, William was breathing the fresh morning air on the deck of *The Emily*. The ship's crew were a hive of activity. William watched as a few sailors hoisted the ship's launch, *Little Fanny*, up from her deck mounts and swung her over the side using the windlass. Having been met by George, William took a walk to the quarterdeck to study the distant British ships. Hundreds of troops were boarding the smaller transport vessels. They were all armed with muskets and well supplied with provisions. It was then William spotted a British warship pulling six large barges in the direction of *The Emily*. It was transport for the slaves.

"Aren't all the sails pretty?" William said to George affectionately, whilst rubbing him under his chin. "Daddy must take a little trip. Yes, he must. To President Moodison's house. Yes, I know he's a buffoon but it's all land for daddy and someone has to keep you in footmen." There was a cough at William's shoulder. "Oh, it's you, Mr Carr," he said, after a quick glance. "Just talking with George about the British. Seems like a lot of fuss to guard one tiny Admiral." At that moment Daniel arrived and handed Carr his spyglass.

"They're loading Congreves, sir," said Daniel, avoiding William's eye. "I thought you might want to warn his lordship."

Carr smirked at Daniel's petty snub of William. As he turned and sighted the spyglass across at the British ships, he muttered something about Daniel being childish. Carr watched through the spyglass as a group of sailors lowered a crate into the belly of a sloop. His gaze then drifted to a group of Red Coats climbing down into one of the crammed troop transports. Carr recognised a few of the faces and he didn't seem happy about it.

"Can you see them?" asked Daniel, eagerly. "Are they rockets?"

"Indeed," replied Carr, turning to William. "What exactly did the Admiral say his job was?"

"Discussions in Baltimore," replied William. "Not that it's any of your business."

"Those soldiers," said Carr, nodding in their direction, "are Wellington's Invicibles."

"Are you expecting this to be my surprised face?" enquired William, pointing to himself. "There is very little I don't know, Mr Carr," he added, "so if it's your intention to point out oodles more obvious facts then I'd ask that you do so elsewhere in order that I may say goodbye to my lion in peace."

Carr's jaw locked at William's offhand remark and he took a breath to compose. "I hope you've thought about this?"

"In great depth," replied William, confidently. "I can assure you it was a most exhausting breakfast." The statement hung for a while until a thought suddenly struck him. "Are you aware of the rare Spanish bat owl? An extraordinary predator. The only bird to actually hunt wearing the skin of another creature." Carr closed his eyes and sighed at William's banality. "It dresses up like a bat, you see, and then sneaks into their caves. The bats don't know it's an owl, of course. Presumably it's a convincing disguise. Anyway, the owl is able to walk right up to its prey to deliver the killer strike. Not sure if it wears shoes that look like a bat's feet."

"Bats are blind!" replied Carr, curtly. "Why would the owl bother to dress up?"

William fell silent, unhappy that Carr's revelation would undermine the logic. "Yes, well the owl doesn't know that bats are blind, of course," he said, peering down his nose.

There was a cry from the approaching British warship and William watched as able seamen from both vessels exchanged mooring lines and secured them to the iron deck cleats. The deck of the warship quickly filled with Blue Coats taking their places. It was as well rehearsed as it was unsettling. For a moment, William was reminded of the efficiency of the British Navy. As the moorings tightened and creaked, the Blue Coats stood to attention and slapped their muskets against their shoulders in unison to the call of the drill sergeant.

"Permission to board?" came a familiar voice from her quarterdeck. It was Lieutenant Scott, and it was clear from his tone that he enjoyed the power.

Carr glanced at William, waiting for him to respond.

"Did you hear a sort of annoying screech?" William asked, frowning. "The type of noise one associates with a constipated dog."

"Permission granted!" shouted Carr, in reply to Scott's request. He then signalled Daniel to prepare the slaves.

Moments later, *The Emily's* main hatch was opened and the iron security grill was winched back. Blue Coats were positioned about the desk with their muskets aimed into the blackness of the hold. The slaves emerged, their chains scraping on the desk. No.19 appeared in the sunshine and winced until his eyes adjusted. He fixed a stare on William. A Blue Coat stepped up to shove him but he was too big to move. After a moment, No.19 dropped his gaze and joined the procession of slaves that were being led across onto the deck of the adjacent warship. Despite everything, No.19 had made it through the voyage alive and so too his wife. What he didn't know was that he and his wife were destined for very different places, of course, and in a few short hours he would be laden like a packhorse and marched, back soaked in sweat, through the Maryland countryside.

William's journal August 19, 1814: It's hard to explain the exhilaration. Maybe it was the war, the chance of adventure, or simply stomach upset from Cockburn's cheap port and his even cheaper cuts of meat. What I was sure about was that we were leaving the security of our beds to face the vast and alien expanse of this strange new world. What is truly worrying it that I have no idea what to pack.

William stood on an orange crate on the quarterdeck of *The Emily* and announced to her assembled crew that he and a select few would be going ashore with the British. It raised little in the way of interest or surprise. William then announced an extra ration of grog for every man not on duty, which received a cheer. "Fickle beggars!" he whispered to Carr, out of the corner of his mouth. "Right, that's it. Carry on knotting ropes or whatever you do."

Daniel appeared through the crowd with urgent news for William. Which, of course, he relayed through Mr Carr despite William standing next to him. "I request you ask his lordship to take Samuel with him, sir."

"You do?" replied Carr.

"He does?" questioned William, to Carr.

"For Samuel's own safety, sir," added Daniel.

Carr relayed the message.

"And why, Mr Carr, should I care about Samuel's safety?" William enquired.

"Please advise his lordship that Barker has expressed

a desire to hang Samuel from the mast and bleed him empty."

"Indeed?" said William, raising an eyebrow. "Perhaps Barker has more balls in his pouch than I gave him credit for."

Carr thought it best not to repeat William verbatim and took another tack with his question for Daniel. "His lordship would like to know if Mr Barker has indicated a reason?" Carr asked, tiring of their silly games.

"Mr Barker," said Daniel, "caught Samuel pleasuring himself to a portrait of Mabel. Mabel is Mr Barker's wife, sir."

"Fruity bugger!" said William, shocked.

"Samuel has a reputation for it," Carr advised. "Your father took to locking pictures of his lady wife away."

"Good lord!" exclaimed William, his lip curling in revulsion at the thought of Samuel's attraction to Mother. "But hang on!" he said, realising something. "That's hardly a reason for me to take the ungodly beast!"

"Please explain to Lord Peel that the crew has warmed to Samuel's simple ways," Daniel advised Mr Carr. "Mr Barker's public disembowelling of Samuel is likely to lead to discord, sir. More discord than I can handle." Carr was about to relay the message when William lost his patience.

"Yes, Yes!" snapped William. "I get the point. Bloody Samuel and his bloody enormous privates again! All I can say is that taking the pea-brain along better not jeopardise things with Mandyson or he will suffer something a damn sight more painful than a disembowelling."

Had William been able to foresee exactly how much

Samuel's stupidity, lack of hygiene, and his enormous privates were going to get them into trouble, however, he would have certainly never let him within a mile of Washington.

William Peel, The Hero of Pig Point

William, Volker, Carr and Samuel were rowed up the Patuxent River by four very red faced stable hands. They joined the fifty or so small ships, launches and barges that the navy had commandeered, which is to say 'pinched' from the local farmers. Some, like *Little Fanny*, were both sail and oar powered, many had no sails and were powered by muscle alone. Volker insisted that the stable hands should be tested on the oars and for that reason they stayed near the rear with the slower, rowed boats. Cockburn had secured a comfortable barge and was as close to point as was deemed safe. The troop supplies were shared out equally amongst the various vessels.

Volker and Carr watched as Daniel saluted them from *The Emily*'s deck. George caterwauled with his paws up on the aft rail.

With the course being somewhat inevitable, William's party had nothing else to do but enjoy the scenery; such that is was. William took the time to catch up on his journal and allowed his mind to drift to Tornbridge. As the landscape rolled by, he wondered whether Mother had made a start with the house restoration and in what season they may arrive home so he could plan his wardrobe.

William's Journal, August 20, 1814: I don't make much of America so far. The scenery never changes. River bank. River bank. Dead tree. River bank. Group of dead trees. A few living trees. River bank. Oh, bush. That's new! It's a relatively flat, uninteresting land. Not dissimilar to France in many respects. There's the usual large buzzing insects and the little silent ones that prey on your exposed bits when you're not looking. Strangely enough they never bother Samuel. I imagine any insect biting on his filthy extremities would soon feel a distinct nausea and curling of the proboscis.

According to Carr, the temperature is touching one hundred and twenty-five degrees, which is just unbearable for anything except a blasted kitchen stove and something I had not packed for. I can actually see my jacket fading and I will have to defy convention by sometimes going without it. It is an odd paradox that everyone loves shade on a sunny day yet they hate it being overcast.

It is a twist by the fickle mistress of fate that I should survive Bowman's torture and secure my freedom only to suddenly find my clothes ruining before my eyes and suffer my hair becoming horribly dry and unmanageable.

Such a strange place is this theatre of war. For all the order and discipline, when viewed from the outside, it really is a preposterous affair. It's little more than people telling other people what to do by people who have, in turn, been told what to do by someone else. And so it goes on. The first night's camp was like watching a comedic play worthy of Aristophanes himself. Naval officers were running about the shore looking for a suitable place to set up camp. After an hour of messages back and forth, Cockburn found a clearing that would do. Presumably the grass was softer and the views nicer. Who knows? Then came another hour of getting the kit ashore, setting up bivouacs, perimeter guards, canteens, camp fires and that sort of thing. It's a little wonder this Barney fellow didn't hear us coming by the shouting of 'Yes Sir' and the smell of smoking pork drifting on the wind.

By Carr's suggestion, we slept on the launch. The evening meal was a revolting stew with very hard potatoes. It took two bottles of red wine, which seemingly travels less well than I do, to eventually knock my lights out.

There was the most God-awful thunderstorm during the night. It nearly washed away a quarter of the tents and apparently sent Cockburn into a fury over damage to provisions.

I awoke early to a morning mist across the water and stomach cramps that felt like someone was repeatedly prodding my guts with a stick. I also felt the unease that comes when one fears a breach. Stepping over Volker and Carr, who were wrapped up in blankets asleep, I jumped ashore to obtain urgent relief. The camp was eerily quiet but I was too busy focusing on the urgent business in hand to pay much attention. The ground was sodden from the night's rain which ruined my favourite Persian slippers. Carr and

Volker had decided that a break was needed from Samuel's stench so he and the stable hands had been ordered to sleep in the navy camp. So after a painful few minutes finding their bivouac in a field of many, I awoke the stable hands and demanded they hurry to a place of privacy with the chamber pot. I note that Carr had insisted I could only bring the pot itself and not the full commode. The fellow is a barbarian!

I had settled on the pot and been started less than a minute when I suddenly noticed a glint of light two fields away. I stopped berating the hands for not holding the blasted pot steady and after a moment of consideration, I recognised what it was. It was a glint of light reflecting from a spyglass. We were being observed. Some blaggard was spying on my potty time. What an ugly business war is. After a moment, the glint vanished but due to the rude interruption, I found the conclusion of my business more of a strain.

As we commenced our journey up river, I informed Carr and Volker of what I saw. They prepared an urgent note for Cockburn which was handed to the cross-eyed stable hand to deliver. He, in turn, passed the note to Samuel who apparently ate it.

William's Journal, August 21, 1814: We reached Nottingham today, which is over half way through the voyage. Cockburn dispatched some twenty heavily armed men ashore to attack some fearsome local militia spotted by scouts. It appears they were little more than farmers with pitchforks who had been spotted in a nearby field. They weren't caught. Not surprising, as most of Cockburn's men, I suspect, like him, couldn't find their buttocks with both hands if they had a friend offering directions. As an expert on military matters, I know that sailors are climbers and can't outrun a three legged dog let alone an American farmer with the British Army at his heels.

Carr discovered an interesting peace of gossip. It turns out that Cockburn was ordered by Admiral Cochrane to enlist local freed slaves to boost the numbers but he spent most of the time lining his own pockets with booty and only raised one hundred and twenty head. It explains why he was so keen to enlist my stock. Bastard! The money he paid for them will be kept off the navy ledger as he used funds raised from American tobacco shipments he seized during the months before we arrived. I have to give him credit for that clever piece of deception.

Note to self: When a moment arises I shall clarify that Cockburn, on Britain's behalf, shall honour any land I may acquire as part of my negotiations with President Middleson (or is it Muddleson). Perhaps, as the monies promised me in payment for my stock is coming from his own coffers, he might be amenable if I waive said costs. Clever William deserves a treat.

I find Samuel the most perplexing of fellows and I have started to view him as a zoologist would study a strange and exotic, if not utterly repellent, creature. For one thing, he makes no effort to obscure himself whilst emptying his bowels. Whilst the rest of the party go to great lengths to find a tree or bush for privacy, Samuel simply drops his breaches and crouches as the mood finds him. For example, as soon as his feet touch the shore. This has led to tensions if he is the first out of the boat. Whereas I am insistent that the stable hands cover the potty the instant my business is concluded, and at which point my interest and involvement in said contents ends, he often makes some study of his produce. I have observed him picking them up for a close look before tossing them into undergrowth and wiping his hands on his britches. Heaven knows what he is expecting to find.

Carr suggested he is likely looking for worms, which would also explain his regular fiddling with his backside. Why or how the poor Lumbricus would set up home in such pipe-work boggles the mind. Then there's his lack of care for even the most rudimentary cleanliness. He never washes his hands, nor his backside after his evacuations. I confess to shuddering with disgust to see him biting his nails or gnawing at the calluses on his palms, which he seems to do with regularity. To be downwind of him is truly eye watering and I have taken to applying small amounts of Byron's Wild Scabbard to a handkerchief which I waft in front of my face whenever I feel the contents of my stomach rise.

William's Journal, August 22, 1814: Carr washed Samuel today. Not being able to cope anymore with the stench of him, he dragged him into the water at first light. Much to Samuel's objection, Carr stripped him naked and scrubbed him as one would an animal, screaming, until his flesh appeared raw. He then provided him new clothes and burned his old ones after we broke camp. I would add that they were quick to flame and burned brightly with many exotic colours. Samuel's only objection appeared to be in his retention of the notebook that I discovered in his pocket at Bowman's fort.

Twice has excitement spread amongst the vessels that Barney and his so-called 'flotilla' have been sighted. Neither came to fruition.

I confess, I am truly bored. My mind wanders again to the lush fields of Tornbridge. They are so dense and handsome this time of year. It is the start of the badger baiting season back home which means outdoor entertainment in the afternoons and the quickening pulse of a wager.

Franny is never far from my thoughts and, of course, Mother. Although not for the same reason. It's hard to believe I've been away for almost three months. How I long for a decent bed, a decent meal, and to bathe for so long that the tips of my fingers become the texture of raisins.

I have come to the conclusion that Volker doesn't like people. Except for Carr, he makes no effort in conversation. He doesn't appear to comprehend that two people exchanging words and sentences is a conversation yet someone talking to him whilst he grunts, isn't, it's just ignorance. When he's not laughing with Carr at the stern, engaged in what I have termed 'private conversations', he simply sleeps, drinks, or indulges his filthy habit of spitting at every opportunity. I confess to preferring him elusive.

The four stable hands talk mostly of girls. They recount tales they've heard from the crew and attempt to pass them off as their own. It reminds me of conversations with that pork loin Byron except his stories were actually true, factually accurate and usually involved married women or men of society and a couple of prostitutes. Beast!

I've also observed that the stable hands snub Samuel and refuse to offer him anything more than a glare of disdain. They too lost their home as a result of his stupidity and he is, after all, the reason they are thousands of miles from home and having to row up a rather dull looking river towards a war. It does appear as though there is some other resentment that I am not aware of. Still, who can say what is harboured in the minds of commoners. It might simply be the social etiquette of peasants that those of standing would never normally observe up close and may never fully understand.

From a close inspection of my jacket, I have learned that the underarms and hem material are definitely a shade darker than that of the shoulders and the arms. Bastard sun!

As night drew in on August 22, commotion spread through the boat crews and lights were urgently extinguished. In the silence that followed, William could make out the faint sound of muskets being readied.

The little fleet was approaching Pig Point where the Patuxent River forked. The west fork, where they were to sail to Upper Marlboro, narrowed as it headed north-west. William and Carr picked up on the commotion and stood like meerkats sniffing the cool breeze.

It wasn't long before everyone could see what had got the crew of the lead ships so agitated. Far ahead, set against the dusk light, was a floating blaze. An assortment of over forty boats and small ships had been put to flame. The British faces were slowly lit up orange by the fire as it grew. The increasing intensity eventually caused people to shield their eyes and one by one the American boats exploded into flames with a deafening roar.

Burning shrapnel rained down about the British hitting the water between the boats with a hiss. One substantial piece ignited clothes on the deck of a launch causing the panicked officers aboard to extinguish it by stamping. It was a mesmerising scene for William but any enjoyment was to be short lived as Volker had a sudden realisation and ordered the stable hands to row with all their might to the shore.

"What is it?" William demanded, as Volker threw Carr his repeating musket.

"Ztay down!" Volker growled, as he and Carr rushed past to the bows and leapt into the long, sodden grass of the bank. Knee deep in sludge, they scrambled to good ground.

William had only glanced back at the river for a second when something caught his eye. An officer on a ship ten yards in front suddenly spun and slumped to the deck. Then another man in a boat to William's right jolted and fell over the side. William's eyes focused on the shoreline as his senses reeled. They were under attack. That's why Volker had bolted. William grabbed a musket and a pouch of powder then leapt from the side of the boat.

"Guard my clothes with your lives!" he shouted at the stable hands.

William found himself running along a banking of long grass in failing light. He had no understanding of where he was headed or what he would do when he got there. His urge to take action had blinded him to the sheer stupidity of acting without a plan. He was running straight into enemy territory knowing that in a few short moments Cockburn's finest would be firing in his direction. He had run about a hundred yards when suddenly his feet caught something and he stumbled to the ground. He had just begun turning onto his back to stand when a large figure drew down on him with his sword glistening.

William raised his musket and deflected the blade but the figure was soon on him again. This time William kicked out and caught the fellow's knee. He felt it break backwards against the joint. The figure collapsed to one knee and grimaced in pain. William scrambled to his feet and grabbed the sword from the grass. Without a pause he turned, cocked his arm, and ran the fellow through. William felt the trickle of warm blood up his arm. Barely had the realisation hit him, that his jacket would be ruined if it wasn't put into soak, when the grass about him was peppered by shot. Smoke from musket fire took to the wind.

The British were retaliating towards the banking. William dived for cover. He buried his head below his hands and cursed at the likely grass stains to his knees. The volley lasted only a minute then silence fell. William raised his head to listen and could clearly make out the sound of people running in water. It was a landing party and they were heading straight for him. He would be dead if they found him. Without a uniform, he appeared no different from the militia. Albeit he was finer dressed. He could hear Lieutenant Scott's voice in the distance,

"It had to be that blighter of all people," William cursed to himself. It crossed William's mind in that instant that Scott might shoot him if he had the chance.

Suddenly, Volker's massive hand grabbed William's collar and pulled him to his feet. "Ve run, now," he whispered, as he shoved William away from the banking.

Beyond the bank was a small settlement of houses with lanterns above the doors. Volker pulled William towards them as shots echoed and ricocheted from all directions. Approaching a small house, Volker yelled his name then booted the door open. Inside was Carr, reclining against a table with his trusty musket across his waist. A dozen militia were huddled in the corner with their fingers interlocked on their heads and fear in their eyes. Volker shut the door and shot the heavy bolt. William took a moment to catch his breath as Carr offered a nod of appreciation to Volker for his efforts.

Suddenly a British soldier peered in through the window and withdrew. "Here!" he shouted to his colleagues. Volker and Carr moved out of a direct firing line as a musket butt pounded the door.

"British Army!" came the cry. "Come out. Arms raised!"

"How bloody dare you. Insolent ass!" barked William,

in reply. "I'm William Peel not a common farmer."

"So you say, sir," came the voice again. "Well if you is not comin' out, then we is comin' in!"

"No, you're damn well not!" shouted William, unusually agitated. "We have a dozen captured prisoners in here. Give the Admiral my name and tell the oaf to come see for himself!"

Cockburn had set up camp in the stables and he had the place so well organised it looked like he had been there for a month. His party occupied themselves with the paperwork associated with taking prisoners as Cockburn himself studied a map intently on the desk in front of him. Busy though he was, he had summoned William to the stables and raised a wry smile when he entered. William had the trophy sword slung proudly at his side.

"I hear again of your bravery," said Cockburn, raising his gaze only momentarily.

"You expect less?" William replied with a typical snoot.

"So too, I see, the famous Peel arrogance."

"It's a failing of the common man that he mistakes arrogance for simply the behaviour of his betters," noted William.

The room fell silent.

Cockburn's eyes fixed on William for a moment but instead of rising to the comment he let out a small laugh. "Barney has fled with his men. Five hundred according to the ones you captured. Barney had been ordered to scupper the craft to prevent them falling into our hands. Lieutenant Scott tells me the militia have removed all portable cannon. I'm sure we'll have the pleasure of those soon enough," he paused for a moment to offer William a cigar, then continued. "We've salvaged some of the flotilla suitable for our purposes. I noticed you have no armour on your own vessel and thought you might like a sturdier craft for the remainder of the journey north. Short though it is."

His eyes dropped to the map again. William nodded in appreciation and was about to leave when Cockburn's gaze lifted one last time.

"I would be honoured if you would sail alongside me tomorrow."

"Then indeed you shall be honoured," responded William, nodding his farewell.

Cockburn's men slept in the houses and outbuildings that night with a watch posted on all approaches to keep an eye for Barney's reprisals. On the way back from his meeting with Cockburn, William reflected on the offer. He assumed, as was his way, that Cockburn was attempting to get into the Peels good books. It even crossed William's mind that Cockburn might possibly be angling to get the slaves for a better price if not for free. Whatever Cockburn's motives, a grateful Admiral, even a Rear one, may one day come in handy.

When William arrived at the house he found Volker and Carr merry with an assortment of liquor they had confiscated as spoils of war. Two of the stable hands were busy over a bowl of water, cleaning the blood out of William's jacket as the other two were dusting the shelves in an attempt to make the squalid place habitable to William's standards. Samuel was in the corner devouring a feast of raw potato and what William thought to be a mixed salad but on closer inspection it turned out to be grass with a few leaves thrown in for good measure. No wonder his bowels were unpredictable, William noted.

William instructed the stable hands who were dusting to charge his glass and he went on to regale the room with the story of how Cockburn would be honoured by him sailing along side. Volker and Carr immediately burst into uncontrollable hysterics. The laughter was so infectious that it spread to the stable hands and eventually to Samuel, whose smile looked like mash.

"What?" demanded William, puzzled. "It's a sign of respect is it not?" which made the laughter intensify.

Volker was soon as red as a beetroot. "Za honour ov vyor company, ya?" which turned him more scarlet and he gripped his sides.

Carr's eyes were bloodshot with tears and he was fighting to get his usual composure. He dabbed his eyes with a handkerchief. "Will you be going off for walks together along the shore?", he giggled, wiping his cheeks. "Discussing matters of military importance."

The laughter soon wore a little thin for William as it was solely at his expense. "Oh, for God sake!" he snapped. "I would expect this from young Daniel but not you. You're all just drunk or delirious from the poison."

"Poison?" questioned Carr, his laughter subsiding.

"The locals have, apparently, been lacing drink with God knows what just to entice the British to their deaths. Perfectly horrible way to ruin a good drink if you ask me."

"I zink you vill find ve haz zeen mozt trickz before," said Volker, taking a gulp and pointing to the stable hands. "Zey zuffered no ill effectz when ve tested it."

"What!" exclaimed William. "You dare test it on the staff?"

After each had regained their senses, Carr felt obliged to clarify. "You're the toast of the hour, true enough," he said, taking a restorative drink. "You're the quickest out of the boats and the fastest with a blade. Cockburn's no fool, he served under Nelson. He knows if you're alongside him he's safer."

William straightened at the thought of his own importance. "Bodyguard to an Admiral, indeed. It has a certain ring to it. Yes, Mother would like that."

"More besides," continued Carr. "Peel stories travel far and quickly. Cockburn won't just be repeating one he's heard, he will be living one. He'll be sailing shoulder to shoulder with you up the Patuxent. He will dine out on that many times believe me."

William took a moment to consider the scene of Cockburn recanting the tale to some society set. A lavish table surrounded by lords and ladies hanging on his every word. Oh, how the ladies gasp, cheeks flushed, at the description of William taking on the Flotilla single handed and not a splash of blood to show for it on his beautiful ice white britches. William was just picturing a young, buxom lass passing out from hearing of such bravery when suddenly he was snapped back into reality. Volker clapped and indicated that the stable hands, and Samuel too, should leave the room.

When they had gone, Volker lit his pipe. "You killed today," he said, blowing out the match. "Za first time, yez?"

It actually wasn't. William once finished off a coal-man with a candlestick after George had not only eaten the sandwich from his pocket but half of his side as well. It was a grizzly sight.

"You vill find it hard to zleep," Volker said, passing him a bottle of Brandy. "Many thoughtz in your head. Not goodt."

Carr took the bottle from William, cleaned the neck, and fixing William with a cold stare, explained. "You were fast out of that boat without a care or thought for yourself," he said, filling William's glass. "We did it thinking there might be trouble, you did it knowing there was. That's a hero. Your father would have been very proud." He gestured that William should take a drink.

"How long had you known him?" asked William, taking a gulp.

"Not long enough," Volker replied, with reverence.

They gave away nothing more.

Barney's men made no nuisance in the night and the camp stirred promptly at first light. Wrapped in a blanket for warmth, William peered out through the distorted glass of the kitchen window. He could see soldiers busily stoking fires for breakfast and canteens coming to the boil on tripods above the flames. Some soldiers were merrily talking in groups. Some were cleaning boots or servicing muskets. They were all preparing for the last leg of the journey. To his left, William heard a commotion as two naval officers had chanced upon Samuel, crouching on the path outside their door, readying his bowels. They remonstrated for a moment then silenced the instant his business started. A second later, the door was slammed in disgust.

The stable hands pulled *Little Fanny* up the bank and secured her tether to a tree before concealing her under branches and bracken. Their new vessel, salvaged from Barney's flotilla, was substantial, sure enough, with its iron clad sides and front but it was almost completely enclosed by the armour and stunk to high heavens of sweat and fear. Even Volker appeared repulsed, although such sensitivity could have been attributed to the entire bottle of rum he had consumed in what turned out to be a late night of cards and storytelling. The stable hands were given twenty minutes to scrub her clean. Samuel expressed no issues as he had been in the vessel a good half hour, eating his breakfast, before the others arrived. The stable hands were in high spirits as they had learned that there would be no more rowing.

The left fork of the Patuxent was narrower than they had previously navigated. The convoy of barges and small ships made their way up the still waters without a soul in sight on land. As agreed, William and his party sailed side by side with Cockburn every inch of the way. Despite everyone being convinced that Barney and his men were hiding behind every bush, there were no skirmishes. The proximity of the banks made Cockburn nervous and he stood, one foot on the bow of his boat, his eyes scanning the banks.

"The blighters are hungry for retaliation," he shouted, conscious of William watching him from the boat alongside.

William glanced back into his own boat. Volker was slouched against a provision sack, sleeping, with a cap over his eyes to keep out the bright daylight. Next to him stood Carr, leaning against the iron hull whilst cleaning the mechanism of his repeating musket with a small brush.

"He needs to keep his damn head down," said Carr, blowing spent powder from the trigger. "Barney might not hear the water break across our bows but he is sure to hear that idiot announcing our passage."

"Is this resentment I hear?" asked William. "The barracking of the lower ranks?"

"His kind are never shot," noted Carr, resting his musket and approaching William. "You'll do well to learn the difference between a hero and a plain fool."

For a moment, they both studied Cockburn at the bows. His back was as straight as a lance as his hands clasped a spyglass. He possessed a noble arrogance, not unlike William's own, but somehow appearing as though he had a huge target on him. It was as if he was actually daring someone to take a shot.

"He's got so many medals earned by the blood of

others that he thinks he's indestructible," said Carr, quietly. "But luck won't hold forever." He smiled then leaned to William's ear, "If you want to study bravery you'll be better instructed by Samuel."

William watched Carr return to cleaning his musket. His gaze then fell on Samuel, who was seated on a sack whilst biting his toe nails short. "Indeed," muttered William, repulsed, as he watched Samuel move on to gnawing at his foot calluses.

The last stretch of the journey up river took less than a day and the party reached upper Marlboro by mid afternoon. They were greeted by a detachment of Ross' troops who were waiting on the bridge to direct them. They offered guard and helped with the transport of supplies. Due to the shortage of horses, everyone had no choice than to make the journey on foot. This was Cockburn's doing. His orders from Cochrane were specific regarding securing the horses needed and enlisting slave labour. He failed in both regards.

Samuel and the stable hands were loaded like pit ponies. Before ten minutes had passed, the British had alighted from their craft and the march across land began. Cockburn, William noted in his journal, appeared restless during the three hour walk and shunned approaches from fellow officers. It was as if he had tired of the journey and wanted action.

"He craves Vwar," said Volker as he, Carr and William strode two rows back from Cockburn and observed his display.

"He craves victory," Carr corrected, quietly. "Has it

crossed your minds that Cochrane picked him for a reason?"

Suddenly, as if sensing being talked about, Cockburn turned and caught sight of William. He beckoned him forward to join him.

"Who the devil does he think he is?" said William to the others.

"The most dangerous man in America, I imagine," responded Carr. "It's a good job he's only here for 'discussions' and not to engage."

"You vorget za militia," said Volker.

"No I don't," Carr replied, with vigour. "Where are they? Is it Madison's plan to let us march where we want? They should have engaged as we landed not wait until we stroll up for a chat on our terms?"

William caught Cockburn up. Giving it a few minutes, of course, just to show he wasn't at his beck and call.

"Scott tells me you won't be accompanying us to Baltimore," said Cockburn, removing his hat to wipe his brow.

"That Scott," replied William, with a snort, "is a blasted, beak-nosed, nosey blighter!"

"He doesn't trust you," replied Cockburn, minding not for the bluntness of his comment. "Well, it's a shame you won't be with us."

"No, I have to go to Washington. It slipped my mind before but I have some interest in land hereabouts." William waited to gauge Cockburn's reaction but observed nothing but a wry smile. "Yes," William continued, quick to quantify. "I suffer from a rather slippery mind, you see, it's a family condition. Anyway, I'd be grateful if such claims were honoured," he added casually.

"How grateful?"

"Well, I don't know," said William, pretending he hadn't considered the question before. "The price of twenty slaves?"

"I really wouldn't want you to go to any trouble," Cockburn replied, with a hint of sarcasm.

"It's only a very tiny patch of land, Admiral. You'd hardly notice it, in fact. Tell you what, how about sixty slaves?" Cockburn remained silent, sensing William was holding back. "Surely you don't expect them all for free?" said William, with a scoff. "I have at least to cover the cost of fetching the blighters over?"

"Ah, the burden of commerce," smiled Cockburn playfully, slipping his hat back on. "Tell me, the paperwork for this land, it's not in Washington is it?" He flashed a knowing smile. Perhaps he hadn't taken William into his complete confidence as once thought.

"You appear to be sporting a peculiar look, Admiral," said William, trying to read his expression. "The same one I observe on George's face when he spots a limping gardener."

Cockburn took a few strides in silence then glanced over his shoulder at Volker and Carr behind. "Why do you suppose," he said, changing the subject, "that your father, one of the cleverest and richest men in the world, would employ such a crew? Has it ever crossed your mind?"

William looked back to see Volker and Carr who

began holding hands and playfully indicating William and Cockburn should do the same. William just rolled his eyes and looked forward. "I have no idea. I sometimes think it must have been the result of heat stroke or perhaps some hefty blow to the head."

"It's because they get the job done," replied Cockburn, alluding to the fact he had overheard William, Carr and Volker's private discussion earlier. "No matter what the odds."

Major Ross had made camp at Upper Marlborough five miles to the east of Woodyard. Hundreds of white bivouacs stretched out neatly across the fields as far as the eye could see. Smoke from fires drifted amongst them as thousands of troops in bright red jackets milled about. William had seen nothing like it and gulped at the sheer scale.

Senior British officers had utilised numerous farm buildings and Cockburn was insistent that William accompany him urgently for a visit to Major Ross.

"I have information you need to hear," Cockburn told William as they approached the door to a storehouse. As the door was opened ahead of them by guards, Cockburn paused and fixed on William's gaze. "Oh, and that offer you mentioned? I graciously accept."

"Oh, you mean your kind offer by which I get to return home with my backside showing? I think not! I'll give you the value of one hundred and fifty slaves and that's my final offer."

"Deal!" replied Cockburn and he shook William's hand

to seal the terms. Before William could question Cockburn's change of heart, they were inside the building and confronted by Major Ross himself who was making his salute.

"Good to see you, sir," said Ross, in his thick Irish accent. "I understand the flotilla provided some entertainment?"

"I confess a satisfaction in making excellent use of those boats Barney didn't burn," Cockburn smiled. "You remember, Lord Peel," he added quickly, as if finding his manners.

"Of course," Ross responded, with a nod in William's direction.

"He's heading to Washington," said Cockburn, "with us."

Ross' eyes narrowed with confusion, thinking he had misheard. "You mean Baltimore, surely?"

Cockburn remained silent perhaps allowing Ross to read his expression or perhaps as he was not accustomed to repeating himself.

"Admiral Cochrane's orders are clear," said Ross, snatching them up from his desk. "No prolonged engagement," he read aloud.

"He also said we're here to make, and I quote, Major, 'a lasting impression on their fears'. He hasn't seen what we've seen. The grand American plan is what? Poisoning us with tampered liquor left on the steps of farm houses? Jesus! The place is wide open."

"There's no advantage in Washington," said Ross,

studying the map on his wall. "Baltimore, here," he pointed, "is their head. We cut that off and Madison will lose all communication."

"Sometimes it's more important they lose their heart," said Cockburn, as he helped himself to a drink. "You clashed with General Winder's troops yesterday? They retreated, yes?"

"Yes, near Long Old Fields."

"They have no stomach for this and no money for heavy guns either don't forget," he said, casting an eye in William's direction. "Not yet anyway. We drive into the heart of the capital and raise the flag."

"You mean occupation?" questioned Ross, hardly believing his ears. "But this is incredible. You think it possible?"

"Send word," ordered Cockburn, as he downed his glass. "We march at dawn." He turned to William. "You will get your land but my men won't suffer at the hand of what it costs you. It's too dangerous for us to wait until Peel money comes flowing in and the weapons flow with it. This way we both benefit, yes?" upon which he left.

For a moment the whole of the conversation replayed in William's mind. The sly old dog, Cockburn, had spotted that William was about to broker some deal that would pour Peel money into the American economy and likely pay for troops and munitions to fight off the British.

It was Ross who eventually broke the silence as he dropped Cochrane's orders back on his desk. "Looks like your slaves would have arrived to find more work than they imagined," he smiled.

"Quite so," said William, still in shock. Fuelled by the urge to just bolt, he fidgeted and blurted out the first excuse that appeared plausible. "If you'll excuse me, Major, I have britches on the boil," and with that, he took one sly look at the map on the wall and then walked out.

William strode amongst the troop tents with singular purpose. He reached the edge of the camp to find Carr airing his shirts on a line, Volker stoking the fire with his sword tip, and the stable hands erecting their tents.

"We're leaving!" announced William, with a loud clap. "Pack up the tents, shirts, ale, and whatever else you can run with," he added, swooshing his hand to indicate the general direction of exit. "We are out of here!"

"Vhat, now?" asked Volker, baffled. "But you zay ve leave fvor Vashington tomorzow?"

"No. No," said William, checking over his shoulder. "We don't leave tomorrow! Four thousand troops do. These chaps," he added, gesturing to the many soldiers in the field. "Noon tomorrow this field of polished bayonets will be seeking out American guts to skewer in Washington. That's right, Washington! Not Baltimore. That old stoat, Cockburn, has led me right up the garden path and hung me out to dry like, like, the best hunting shirt of the rare bat owl."

"We can't just leave," said Carr, indicating William's attention to Lieutenant Scott who was loitering by some nearby latrines and trying desperately hard to look like he wasn't spying. "What would be the reason?" Carr continued, quietly. "Cockburn would surely hunt you as an American sympathiser. Not to mention the risk of us running headlong into the militia."

William had had enough of Scott's nosy-parkering and he ordered Samuel to drop his britches and scare him off with his enormous privates. Samuel did as ordered and it had the desired affect. Scott even managed to trip over a tent peg in his hurry to escape. "Winder's force," continued William, without missing a beat, "is camped at Long Old Fields. We stick clear of the roads and head west until we hit the ferry at Alexandria. It's no more than ten miles. I've seen the map."

Carr let out a sigh, which William took as an insult against his map reading prowess, which, of course, it was. "Head back to *The Emily*," urged Carr, "cut your losses. Tell Cockburn it would be bad for business to go further. He will understand."

"Just go home you mean?" asked William, anger brewing. "Oh, no. I have to salvage something."

"You have some 'brilliant' scheme?" noted Carr, reading him with suspicion.

"Any brilliant schemes I might have, or might not have, are my business, not yours, and certainly not blasted Scott's," said William, avoiding Carr's eye. "Besides if I did have a brilliant scheme, which, I'm not saying I do or I don't, it would involve a nice leisurely meeting with The President at his house. I doubt it now though. Oh, no! Not when bloody Ross' troops march past Mandongton's front window and start shooting his servants. BASTARD!"

William paced faster and faster until, in a moment of

rage, he began tearing at the tent, eyes steeled, jaw locked. It was a classic William tantrum that saw the tent shredded in moments, Samuel's backside raw from a boot, and pots and pans away across the field. William then proceeded to chase the fat stable hand with a loaf of bread whilst attempting to clobber him around the head with it.

"Sir! Sir!" Carr pleaded, keeping in William's eye line, dancing between him and the stable hand who cowered in fear. "This isn't the way."

"Shitty! Bastard! Arse! Toss!" shouted William, and made a break for Samuel. Samuel let out a yelp as William clipped him on the side of the head with the loaf.

"Sir?" said Carr, pulling Samuel away. "If we do this then I need to know your plan."

"La-la-la – lalalalal- la-la-la – lala," sang William, fingers in his ears.

William did have a plan and it was just as 'brilliant' as all his others. Which meant, of course, that it was dangerous for everyone concerned and destined to end in a spectacular disaster.

Commodore Barney of the Flotilla

Once William had learned of Cockburn's intentions to march on Washington and hoist the British flag, he knew he needed to show him a clean pair of heels and get to the capital before him. In William's mind, his brilliant plan was still possible. If he could only get to Madison before the British, he would find a President desperate for money to buy weapons. William knew he had to escape the British camp but the trick was to do it without appearing as though he had simply run off in the night to tell The President about Cockburn's plans. He was also aware that Lieutenant Scott was likely hiding in the bushes somewhere and spying on his every movement.

After pondering the predicament over a couple of cheroots and a modest cheese board, William gathered the party about him and explained his brilliant plan. Although William initially considered simply shouting, "Look! American militia!" whilst pointing with conviction to a bush in a far away field, he eventually settled for the tried and tested classic of simply starting a fire near a place of importance. In this case, the fire was to be started near a barn utilised as a British Army munitions store. At 7.30pm sharp, Samuel crept his way around the barn to the exact point where the diversionary fire was to be started. Meanwhile, Volker and Carr had strategically positioned themselves amongst the troops so as to call 'fire' and raise alarm to maximum effect. The plan, however, went horribly awry.

It's not exactly clear how Samuel got the instructions wrong, although, the fact he was a village idiot was the most likely answer. Instead of taking straw from the barn to start a fire outside, Samuel mistakenly set fire to the straw inside the barn instead. The subsequent blaze took hold very quickly and ignited not only the powder kegs but also a dozen Congreve rockets. At approximately 7.40pm, the barn exploded with a deafening belch that saw the stone roof tiles scattered a mile in all directions. As the British troops were diving clear of the falling masonry, William, Carr, Volker, Samuel, and the stable hands were heading off at break-neck speed into the woods to the north.

William's journal August 23, 1814: Franny, would have been appalled, bless her, to see me sprinting through the long grass. 'A gentleman never has runs' she would repeat in her French accent whenever she caught me sprinting spiritedly across the great hall to the sound of the dinner bell. Well I ran this evening. Like the hard-boiled clappers. Straight through the woods that bounded the camp and then down a slow bank into a field of rough grazing land. Carr was the fastest, blast him, closely followed by myself and the stable hands (even the fat one, which was surprising). Blast them for keeping the pace despite being laden down with packs. Then there was Volker, his face red and neck veins throbbing from his love of leaf and beer. Last was Samuel, which I attributed to his 'handicap' and my mind recalled the image of Scott's terrified expression at the sight of it. Blast Samuel too for his enormous privates!

William and the party ran flat out for half an hour until Carr called a stop and they concealed themselves by a hedgerow to regroup and take a rest.

"Long Old Fields is two miles that way," said William pointing north, breathless. "We better watch for scouts."

"Zat way, I believe," said Volker, pointing north-west instead.

"Yes, of course, William replied. " I was being indicative. Anyone else have a stitch?" he asked, clutching his side.

"I don't like this," said Carr, taking a drink from his canteen then wiping his mouth. "We don't know if there's still a ferry service across the Potomac at Alexandria or even if they will let us on. They might just kill us."

"Then we follow the river road north towards Washington anyway," said William, with conviction. "It looked about five miles, seven at the most."

"We still need to cross to the west," said Carr. "Washington is on the other side of the river."

"Indeed, Mr Carr, and we have two bridges to choose from," William replied, curtly.

"Assuming zay are not blown," said Volker, cheerily.

There was a moment of silent reflection amongst the party. The destruction of the bridges was a very real possibility that William hadn't considered.

"I never pitched you as a glass half-empty chap, Volker," said William.

"Can I suggest we keep moving," cut in Carr, with urgency. "We don't want to go through all that again!"

The party reached a wood two miles east from the Alexandria ferry crossing at dusk. Progress had been slow due to the militia scouts on the footways and roads. All of which had been avoided with great success thanks to Carr's keen eye. With good cover afforded them by the dense trees, Carr suggested the party keep low and hide as he went ahead to scout the way. He knew there would likely be more militia to be avoided the nearer they got to the ferry. It was decided they would eat first to kill some time until the light failed and Carr could use the cover of darkness. There was, however, a thirty minute diatribe from William as the stable hands had seemingly left the pâté by mistake, therefore, William would be without a suitable first course to follow his sherry.

Carr returned about midnight to find the rest of the party asleep from the day's exertion. He approached William in the darkness and woke him gently by covering his mouth with his palm to keep him silent.

"What the devil!" barked William, slapping Carr's hand

away. "How dare you touch the lips of a Peel!" He quickly wiped his mouth with his handkerchief. "Never touch my lips! Or my face! Or my bare arms for that matter."

"We must wake the others," whispered Carr. "The ferry is closed but I've secured a launch."

William glanced at the stable hands, who were all sound asleep and snoring like pigs. Angered they weren't keeping watch as he instructed, William kicked the gaunt one. "Why are you not keeping look out?" he growled. "You test my famous patience you emaciated ass!"

The gaunt stable hand rubbed his eyes and yawned. "Beggin' your pardon, sir, but we got Samuel to take a turn."

William and Carr looked about for him and came to the same dreadful conclusion at the same time. Samuel was nowhere to be seen.

Suddenly there was movement all about them; the sound of dry twigs breaking under foot and American voices hushed in the distance. It was the militia. Carr woke Volker in silence and they aimed their muskets into the darkness. Wherever they heard a noise, they changed direction to aim at it. The scene fell deathly quiet. No movement. No sound. Just a curtain of blackness about them.

It was possible the militia had moved past them unaware that they were only feet from their quarry. Suddenly, only twenty feet from William and the rest, a high pitched fart was followed by a loud straining noise. In a flash, a row of lanterns were opened in unison and light poured down onto Samuel who was crouched with his britches around his ankles. Militia muskets raised to take aim in his direction as Samuel's dopey expression slipped into a smile for their benefit.

"Drop the weapon!" came a stern American voice from behind a lantern.

"Not weapon," replied Samuel, opening the fingers of his outstretching arm and allowing the suspected weapon to roll off his palm. "A long Bab."

"Jesus Christ!" came the reply, followed by an instant convulsion and a dropped lantern.

A moment later, an army of at least five-hundred men stepped out of the blackness and one by one their lantern shrouds clicked open. The wood, and William's party, were bathed in light as bright as day. William was caught, again, and he knew it. Two militiamen marched up and snatched both Volker and Carr's muskets. Another figure then stepped forward and stood above them. He slowly raised his lantern aloft so they could see his face. He was a stocky figure with long, unkempt hair and a chubby face. It was none other than Joshua Barney and he let out a loud laugh when he saw Carr.

"Bring them!" he ordered, and closed his lamp.

"Oh Sparkling!"

William's group were marched north along the road that traced the Potomac from the ferry crossing at Alexandria up to the small town of Bladensburg. Each prisoner was bound by the wrists to ropes that were strung off the provision carts.

Samuel and the stable hands were lashed to carts ahead of William, Carr was beside him, and Volker behind.

Barney was the only man on horseback. The rest of the flotilla marched on foot. They were a ragbag fighting force. Most were farmers, going by their clothes, and they all looked like they hadn't slept or eaten well for days.

Five miles into the journey, William caught sight of Washington to his left across the river. They were close enough to see the buildings but it could have been a hundred miles away for what good it did him. The street lanterns were lit but there was hardly a person to be seen. The only visible activity was a group of workers at the docks who were loading a sloop. The stone Capitol building stood proudly on its lush, tree covered hill. To its left was The President's House. It was bound by grassland that stretched down to the river. Both bridges into the capital had been destroyed hours before and were little more than smouldering abutments. It was the first evidence William had seen that the Americans were preparing for the British arrival.

Washington wasn't as grand as William had envisioned. The plan he had seen in the document room of Peel Manor showed a huge, interlacing grid of buildings, akin to a geometric spider's web. Apart from a populated section between The President's House and Capitol Hill, the rest appeared almost rural; nothing more than a scattering of houses down the wide streets. William soon lost all interest in it and his mind wandered to the two lovely French twins with the soapy sponges that he had met on his voyage to

Sicily. Unintentionally, he had also imagined them being joined by a bare breasted Franny, brandishing a fruit salad and fluttering her eye lashes. William was considering the etiquette of engaging a governess in such activities when a musket butt was jabbed into his ribs.

"Move it!" came a rough voice at his ear.

"Yes, yes." replied William, as the militiaman shouted a few disparaging remarks about the British. William caught sight of Samuel who was lashed to the cart ahead.

"I blame your backside," snapped William. "If it's not setting fire to my house or knocking me off my blasted boat it's alerting the enemy to our presence with a chorus!" Samuel flashed his pea-brained smile.

They arrived at the outskirts of Bladensburg a little before two o'clock in the morning. A crooked signpost indicated Washington was six miles to the south-west and Baltimore thirty miles to the north. To their right was a steep hill littered with the lantern lights of a large troop encampment. Despite the angle William had of it, the number of tents looked to match that of Ross'. It was then William saw a group of soldiers by the side of the road wearing blue uniforms. The uniform itself was familiar but for the life of William, he couldn't remember where he had seen it before. Then it hit him.

"The French!" he exclaimed, suddenly remembering.

"Don't be fooled," said Carr, "they're just borrowed uniforms."

"But isn't that..?" William stopped himself, puzzled by the obviousness of the point he was about to make.

"What?" questioned Carr, "really stupid to dress like the French?"

"Exactly! To use the one uniform that the damned British are well versed at daggering."

They turned left at the junction and headed on into Bladensburg itself. In its day, it was likely a thriving settlement with sturdy brick built houses and businesses along the roadside. Such days had long since passed. Even by lantern light, the place looked down at heel. Many of the houses appeared long deserted. As the road veered right and the lanterns became more frequent, there were signs of life through the shuttered windows. Slowly, the street seemed to fill with people, eager for news, who stepped in towards the procession. The sound of distant conversation and debate drifted on the breeze. A few locals spat and cursed at William's party who they believed to be British prisoners.

To the south-west was a rickety wooden bridge. It was a hundred feet long with stone abutments that churned up the fast flowing river below it. Downstream, past a watermill, the river dwindled down to little more than a wide stream that was bound by woodland and scrubland for rough grazing. It was then William saw the soldier's bivouacs stretching to the limit of his sight across the fields beyond the bridge. By the sheer scale, it was a force that greatly outnumbered Ross'.

"It will be decided here," said Carr.

"What will?" William enquired.

"Whether Cockburn gets to march on Washington."

The carts drew to a stop just short of the bridge.

Locals milled about the party exchanging views and sightings of the British forces. There were families, husbands, wives, and children. Everyone's view was different and every face was filled with dread and fear. They encircled William's party and demanded answers. A woman lashed out at Carr and had to be pulled away by one of Barney's flotilla. As William and the rest were marched away, he could hear arguments break out behind them. No one knew where the British were or when they were coming. No one knew except William and his party, of course, and they kept their mouths tightly shut.

William and the gang were escorted by armed guard inside an old courthouse. The corridor stank of damp and the floor was littered with flyers warning people to be vigilant for British scouts. The group were escorted into a chamber set out for public meetings. Barney pushed them across the room then shoved them down into seats. His men quickly tethered their hands behind their backs. When Barney retreated, muskets were raised and levelled on the group. He wasn't taking any chances. Without a word, Barney then left the room through a door at the back, which remained open. William suddenly realised that there was no reason for their silence so he turned to Carr.

"You know that sour looking fellow?" he asked.

"Joshua Barney! The flotilla commander? He's either not sure what to make of you or he recognises you as the hero of Pig Point. Either way he's lost a lot of weight since I saw him last."

Volker nodded in agreement, "Two stonz at leazt."

"What? Oh, sparkling!" William sighed. "If the chap doesn't mind enough that we've caused him to burn his precious little boats, you're going to poke a nerve by being discourteous about the fellow's physique."

William glanced over his shoulder and caught sight of Barney through the open door talking to another man. The man was busy packing and wasn't still long enough for William to see him properly. William then heard a woman's voice. She was protesting tearfully. A moment later she appeared visible through the doorway. William gulped at the sight of her. She was beautiful. Dressed like an English lady complete with a blue summer bonnet and lace gloves. In a moment, her piercing blue eyes turned to William and the pair exchanged a lingering look. It was love at first sight but before William could comprehend the meaning of it, the door creaked and closed on a draught. William's eyes dropped for a moment then his heart lifted again as the door opened once more. The girl had vanished though and Barney entered carrying Carr's Japanese sword. With his free hand, he purposefully removed a pair of pistols from his waistband, cocked them, then placed them on the table at the front of the room. He was expecting trouble and looked like he could handle it. He stepped forward and stared at William.

"I'm Commodore Barney," he said, with a rough American accent. "You're a British spy?" he added, pausing to feel William's lapel. "A lady too going by your smell and fancy clothes?"

"I'm Lord Peel of Tornbridge. I'm not British. It's a partially independent autocracy. I would explain the meaning in a way you could understand if only I had a crayon and an hour to spare. In the meantime I would be grateful if you would untether me from this softwood chair."

"I bet you would," chuckled Barney, as he took a seat and put his feet up. "Tell you what," he said, sliding Carr's sword from its scabbard. "You tell me how a 'Lord' such as yourself finds company with the butcher of Aspern-Essling," he said nodding at Volker. Volker looked at William and shrugged it off as if it was nothing. "And this peculiar, retarded creature," said Barney, pointing to Samuel, "who appears to be as dumb as a potato yet blessed with at least a foot of prick." Samuel let out a laugh and winked at William with drool seeping through his smile. Barney studied the sword for a moment. He watched as the light drifted along the highly crafted steel edge. "Finally, this man," he said, nodding at Carr. "A man wanted for desertion by both the French and Dutch." He pointed the perfect blade in Carr's direction. "Not to mention dishonouring my fiancé. An innocent woman he beguiled."

William threw Carr a glance and mouthed "*His fiancé?*"

Carr smiled then quoted a line from Shakespeare. "Love sought is good but given unsought is better."

Barney took a hurried step forward and poised the sword against Carr's cheek. "This sword remembers being here before," said Barney, eluding to Carr's scar. "Your damned fancy ways turned her head!" he said, contemplating a killer strike. "I told you what I'd do if I saw you again." Carr didn't give him the satisfaction of seeing fear in his eyes.

At that moment the door opened and the figure who was packing in the back room entered. He was as shocked to see William as William was to see him. Although William couldn't initially place his face.

"Well, well!" said William, with great enthusiasm, "Arnold Hughes as I live and breathe. Why, simply the finest glove maker in London," he said. "So what brings you here, Arnold? Is it mittens for the militia?"

"My name is William Winder, my lord," replied the figure.

"Winder?", pondered William, repeating his name several times. "Wait a minute!" said William, with vigour. "Not the animal juggler who dropped a kitten down Caroline of Brunswick's cleavage on my seventeenth birthday?"

"No, my lord. General Winder. I visited you on your eighteenth birthday with James Madison, the American President."

"Mr Winder, of course," said William, as the penny finally dropped. "Well, that's perfect. Then please confirm to your asinine friend here that I am no danger to these lush lands and therefore don't deserve to remain bound like some out of control woman."

"You'll damned well, keep silent!" shouted Barney. Winder, sensing clarification was needed, approached Barney for a private word. William couldn't hear the conversation but Barney's cries of "he's a Goddamn what?" and "but he's a horse's ass" indicated that Barney didn't like what he heard. Winder then signalled to Barney that William should be untied and after a few muttered curses, Barney did as he was ordered.

"Apology accepted," said William, rubbing his freed wrists. "Never let it be said that William E. Peel holds a grudge."

"How, may I ask, did you come to be here, my lord?" Winder enquired.

"I was on my way to Washington with those slaves you wanted," said William, doing a few stretches, pained. "Hang on a minute. My blasted backside's gone to sleep." William took a moment to do a few squats before continuing. "Where was I? Oh, yes. We were minding our own business enjoying your varied countryside when we were suddenly captured by Major Ross of the British Army. I won't bore you with the dangerous and explosive nature of our escape but needless to say it was executed exactly to my plan. We had hoped to reach the Alexandria ferry and then head north to Washington and safety but..."

"The southern bridge has already been destroyed," cut in Barney.

"When was this?", Winder asked, stepping towards William, eagerly. "When were you caught?"

"Well, let me think." William wracked his brain for some convincing details. "We disembarked at Benedict and saw no trouble until we reached a wood yard south-east of here, yes. About fifteen miles away. That was eight-ish last night." Winder and Barney exchanged a knowing look. "There is something else," added William, straining to touch his toes. "Something I overheard when they were torturing me." Carr and Volker raised their eyebrows worried that William was laying it on a little thick. "The British are to march on Washington," said William and Winder and Barney blenched. "I escaped so I may warn you. That was, of course, before I was apprehended and tied to a cart by this elephant's ball bag," he said, pointing a thumb in Barney's direction.

"They could be here by dawn," suggested Barney.

"Baseless supposition," said Winder. "We must send scouts immediately."

"What of them?" Barney asked, throwing a glance to Carr and the rest of the group.

"Well, untie them, of course," said Winder, as if Barney shouldn't need to ask.

As Barney moved to free Carr, the pair exchanged a look. It was obvious that Barney felt cheated from the chance to settle his old score.

"Commodore?" said Winder, filled with purpose. "Tell Stansbury we will withdraw across the river bridge and blow it within the hour. He has to hold the British from the hill at all cost when they show. Mark that." He moved to the door then stopped and turned to William. "The British will know you revealed their plan. You have my word I'll do my best to keep you from harm's way." William didn't have time to respond as Winder and Barney vanished through the doorway.

As William and his party were led out, he could see immediately the action his news of the British had brought. Families who had been hiding in the buildings were rushing, ladened with their belongings, towards the bridge. "The

British are coming!" was the repeated cry as people banged on every door they passed. It became a crush as an endless stream of people appeared between the buildings. There was shouting and the cries to loved ones separated in the stampede.

Glancing back towards the courthouse, William could see Winder and the mysterious girl emerge with two militiamen carrying their bags. Her eyes once again found William's and the crowd seemed to part between them. As if William wasn't in love enough, she smiled timidly through her pretty lips. Before William could smile back, Winder, oblivious to the loving sparks, urged her quickly into a carriage. Winder's gaze then searched the crowd and his eyes too caught William's.

"Take the Georgetown Road, right as you leave the bridge," he shouted, before passing a note to a messenger. "You may have my quarters," he continued. "I'm going to Washington to update The President. Keep this note with you. It says you have my trust. It might keep you alive before we meet again." Upon which he swung into the carriage and shut the door.

"Can you take me to him?" William shouted.

"Visit us in Washington tomorrow," Winder shouted out of the window, as the carriage pulled away. "I am sure The President will be thrilled to see you."

William let out a little sigh as the carriage made off through the crowd. "Isn't she just the most delightful flower?" he said, turning and finding Samuel's lecherous gaze on him. "And you can cut that out before it starts. Filthy beast!"

"Hardly an orderly force," Carr said looking at the militiamen as they passed by.

"Nein."

Winder's messenger pushed through the crowd and thrust the letter into William's hand.

"But it doesn't need to be," said Carr.

"What doesn't?" asked William, distracted by reading the letter.

"Lowndes Hill," said Carr, pointing east. "We passed it on the way in. So will Ross. It's an excellent vantage point for the militia. So too this street of houses. With the bridge gone, and the American numbers as they are, the British shouldn't stand a chance."

William was about to debate tactics when Barney drew up in a horse and cart. "I don't care if you claim to be Dolly Madison herself," he snarled. "This belonged to Thomas Sheppard," he said, holding up William's trophy sword. "Which means you were at Pig Point and you're a liar. Eli and his boys," he said, thumbing in the direction of a surly militiaman who was perched on William's bags on the back of the cart, "are the last defence on the Washington Road." Eli kicked the bags and muskets off the back of the cart and into the dirt. Barney threw William the sword. "You wanna get to Washington, you're gonna have to get through us."

Volker stepped forward ready to go through him there and then but Barney whipped the reins and the cart jerked away. All Volker could do was grunt with anger and spit at the ground with venom. As the cart sped away across the bridge, William watched as Eli drew a finger across his throat as if it were a blade. William would be a dead man for sure if they met again.

"Shall I summarise?" William asked, staring at his bags in the dirt, "or is everyone pretty clear on how dismal our prospects are?"

"Things could be a lot worse," said Carr, picking up his musket and checking the sights in Barney's direction. "With the Bridge gone, the British can't reach Washington. So whatever your brilliant plan is," he paused to sight a clear shot at Barney's back, "you're a hell of a lot closer to it."

"And what about him?" asked William, watching Carr contemplate a shot to the back of Barney's head.

"Well, I think you leave that with me," replied Carr, lowering his musket. "His time will come."

"Zhere is just one small point," said Volker, taking out his pipe. "Ve haz to get passezd Barney to get to Vashington. He is guarding za only way. Once ve cross that bridge ve are trapped."

"Oh, heavens!" sighed William. "I feel like an arctic snow badger. Now, stop me if you know about this creature. During mating season the males all fight over the bitch. They bite at her and pull her this way and that. All to get dominance, of course. By the end she's literally pulled apart. There's nothing left but blood soaked snow. It's apparently very horrible."

"Zat iz not goodt."

"Quite so," said William. "But that's like me, you see. I'm pulled in all directions until what's left? Nothing but a slow, miserable extinction." Sensing he had confused them, he made a loud clap. "So the plan is to stop the Americans from blowing the bridge thus allowing the British to cross." Both Carr and Volker stared at William in disbelief. "It's very simple my dear acquaintances. The enemy of my enemy is my friend. An old Indian expression, or maybe Arabic. Some clever chap anyway."

"Get the British to knock out Barney?" asked Carr, genuinely impressed. "Clever tactic."

"Courtesy of Uncle Wellington."

"Of course the British won't be able to cross if the militia still hold the higher ground," said Carr, nodding in the direction of Lowndes Hill.

All eyes fell on William, waiting for his lead. "Come on," he shouted, as he started walking off against the flow of Americans. "We have less than an hour to save the bridge!"

The stable hands picked up the backpacks hurriedly as everyone followed a very determined William Peel.

"Vhere?" asked Volker.

"That chap, Stansbury, of course," William replied. "I have to convince him to get his chaps off that hill." Volker and Carr stopped in their tracks and just looked at each other like William was crazy.

"Even if you make it up the hill," said Carr, "they'll never let you see him."

"You underestimate the Peel cunning," replied William with his usual confidence. "Remember, I am skilled in the highest levels of diplomacy." William had walked a good distance when he realised Volker and Carr weren't following. He stopped and turned. "And I have this, of course," he shouted, as he held up the letter from Winder. "It states that I'm to be trusted. Shall we test it?"

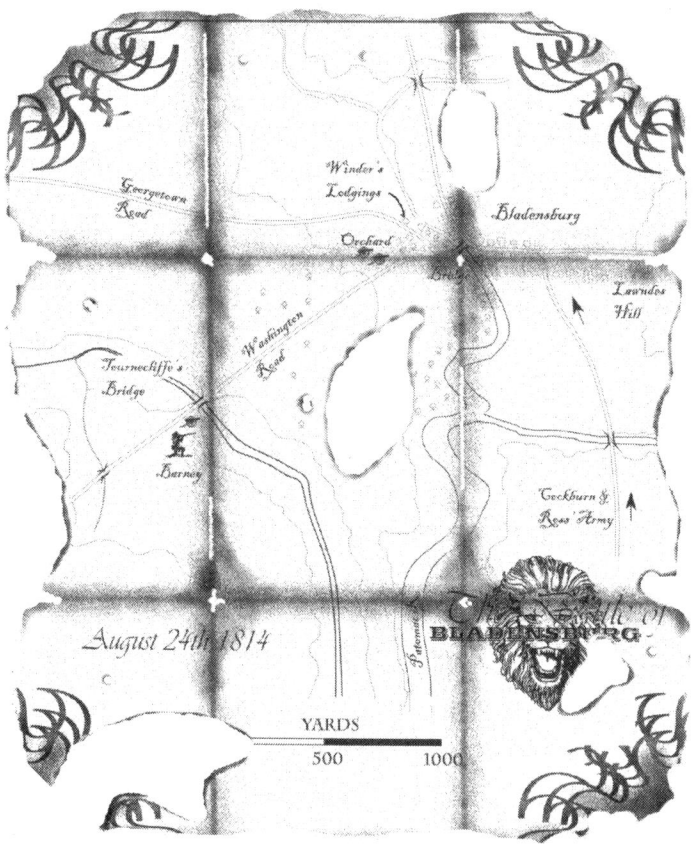

The Battle of Bladensburg

William's gang puffed and panted as they ran up the steep incline of Lowndes Hill. William led, followed by Carr and the stable hands. Volker was close behind and Samuel, who was hampered somewhat by his painfully chaffing privates, brought up the rear. They passed amongst the militia tents and bivouacs without challenge and were close enough to see the sleeping men inside. William was almost at the top of the hill when he was stopped in his tracks by a musket thrust in his face. The musket belonged to a very young militiaman, no older than fourteen, who was trembling so much that his weapon rattled.

"Hold it there!" came the nervous cry.

"Stansbury?", enquired William, breathless. "I have information of great military importance." The young militiaman was naturally reluctant. "Chop, chop!" William insisted. "No time to hang about waiting for your moustache to sprout."

Brigadier General Tobias Stansbury studied Winder's letter to William with great interest before passing it back. He was a slight man and although only mid forties, he was grey haired from worry. Stansbury's troops had occupied a small settlement of farm buildings and he had claimed the farmhouse itself as his headquarters. The walls were littered with hunting trophies whose dead eyes seemed to follow William wherever he moved. Especially, William felt, as he eyed up a rather enticing cheese selection on a side table.

"What's so urgent, son?" Croaked Stansbury, lighting a cigar. "You've picked a hell of a night to call."

"Brigadier Winder..." began William, but was cut short.

"Just call him Winder, for God sake!" said Stansbury, who turned to warm his hands near the stove. "It'll make things quicker."

"Winder has you defending this post at all costs, does he not?" asked William, taking a moment to slyly inspect the cheese board.

"You have a familiar tone. Don't know if I care for it yet, sonny," said Stansbury, turning back and almost catching sight of William's hand reaching for the stilton.

"May I?" William enquired, nodding towards the cheeses.

"Are you about to make a point, Mr Tornbridge?"

"The plan is flawed," William replied, fighting the urge to correct him regarding his name. "Ross' force includes locally recruited peasant commoners. One thing we Peels know about is the peasant commoner. That and cheese, of course. Do you mind if I chop off a corner?"

"What about commoners?" asked Stansbury, impatiently.

"Well, they are a pretty close lot, you see. Comes from being too lazy to walk to the next village to find a wife. That's why many have ears on their cheeks, webbed toes and thumbs halfway up their forearms. Once such kinfolk meet on the battlefield, well, they'll simply turn and run. Sure as eggs go with bacon."

As Stansbury turned away to contemplate the information, William snipped off a lovely stub of Stilton. He was just about to snatch it up when Stansbury turned back and William was forced to abandon his prize.

"You're saying that what's left of my militia wont be enough to hold the British regulars?" Stansbury asked, pouring himself a large glass of port.

"Frustrated that the bridge is burned Ross' troops will be forced to turn on yours. It will be the proverbial bath full of blood. The British are a savage race. Anyone who has dined with them would testify to that."

It was a bold gamble on William's part. The truth was Cockburn had only managed to recruit a handful of local sympathisers and William didn't know that American scouts hadn't relayed that.

"God damned British!" said Stansbury, bracing himself against the chimney breast, crestfallen.

"All burning the bridge will do is cut the British off," continued William, taking his chance to wolf down the Stilton.

"Winder's a lawyer true enough, not a tactician," remarked Stansbury, staring deep into the flames. "I've said this again and again but Madison won't listen."

"I have been schooled in tactics," said William, slyly taking a gulp of Stansbury's port. "If you were on the other side of the river and the bridge were open, well, the British could be funnelled and managed." William paused for a moment to savour the taste. Unable to resist the urge to binge, he put what was left of the Stilton in his mouth in one go and swilled it down with the rest of Stansbury's port.

"There are strategic reasons to keep the bridge open, true enough, son," said Stansbury, turning back to William. "Winder forgets that. If the eastern bridges are destroyed, communications will be severed between Washington and Baltimore." He paused for a moment, baffled by why William's cheeks looked bloated. "You feelin' Ok, son?"

William could make no other sound than a "hummm" whilst offering a big thumbs up. Stansbury continued. "We'd be fighting blind to British movements." It was then Stansbury spotted the Stilton crumbs on William's lapel and the empty port glass on the table. He watched as William swallowed the evidence down in one painful go.

"Why, why, why, would Winder write this letter?" he quizzed, snatching it from William's hand, "only for you to scurry here and eat my cheese."

"You offered," said William, dabbing the corners of his mouth with a handkerchief.

"I most surely did not!"

"I'd say, Stansbury, that platter is the least of your problems." William stared at him down his long nose. "If you're still here when the British arrive then they will most likely use that platter to serve you your privates. And I'm not talking about your lower ranks."

Stansbury's glare of thunder slowly turned to a chortle and he charged two glasses. "You're crazier than a sun-struck Chesapeake Bay retriever." He passed a drink to William. "You tell me how we're ever gonna win this war," he said, taking a big drink, "if we listen to weak backed, nut brained, goofs like Winder and Armstrong? Secretary of War, my ass!"

"The secret of your conundrum, my wispy haired American eccentric, can be found with the bald, African jungle beaver?"

"Does this little creature by any chance abandon its hill when it's invaded by a superior force?"

"Quite so."

William made his way down the path away from the farmhouse to where the gang were huddled under a lantern.

"Vot now?" asked Volker, yawning.

"You ever asked why we're all fighting for pieces of this wretched place?" asked William, as everyone stood and dusted themselves off. "Most of it is just plain boring and the inhabitants are madder than, well, Uncle George. Which is some bar to hit."

"You convinced him?" asked Carr, stretching his back.

"I think he convinced himself. Crazy old stoat. Whether he can muster two thousand sleeping troops in time, of course, is a completely different cheese."

Looking down across the road and river, William and his party could see the great military camp of the militia. The faint light from the lanterns flickered off the tent fabric.

Thousands of militiamen were sleeping oblivious to the British troops most likely preparing to march. The whole place looked eerily quiet. The night air was still and fresh. In the distance, just west of the river bridge, was a small settlement. Smoke drifted from the crooked chimney of a cottage and the windows flicked orange with candlelight. William and the party walked down Lawndes Hill and passed, once more, through the camp of snoring militiamen.

William and Carr found themselves side by side and Carr explained the plan they had agreed when William was away meeting with Stansbury. Volker and the stable hands were to wait for those tasked with blowing the bridge. Carr would take to high ground to the north of the town and use the wind direction to mask the sound of his musket shots. Volker would then dispose of the bodies. It seemed an unbelievable plan but William knew better than to question it. If anyone could rattle off accurate shots in quick succession, from a great distance in a prevailing wind, he knew Carr could.

"Is it common do you think," William asked, quietly, "to see a girl and feel a weakness to the hips and legs?"

Carr took his time to compose an answer. "No, it's not common. It's more precious than any Peel wealth. It's love."

"Really?" replied William. "I thought love was what the French twins did with a sponge?"

"No," Carr smiled. "But sometimes it's a substitute."

The party reached the road at the foot of the hill and then followed it north into Bladensburg itself. The town was deserted. Window shutters swung on the breeze and the road lamps creaked on their brackets. Suddenly, Carr signalled to the party to move into the shadows of the buildings. He slipped his musket off his shoulder and carried it ready to raise and fire in an instant. His senses were reeling as they crept on through the town. He had the smell of something and everyone froze in silence as he cocked his musket. A second later there were voices in the distance.

A hundred yards away, two militia scouts were checking the empty buildings. One quietly pushed open the door as the other peered inside with his musket ready. When they were satisfied that the coast was clear, they moved on to the next house.

Carr took up an aiming position and readied a shot. He studied their pattern as they checked a couple of houses. Carr prepared to fire at the point where he could get both with a single shot. His finger was poised on the trigger.

The man checking inside the houses then appeared with a bottle of whisky. The pair proceeded to fight over the drink. A minute later they were both necking the contents and arguing about who was having more.

Carr lowered his musket. Even though the militiamen had no idea what was about to happen, Carr and Volker did. The scouts' cries of merriment soon turned to gurgles of pain as they clutched their throats and dropped to their knees. The bottle smashed on the ground as they arched backwards in agony. Less than a minute later, they were dead. The drink was poisoned. Once Carr was happy it hadn't drawn any attention, he gave the signal for the party to start moving. As they passed the bodies, William shuddered. Their spines were arched so far backwards they appeared broken and their faces were contorted from the agony.

The river bridge was deserted and the roads to Washington and Georgetown likewise. A faint mist clung to the banks of the river and the light from the camp fires cast shadows in the trees that bound it. As the party concealed themselves at the side of the old court building, Carr did a sweep of the bridge for militia. Poised down the sights of his musket, he ran to the parapet in silence and checked in all directions as he went. A moment later he gave a signal and William and the rest made double quick time to join him on the creaking deck timbers.

"This is where we leave you," whispered Carr.

Volker saluted William by way of a goodbye whilst the stable hands bowed in some half-hearted show of respect. William soon realised that he was being left with Samuel. Samuel smiled up at him through his rotten teeth.

"You do realise," William said, under protest, "that Winder will likely have some polite company."

"Samuel knows some jokes," Carr teased, relishing in William's predicament. "Ask him to tell the one about the lady and the pianist."

"Don't let him play shapez," said Volker.

"Shapes?" queried William, curtly.

"You need a pencil and paper," clarified Carr. "Samuel starts drawing an object and you have to guess what it is."

"What kind of objects?" asked William.

"I have to admit," said Carr, leaning in and whispering.

"I don't know where he's seen the things he draws but I'm glad I wasn't with him."

"He hazt made people zick."

Carr nodded to confirm he had seen it happen. The stable hands nodded too and their faces indicated the horror of it. Samuel smiled at William then produced a rather tatty looking pencil, which William took from him as if removing a weapon from his grip.

"I'll keep this, shall I?" said William.

"No Shapes?" asked Samuel.

"No Shapes," replied William.

Volker then signalled to the stable hands who loaded Samuel with William's pack. They then lifted the remaining packs onto their own backs.

"Good day, brave fellows," said William. "We'll meet this evening in the woods by Tournecliffe's bridge on the Washington Road. Providing the British turn up of course."

"They'll show," said Carr, swinging his musket strap over his shoulder. "Have no fear there."

William watched as Carr, Volker, and the stable hands turned and hurried off into the darkness. "Well, Samuel, my somewhat unsanitary companion, it looks like it's just us again." Samuel let out an excited noise that was somewhere between a laugh and a belch. "Hummmm," pondered William, as he watched Samuel swallow whatever it was he had burped up. "Perhaps best if you don't make any noise from now on."

William and Samuel followed the Georgetown Road as instructed by Winder. At the junction with the Washington

Road was an orchard. By the faint light of the moon, William could see heavy artillery hidden amongst the trees. The guns were aimed towards the bridge. Riflemen were milling about in the shadows, some were talking in groups, some were catching a few moments of sleep at the foot of the trees. No one seemed to care about the two solitary figures walking past at that time of the morning.

William proceeded to lecture Samuel on how, with his own vast experience of military tactics, it made no sense at all to guard a little bridge with six-pound guns. Samuel hung on his every word.

"You should be a genital," said Samuel, followed by his peculiar excited noise.

William cast him a confused look then suddenly twigged. "Ah! You mean 'General'?" he said, with some relief. "Well, I won't deny I have a certain pull where leadership is concerned. People follow me, you see. It's my coolness under fire. The Indians have a name for it. Something to do with feathers, I think."

They arrived at a small group of farm buildings to find no sign of life. The watermill, the barn, the cottage, all had just a small lantern by the door but nothing else to indicate life inside.

"Arses!" shouted William. "There was a bloody light on only a few minutes ago!" As William wasn't sure exactly which one of the buildings would be Winder's lodgings, he chose the cottage and knocked lightly. The quaint door was immediately opened by an ageing servant named Folsom who invited them inside and locked the door behind them.

He then indicated towards the stairs.

"The name's, Folsom, sir," he said in a perfect English accent. "Will you be requiring separate lodgings for your man servant?"

"Best not," replied William, heading up the stairs. "He has some peculiar morning routines which may offend those with less than iron guttering."

"Very good, sir," Folsom responded. "The Brigadier General is to have an early luncheon at eleven."

"But he's left for Washington, surely?" questioned William, pausing on a step. "He told me so himself."

"He changed his plans, sir," said Folsom, urging William continue. "Miss Hooper has suggested he entertain his senior officers, their wives, and some friends, sir. I am to extend an invitation to you, also."

"I accept, of course," said William, as they reached the landing. "What time, might I ask, is the good Brigadier General expected to rise?"

"He has ordered breakfast for eight sharp," said Folsom, pointing them into a room. "If that will be all, I'll bid you good night, sir."

"Just one more thing, Folsom, if I may," requested William, gingerly. "Miss Hooper? A flaxen haired girl is she? Sort of curly? Blue eyed?"

"Indeed, sir."

"Is there - hang on," at which point William pushed Samuel's inquisitive face into the room and pulled the door closed. "Is there anything an interested party needs to know?"

The pair gazed at each other for an awkward moment. So long in fact that William was beginning to wonder if his subtle question was too subtle. Either that or Folsom had nodded off. Suddenly, Folsom replied.

"I'm afraid there is a code, sir," he stopped dead as William slipped a Five Guinea piece from his pocket. "I say code, sir," Folsom back tracked. "I'm sure if the information weren't too salacious there would be no harm."

"Quite so."

"She has a suitor, sir. An American gentleman. An ill-suited match but one which appeared to have sufficient legs to go the distance."

"Appeared?" enquired William, with a look that a spider would give a lame fly.

"The gentleman has not yet returned from a mission to Africa, sir. He was expected home a week ago."

"Mission?"

"To buy slaves, sir. Miss Hooper is Governess to Mr William Thornton, the Washington architect. The slaves are needed for urgent works to the capital and the gentleman was no doubt hopeful that securing them would win him favour."

William extended the coin but resisted Folsom's efforts to take it. "You said ill-suited?"

"Miss Hooper, like a good many healthy women her age, sir, has a weakening disposition where men of action are concerned. The suitor intended to prove such credentials. However, if I may say, sir, he probably tripped on his shadow and died before he left the country."

"Thank you, Folsom," said William, letting go the coin.

William stepped into his room and closed the door. He listened for a moment to ensure Folsom had retired. William then turned to find Samuel staring in awe at a portrait of a lady in a Mother of pearl frame. William, suddenly remembering Samuel's proclivity for portraits of women, quickly snatched it from the dresser.

"Come now, Samuel," he said, steering him away towards a blanket on the floor, "I'm sure you'll be far more comfortable down there on the oak." At which point William put on his business face. "Now, Samuel. I want you to listen carefully," he said, lowering his voice. "These people will be expecting a gentlemen of my standing to have, well, staff. Which, under the circumstances, means you."

Samuel's mouth fell open into a grin. "Samuel knows," he said, winking and tapping his grubby nose.

William took a moment to compose the right words. "Quite so. Thing is Samuel," he paused again, coughing, "it's imperative that this meeting with Winder goes without a hitch." Samuel winked again. "So I insist that you wear trousers at all times. And absolutely no emptying of your bowels within, at least, a hundred feet of the cottage."

"Master William will set Samuel on as his servant, he will," said Samuel, sniggering.

"Let's put that aside for a moment," said William, moving in as close as Samuel's breath will allow. "And to put this delicately, I absolutely forbid you to," he paused to find the words, "fiddle with your little Samuel," he added, nodding in the direction of Samuel's crotch. "No touching him or his two friends. Understand?"

"Wee-wee wand?"

"If that's your name for it, then yes. We are guests, Samuel. We are poised, nay, teetering, between two sides on the brink of battle and we dare do nothing that might jeopardise my chances of making some money out of it."

William's Journal August 23, 1814: This is the eve of one of the most important days in history. The future of Washington will depend on it. Whatever happens I must keep Winder from discovering that the bridge to Washington still stands. God I hope Carr and Volker met with success and saved it from the militiamen's sabotage. I have a tough and unusual job tomorrow and I'm not convinced Samuel completely understands his part. Despite my detailed explanation of what's expected of him, I believe, unless my ears deceive, that Samuel is disobeying the very last of my explicit requests as I write this entry. What's more, I have just noticed that the portrait has gone from the dresser. Filthy beast! Oh, Mrs Forbes? What on earth is the correct etiquette for such an occasion? Perhaps best that I just bury my head and try not to picture him.

The morning of August 24 started well for William Peel. Firstly, he had managed to obtain enough warm water from

Folsom to allow him to bathe. Normally it fell upon the stable hands to perform this duty but as Samuel was all William had to hand, he was instructed to roll up his sleeves, soap up his paws, and sponge away. William had also intended to shave, all for the benefit of the fair Chloe, of course, but it was already stressful enough to let Samuel loose with a sponge let alone allow the idiot anywhere near his neck with a razor.

Once bathed and suitably towelled, William dressed and headed off downstairs with the hope of catching Winder having his breakfast. It turned out that Winder had had even less sleep than William that night and had spent most of it out and about engaged in war preparations. According to Folsom, Winder had lodged elsewhere but returned early for yet more meetings. William was knotted with apprehension as to whether he had seen the bridge standing. Perhaps not, he thought, if he had come from Washington. William had also learned from Folsom that the lady's portrait in his room was Dolley Madison, the First Lady. There was a portrait of the Madison's framed in the dining room of the cottage. William had to smile to himself as he peered in close to Dolly's stern expression. 'Looks like Samuel's a social climber,' he said to himself just as the door opened behind him.

"You spotted that, did you?" said Winder as he entered.

William was of a mind to comment that it was the only painting in the room and in such a prominent place that one would have to be blind or French to miss it.

"A good man," said Winder, drumming his chest with pride, "Dolly too. Well, a good woman," he said, clarifying. "Did you notice the picture of the First Lady in your room?"

"I did, yes," William confirmed. "My servant came across it last night," responded William, missing the literal meaning of his own comment.

"She's a fine woman, just fine." Winder seated himself for breakfast and beckoned William to join him. "I'm hoping, Lord Peel, that despite your previous meeting with The President, you may still choose to support our cause." As if by clockwork, Folsom entered with a tray and placed two bowls of porridge and some toast on the table.

"Forgive me, sir," said Folsom, "but Miss Hooper has left to meet her friends. By escort, of course. She said she will be back in time for luncheon as agreed."

"Thank you, Folsom," Winder replied. Once Folsom had gone, Winder returned to the topic at hand. "The country needs money, Lord Peel. Without a bank, we have no ready reserves of our own." He paused for a moment to stir honey into his porridge. "That's why we came to you. Not just to fund the war but for the money to complete the capital."

"Ah, yes. The vision!" said William, as he seated himself and pulled the napkin over his lap. "The President and I didn't exactly part with the warmest of embraces."

"That was then," said Winder, flashing a knowing smile. "I have his ear. Leave that to me. I'll get you that meeting."

William found it hard not to smile. The deal was within his grasp. It was perfect. Not only had the fool, Winder, missed spotting the bridge standing but he was going to do the ground work in buttering up The President. In addition, with the British likely to arrive at Bladensburg at any moment, Madison would be eating out of William's gloved hand. William could hardly wait to see Mother's face when he returned and calmly explained that he had secured some considerable acreage in America. It was brilliant. William paused and composed himself. He still had to keep Winder from leaving the house and knew that it wouldn't be easy. He needed a ploy. Some clever ruse. Just when he thought the morning couldn't get any better, the answer presented itself.

"Forgive me, Lord Peel," said Winder, wiping his mouth of crumbs, "but this hospitality is not entirely without motive. But then you're a sharp fellow so I figure you had read my mind."

"No."

"You have knowledge of Ross and Cockburn?" Winder asked, cooling his porridge with a light blow.

"Some."

"I like to know my enemy any chance I get."

"I'll offer what I can, of course," said William, conscious that he must, at the very least, appear to be on the side of America. "Both are experienced men. Ross has a large number of Wellington's men under his command. Did you know? Ross himself was a prodigy of my Uncle Wellington?"

"No, I didn't know that. I've heard of Wellington, of course. Your Uncle you say?"

"Point of note," said William, with a cheeky wink,

"should you find yourself face to face with the Iron Duke, aim a kick for his groin. He's particularly sensitive there."

"Indeed," replied Winder. "Useful to know."

Both ate in silence for a while. William's mind turned to the subtlety of the dilemma. Should he big-up the British Army? That would likely put such a fear of God into Winder that he would scurry back to Washington and board up the windows. That would, no doubt, also mean a harder fight for the British. Or, on the other hand, should he play the British forces down? That would likely allow Winder some confidence and cause his men to fight with more zeal. William was, however, sure of one thing. That the more he could hold Winder's attention, the better chance he had of keeping him from walking off with the hope of lighting a cigar off the burning bridge. The bridge which actually wasn't burning.

"Let me start with what I know of the troops," said William, preparing himself for the longest account of plausible bilge he could muster.

It was a passionate and often animated account that lasted a little over two hours. At one point, William used a bread roll to represent a Congreve rocket and hurled it across the room into the fireplace. Winder was captivated as William went into great detail about the navy and the training of the infantry. All complete and utter fabrications, of course. About an hour in, William really found his stride and the usually dangerous, automatic part of his brain was at last serving a useful purpose.

At one point though, he did feel he had gone a little

fast and loose with the truth when, during his detailed account of officer training techniques, he described how chaps were put in a cage with wolves whilst asked to place various wooden shapes into a box with corresponding holes. The exercise, as William explained, was to teach decision making under pressure. Winder just soaked it up and, save for the occasional whispered response such as "mighty incredible" or "you don't say", he remained silent throughout. William was just explaining that naval captains would personally oversee the casting of any new cannon when he realised Winder's eyes had glazed. He waved his hand in front of Winder's face with no reaction.

"Extraordinary!" said William.

It was like the man was in a trance. William glanced about to check he wasn't being observed then moved in closer to gaze deep into Winder's eyes. After William had pulled a few of his funniest faces, and received no reaction at all from Winder, he leaned back in his chair and declared to himself that it was amazing. William was about to leave things there when it occurred to him that Folsom was bound to enter at some point and find it a little odd that William would just sit there and not get help. So without a moment's thought, he took the spoon from his saucer and pressed it against one of Winder's gazing eyes. He returned it casually to its saucer as Winder's attention snapped back into the room and he screamed.

"Well, I think that's pretty much everything," said William, casually lighting a cheroot.

"What the hell!" exclaimed Winder, clutching his eye in

pain.

"Forgive me. You were lost to the world. I was forced to touch your eye with my spoon. A trick used with great success on Mrs Forbes my childhood Governess. She was often overcome with a similar malaise. One has to be careful the spoon is cool, of course."

"So I would imagine. My God!" said Winder, rubbing his watering eye.

"Did my summary satisfy your curiosity?" enquired William, sipping his tea.

"Well you're thorough, I'll give you that," said Winder, blinking his sore eye. "And you got all that from less than a day with them? Jesus! You're like... like a human mind sponge."

Whatever that was, thought William, at least Winder was convinced.

"Excuse me, Lord Peel," said Folsom, appearing at the door. "Your man servant wishes to speak with you. Quite urgently, I should say by his demeanour."

William appeared hesitant.

"Go on," said Winder, stretching. "I might take the air before our guests arrive. See how the land looks."

William excused himself, quickly, to find Samuel in the hall holding the seat of his pants with some discomfort. "What the devil are you doing?" barked William, as loud as he dare. "Can't you see I'm in the middle of a very important military discussion. Do you want to ruin everything. Do you?"

"Samuel, needs to make dirty," he said, sweat popping on his brow.

"I never said you couldn't, you know, do that!" William responded, checking they weren't overheard. "I just meant you couldn't do it on the bloody step." William yanked the back door open, grabbed Samuel by the collar, and sent him packing towards the bushes with a hearty kick to his britches. Still angered, William turned and shoved the dining room door open. It abruptly stopped with a thud and there was a yelp from the other side. William peered around the door to find Winder in shock and holding his bleeding nose.

"What the hell!" cried Winder, before he keeled over, unconscious.

William froze for a moment, glancing about him, the horror of the situation soaking in. In a flash, he grabbed Winder's arms and dragged him into the middle of the room. He lifted him up onto an oak chair and, tilting back his limp head, pinched Winder's nose to stem the bleeding. After a minute had passed, William thought Winder needed some encouragement to regain consciousness and he began slapping him across the face with ever increasing vigour. He was just at the height of a backswing when in walked Folsom. Both immediately froze.

"It's not how it looks," gasped William, suddenly hiding his blood soaked hand behind his back. "I knocked him unconscious, you see, with the door. Look, grab his legs will you, there's a good chap."

"I'm afraid I have a code for this sort of thing, sir," said Folsom, stiff backed as usual.

"What?" exclaimed William. "Oh, I see. Payment you mean?" He quickly searched his pockets for a coin he might have missed but had no luck. "Don't suppose I could owe you?"

"In which case," replied Folsom. "Etiquette dictates that I make a quick exit, sir, shouting foul play."

"What? No!" cried William. Folsom turned on his heels and made good his exit. The whole horrible situation flashed before William's eyes. If he were caught covered with Winder's blood it would put an end to any chances with the fair Chloe. Nothing less likely to stand a suitor in good stead than one who has put his host's nose across his face. Not to mention putting an immediate end to discussions with Madison for which Winder was key.

William was across the room in a flash and, in one smooth motion, he grabbed a fire iron from the hearth and cracked Folsom around the head with it. Folsom stumbled a few steps then dropped like a felled tree with blood pouring from a hole in his head.

"Oh, sparkling!" William sighed, as he threw down the iron. His gaze drifted between Folsom's twitching body and the unconscious Winder who was slumped back in the chair with his face smeared in blood.

William had less than a second to marshal his thoughts when his eye caught sight of Chloe standing with a group of ladies at the end of the long path that led to the front door. They were busy in merry conversation but for how long, William had no way of knowing.

Without a moment to lose, William rushed from the room and out of the back door. His eyes searched the hedges for Samuel's crouching figure.

"Samuel!" he repeated, as loud as he dare. "Get back in here this instant!" There was nothing but silence. Cursing under his breath, William turned to go inside and found Samuel at his elbow, grinning up at him. William grabbed him by the shoulder and shoved him quickly into the dining room.

Checking through the window, William could see the ladies making their way up the path. He ordered Samuel to grab Folsom's ankles and they dragged him across the room and rolled him up in the rug.

"Is that his thinking box?" Samuel asked, prodding at Folsom's brains through the hole.

"Yes, that's his thinking box," said William, grabbing the rug at the foot end. "Lift, damn you!" The pair manhandled the body through the doorway into the hall. Once outside, they took him over towards the hedge. "This is turning into a bloody terrible morning!" commented William, as the pair started to swing Folsom between them. After a few big swings, they let go and the body tumbled off down the hill with gathering pace before vanishing with a thud into the bracken. William rushed back inside to find Winder coming to in a state of confusion.

"Oh, my Lord!" cried Winder, pained, "What the hell happened?"

"A sudden nose bleed," explained William, fighting to catch his breath. "When you stood to get some air you passed out. Fell by the door, see?" he pointed at Folsom's puddle.

Winder, very shakily, took to his feet. "What the hell

did you do? Stick the spoon handle up my nose this time?"

"No, no," laughed William, nervously, as he suddenly spotted the blood-stained fire iron on the floor. Turning Winder to face the window, he frantically pointed Samuel's attention to the iron then offered Winder a napkin off the table. "Here, man," said William, "keep your head back. That's it. Pinch, man, pinch." Turning to see Samuel's progress, he found him stood by his elbow holding up the iron as if he had simply asked him to pass it. As the door opened, William shoved the poker up Samuel's tunic and he yelped in pain.

The ladies entered. They were all cotton summer dresses and bonnets. Their bosoms heaved with concern at the sight of a pale Winder, his eye bloodshot and his face smeared with blood. They rushed in on him at once, encircling.

"Oh my dear, lord," said one, in a thick southern drawl.

"See now, you just sit yourself here," said another, indicating Winder to a chair.

"I'm fine," said Winder, not happy with the fuss. "Where's Folsom? Tell him to fetch a brandy, damn it!"

It was then that the ladies noticed someone else in the room. They all turned to William and fluttered their eye lashes in unison.

"And who might you be?" asked Chloe, as the other's giggled.

"William Peel of Tornbridge. Lord Peel, that is," he quickly clarified.

"Chloe Hooper," she beamed, through an angelic

smile. "Miss Hooper that is," she added, quickly, her eyes dropping to the floor and cheeks flushing.

William bowed and took her hand. Fixing his gaze on her, he could feel his heart flutter and knees weaken again as if his very soul was being drawn into her pretty blue eyes. She too was transfixed on him. It was a second that felt like an age. This was what William had been waiting for all his life. Not the forced hand of marriage for the sake of tin exports. Mother was wrong, William could find a suitable bride for himself without paying for her. For there she was, Chloe Hooper. She was a beauty with poise and grace. She had no obvious signs of disease and possessed her own teeth.

"First things first," cut in Winder. "Never mind that nonsense. Where the devil is that fool Folsom? Something's not right here." He had just taken a step to the door when an almighty explosion shattered the windows and showered everyone with dirt and glass. The blast blew Chloe into William's arms and the pair were thrown across the room. The front of the building suddenly collapsed and became a shower of masonry and dust. Everyone was knocked over by the force but by some miracle no one was seriously injured. The dust hadn't settled when a young militia officer dashed in full of his own importance. His name was Clarke, a flashing blade, who held his heroism and perfect hair in the same high regard.

"The British, sir," he said, quickly helping everyone to their feet. "They're launching rockets from the east bank. I took out a couple with my trusty rifle."

Winder steadied himself. "How the devil did they get that far? What the hell is Stansbury doing?"

"Stansbury, sir?" questioned Clarke, dusting himself off. "He's dug in south-west of the river repelling fire."

"Jesus!" exclaimed Winder, shocked. "If he's not on the hill then we've lost tactical advantage."

"Then you have my word, sir," said Clarke, quickly throwing in a salute for good measure. "I shall place the very heart that beats in my proud breast into harm's way for the cause."

"Yes, yes," Winder replied. "Duly noted but the only hope now is to push the artillery north-east to defend the banks."

Clarke's face froze with disbelief. "Sir, surely the British will just cross the bridge?"

"WHAT!" Winder turned scarlet. "The bridge still stands!"

"What does that mean?" asked Chloe, anxiously as she clutched William with fear.

"Bladensburg may fall," responded Winder, moving to the hole that was once the window, "and Washington will surely follow." The distant sound of musket fire filled his ears. He turned in a flash. "You must be guarded, my dear."

"It will be my honour," said Clarke, saluting again. "And may I say there are no safer hands in the entire militia, sir."

William noticed Chloe's cheeks flush and, remembering Folsom's advice about her healthy proclivity for men of action, he took a step forward.

"Then the bridge must be destroyed," William said, his eyes steeled and his chest heaving.

"It will be impossible," said Winder, pained. "It would be a suicide mission now."

"Then I have just the man for it," responded William, turning to Chloe. "I will try and buy you time," he whispered.

"You hardly know me, sir, yet you risk so much," she trembled, tears filling her eyes.

"If it means sacrificing a life for a mere moment in your company, I will do it gladly," said William, and for a moment he forgot the musket shots and gurgling screams of death just a stone's throw away. The other ladies quivered at such a display of bravery. Presumably, they didn't register that it wasn't his own life he was preparing to sacrifice.

"War can make the amateur act foolhardy," said Clarke, keen to regain some points at William's expense. "But rest assured I'm an expert and will treasure your safety even if it comes at the cost of my own."

William took a step and called for Samuel who appeared at the door in a flash and handed William his sword. "We're leaving," William said, as he slung on his trophy sword. "Until we meet again, Miss Hooper," he smiled, and blew her a kiss.

William and Samuel walked back along the Georgetown Road, which traced the river south-east towards the bridge. To their left, between the road and the river, was a wooded embankment. It was another baking hot day. William dabbed the back of his neck with his handkerchief and berated Samuel for doing nothing about his own sweaty face. Ahead, through the trees, they could see the blue and red of Cockburn and Ross' troops taking positions on the east bank. Congreve rockets screeched overhead from the British line. Spiralling on the edge of control, they slammed into the earth and exploded with great violence in a cloud of fire and dirt. Just as William and Samuel neared the bridge, a rocket landed amidst advancing cavalrymen a hundred yards down the Washington Road. William and Samuel ducked under a mature oak for cover as the sky above them filled with men and horses engulfed in smoke and fire. Blood curdling screaming seemed to echo about the all consuming smoke. When the smoke cleared, a dozen men and horses lay dead or wounded. One cavalryman trapped beneath his lame horse shot it where they lay then used another pistol on himself.

William looked around the tree and eyed up the bridge ahead. The barrels of gun-powder were still strapped to the bracing. Ahead, he could see the red of Thornton's light infantry advancing towards the bridge from the north, muskets levelled, exchanging fire with the Baltimore artillery in the orchard.

"I have a job for you," said William, ducking as shots whizzed above them. "See those barrels?" he asked, pointing to the bridge.

"I thought we needed the bridge?" asked Samuel, digging something out of his nose.

"You needn't concern yourself with the complexities of warfare," responded William, slapping Samuel's hand away from his nose. "Take these," he said, passing over some matches.

"Samuel not allowed to make fire."

"I won't lie, Samuel, there's an element of danger to this but I don't want you to worry, I'll be far enough away should it blow early. I'm sure you'll agree that the fair Chloe is worth the risk. Yes? And the last thing I want is the smell of smoke in my hair when we next embrace." Samuel grinned and grunted, thrusting his crotch into the tree trunk. "Alright, enough of that. Now go! Go! And think nothing of your own safety."

Samuel slipped off his backpack and gripped the matches in his dirty paw. He took care to push them deep into the pocket of his britches. He winked eagerly at William then sprinted off towards the bridge like the simpleton he was. William urged him on as a punter would his horse in the final furlong. Beyond the bridge, the British infantry were taking casualties from the heavy cannon fire but still making good their advance.

"It will be close," William said, to himself. "Come on! Come on!" He shouted to Samuel. Suddenly, Samuel came under fire. Shots peppered about him as he ducked and weaved like a rugby forward sprinting for a try. He had reached the bridge but much to William's horror he appeared to be heading for the eastern embankment; the side closest to the British. "Oh, the bloody fool!" William muttered to himself, taking cover from a barrage of shots. "Other Side!"

he repeated at the very limit of his lungs, before ducking back for cover. "For the love of God!" he grumbled. "The fellow is a complete imbecile."

Samuel tip-toed amongst the shot that pounded the earth about him as he backtracked to the other side of the bridge. Lead shot splintered the bridge timbers as Samuel slipped down the embankment on the west side. Losing his footing a few times in the mud, he scurried down the banking. Stopping at the wooden piers, he gasped for breath. He could see the barrels lashed to the bracing. After receiving what he believed to be shouts of encouragement from William, Samuel waded out into the river. The water got deeper and deeper as he reached the underside of the barrels.

Meanwhile, Major Ross of the British Army was in one of the abandoned houses in Bladensburg observing the battle unfold through his spyglass. He suddenly came upon William and witnessed what he believed to be the young lord shouting orders at Samuel.

"The place is deserted," said Cockburn, appearing at the doorway.

"Unless my eyes deceive me," said Ross. "That eccentric Tornbridge Lord is braving the intense fire of both armies to disarm what looks like the American's attempts to blow up the remaining bridge."

"Such heroics won't please Lieutenant Scott," responded Cockburn. "Perhaps William's not the pompous, self-obsessed ass his personality would convincingly have us believe."

"I've never seen anything so selfless," said Ross, offering Cockburn his spyglass.

"What did I say, Major? Such an extraordinary family," he said, with a sigh. "Right, well, if the bridge is safe let's get across it."

Back at the bridge, Samuel was wading shoulder height through the water. If it hadn't been for his hand reaching out for the timbers at the last moment, he would have been caught by the current and washed downstream. Fighting the wash that broke on the pier, he grasped the bracing above him and pulled himself up with all his might. Climbing amongst the timbers, he moved to the barrels. The fuses were set and ready. He laughed to himself that he had made it then stuffed his hand into his pocket to retrieve the matches.

William waited with bated breath but no explosion came. Across the river, he could see the British artillery being withdrawn. The cannons were being fixed between horses and towed away under the cover of musket fire. The British were readying to storm the bridge. American gunfire intensified around William at that point and, realising that the British crossing the bridge was inevitable, he buried his head expecting the explosion only moments away. Suddenly, a squelching wet figure cast a shadow over him. Hearing the water drip, William looked up to see Samuel's gormless smile. In Samuel's outstretched grip were the soaking sticks that were once matches; the sulphur ends had all dissolved.

"Samuel needs more," he said.

"What!" barked William. "What the devil did you do,

wade into the river with the matches in your pants?" Samuel just shrugged. "Typical," said William, taking to his feet. "You manage to burn my entire house down in your sleep and yet here you can't light a simple fuse when armed to do so. What are you?"

"Samuel," he replied, pointing to his chest.

"A giant, ass-headed idiot!"

Samuel nodded.

It was too late for another attempt. The British were charging the bridge. William pulled Samuel behind a tree as President Madison himself led the counter attack up the embankment from the lowland wood. His mount reared as he reached the Washington Road and William later noted in his journal that The President looked the most heroic sight. His large white colt stood defiant against a backdrop of smoke and muzzle flash. Of course, Madison appeared to have misjudged exactly how quickly the British were marching and soon had to crack the reins and yank his mount clear in order that the regiments in the orchard could get a clear shot of the advancing army.

As Stansbury's troops advanced north towards the British, they were met by a barrage of rocket fire from the eastern bank of the river. It was a deafening noise that seemed relentless. Pounding guns, smoke, the stench of powder on the wind and the distant calls of orders to the sound of the British drumming.

William knew there was little time. They were moments from being trampled, either by the British or the Americans, depending who advanced the quickest. He and

Samuel hurried back along the tree line. They stuck close to the river as far as they could then headed double-time back along the road towards the cottage. Suddenly, William caught sight of his dusty clothes and stopped.

"Oh, for the love of God!" he shouted, patting the dust off his thighs. "This is insufferable. How can I present myself to the fair Chloe looking like one of your chimney sweeping relatives?" Samuel just shrugged. "Is that all you can say?" Glancing over his shoulder, William could see the British advancing at pace. They had cleared the bridge and, like an army of ants out of a crack in a wall, they were pouring across the river.

William and Samuel arrived at the cottage to find the door locked and bolted. Even the windowless dining room had its internal door barricaded from the hall side and was too solid to kick through despite William making several attempts. Which is to say, Samuel made several attempts with William shouting words of encouragement in his ear such as 'You really ought to put your back into it' and 'For God sake, you set about it like a malnourished girl!'

William called Chloe's name up at the windows several times but assumed she must be boarded up in a room somewhere and unable to reply.

Like a bolt from the blue, a thought suddenly jabbed William's brain. "Folsom!" William exclaimed, turning to Samuel with a click of his fingers.

"He's sleeping in a carpet," said Samuel.

"Never mind that," William replied, dismissing Samuel's stupidity. "Listen! We find him then we find his keys." And with that, William dashed around the back with Samuel at his heel like a puppy. Making his way down the banking, William retraced his earlier steps. "I better not find myself confronted by your dung," he said, as his eyes scanned the bracken. "There!" he declared, pointing to a corner of the carpet. He hurried down and ordered Samuel into the thick of it. "Never mind the nettles, you pilchard. Get his ankles!" A few minutes later they had carried Folsom to a clearing and the search began. Pocketing the gold coin he paid Folsom earlier for information about the fair Chloe, William then came across the keys. "Sparkling!" he said, grasping them in his fist.

"He doesn't look good," said Samuel, pulling earth out of Folsom's open mouth. "Should we wake him?"

"Best not," responded William, not sure how else to answer. "He's having the longest sleep of all."

"Like a Sunday?" asked Samuel, with excitement.

"If you like," replied William, casually, getting more used to disregarding Samuel's stupid comments.

With Folsom discarded back into the bracken, the pair went into the house and conducted a room by room search. They found nothing. The house was empty. When they reached the back door again they saw Winder approaching on horseback. He was charging across the open field to the west of the cottage amongst a huge force of cavalry, infantry, and riflemen. He took a detour and galloped to William.

"She's safe," shouted Winder. "I'm assuming it's Chloe you came back for?" he asked, drawing on the reins. "As we speak, she's with that brave officer, Clarke, in a carriage on the way to Washington. I've organised secure lodgings at The President's House till this blows over."

"Blows over?" questioned William, with a look of surprise.

"I saw what you tried to do at the bridge. It was mighty brave." Without another word Winder dug in his heels and galloped off in a cloud of dust to rejoin the cavalry.

"But the meeting with The President?" William shouted. It was too late, Winder was gone. "Bloody idiot!" William said, to Samuel. "Blows over! It's ten thousand men locked in mortal combat not a blasted tavern argument over spilt ale!"

William ordered Samuel to grab what provisions he could from the house. After stocking up with food, water and a musket, the pair took off up the hill west of the cottage. By keeping to the woods they managed to avoid the various pockets of Americans who were firing all they had towards the advancing British line.

Apart from the occasional deserter, running, coat turned inside out through the woods, William and Samuel came across no one else for a good twenty minutes. In the distance they could hear the war raging. Musket and cannon fire was carried on the wind along with the screams of the victims. There was some peace in the woods though. The baking sunlight pierced the canopy and cast green shadows on the lush woodland floor.

"I'm the furthest any Boyle has been from home," said Samuel, as he hurried to keep up with William's pace. "Except Uncle Boris. He went on a trip when the mine blew up."

"Really?" replied William, more of an automatic response than one of genuine interest.

"We don't know where he is. Dad says he'll probably let us know where he is when he gets there."

"I'm sure he's right," said William, still not really listening.

"You think I'm further than him?" Samuel asked, eagerly.

"Probably."

"I think war is a bad thing," Samuel prattled on. "Don't you think war is a bad thing?"

"I think it is when you're up to your teats in it and not profiting on it from behind a walnut desk in Tornbridge, yes." Ahead, William caught sight of the road and pulled Samuel down to get cover. "Glass!" he ordered, like a surgeon barking orders to a nurse. When he was presented with a drinking glass he sighed. "Not that, onion brain. The spyglass!"

The British forces were clashing with the militia on the far side of Washington Road. It was close quarter stuff with sword against sword and bayonets glinting in the bright sunlight. Looking closer, William recognised some of his negro cargo fighting with little care for it. Anyone pushed to the edge of the battle were simply deserting. Dozens of men were running off any chance they could. William's heart sank as he fixed the glass on an upturned carriage on the road. He had not had a moment to think of the fate of poor Chloe when the glass was suddenly snatched from his grip and he was confronted by three militiamen with their muskets sighted at him.

"Hope we're not disturbin' you non?" came a thick southern voice. "You two being lovers, an all."

The other militia joined in with a laugh.

"What!" exclaimed William, confused. "He's the man who carries my blasted chamber pot."

"Why don't you shut up and strip," said the third man, "be a shame to spoil those lovely clothes."

Samuel dropped his pack and began stripping.

"Not you, Goddamn it!" came the quick reaction. "Your clothes is worse 'en mine. I'm talkin' to this fancy fella," he added, nodding towards William.

William was considering his options when suddenly a musket cracked and shot splintered the tree next to him. A not too subtle reminder.

"That's right! We're waiting," came the shout.

After a reluctant sigh, William turned to Samuel. "Would you take my jacket," he asked, holding out his arms as if being undressed at the end of the day. Suddenly a shadow passed to the side of William and there was an unholy crack that caused him to turn. In a flash, there was another crack and William glimpsed a figure moving quickly past a tree. Two of the militia were on the ground, unconscious, and as the third turned his musket into the shadows to fire, he suddenly found a thick branch strike his neck that knocked his head sideways. The impact was so violent that he died instantly.

William turned to find himself face to face with a large

black figure in a British Army uniform. As the figure drew himself up to his full height, William recognised him at once. To his horror, it was No.19. The muscular slave responsible for the uprising on *The Emily*. William was understandably concerned that the man might carry a grudge and was certainly armed and suitably capable to exact a most horrible revenge. During a moment of eye contact, William slowly moved Samuel in front of him by way of a shield.

"It was you on the boat that brought me to this place?" said No.19, in rough pigeon English. "I remember your face. The man with the lion."

"Yes, and I remember you," replied William, thinking it best not to refer to him by his number. "Fancy bumping into you again. Especially here. In these secluded woods."

"Ndeh!" the man shouted, pointing to himself. His eyes were wide with adrenalin. "And my child's name was Abena."

"The little girl who died," Samuel whispered to William.

"Yes, I know who he means," William replied, moving Samuel out of his sight.

"She had disease," added Ndeh.

"I know," responded William, not sure of the etiquette. "Unpleasant business. One sympathises."

"The doctor in our village said she would not last a week."

It suddenly hit William what Ndeh was saying. It was Abena who carried the sickness on board *The Emily*. She had it when she was taken from Africa.

"My wife Rabia is alive because of you," said Ndeh, stepping forward and removing his army issue jacket. "You killed your own because of what the big man did. You are a great man." William wafted away the comment as if it were all in a day's work. Not that he had ever done a day's work, of course. Ndeh grabbed the militiamen's muskets and slung them over his big shoulder. He then paused sensing that William was somewhat lost for words. "You are surprised that I do not hate you?"

"Well, I had imagined some umbrage," replied William, clearing the lump in his throat. "However misplaced."

"You saved Rabia because you knew it was right. This business, slavery, will end one day. I believe that in my heart. It will only do so by men like you. Men who see something wrong and fix it. For the sake of my children, I cannot hate such a man. Your God be with you." Without a pause, he turned and walked away into the woods. "I go now to find Rabia," he added, over his shoulder.

"Nice man," said Samuel, fiddling with his backside as he watched Ndeh vanish.

"Yes," William replied, with a discrete sigh of relief. "And will you leave your bottom alone, for heaven's sake!" William smoothed his jacket and ordered Samuel to load up with his pack.

Beyond the carriage they could see the battle waging. It was seemingly leaderless. The rough grazing land beyond the road was littered with militiamen falling foul of British Red Coats. The screams of agony and musket fire were never ending. Every few seconds, the ground felt to shake to the British big guns as they let loose across the river. William and Samuel quickly took shelter behind a tree as a stray

Congreve spun wildly out of control and exploded in the canopy above them. They were showered with sparks and ash.

Chloe's carriage was on its side with its wheels in the direction of the woods. Ahead of it lie the horse, shot and bleeding. The British were only minutes away from advancing past it and William knew he needed to get Chloe out before the carriage itself was consumed in cross-fire. He watched for a moment as a stray shot clipped a wheel and ricocheted off into the woods.

"Stay here until I signal," said William, with authority. "And guard that chamber pot with your life. I fear I may have an abrupt need for it."

In a sudden rush of chivalry, William made a dash for the carriage and to the fair Chloe's aid. After a good minute attempting to pull his podgy frame up onto the side of the carriage, William gave up and beckoned Samuel sternly as if it were all his fault.

"This damn shoulder," he said, pushing Samuel to the dirt and taking a leg-up from his back.

Once on the carriage side, William yanked open the door and threw it back. The inside was empty except for Chloe's scarf. He cursed and moved to the front where he saw Clarke half trapped under the seat with his thigh badly crushed. William presumed he had tried to jump clear before the crash but hadn't made it. William climbed down and took the canteen from Samuel's backpack.

"Taken!" Clarke gurgled, as William knelt beside him. He tried gripping William's jacket but his fingers were soon peeled off and placed on the canteen.

"Who?" queered William, as he tipped some water into Clarke's dry mouth. William took great care to make sure Clarke's blood-stained lips didn't touch his canteen.

"Chloe."

"I meant who took her, you ass!" William replied.

"Naked savages. Niggers. A dozen. Brutish men. Too many to elude," he said, straining. "What kind of animal would just snatch someone like that? And to what end? To serve what vile purpose?" he added, through gritted teeth. "Christ man! I can't feel my body!"

"Probably because you have a carriage on it," responded William, not oblivious to the irony that 'the savage', as Clarke called him, was himself most likely enjoying the sun in his garden a few months earlier until some Barbary raider kicked his hut door in and dragged him off for selling. If 'the savage' was lucky enough to survive the Atlantic crossing, he was then kicked out onto a battlefield and ordered to fight for a purpose he knew nothing of, nor cared about. His first thought, as anyone would expect, would probably be for getting his black, malnourished backside back home.

"You must save me," Clarke piped up, grabbing William's lapels again. "Quick man! You gotta saw off my leg."

"What!" exclaimed William, looking at the cart seat that trapped Clarke across the right thigh. "I'm not sawing anything off. It's likely a very messy business."

"Then he must," responded Clarke, his pained eyes

glancing in Samuel's direction.

"Oh, I really wouldn't advise it," William resisted, ducking as a barrage of shot peppered the carriage by his head. "Not if it's anything like his dentistry."

"It's the only way," Clarke gurgled. "A hero's way." William turned to Samuel who had caught the gist of the conversation and was holding up one of William's silver dinner knives.

"You're not blunting the family silver on this oaf." responded William, with resolve. A resolve that soon faded to a sigh. "Well, I best not be splashed with the juices," he said, and sought shelter around the back by the wheels.

A moment passed. Distant shots rattled about them. Then came Clarke's ungodly, gurgling scream, which seemed to go on and on. William took as much as he could bear then decided he couldn't ignore it any longer. Making his way around the front, he could see Clarke grimacing with the veins proud on his neck. His eyes were pained and watering. Samuel was crouching over him with his elbow going like a piston.

"What the hell are you doing!" William queried, moving behind Samuel to take a look. "Tell me you're not sawing the wrong damn leg?"

"Not even through his britches," replied Samuel.

"Jesus in pyjamas!" William protested. "This is ridiculous. Look Clarke, you sorry excuse for a man. If you can't even cope with the pain of having your britches cut what do you think will happen when he takes my cutlery to the meat?" Suddenly a cannon ball landed close by and showered them with dirt. "The fair Chloe is in peril," William cried, "and she doesn't have time for this twaddle!"

"Don't you leave me!" shouted Clarke, as William stuffed the canteen into Samuel's pack. "My death will be on your conscience."

"I am leaving," said William, brushing himself down. "And no, your death won't be on my conscience because I didn't trap your fat leg under your own stupid carriage. And if you were the hero of your persistent claims then you would have had the decency of turning your pistol on yourself. A fat head like yours would be hard to miss!"

"You utter bastard!" shouted Clarke.

"Oh, dry your eyes," replied William, before he and Samuel made off up the road.

By the time William had reached the woods to the north of the Washington Road, it was clear that the American forces were pretty much fragmented and chaotic at best. Ross' troops were marching down the Washington Road unchallenged and taking prisoners and horses where they could. Most of the militiamen had run off back to their families and the only resistance appeared to come from the hill south-west of Tournecliffe's Bridge. As Ross' troops came within range, the American guns opened fire. It was Barney, guarding the bridge as he had vowed. William could not quite believe anyone would be so bonkers as to stand five hundred boatmen against the might of Wellington's Invincibles. It was to William's benefit, of course, as he needed Ross to kick Barney into touch in order to clear the way to Washington.

William grabbed Samuel and pushed him onwards behind the tree line towards the river bridge. Up on the hill, William could see the militia unleashing their three-pound guns on the British. The British took casualties but held their line and set themselves for a volley of musket fire.

"Fire!" Ross cried, and a second later another line of soldiers stepped past the first and took aim. "Fire!" he cried again and the militia were falling like swotted flies.

Cocking his musket, William moved about the dense trees. His breathing was shallow as his eyes scanned for signs of an ambush. His caution was soon to be justified as a musket came into view from behind a tree ahead. The militiaman spotted William and took aim. In a flash, William fixed on him and fired. It was a clean shot through the fellow's throat and he fell, blood spurting, to the ground. William quickly reloaded. Suddenly, there were footsteps in the distance. The sound of men approaching. William quickly tapped powder down the barrel and had just dropped in the shot when a figure emerged brandishing a sword. William cocked, turned, aimed, and - BANG! The ugly brute took one in the chest and stumbled a few steps before collapsing. William did his best to reload but it was too late, another militiaman was on him with his sword slicing the air. William ducked as he drew his own sword. Blades clattered and slashed. It was a tiring business and after a few minutes of keeping his quarry at bay, William faltered and the sword was sent rattling from his grip. A smile spread across the dirty face of the militiaman as he savoured the last few moments.

"Now, hang on!" said William, his outstretched palms urging for calm. "I'm not your enemy."

"Tell them," growled the American, indicating to his dead colleagues.

"Yes, well. I grant you that looks bad but they jumped me."

The militiaman took a step towards William and raised his sword. William's self defence training kicked in. "Oh look!" he cried, pointing over the militiaman's shoulder. "A pair of mating Badgers!"

The militiaman quickly glanced over his shoulder but as he turned back, William jabbed him hard in the eyes with a fingers. In that instant, Samuel jumped the man from behind and wrapped his legs and arms tightly around him. The militiaman screamed in agony as Samuel sank his teeth into his neck. William stood back with revulsion as blood poured from the bite. The man flailed his arms and spun madly in an attempt to shake Samuel free but to no avail. Conscious that the fellow would bring attention, William stepped up and kicked him as hard as he could in the crotch. The militiaman's once flailing arms flew to comfort his aching manhood and he dropped to his knees. Samuel slipped off, his teeth red with blood. William stared into the militiaman's pained eyes. Both were bleeding from William's nails. Suddenly, an object struck the fellow's head from behind and shattered. As the blaggard fell forwards into the grass, William noticed the broken handle of his ornate chamber pot in Samuel's hand.

"Oh for pity's sake, Samuel," sighed William, looking at

fragments of ornately decorated porcelain on the ground. "Could you not have grabbed a rock, you dullard!" But Samuel wasn't listening. Instead, he was staring off into the woods over William's shoulder.

"Angry men," Samuel trembled, with his finger pointing.

"Don't change the subject," said William, annoyed. "You do realise what you've done, don't you?"

"Mr William, quick," said Samuel, tugging the arm of William's jacket.

"What?" responded William, slapping Samuel's filthy hands away. "Never touch a Peel, ever! And look at me, damn you, when I'm taking the time to improve you." It was then he saw the urgency in Samuel's eyes and turned to follow his gaze. As he did, he felt his stomach churn. "Oh, God!" he gulped, as he stared at a group of half a dozen armed militia running in their direction through the woods. "By some irony I feel the need of that pot."

"Angry men, Mr William."

"Yes, yes," said William, pointing to the back pack with urgency. "Perhaps a tactical retreat." And with that, William ran full pelt in the opposite direction to the charging militia. Samuel snatched up the pack and ran after him. William had got about forty feet when a barrage of shots rang out ahead of him and he dived behind a tree for cover. He turned back to see Samuel running past.

"Get cover, pea-brain!" William shouted. With shots coming from all directions, William had no option but to get low and hope for a miracle. He watched as the chasing militia raised their muskets ready to fire. They were nearly on top of William when suddenly a volley of shots rang out from nowhere and all the militiamen were peppered. They fired their last shots by reflex as they spilled to the dirt. Five died instantly and the other clasped his chest. As both William and Samuel hurried to their feet they saw Volker, Carr and the stable hands appear from behind the trees. Carr's repeating musket was smoking.

"You're early," said Carr, coolly, as he sighted in the injured militiaman and put him out of his misery with a clean shot to the chest.

"On the contrary," responded William, pointing to Washington Road. "Looks like we're just in time."

The British were advancing across Tournecliffe's Bridge and although they were taking heavy casualties from the deck guns stripped from the flotilla, their progress was relentless. The air was thick with smoke that blew through the woods like a fog. Just as William had planned, Ross was punching a hole through Barney's defences that opened up his way to Washington.

"Zis way," said Volker, urgency in his voice.

"We found a way around the militia defence," said Carr, as they headed off. "We must be quiet and quick but there are boulders on the river we can use to cross."

"What of the rest of the militia?" queried William as he followed.

"Dispersed," replied Carr. "Barney's flotilla is the last real resistance."

"Cockburn was right," William smiled. "He said he

would have the pleasure of those deck guns again." And with that, they all fell silent and ran the last fifty yards towards the edge of the woods. True to Carr's word, there were large rocks in the river with water breaking about them. One by one, the party leapt from one to the other then regrouped at the toe of the bracken covered banking at the other side.

The timing was perfect. Just as William and the party were reaching the top of the bank, the British had breached Barney's defences and the close quarters fighting had begun. Barney's men charged the British with swords raised and clashed head on. A wave of clattering steel and pistol fire erupted as near on a thousand men engaged toe to toe. It was a bloody affair and Barney put himself right into the thick of it with his bayonet.

Carr watched for a while before taking cover behind a hedgerow. The battle noise soon faded behind them as they followed the hedge a quarter of a mile south. They then dashed, heads low, to a wall that bound the road to Washington. Suddenly, William's eye caught something blue ahead in the distance. Grabbing the spyglass from Samuel's pack he sighted it in. It was Chloe, draped across the saddle of some militiaman's appaloosa as they galloped off over the brow of a hill towards Washington.

"A dozen savages indeed, Clarke," muttered William. "My lion's loin hair!" he cursed, as he passed the glass to Carr. "We must save her."

The group had only followed the wall a few yards when Carr suddenly dropped to one knee in pain. At first, William assumed he had stumbled then he saw dark blood running down his jacket and over his thigh. Carr's jaw locked in the agony of it. He tried to take another step but faltered. Volker quickly threw his friend's arm across his shoulder and they all took cover by a nearby pile of logs. As Samuel undid Carr's jacket, Volker looked around with his spyglass. After a moment scanning the scene, he found what he was looking for. It was Barney and as soon as he saw Volker had a glass on him, he took another shot that splintered a log only inches from his head.

"Za dog!" shouted Volker, ducking.

"No need for a field physician, my lord?" laughed Carr, pressing his palm against the pouring wound.

Volker pulled Carr forward to see the wound from the back. It was serious. He cursed in German then tore a strip off Carr's shirt to make a dressing.

"No, no!" said Carr, resisting. "The girl. You have to go. You can't fix this."

"I am za captain. You do az I zay!" barked Volker, still trying to dress the wound.

"Not for this voyage, old friend," said Carr, pushing Volker's hands away. One of the stable hands rushed in with a canteen and Carr took a long, soothing drink. "Get to Washington," he ordered, wiping his mouth. "You have to finish this!"

"Samuel carry you," said Samuel, pointing to himself.

"I'll sooner see my end here in comfort," laughed Carr, "than a mile down the road on your back, my friend."

Volker's teeth gritted and he smashed his fist so hard against the logs that they shook. Wiping a tear from his eye, he grabbed Carr's musket from the ground and clasped it into his friend's blood soaked hand. "Firzt Mate, alwayz."

"Take care of Daniel, will you?" Carr asked William. "He's impulsive but a good man."

With a last, affectionate slap on Carr's shoulder, Volker rallied the party and indicated that they were all to move out. Although the closest of friends, both were professional to the last. Each of the stable hands gave Carr a rather shoddy but heartfelt salute as Samuel rushed over to give him a hug goodbye. Carr patted him warmly on the back then Volker gently pulled Samuel clear.

"I vill see you again," said Volker, squeezing his friends hands.

"Don't be in a rush, though. Ok?" Carr replied.

With a nod goodbye, Volker and the rest ducked down and ran back to the wall that bound the road to Washington.

William stayed, he felt the need to offer some last, comforting words. Nothing obvious came to him though. In the end it became an awkward silence. "Are you in pain?" he finally enquired, his brain slipping into automatic. Carr ignored the question. "Feeling cold in the lower body? Light headed?" William added. "Past flashing before your eyes, that sort of thing?"

"None," said Carr, coughing. "Apart from the hole in my guts I feel pretty good," he added, with a laugh. There was another silence and Carr put his head back. He tried to relax as best he could considering his wound and the war raging only a few hundred yards away.

"Did you love her?" asked William. "Barney's bride to

be, I mean. I assume you did."

Carr remained silent as memories of her flooded back into his mind. Just when William thought he would never get an answer, Carr lifted his head.

"When we were apart, it was as if I were becalmed. You understand?" William nodded. "When the sails sit so still there's not so much as a flutter. It can be a minute, an hour, a day. Then you see the wind come. Feel it hit you. Your heart tightens and races. Your sails fill and, well, it was like she was the wind to me," he stopped, savouring the memory.

"Yet you didn't pursue her?" William asked, bluntly.

"No," Carr replied, his face filled with regret. "I chose a career in the French Navy. She died two years later. The irony is she's probably still waiting for me upstairs," he pointed up to heaven. "I'll never get there." He chuckled to himself, reflecting on a life of dubious adventure.

"Oh, I think you're a pretty sparkling fellow Mr Carr," said William, his back straightening. "You've not been easy at times, but I would say you've done enough good to make up for earlier transgressions."

Carr's sprits lifted. It was about as good a compliment as anyone could ever hope to get from a Peel. He weakly held up his hand for William to shake. William approached with trepidation on account of it being covered in blood. After a moment considering his options, William grabbed the very tips of Carr's fingers and gave them a little shake.

"Ugly business," he said, indicating to the wound. "If it's a comfort, I don't mind helping your passing," he added, picking up a lump of stone. Uncle Wellington advocates a violent, upward strike to the back of the head, just at the top of the spine." Carr's expression was enough to make William stop talking and drop the stone. "I see that you're a 'pass quietly' type of fellow so I will leave you with your thoughts."

"I have a score to settle first," croaked Carr, pulling his musket in close.

William sensed it was time to leave and without uttering another word, he ducked low and ran to the wall.

Carr took a few deep breaths and checked his musket sights. "Aim true," he whispered, and kissed the barrel. He pulled himself to his feet but grimaced in pain as he did so. After a few more restorative breaths, he turned and took aim towards the battle, but before he had chance to cock the hammer, he sighted on Barney preparing to fire a shot himself. "You son of a bitch!" he uttered.

A single shot carried on the wind and stopped William in his tracks. After a brief but reverent thought for his companion, William carried on running to catch up with the others.

The plan was simple as far as William was concerned. Once he had rescued the beautiful, and no doubt very grateful, Chloe, it would then be a simple stroll into Washington and a late dinner with President Madison; providing William could get his name right, of course. With any luck, William could be in, fed, and out again laden with land deeds before Cockburn, Ross, and the idiot Lieutenant Scott, had so much as a sniff of Capitol Hill. How could it fail? Winder, The President's close advisor, had witnessed William risking life and limb to destroy the bridge. Chloe, governess to the children of the Washington architect, was soon to be rescued and thus cementing William's heroic status. With the British only hours from the capital it was more than likely President Madison would welcome William Peel's money with open arms. It was a perfect plan and William afforded himself a little victory dance in the road. In fact, the only slight glitch in William's scheme was that in doing his victory dance, he had lost his bearings regarding the direction of Washington.

John Lewis

Bladensburg fell to the advancing British on the afternoon of August 24, 1814. The militia were smashed and those who survived fled back to their loved ones. The last of the musket smoke had dispersed on the breeze and Major Ross made camp to take stock of his losses. There was no sign of President James Madison, Tobias Stansbury, or Brigadier General William Winder.

By late afternoon, William and the party passed Washington's two mile marker post. The air was warm and still and, except for bees buzzing about the hedgerows, the scene was silent. They had run since leaving Bladensburg and, after the sad loss of their friend and colleague, John Carr, all were wearier than they would freely admit. Apart from taking to the woods to avoid the occasional scout, the party's journey had been uneventful. There had been no sign of the villainous militiaman or the appaloosa over whose saddle the fair Chloe had been sighted hours before.

William was entertaining the thought that Chloe might be lost to him when the distant snort of horse had him stopping in his tracks. Sure enough, it was a black spotted, white appaloosa. It appeared to all concerned as though the creature had just been abandoned. Ducking out of sight behind a hedge, the party watched as the horse grazed in pastureland. It was saddled but roamed untethered. Beside the field was a small cottage that was only a stone's throw from the road. There was no sign of movement through the windows or smoke visible from the crooked chimney.

William and Volker exchanged a look, both concluding at the same time that it all appeared too easy. Suddenly, there was a clattering of pans inside the cottage and the startled horse bolted. William leapt into action and, without thinking, he was away through the gate in the direction of the cottage with his sword drawn. Volker cursed at him under his breath. He slipped the musket off his shoulder and ordered Samuel and the hands to stay hidden. Instead of taking the long way around, Volker simply pushed this massive frame through the hedge.

William pressed his face up against the glass of a side window and peered in. It was the living room. There was simple pine furniture with a threadbare couch under the window and a calfskin rug by the fireplace. Volker arrived at his elbow and the pair moved silently towards the rear of the house. Suddenly, there was a loud crash followed by an outburst of profanity in a rough American voice. William was just about to check through the next window when the glass shattered outwards and a pan bounced along the grass only yards away. Quick as lightning, Volker and William were backs to the wall with their weapons readied.

"English bastards!" was the cry from inside, followed by more smashing of crockery.

"You shouldn't take on so," came Chloe's calming voice and William was so taken with joy at hearing it, he quickly glanced in through the shattered window in the hope of seeing her. In an instant, a pistol shot cracked the frame above William's head and splintered the timbers. He ducked down for his life.

"You hear me!" called an angered voice from inside the cottage. "You British soldiers who are raping my Motherland! Biting her teats sore!"

William cast a look at Volker. He was somewhat revolted by the thought of a Peel biting America's teats. There was more smashing of crockery and what sounded like a table being upturned in rage.

"You think you can break us?" the rant continued. "You think we'll stand by and let you march on our beloved capital. Then you, sirrrs," said the man, slurring his words, "do not know who you're up against."

"The fellow's stinking drunk," whispered William. But when he turned to seek Volker's opinion, his companion had vanished.

Suddenly, a commotion erupted inside and a shot rattled through the roof slates. There were sounds of a struggle and cries of pain. A moment later a body flew through the window above William and took the remainder of the glass with it. William dived for cover as the figure landed in a heap on the verge. With some fight left in him, the figure slowly took to his unsteady legs. He was a big man, in his mid thirties, with a week of stubble and unwashed hair. His cheeks were crimson from drink and temper and they puffed when his gaze fell on William. The man's eyes were heavily bloodshot and looked as if they would be painful to see through. He squinted as he focused on William. With his rage building, he moved towards William with his fists clenched.

"By God!" the man shouted, jowls wobbling. "I'll teach you what Madison can't." With his anger aroused, he charged at William. The man's senses were clearly impaired by him being blotto, however, and instead of tackling William head on, he missed him entirely and ran full pelt into the house side. As the man collapsed backwards, William looked in disgust at the patch of blood left by the fellow's nose on the wall.

"Za girl is, ok," said Volker, appearing at the window.

William didn't have time to answer as the fellow was quickly on his feet again and ready for a fist fight. Wiping his blooded nose, the man put his dukes up and attempted to coordinate his movements.

"Dirty fighter!" he said, making a few drunken jabs. "Well, come see what John's got for ya in his bag of pain." He stepped towards William and swung a hard right hook. Instead of striking his intended target, however, he cracked his fist hard into the window frame. "Christ!" He yelped, moving back. After rubbing his eyes for better focus, he moved in again with a fully committed left hook that missed William completely and landed with a crack against the brickwork. He staggered back, crossing his arms with the agony of his bleeding fists. "You have done me," he said, with his knees trembling and his eyes filling with tears. "Why do you wait to claim your prize? Damn you!" he added, before collapsing face forward onto the grass.

Chloe appeared from the front of the house. "My dear, John," she shouted, rushing to his side.

"There were too many," the man slurred, before passing out.

Chloe let out a huge sigh then turned to see William leant back against the side of the house as he casually watched the show.

"William!" she exclaimed, her face lighting up with joy as she rushed to him. The pair embraced with tenderness. William had a mind to lift her in the air with joy but felt his back twinge as soon as he took her weight. Instead, he pulled her into another embrace and quite unintentionally his lips found hers. He felt her body heave and her grip tighten as her breasts pressed into him. It was all he had hoped and dreamt it would be. Sure, it wasn't his first kiss but it was his first fired with such passion. Neither the French twins nor Kyra ever kissed him like that, although, what they did do left a lasting impression. Chloe's eyes sparkled with devotion as he drew her once more into a breathless embrace.

As the stable hands carried the unconscious militiaman into the cottage, Chloe had time to explain that he was John Lewis, none other than the grandnephew of George Washington himself. If there was any man in the country that hated the British more, she explained, he has never shown himself. William had it in his mind to question why such a revered man with a passion for his country would get so rat-arsed at a time when his country needed him most. Considering Chloe was American and appeared to like the fellow, however, he decided against saying it.

After checking over the cottage, the group found the larder stocked and decided a rest was needed.

"Ve can afford an hour at za most," said Volker, standing his musket by the front door. "Ross will not rezt his men long."

And so it played out like a well oiled machine. Two of the stable hands cleared the broken crockery out of the kitchen and set the upturned table. The third, the gaunt one, tended to the appaloosa and put it out of sight from the road. By a stroke of fortune, the fat stable hand found chickens in the garden and set to work breaking necks and plucking. Samuel was given the task of chopping wood for the stove, despite William's concerns over the idiot being in charge of a sharp axe. Volker took up position in the dining room at the front of the house in order to keep watch on the road. William was with Chloe in the living room. He watched her tend to John Lewis' wounds as he snored on the couch.

"That fool Clarke," said Chloe, cleaning John's blood-smeared knuckles. "It was his fault. All was going fine until he decided to show off by swerving the carriage this way and that. All to make me giddy. Next thing I knew, the seat had vanished below me and the world was up ended. So I ran. I ran for my life. I was eventually found by John."

"I'm afraid to say Clarke was still full of pomposity when I arrived," replied William, helping himself to a brandy. "He even begged me to saw his leg off. Idiot!"

"He wasn't a real hero," said Chloe. "Not like you."

It was just those few words that made William's back stiffen and his chest rise with pride. He was indeed having an adventure destined to rival those told by his father. William watched Chloe's beautiful profile as she took a moistened cloth to John's blood soaked hands. She was an enchanting creature and William couldn't help picturing her laid bare on the hearth rug littered with exotic fruit pieces.

"Perhaps," said William, pausing to down his drink, "you would care to return to Tornbridge with me."

Chloe took a moment to think as she put the cloth in a bowl of water by her feet. "Why, sir," she replied, cheeks blushing, "what is it you're saying?"

William moved forward and, after passing her a towel so she could wipe her blood-stained hands, he pulled her up into an embrace. "I'm asking if you will come back to Tornbridge with me," he said, assuming she just hadn't heard him properly. Chloe pulled away, her head spinning with excitement and apprehension.

"Why, I hardly know you, sir," she said, wringing her hands as she stepped to the window. "Save that you are rich beyond imagination, evidently heroic, and unquestionably handsome."

"Did I mention the splendid house?" added William, failing to say it had been gutted by fire, of course.

"I am from simple, God fearing stock, sir," she said, voice trembling. "To form a union with a man such as yourself, well, I would fear the implications. What of the gossip? What of your good name?"

"Nonsense! Men of note marry beneath themselves all

the time and besides," said William, slapping out a quick tune on his belly, "we Peels have breeding enough for the both of us." He then gathered her in his arms and stared into her pretty eyes. "As for the gossip, no fear there, we can just have them killed."

"No, sir, you can't!" she protested.

"It's fine. Parsons knows a fellow."

"Although my heart says yes, yes, yes, I fear it would not be right," Chloe withdrew and turned her back. "You must know that I am a Quaker, sir, and to marry an outsider would mean expulsion from the Society of Friends."

"So?" William replied, ignorant to how it mattered.

"I must discuss it with someone who has experience of such things."

"Rot!" William exclaimed. "What is religion when compared to love and a big house? Besides, one imagines your average Quaker would advise against our union. One less backside on a pew and so forth. You do go to church, I assume?"

"I shall seek counsel from Dolly Madison," said Chloe turning in a flash. "She made the same choice when she married The President. Yes, I will leave our future happiness in her hands." She watched William for a moment, his lip increasingly curling as the idea sunk in. "You must have faith," she added, taking the silk scarf from around her neck and placing it in his hand. "It is a little thing, I know," she said, folding his fingers around it, "but it's often the simplest things, isn't it?"

"That what?" enquired William, expected her to finish

the statement.

"Why, 'that mean the most', of course."

"Oh," replied William, deflated, "that old chestnut."

With a quick kiss on William's cheek, Chloe returned to the couch and tended to John Lewis.

Volker was seated on the dining room table, musket across his lap, surveying the distant road beyond the window. He missed his friend and appeared more withdrawn than usual.

"Just sparkling!" said William, as he entered the room. "If it isn't the prick end of the needle," he added, leaning against the door frame. "You meet a girl. You like her. She likes you. She's pretty, witty and charming. She has all her own teeth. Lips like roses and breath to match. Suddenly, bam! Your future ends up resting on the whim of the wife of The President of America. Go figure. A man to which yours truly is about as welcome as a squirrel is to a man who collects nuts and keeps said prized collection next to an open window facing a wood."

"I do not underztand," replied Volker, his sad eyes never moving from the window. "Andt now I do not haz Mr Carr to explain vhat you are talking about."

"It would appear that, indirectly, President Mandingelson has my nuts."

After a pleasant meal of chicken and boiled potatoes, with a cheese selection to finish, they packed what provisions they could carry and set off for the capital. William had assumed the house belonged to John but Chloe informed him otherwise. Like most property in the area, it had simply been abandoned. The owners, terrified by the distant sound of guns and the smell of cordite on the wind, had packed what valuables they could and headed off for the refuge of Salona.

With their bags packed, the gang contemplated the problem of John Lewis. Everyone stood quietly in the living room watching him snore like a baby on the sofa. They pondered what to do for the best.

"You leave him here he'll be killed," said Chloe. "The advancing British will murder him in his sleep."

"That's settled then," said William, as if she was offering a suggestion rather than stating a fact. "Seems to fit the bill," he added, clapping his hands.

"William!" protested Chloe, disappointed.

"What?" he queried, unsympathetic. "The drunken ape nearly shot my scalp off. What happens when he sobers up and get's his eye in?"

John was carried unconscious to his horse where his hands and feet were bound. He was secured to the saddle with ropes across his lap that would prevent him rolling off until he woke.

The group set off along Washington Road with Volker leading the appaloosa by its reins. William and Chloe followed behind them with Samuel and the stable hands bringing up the rear. There was no longer the need to hide from scouts. Chloe and Lewis' presence offered an obvious validity to their presence. William spent the two mile journey talking about himself, his rather splendid house, and how he missed his pet lion. Chloe hung on every word, even through his rather graphic description of George devouring a gardener.

"You can't blame the lion, of·course," said William, spraying himself with a fine mist of Wild Scabbard. "Think of it like an afternoon snack."

The Maryland countryside was deserted. They never saw another living soul except for a few cows grazing in a nearby field. Volker joked that Cockburn and Ross would likely be having steak that night. The peace was shattered though, the moment they caught sight of the Washington Turnpike.

"What the devil!" shouted Lewis, waking with a start. The group stopped in their tracks and congregated about his horse.

"Fear not, John Lewis," urged Chloe, touching his leg. "These men are not British. You are being taken to the safety of the capital. See?" She pointed to the wooden building at the turnpike gate where the sign read 'Washington'. Volker slipped a blade from his belt and held it to the rope that secured John into his saddle. He paused waiting to gauge William's reaction. "These men are loyal to The President," said Chloe. "Do they have your word that you will be calm?"

John reluctantly nodded his agreement and after William gave Volker the nod, the ropes were cut. After loosening himself from the remainder of his bindings, John Lewis slipped his hand into his rifle sheath. Volker quickly grabbed his musket and took aim. There was a moment of unease as all eyes flicked from one to the other. Slowly, John withdrew his hand from the sheath. Instead of brandishing a musket, however, he produced an almost empty bottle of scotch. All sighed with relief.

"Medicine," said John, popping out the cork with his teeth.

It was dusk by the time the party found themselves walking down Maryland Avenue. The straight, tree-lined street was bounded by a scattering of deserted houses and boarded up businesses. There was nothing between the buildings but marsh and scrubland. The wide avenue itself was littered with belongings. People had been in such a hurry to leave that they hadn't bothered stopping for whatever fell from their carts. There was even an animal carcass or two. Poor creatures mistaken for British scouts in the confusion of darkness.

"This is a joke, one presumes?" asked William, stepping around a dead cow. "This is The President's great vision?"

"Every great place gotta start somewhere," grunted John, as he finished off the last of his scotch.

"I'm not surprised everyone has split," William added. "I'm filled with the urge to follow them."

"Not everyvone." Volker said, resting a hand on his pistol." Ve are being vatched!"

"I don't see anyone," said William, glancing at the empty houses.

Volker stopped in his tracks and studied the straight road ahead. Something was approaching them. A distant shape gradually became visible. There was the sound of approaching hooves and the rattling of cart wheels. Less than a minute later, a horse and heavily laden trap charged past with no intention of stopping. The man driving lashed the reins as he held his wife tightly around her waist.

"Are the British far?" he cried, as they approached.

"Bladensburg," shouted John Lewis, as the cart passed by. "What of the militia?" he asked, but never received a reply. The cart quickly vanished into darkness and the scene fell silent once more.

The further the group travelled into the heart of the capital, the more people they fleeing. One young woman ran to John Lewis and thrust her open locket towards him.

"Have you seen him?" she begged. "Have you seen my husband!" She repeated his name and description as she rushed to show the locket to everyone in the group.

Some residents were busy nailing closed their window shutters whilst others packed what they could onto whatever they had with the wheels or hooves to move it. Just like it had been with Bladensburg the previous night, the locals were confused and terrified.

Capitol Hill itself towered over them with the massive The Capitol Building situated proudly at the top. Its huge dome and Corinthian columns doffing it's hat only to the grandeur of St Peter's in Rome. Scattered around the building itself hundreds of militiamen were lounging on the grass without order or discipline. Many had been drinking and small pockets of fighting broke out. As William and the party headed towards Pennsylvania Avenue, they passed groups of residents arguing at the top of their voices.

"Madison has failed us!" one cried.

"He's a coward!" shouted another.

"It's not one man's fault!" cried someone else.

William, of course, knew differently. He knew Madison had gambled on the British being too stretched fighting his Uncle Boney to care about a silly war with America. The gamble had failed catastrophically. Madison had declared war without the stability of a central bank to fund it or a regular army to fight it. Whilst Britain's forces remained weakened from engagement across the globe, the Americans could just about hold their own. That had changed though thanks to William pulling the Peel plug on financial support to his Uncle Boney's European campaign. Boney's subsequent abdication meant the British could finally devote their resources to kicking Madison's backside inside out. William, of course, had forgotten all about his part in events. America might have started the war to show it had a place on the world stage but Cockburn was about to bring down the curtain. Washington residents were right to feel vulnerable. There was an army heading their way that they couldn't stop and after Bladensburg fell, Madison, and the other leaders, feared Washington would be next.

"You can't tell me that ain't a vision." said John Lewis, pointing his empty whisky bottle up at the House of Representatives.

"I'm suspicious of all architects who use domes." William replied. "They were obviously left on the teat too long or not held enough by their nannies."

As William and the party made their way up Pennsylvania Avenue towards The President's House,

Volker picked up a flyer that the wind had blown against his leg. On it was a picture of Cockburn with the caption, 'Death to the British'.

All the shops and businesses they passed were boarded up. Even The National Intelligencer building, which, ironically, had a headline stuck to the window claiming that the capital was safe. Volker smiled when he spotted it and he nudged the stable hands' attention to it.

It wasn't long before the party found themselves at the 15th street bend where the avenue was interrupted by the grounds of what later became known as The White House. The grounds, like Capitol Hill, were grassed and peppered with trees and grazing sheep. Save for a low stone boundary wall along the roadside, and a very flimsy looking post and rail fence that bounded the drive, there was little in the way of an obstruction to any advancing force. The drive to the front of the property was busy with house staff loading belongings onto carts.

The house was clearly going to be abandoned and everything of value was being stripped out. The grass around the house itself was littered with pockets of militiamen who were being heckled by groups of irate residents. The locals protested that the militia were on their backsides drinking and not keeping the British from their doors. Tempers grew as argument turned to anger and fights erupted out of sheer frustration.

The President's House was neo-classical in form with its pediment topped windows to the ground floor and the cornice and parapet around the roofline. Unlike the House of

Representatives, The President's House was altogether more modest. William was surprised that there was no columned portico nor grand entrance to shield residents or visitors from the rain. Instead, there was simply a small stone bridge spanning the path serving the lower ground floor. The bridge met the front doors in the middle of a row of four columns with a pediment above. The pediment, William noted, was without a scene depicted in the freeze. Very cheaply done, he was quick to point out to Chloe.

William suggested that Volker, Samuel and the hands wait outside as he, John and Chloe visit The President. William's thinking was that John and the fair Chloe's presence might warm The President's spirits. It appeared logical as John was from such a respected family and Chloe was a close family friend. This was preferable to the likely look of fear on his face as Volker's massive frame ducked under his doorway. Not to mention the likelihood of Madison retching up his stomach contents when he caught the scent of Samuel's britches.

William, John and Chloe made their way up the stone steps to the north entrance. They were passed by a line of staff hurrying by with files. Once one cart had been filled, the driver would crack the reins and be off in a cloud of dust. The next cart in line would then quickly draw forward. William was about to step through the front doors when he had to move aside quickly as three young men ran past carrying a pair of long, velvet curtains.

The entrance hall of the house was a hive of activity as staff with step ladders removed pictures and portraits from the walls of the grand Cross Hall. The Cross Hall was the east-west corridor that supported the floor above via a row of Doric columns.

The scene reminded William of a painting of the French Revolution that Uncle Boney had given his father that hung in the library of Peel Manor. The painting was a depiction of peasants looting some noble French house and making off in all directions with anything that appeared valuable. There was a naivety to the place too. William Peel, a stranger in the land, had arrived unchallenged at The President's own house. If this had been Peel Manor, William told Chloe, an unwelcome stranger wouldn't get past the gatehouse let alone be able to get into the hall. If he had, he would soon be stopped by Able and escorted away by the collar, quizzed with great intensity by Mother, or eaten by George.

William was glancing at the many doors in turn and pondering where to look first when Madison's raised voice echoed from a room to their left. It was the East Room, a vast, bright space that covered the full depth of the house and almost a quarter of the width. William entered to find Madison engaged in a debate with three men. One was General John Armstrong, the Secretary of War. Armstrong was mid fifties with wispy grey hair to the sides of his head but almost completely bald in the centre. The other man was the Secretary of State, James Monroe. Monroe was also mid fifties, grey haired and had a strong, muscular jaw. William recognised Winder, of course, who was rubbing his stressed temples and lost in contemplation. They were on their own in the room. All furniture had been removed except a large piano that stood near the front windows. It was presumably too large to move in a hurry and unlikely to be a popular choice with looters. The men were standing around the fireplace to the rear of the house and were so engaged in their own business that none sensed William or the others enter. It was then William noticed the brightly coloured bird which was caged in the corner behind him. It was a parrot, if he remembered correctly from Franny's pop-up book of birds.

"How extraordinary!" William whispered to Chloe upon sight of it. He approached the bird despite strong objection from Chloe.

Meanwhile, Madison, Armstrong, Monroe and Winder debated the future of Washington oblivious of their presence.

"I say we hold the capital," said Armstrong, "fortify what we can. Dig in deep."

"Oh, for heaven's sake!" blasted Monroe, "and watch as the British take everything around us? The city is too vast to hold completely."

"Then we hold up in The Capitol Building," replied Armstrong"

"They'd starve us out in a day," snapped Monroe, with impatience.

"We have loyal militia," said Armstrong, with passion, "who will fight to the death."

"It's already lost," replied Monroe, "and we both know why," he added, his jaw tense.

"No," sighed Madison, despondent, placing his hand

on the mantel for support. "I could never have believed it had I not witnessed with my own eyes the scenes of this day. The difference between the professional soldier and our militia is vast."

The room fell silent in contemplation. A silence which was shattered by a bird squawking in distress and the sound of its wings flapping against the cage bars. Madison and the party turned at once to see William with his fingers trapped in the cage and the bird flapping so violently that the cage rocked on its hanger. William cried in pain then began prodding the bird with a pearl handled comb.

"Casse-tio," squawked the creature as its feathers were flying off in all directions

Madison rushed over and, as Monroe and Armstrong held the cage, he yanked William's hand free.

"You!" exclaimed Madison with surprise, as he suddenly recognised William.

Chloe ran distraught to Winder for a hug as William clutched his bleeding fingers and cursed the bird.

"What the hell are you doing here?" Madison demanded.

"Extending the Peel hand of support," William replied, pained. "That was until this buzzard took a dislike to it." He was about to add something about John Lewis but turned to find he had vanished.

"It's a macaw!" Madison snapped, angrily. "And I asked what you are doing here? I thought you made your feelings on America clear when we met."

"I'm surprised to find one carnivorous," said William,

sucking a finger. "I thought they liked seeds and fruit, that sort of thing."

"Will you forget about my damn pet!" Madison growled.

"I invited him," said Winder, unwrapping himself from Chloe's embrace. "Lord Peel graciously excepted."

"But why?" asked Madison, closing the gap on William who recoiled. "Why are you facing all this death and danger to be here now in my house?" He studied William's eyes for a clue. "Is it your wish to witness me driven out?"

"Oh, don't be an ass!" William scoffed. "I'm here despite great personal peril. By invitation, I might add. And what do I get? The old 'Icelandic deltoid' from you and, unless I'm mistaken, a 'sod off' from your jumped-up canary."

"Please," said Madison, his stress levels rising. "Just leave us. We have to decide on a way forward. We are much vexed by the events of this day."

"Then perhaps a song?" asked William, indicating to the piano. "Yes, some rousing number to lift one's spirits. 'To Anacreon in heaven'. Do you know it?"

Madison didn't reply. Instead, he and the others just walked away. William was contemplating taking his boot to the ungrateful oaf but Chloe's pleading eyes tempered his white hot rage. The last thing she needed when she was about to seek marriage counsel was to have her prospective husband grip someone by the throat and tan their backside. Especially as the said someone was The President of America.

"Ta Gueule," squawked the Parrot, as William turned

to leave the room. William, checking Madison wasn't looking, shook his fist at the macaw and gave it one last jab through the bars with his comb. The bird flapped again violently but by the time Madison had turned to look, William was long gone.

Leaving Chloe to take counsel with Dolly Madison, William took a few breaths of evening air. He stood by the front door for a moment watching the staff hurry about. He then spotted John Lewis on the drive talking to an ageing Naval officer.

"What happened to you?" demanded William, as he approached. "I turned around and you'd vanished like snow on a white door."

"I suddenly realised I wasn't drunk enough to listen to the prattle of politicians."

"Oh, sparkling!" said William. "Well, are you drunk enough for whatever you're scheming now?"

"Almost," he replied. "Captain Tingley here has something he needs destroying."

"Big stuff is it?" William enquired, with a devilish glint in his eye.

"They don't come much bigger, sir," responded Tingley.

"Sparkling," said William, with a grin. "We Peels are experts where destruction is concerned!"

Sabotage at the Ship Yard

William clung to the open carriage for dear life as it charged through the crowds around Capitol Hill. The driver was one Captain Thomas Tingley who cracked the reins and barked at the horses as if the devil himself were in pursuit. Despite being in his sixties, Tingley had lost nothing of his thirst for action. His eyes steeled as he shouted at anyone in their path to clear aside.

With the wind drying his eyes, William glanced over his shoulder to see Volker, Samuel and the hands in the back, bracing themselves against anything solid. Even John Lewis looked worried as he brushed the wind swept hair from his face. The cart picked up even more speed down Capitol Street as Tingley lashed again at the backs of the horses that were already glistening with sweat. It was at that point that William had an inkling of their destination. He could see the flag flying over the harbour and the towering buildings of the boatyard in the distance.

As they thundered on through a residential district, locals dived clear to avoid being trampled. Making a sharp turn right, Tingley drew back tightly on the reins and brought the horses, hooves skidding, to a sudden stop. Within a moment, he had leapt from his seat and was urging everyone else to do the same.

They followed Tingley down some steps and through a door that led into the huge boat shed. It was a white, lattice sided building big enough to build a warship in. He quickly grabbed a couple of lanterns from the wall and lit them. Passing one to Volker, he set off running again. Beyond the shed was the jetty itself and the slipway which dropped down to the river. Tingley led them down some wide steps to the boatyard. The yard was surrounded by large stores and work sheds. Tingley passed his light to John Lewis then approached one of the stores. With great purpose, he pulled at one of the massive sliding doors. Much to his frustration, it was immovable.

"Blast!" he cursed, in his polite English accent. "Perhaps if we could all take purchase?" he asked. Volker stepped forward and indicated that the good captain should move aside. "It's slipped off the runners," said Tingley, as Volker's thick fingers slipped into the gap between the doors. "It will take four of us." He silenced once the door started screeching open.

The whole group then recoiled in fear as their lanterns illuminated the contents. The shed was packed with gun-powder kegs which were piled from floor to rafters. There were hundreds of tonnes. Enough explosives to put a hole in the world let alone level a shipyard.

"He built the yard," said John, as he leaned into William's shoulder. "Captain Tingley's life's work is what you see around you."

"Which is why it falls on me," said Tingley. "To undo what it has taken my all to do."

"Zen vhy?" Volker asked.

"William Burns is why," replied Tingley, with a sigh. "The Secretary of the Navy deems the yard a risk. It could be used as a base by the British to repair their ships." Tingley rubbed his neck and sighed as Volker pushed back the other door. "Madison's decision to retreat," Tingley continued, "has effectively given Washington away. You ever heard of such a thing? For a country to abandon its capital without a fight. What would Washington himself say, hey John? That not one American will stand and fight when the British come."

John's jaw tensed and his knuckles whitened. "Is there nothing to drink in this blasted place!" he cursed, wetting his lips.

"America needs every man sober," Tingley replied, with a sympathetic smile. "This is our darkest hour."

Tingley grabbed a sack cart from the shadows and began loading barrels. Volker and John stepped forward to help and William indicated that the stable hands should do so as well. When Samuel stepped forward, William slapped him around the ear and yanked him back by his collar.

"Not with your track record," he said. "You keep your hands in your pockets and your eyes on your shoes." William paused, staring down at Samuel's bare feet. "Where are your shoes, anyway?"

"They fell off," replied Samuel.

"Oh, well keep your eyes on your grubby, webbed feet then." William ordered.

For almost forty minutes, the gang worked themselves into a lather. Each of them carried barrels and piled them in the sail loft, the sawmill, and the paint shop. It seemed endless. Hundreds of tonnes of powder was moved. Even when the other buildings were set with enough powder for the job, the main store looked only half-empty. William had found a bottle of port in the office and decided to observe proceeding from a comfortable chair.

"Best drink this before Mr Lewis finds it," he said, watching Samuel pour him a glass. "Don't want him blowing a gale again."

"Angry man," said Samuel.

"Yes, well," replied William, looking disappointed at his right boot. "What say you try and get a shine on these?"

As Samuel knelt and buffed away eagerly at William's boot with his sleeve, William reclined. His tired mind soon wandered to the fair Chloe. "I have asked for Chloe's hand," he said, indicating to Samuel that he had missed a patch on his heel. "And before your simian-like intellect takes that to mean 'her actual hand', I am, of course, referring to marriage."

"Pretty lady," replied Samuel, touching himself.

"Yes, quite enough of that," said William, sternly. "I don't want you to do that again, understand? Good. Ah, I can't wait to see Mother's expression when Chloe first steps from the carriage at Peel Manor. A very proud day indeed for W.E.P."

William watched as Tingley started cracking open the tops of a dozen barrels that had been piled on a cart. He then climbed up and kicked them over. As the powder poured out onto the ground, the stable hands pulled the cart towards the jetty where two ships, the Argus and Columbia, were moored. It wasn't long before there was a train of powder all the way to the two naval ships. Volker and John were each making a powder train from the ship's magazine up onto the deck to complete the fuses. Each of the building's had a powder train that converged in the middle of the yard. All it needed was one spark and the order to make it.

By approximately 7.45pm all necessary preparations were complete and as daylight failed, Tingley climbed a ladder to light the three large lanterns that hung on high brackets. Just as he had lit the last, a horseback messenger charged into the yard. Conscious of the fuses, Volker quickly grabbed the horse's reins and pulled it to a stop.

"A message from the Secretary, sir," came the messenger's breathless news. "Do not light the yard. There is still hope. Hold out as long as you deem appropriate."

"What of The President?" asked William.

"Still at home, sir," the messenger replied, patting his horse's neck. "He is to dine with his senior staff."

"And the British?" asked John Lewis.

"No news, sir," the messenger replied, taking back the reins. "The streets are silent save for a few stubborn residents. I must haste. Goodnight gentlemen," he added, eager to be off. "May God keep you safe this night."

As the messenger charged away, William inspected the lustre to his boot toes then pushed Samuel into Volker's grip. "Mr Tingle, if you have no objections I would like use of your carriage to return to The President. I have urgent business to conclude before the British arrive and cock their leg."

Tingley raised no objection, despite William getting his name wrong, and after everyone had shaken hands, except William, of course, the party made their way back up the steps towards the road.

Washington was a very different sight from that of an hour before. The darkness cast strange shadows in the deserted streets. Houses without shutters were crudely boarded and distant sounds of smashing glass and hurried feet meant only one thing, looting. The militiamen who had lost their homes, and worse at the hands of the advancing British, were exacting their own revenge on the rich families of the capital.

It was almost dark when William drew up outside The Presidential House and Madison himself was loading some official papers into a cart by lantern light. Madison glanced at the party in the carriage and gave a subtle nod of respect and recognition to John Lewis. He blanked William completely.

"Going somewhere?" asked William, as he slipped from the carriage seat.

"Not yet," Madison replied, with disdain, "but my personal papers are, yes."

"And Chloe?" enquired William, peering past him for signs of her inside. "She's quite enchanting by moonlight I imagine."

"She's inside, yes," said Madison, his demeanour even frostier than William remembered.

"I'll just say a quick hello," said William, indicating he was about to head off walking. Madison, however, had other plans.

"I have considered your position," said Madison, stepping across William's path. "I will, no doubt, be judged for events that have unfolded here. I cannot change what is already done. I can, however, change what is not yet done. And to offer you land or see Tornbridge profit one dime more off this fair country is an error I can correct. So too your proposal of marriage to Chloe. A proposition that leaves me angry."

"Rot!" William scoffed, "have you completely lost yourself?"

Madison took a step towards him and casually revealed a pistol on his belt. It was a subtle threat, which William failed to recognise. Volker, on the other hand, did not and quietly cocked his musket.

"What?" queried William, pointing at Madison's jacket lining. "Am I expected to comment on the cheap tailoring?"

Madison swept the hem of his jacket behind the pistol and rested his palm on the pearl handle.

"Oh, I see," William said, spotting the weapon. "This is some kind of tough talk, is it? Predatory aggression. What next? Will you be beating your chest and urinating up my britches?"

"You are hence forth banished," Madison said. "On pain of death."

"Oh don't talk such claptrap, you halfwit!" said William, moving around him to go inside. "I intend to see Chloe even if it means treading on your fat head."

Madison drew his pistol and levelled it at William's chest. Volker quickly moved to a firing position, but immediately felt John Lewis's pistol press against his temple and be cocked.

"Of all the rudeness," said William, as he glanced about at the standoff. "Well, if this isn't the steam off the potty. Very impolite, Muddyson. Poor form, I have to say."

"Is it not 'impolite' to prey on innocent women?" questioned Madison, cocking his pistol. "Just as their suitor's are away serving their country?"

"No!" William casually replied.

"To unbalance her mind with your lion, jewels, and portly frame?" continued Madison.

"Leave my portly frame out of this!" said William.

"To molest a man's innocent bird?" Madison went on.

"It told me to sod off!"

"By God, sir, you are the worst kind of scoundrel," said Madison, fighting the urge to shoot him. "Mr Lewis?" he called.

"Yes, Mr President?"

"Are you sober?"

"Yes, sir, I am."

"And do you love your country and the values for which it stands?" questioned Madison.

"Yes, sir, and I hate cruelty to animals."

"Oh for heaven sake," William cut in, sensing this was

all building to something unpleasant. "I only jabbed the damn thing with a blasted comb. It bit me. See? What of cruelty to lords?"

"Mr Lewis," Madison requested, "please take this turd off my lawn and escort him to the Washington Road Turnpike."

"Yes, sir."

"And Lord Peel," added Madison, uncocking his pistol. "If I see you again, even so much as a glance, I will not be responsible for my actions. Am I clear on that?"

"No, not really," replied William, causing Madison's eyes to widen. "What if I see you tomorrow when I pop back early to see Chloe?"

Madison bared his teeth. His jaw shivered with anger. "WHAT!" he exclaimed, only moments from combustion.

This time it was William and his party, not John Lewis, who was bound by the wrists and feet and tied to a horse. It's fair to say that the Peels were rarely banished. Especially as banishing a Peel meant also banishing their fortune. Most people were not so stupid as to stand firmly on their principles.

It was pitch black as they trotted back up Maryland Avenue towards the turnpike. John Lewis followed behind them on his trusty appaloosa checking the empty whisky bottle in his rifle holster with the hope it had perhaps a few drops left he had missed.

"You as rich as they say?" Lewis asked William. "How does someone get so rich?"

William had it in mind to ignore the question but something was just niggling him. It wasn't the fact that he had been bound against his will, he was getting strangely accustomed to that, it was something fundamental. He was in America on business. It was a fair business and, as such, he was aggrieved that he was being treated in such a fashion by a man who knocked on his door only a matter of months earlier and flashed his threadbare pockets.

"Breeding," replied William, with a pleasing sarcasm. "Without breeding, well, I don't know. There are books, of course, if it's possible to improve the common mind."

"I don't need no book," Lewis laughed. "I don't hear the jingle jangle of American land in those pockets of yours."

"A mere glitch," William replied. "Nothing, more. When President Mudelson reflects on his decision, well, he will be back on a boat to Tornbridge faster than he can say 'good lord, am I on a boat to Tornbridge already'. Mark my words there's about to be a sudden change in fortune where William E. Peel is concerned. We Peels have a nose for such things."

"Well," replied Lewis, smiling at William's bluster. "I'd sure like to drink to that," he said, tossing the empty bottle into the gutter.

They had got a few hundred yards out of the capital itself when suddenly they were stopped in their tracks. Ahead, armed militiamen appeared from around the houses with lanterns aloft. John Lewis turned in the saddle to see the same number of militia behind them; they were surrounded. A dozen muskets suddenly cocked in unison. Volker's huge arms tensed so much that his bindings creaked but they were still too strong to break. William couldn't make out faces behind the lantern light but as they stepped closer he saw one face he knew. It was Eli of Barney's flotilla. The man who threatened to cut his throat at Bladensburg.

"Nice evening," said Eli, spitting out his chewing tobacco. "What's going on here, John?" he said, petting the neck of the appaloosa.

"Long story, Eli," John Lewis replied. "By The President's orders, these men are banished."

"Banished huh?" queried Eli, casually. "They must have made all kinds of nuisance, right?" he sniggered with more menace than merriment.

"Somethin' like that," Lewis replied, warily.

"That there dandy fella is one William Peel," said Eli, pointing with his musket. "That man shot and damn neared killed Joshua Barney."

On hearing this, the militiamen stepped in closer and steadied their aims. A smile spread across Volker's lips at the thought of his old friend. Carr, it would appear, had almost got his revenge.

"Yah!" cried Samuel, suddenly, and dug in his heels with a mind to galloping off but his horse remained still. "Run!" he shouted, rocking in the saddle as all eyes fell on him with bewilderment. "It won't move," he called to William. "Let's just run away." Eli quickly approached Samuel and knocked him unconscious with the butt of his musket.

"I suggest you go on, John," said Eli, walking back to John Lewis. "It's my business now. I'll say you let them go beyond the Turnpike gate. My friends here watched you do it."

Eli stepped forward to Volker and cracked him too in the temple with his musket butt. He was surprised when it didn't knock him out. Volker just shook his vision straight.

"I got orders, Eli," said Lewis, shuffling in his saddle, "and there ain't none higher."

"These men are cowards, John," said Eli, spitting again. "Playing one side 'gainst 'tother."

"Untie zese," replied Volker, offering up his hands, "and ve'll see who iz za coward."

"Oh, you had your chance for a fair fight in Bladensburg big fella," said Eli, approaching him, "but you scurried 'cross river instead of charging the bridge like the British." He took two more cracks at Volker's skull before he eventually knocked him out.

"You go, John," said Eli, beckoning to one of his men who tossed him a half drunk bottle of whisky. "You don't need to see this." He offered the bottle to Lewis.

John Lewis watched the group for a moment. His lips moistened at the thought of the cold bottle neck touching them. All eyes fixed on his in the flicking light of the lanterns. Waiting. Wondering. They watched as he weighed up his duty against a bottle of God knows what percentage proof. Wetting his lips once more, Lewis snatched the bottle from Eli's grip.

"I'd rather be drunk in hell than sober in heaven," John Lewis barked. He then turned his appaloosa around with a yank on the reins and galloped off into the darkness.

When he was gone, Eli signalled his men and each stepped up and knocked out the rest of William's group. As they slumped one by one on their horses, Eli turned to William and flashed him a smile blackened with tobacco. "I'm gonna go to war on you, son. You got a debt to pay." And without waiting for an answer, he cracked William on the side of his head too

William came to with a screaming noise in his ear and an unbearable headache worse than any Spanish wine he could remember. His eyes could focus on nothing at first just a haze that seemed to match the screaming. He slowly gathered his senses. There was a sack over his head, which smelled of bread. He was tied to chair arms by the wrists. He was inside a building. There were floorboards beneath his feet, creaking with the movement about him. There was a lantern to his top left. He could make out shapes through the cloth. Some people in the room were talking. Others were whispering. It was then William heard it. It was a noise that dried his mouth in an instant. The sound of steel being dragged across steel as two knives were drawn against each other.

"You hear that?" came Eli's voice, unexpectedly at William's ear. "You hear how sharp that sounds?" William felt the point of a knife touch his leg. "You feel that, huh? You feel the very point of the blade?"

"What kind of man?" asked William, sternly, "binds a man powerless to a chair then threatens his britches. If it's money you want then state your terms and stop all these juvenile theatrics." William yelped as Eli stuck the knife into his leg at least an inch. It was deep, so deep there was a squelching noise as Eli pulled it out. William gritted his teeth with the pain and struggled against his bindings. His efforts were useless and Eli knew it.

"This is what awaits the British," said Eli, as he brought the cold blade up to William's throat. William felt the steel press hard onto his skin and burn as it was readied for the big cut.

Suddenly, a far away noise was carried through the window on a breeze. It was the sound of a military drummer. The lanterns quickly clattered shut and the room fell into darkness. William felt the blade vanish from his throat. There were whispers amongst the militia and the sound of movement about the room. Outside, the drums got louder and louder. William knew in an instant what it was but also couldn't believe he felt thrilled to hear it. It was the British Army. He could hear the militia taking action. He could feel the energy in the room rise. Something momentous was about to happen.

"Wait!" urged William, sternly. "Those drums offer parley. If you fire you will discount the chance for any terms."

"What do I care of terms?" said Eli, as he cocked his musket. "There's only a handful of 'em."

The room suddenly filled with the cracks of muskets and the smell of spent powder. Outside there was a scream. Someone was hit. Then another. Excitement spread amongst the militia as Eli and his confederates were filled with a blood lust.

"FIRE!" came a call from outside. It was an Irish voice that William recognised immediately. It was Major Ross himself. In an instant, the room was peppered with shots and thuds as the militiaman were hit. William struggled against his bindings as he could hear the groans of men writhing on the floor from their injuries. Outside there was a call of "ceasefire" and William leaned forward to see if he could pull free the sack from his face. With his head as low as it would go, he grimaced as his hands stretched up, touching the cotton with the tips of his fingers but not enough to find purchase. After a minute of effort, he gave up with a frustrated sigh.

"Volker?" William called out as loud as he dare "Samuel? Stable hands, whatever your names are, are you alive?"

"Yes," came a series of replies.

William was about to say something else when the room was filled with another volley of shots. This time hundreds, thousands it seemed. A never ending shower of lead that whizzed and whistled about their heads. William closed his eyes as tight as he could as shrapnel of all sizes rained about them. The noise outside was like the New Year's Eve fireworks displays they used to have on at Peel Manor. It ended a minute later and silence followed. The room stank of dust and smoke. The air was so thick with it that William and the rest coughed and wretched. What William heard next had him scrabbling with increased effort at the sack on his head.

"Congreve's if you please, Lieutenant Scott," shouted Ross.

William finally tore the sack from his head and what he saw he could hardly believe. The entire room was riddled with holes but not a single shot had hit them. He stood up with the chair still attached and turned to see the others glancing about in shock at the miracle. Without a moment to lose, they all hobbled out over the bodies and onto the landing. Still attached to the chairs, they thundered down the stairs. An instant later, rockets were fired through every window behind them. In a blinding flash, the house shuddered and began disintegrating. All William and the gang could do was dash full speed for the back door as an avalanche of masonry and sparks showered down about them.

The group had got ten feet into the garden when there was a volley of shots ahead of them from the lawn. They had run straight into a unit of six British Red Coats. In a flash, Samuel dived in front of William and took a shot in the chest. From the light of the burning house behind them, William could see the group of Red Coats hastily reloading their muskets. William's world slowed as the feeling of dread washed over him. He knew that once the muskets were reloaded they would all be dead. He turned to see Volker charging, growling like a beast. Three soldiers toppled like skittles as his massive frame hit them full force. As Volker tumbled to the ground the other three Red Coats were on him with their bayonets. They stabbed him repeatedly as he writhed on the grass against his bindings. Like an upended turtle, he was powerless to defend himself.

Despite his own wound, William found the strength in his Peel legs and he too charged at the Red Coats, head down. The other three soldiers were on their feet again and levelling their muskets ready to meet William's advancing charge. He was less than six feet from the gleaming tips of their bayonets when the ground felt to give way beneath his feet with a rumble. Ahead of him, the soldiers looked uneasy too. In a sudden flash, the whole sky lit bright orange with the boom of some distant thunder. The soldiers, unsteadied by the shockwave, lowered their guard and William fell to the floor only inches from their bayonet tips.

Looking up, William could see huge fireballs blazing across the glowing night sky like comets. Moments later there was another explosion, then another soon after that. Each sending tremors through the ground like massive earthquakes. William turned to see Volker writhing on his back as he gasped for breath from his bleeding chest wounds.

"WAIT!" cried William, rolling onto his side. A moment later he felt a blade cut his bindings and two British soldiers pulled him to his feet.

"The Americans are destroying their own ships," said Cockburn, greeting William with a smile.

"Never mind, you ass!" replied William, wearily. "Look

what you've done to my captain."

"Major Ross?" shouted Cockburn, straightening. "These men aren't to die, understand?"

Looking back to the house, William could see Samuel being cut from his chair.

"I fear we may be too late," Ross replied, as Samuel rolled lifeless onto his back.

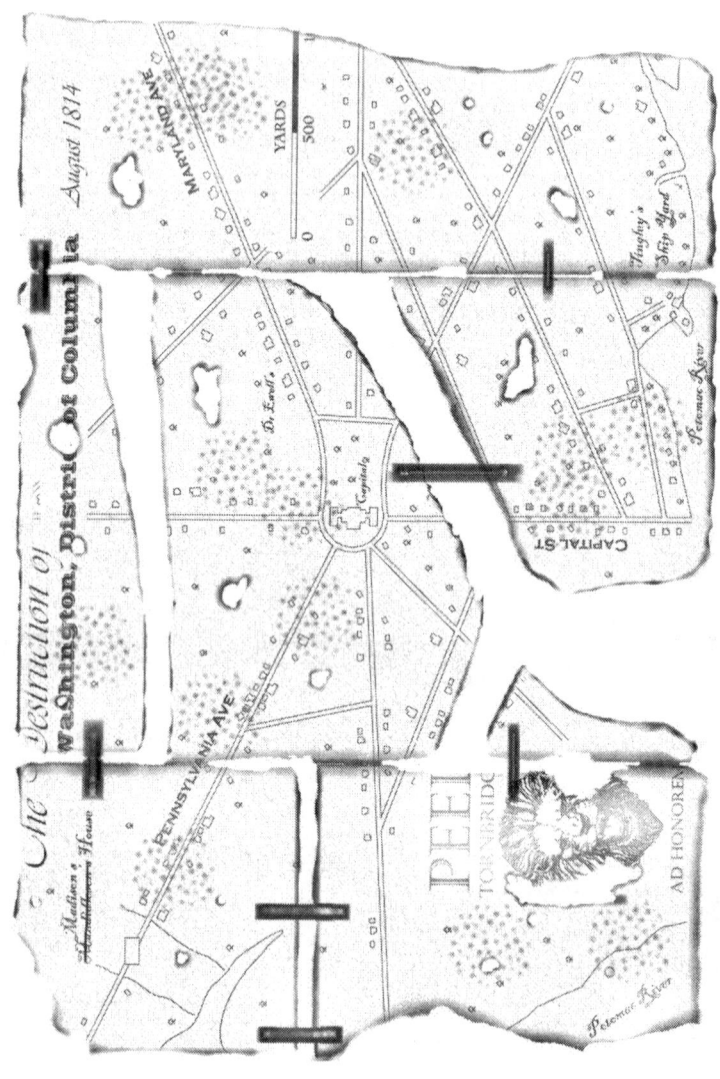

Washington Ablaze

William limped alongside Cockburn as they climbed the grass embankment of Capitol Hill. The fire from the naval shipyard was spreading to adjoining buildings and growing so bright it was like daytime for Cockburn's men. Cockburn stopped on a flat section of ground and turned to watch the troops below on the street as they fell into rank and file. They comprised of the 3rd infantry brigade, marines, seaman and most of the 21st Foot. Upwards of one and half thousand men. Most had not seen action and the earlier militia attack under parley had dispelled any conscience about laying siege to the capital.

Tingley's sabotage was perhaps a little too effective, thought William, as he watched embers from the shipyard fire dance across the nearby rooftops. Another thought then struck him. What of the fair Chloe? He hoped to God she couldn't see him. It would certainly put into question his allegiances if she were to see him shoulder to shoulder with none other than Admiral Cockburn.

For the first time in his adventure, William was on his own. Volker and Samuel had been stretchered off by medics and William had ordered the stable hands to stay with them.

Had William been a smarter man, he would have probably realised the precarious position this put him in. As it was, it didn't enter his head that without Volker and Carr, he had no personal guard. What's more, William was back in Washington against the express orders of The President and, if that wasn't dangerous enough, he was there as a guest of the invading army. It was no wonder that he felt the most peculiar sensation of being watched. Cockburn, as it happened, had felt it too and immediately beckoned Major Ross up the hill.

"Yes, sir?" replied Ross, approaching.

"Make a search. Every building."

"To what purpose, sir?"

"Anyone found with weapons will have their houses torched."

Ross saluted his reply and set off back down the hill to gather troops for the task. Cockburn was then silent as he soaked up the magnificence of the situation. The British had reached the soil of Capitol Hill and their flag flapped gently in the wind above it. Cockburn could have been forgiven for a moment of smugness considering the historic implications of his achievement. William, however, failed to be impressed on account of his throbbing leg wound.

"Is this it?" asked William, adjusting his field dressing. "Fingers crossed for you having a shiny new medal, but," he paused, catching Cockburn's eye, "it's all a little tedious."

"Tedious?" Cockburn enquired, puzzled.

"Quite so." William paused, sensing Cockburn was not impressed with his summary. "The truth is, you've come here all dressed up and there's no one to impress." Cockburn's stony-faced expression suddenly cracked into a chortle.

"These men don't do 'tedious'," he replied. "If you're up for the climb, I'll show you what they do."

Cockburn led William up the hill and around to the front of the Capitol Building itself. It was impressive for its time, especially close up. It comprised two wings, Senate and House, either side of a central rotunda. The grandeur of the upper two floors was represented by Corinthian pilasters (columns built into the facade). It wasn't the architecture that brought a sudden lump to William's throat, however, rather the hundreds of British troops positioned facing the building with their muskets aimed. Cockburn casually nodded to an officer who responded with a salute and a loud call of "FIRE!" The troops opened up with a volley of shots. Sparks exploded from the stonework as glass shattered and tumbled down the side of the building. Moments later, a second wave of shots rang out. Cockburn observed the building with a spyglass to check for signs of life. There were none. The place was left without guard.

"Right!" shouted Cockburn, sliding shut his spyglass. "Let's be in then."

Within a few seconds, the heavy front doors were hanging off their hinges. With a resounding cheer, a group of marines rushed into the inner rotunda with their muskets poised. A few moments later, the cry of "SECURE!" came from inside.

Although the grand, neoclassical architecture was lost on the common foot soldiers, for the senior officers it was like a sightseeing trip. Once inside, they dispersed to tour the great halls and chambers with their lanterns aloft.

"Still finding things tedious?" Cockburn asked William, as they stepped inside the rotunda. "Do be careful of the broken glass, wont you." He headed off, hands clasped loosely behind his back, through the high doors to the west wing.

William turned to find the stable hands waving at him from across the room. They indicated his attention to two stretchers making their way through the crowd of troops. William walked over as Samuel and Volker's injured bodies were directed to a young medical officer.

"Are you a doctor?" enquired William, as the young officer, Palmer, was clearing off a table and indicating the men be placed there.

"I intend to be, sir," replied Palmer, beckoning forward an even younger looking officer. "The Admiral wants a report," said Palmer, and the younger officer quickly took out his notepad and pencil.

Volker was conscious, barely, but covered with blood that appeared to seep from all over his body. "Multiple puncture wounds," said Palmer, indicating that he wanted that noting. He then ripped Volker's leather waistcoat open sending the buttons scattering across the polished wooden floor. "Jesus!" he whispered, when he saw the extent of the injuries. "Get him clean!" he ordered, to the men who stretchered them in. "Keep pressure on the wounds!"

Palmer then moved to Samuel and tore open his tunic to reveal a bleeding hole just below his ribs. Unlike Volker,

Samuel was unconscious and already looking grey. "Roll him!" he ordered, and he checked Samuel's back to see if the shot had gone through. It hadn't. "Musket shot stuck behind the ribs," he commented to the officer taking notes. "I'll need to operate," Palmer concluded, "but not here."

"Will he live?" asked the gaunt stable hand, full of concern.

"I don't know," replied Palmer, washing his blood soaked hands in a bowl of water. "It's in God's hands more than mine."

"He'll heal," said William, spotting a small leather bound notebook poking from Samuel's inside pocket. "Even rice pudding has the wit to get a skin on it."

The last time William had seen the notebook it had been in the cage at Bowman's fort; the evening he and Samuel had swapped clothes. The clearest memory William had of the book was how vehemently Samuel guarded it. William was just about to reach for it when a voice cut his train of thought.

"That will need stitching, sir," said Palmer, his eyes indicating to the wound in William's thigh.

"Quite so," said William, "but by a more skilled hand than you are blessed with," he added.

"Three stitches at most, sir, I assure you," Palmer replied.

"And what exactly do you know of pant repairs?" snapped William.

"None, sir," said Palmer, with a smile. "I'm talking about your leg."

"Oh, I see," said William, finally catching on. "Very well."

He took the notebook and began to flick through the pages. Most of the childlike images he didn't understand, and didn't really want to, but a few pages in he stopped. Samuel had added more drawings since William had last seen the book. There was a small picture of William and Samuel being dragged along by camels in the desert of North Africa. All figures, camels included, were depicted with smiles on their faces. The next page was an image of William and Samuel running through the woods at Bladensburg. The next, was William reading poetry to Samuel on *The Emily*. The last drawing was of William, George and Samuel. They were holding hands on the deck of *The Emily*, waving, as they were going home. At that instant, it struck William that Samuel hadn't seen his trip as a penance for the fire at Peel Manor. Samuel had had an adventure. Sadly, an adventure that was close to claiming his life.

"Bastard!" screamed William, suddenly, as he glanced down to see Palmer sewing his thigh.

Later, William followed Cockburn's route through the corridors of the Capitol Building and found the Admiral in the huge Hall of Representatives. Cockburn was lighting candles on one of the two lowered chandeliers.

"A tad more grandiose than the house of Commons?" he said over his shoulder at William. "Doesn't appear in keeping with republican simplicity, does it?"

William couldn't be bothered to enter some political

debate. Especially as political debate was far from his strongest subject. Instead, he pondered to himself why Cockburn would bother to light candles when the room was already lit well enough by the flames of the burning city clearly visible through the huge, shattered windows.

"How many slaves?" enquired Cockburn, "did it take to build such a place do you think?"

William remained silent. He wanted to note that it was no more ironic for a country to value liberty and freedom and celebrate such with a capital built by slaves than it was for the Admiral of the British Navy to question it. It was, after all, the British who were responsible for over half the Atlantic slave trade. Considering the Peel family business had profited handsomely by the slave trade over a long number of years, it also seemed ironic that Cockburn should ask William's view.

"How are your friends?" enquired Cockburn, as he blew out his match.

"Samuel makes more of it than it is, I'm sure," William replied, "but both require a surgeon's skill."

"Then we must not waste time," smiled Cockburn, with resolve.

At that moment, Lieutenant Scott entered in search of Cockburn. He was surprised to see William and threw him his usual glare of mistrust. "Still with us, I see, Lord Peel?"

"Quite so," replied William, with a false smile. "You haven't blown yourself up then by one of those damned noisy rockets?"

Scott was set to blaze into William with a barrage of ill-considered insults when Cockburn intervened.

"Lieutenant?" he queried, wise to the tensions. "Lord Peel and I were just discussing the beautiful architecture."

"Sir," replied Scott, with a salute. "What are your orders?"

Cockburn pondered for a moment. His eyes traced the craftsmanship poured into every fitting and fixture. "Burn it!" he replied, with a smile. "I'm sure the men would enjoy that."

Torching the Capitol Building wasn't as easy as Cockburn had thought. Several attempts were made to start fires without much success. Scott had tried firing Congreve rockets into the ceilings of both the Great Hall and the Senate Wing with no luck. He blamed the curtains for being too damp, the hardwood chairs for being too hard, and he even went as far as suggesting that the neighbouring fires were using up all the good air. William dismissed him for being an ass and left him to it. Cockburn, however, was far less jovial by the notion that it couldn't be put to flame.

William was enjoying a cheroot in the rotunda when Cockburn appeared. He was eagerly followed by Scott and it was clear that Cockburn was far from impressed with the progress. As they passed by, William suggested that the best course of action would be to fix up Samuel's injuries and let him have a crack.

"The fellow managed single handed to destroy my entire house and stables with just his backside and a small oil lamp."

"It won't hold a flame!" Scott explained, following Cockburn's purposeful strides through the entrance.

"Then we use powder!" Cockburn ordered, his patience gone.

The pair had only taken a few steps outside when they were immediately faced with a commotion. A large number of angry townspeople were being held back by soldiers. There were raised voices and tearful protests. Cockburn was just getting a measure of it when Ross appeared through the crowd with several elders. One frail old lady quickly squared up to Cockburn. She recognised him instantly from the propaganda literature.

"Are you a devil, sir!" she shouted. "As you are surely no gentleman!" she added, pointing a bony finger at the powder barrels on the grass. "Is it your intention to explode this building? Then what of the houses nearby?" Cockburn removed his hat to smooth his hair. He was about to reply when the woman continued to berate. "This fella here? There. Him," she added, pointing to Ross. "He gave us your assurance that if we cooperated then no harm would come to us or our property. I'm seventy-one years old, young fella. I ain't got the years left to start again."

"My dear lady," said Cockburn, so quietly that she had to lean in closer. "You are right, of course. And you have my word."

"I do?" she said, recoiling. She had expected a harder fight. "Well I'll be."

"You're very welcome," replied Cockburn. "Now, be so good as to direct me to a local physician."

In the end, the solution to starting the fire in the Capitol Building was suggested by William. He had got fed up with Scott's ever growing list of excuses so he stepped into take charge.

"Oh for heaven's sake!" William snapped, as Scott blamed the proximity to the river. "The only thing damp about these soft furnishings is the trout holding them!"

Fortunately for William, he had remembered his long chat with the Tornbridge magistrate overseeing the Peel Manor blaze inquest. William was, however, surprised about how much of the boring afternoon had stayed with him. He didn't say that, of course. Instead he blustered on as if presenting a great lecture on the subject. A ready expert, as ever, on subjects he had only heard of in passing.

Under William's direction, the stable hands created two huge piles of chopped furniture and soft furnishings in the centre of the Great Hall. Rather than using black powder as an explosive, the stable hands covered the furniture with it to act as an aid to incendiary. The same plan was copied for the Senate Wing. Rockets were set facing into the heart of each pile and, once the building was cleared of soldiers, a match was put to the fuses. The fires soon took hold and within a matter of minutes the entire building was ablaze. Flames burst from the windows as the inferno grew ever more intense. Cockburn did not stay to enjoy the spectacle. For him it was only the beginning.

Dr Ewell, of Pennsylvania Avenue, was another objector to British conduct and demanded an audience with the Admiral as the soldiers were descending Capitol Hill. When it transpired that the good doctor had a large, comfortable residence close by, Cockburn suggested that the best way to prevent any further discord was for himself and William to take lodgings there. It was also agreed that Dr Ewell would tend to Volker and Samuel's wounds in exchange for William's guinea. William's only stipulations to the deal were that the doctor throw in a new chamber pot and give him the best bedroom.

The doctor was a middle-aged, athletic man, who, according to William's journal, had a nervous demeanour. William later corrected the note stating that anyone who opens their door to find a thousand troops on their front step might be forgiven for getting sweaty palms and tripping over their tongue.

As William's guinea had paid for the doctor's own bedroom, the cramped box room became a surgery for Samuel. In preparation for his operation, the unconscious Samuel was washed by the stable hands. They appeared determined to ensure his lack of hygiene didn't have a detrimental affect on the operation, nor the doctor himself, who would have the unfortunate job of having his nose less than a foot away from Samuel's naked frame. William watched the preparations from the doorway until it came time to remove Samuel's britches. William left as soon as the stable hands started giggling at the sight of Samuel's ungodly large privates.

On his way down the stairs, William paused to look out of the landing window. It was an incredible sight. To his right,

The Capitol was well ablaze and the wind carried great tentacles of flames to the neighbouring buildings. Even the trees on the hill were burning. In the distance, William could see Tingley's naval yard. The boat shed was bright red with flame and the two ships themselves were afire by the jetty. William's mind wandered to the plight of his fair Chloe. She was no doubt scared half to death watching the same scene from some attic room in The President's House. As William turned to head back downstairs, he passed Dr Ewell on the landing. The doctor was all scrubbed up and ready for surgery.

"Best of luck," said William, as he stepped aside. "And don't be surprised if Samuel's contents don't appear normal."

Ewell offered little more than a grunt in response as he vanished into the box room.

Less than an hour after Cockburn and William had lit the fuses to the rockets in the great halls, they were sitting with a glass of sherry and a cigar in the Ewell's lounge.

"You impress me, Lord Peel," said Cockburn, wetting the end of his Havana.

"Of course," replied William, wondering if Cockburn was fishing for a compliment himself in return. If he was, he wasn't going to get one.

"When we first met, I had doubts," Cockburn continued, sipping his sherry. "Then when you took on Barney's men at Pig Point, well, I saw you differently."

William suddenly felt uneasy and tried to peer through the hall doorway to ensure they weren't being overheard from the kitchen where Mrs Ewell and the servants were preparing a supper. The last thing William wanted to do was to stir up all that business with the flotilla.

"Then you proved your metal at the Bladensburg bridge."

"I did indeed," replied William, full of himself.

"Which is why I intend to mention you in dispatches," said Cockburn

"I'd rather you didn't," replied William, quickly. "They have a tendency of going missing in war and compromising those involved." He had another quick peer through the doorway again before continuing. "Not that I hold out much hope of reconciliation with the idiot, Mandidleson, of course, he seems to view me with the same contempt as medieval knight's viewed rust to their underarm joints. God knows, I'd like to return home with something in the bag."

"So you will soon leave for Tornbridge?"

"Gladly," William replied, blowing a smoke ring, "were it not for the fair Chloe. I'd like an answer from her own pretty lips. I can't honestly see the whole Quaker life being a bigger pull than a life with servants tending to her every need in the opulence of Peel Manor. True enough, Peel Manor currently looks something like the Hall of Representatives will look like in the morning but..."

At that point the doctor entered wiping his blood soaked hands on an apron soiled enough to befit a butcher. He wasn't smiling either.

"It's not good, I'm afraid," said the doctor, charging a shot glass with whisky. "I got the lead out and fixed him up but there's little sign of life."

The thought hung for a moment then William leapt to his feet and clapped his hands with joy. "Doctor, this is excellent news!" he said, rubbing his hands warmly. "There's very little sign of life on a good day. Is he, per chance, drooling?"

"Why, yes," the doctor replied. "As a matter of fact, I thought it was a stroke during surgery."

"No, no," said William. "Rest assured it's a healthy vital sign in a creature such as he."

As the doctor left to clean up properly, William spotted the stable hands by the hall door. Their eyes were filled with concern. From time to time William has been at a loss to understand the common man's mind. Never was this more evident than with the stable hands shift in attitude towards Samuel. From the outset of the voyage, they seethed whenever Samuel was present. They never involved him in any discussion and threw the obligatory 'dirty glance' at every opportunity. At that moment in the Ewell's doorway, however, they looked more akin to concerned relatives than estranged companions.

"Beggin' your pardon, sir," said the one with the crossed eyes.

"Can we speak with you, sir, please?" said another. William wasn't sure which.

Sensing they wanted some privacy, William ushered them outside into the street where the sky was still orange from the flames and groups of British soldiers were in discussions with the locals, bartering over food and so forth.

Whenever the stable hands were in groups it was difficult for William to tell which one it was who was speaking as the conversation seemed to flick from one to the other as if it were a single stream of consciousness. Like some mythical four headed servant creature, William once wrote.

The creature spoke:

"Beggin' your pardon, sir."

"There's an injustice, sir."

"With Samuel."

"And us."

"All of us."

"And well, sir."

"Being that Samuel is so close to death and all."

"After him being so heroic on your behalf, sir."

"Well, sir, there's an injustice, sir."

William could feel his headache returning and was none the wiser regarding what the hell they were outside to discuss. He settled himself with a sigh. "And the injustice is?" he asked, with trepidation.

The creature continued:

"The fire, sir."

"At Peel Manor, sir."

"We testified to it being Samuel, sir."

"But it wasn't his fault, sir."

"Not directly, sir."

William rubbed his temples, "Are you saying it wasn't Samuel who started the fire?"

The creature was quick to clarify:

"No, sir, it was Samuel, sir."

"Indirectly, sir."

"What happened was, sir. We had a night off, sir."

"With some of cook's brandy, sir. Ouch!"

(Someone elbowed someone)

"We was away drunk, sir. By Lake Winston, sir."

"And when we got back we played a game with Samuel, sir."

"Him being flatulent and all."

"We decided to try and light it."

"His flatulence that is, sir."

"But we didn't reckon on him being so flatulent, sir."

"We misjudged it."

"By ten feet, sir."

"First we knew of what we'd done."

"Was the strange smell."

"And the flames at the top of the stack of hay bails."

"So we made Samuel swear not to tell, sir."

"Told him we'd lose our jobs."

"Then we rang the bell, sir."

"The story of the oil lamp just happened."

"Him having a singed backside already and all, sir."

William took a step away as his head swirled with the prospect of such treachery. Firstly, he was of the mind to take a shoe to them for their effrontery. Then he admired their courage in telling him the secret when it could have gone with Samuel to his grave. William changed his mind again and stepped in with a desire to take both shoes to them for sitting silent as Samuel bounced down Gout Hill in a barrel as his punishment for the Peel Manor blaze. William stepped away once more thinking that with Samuel injured, and the potential of his footwear doing serious damage to the stable hands, he would be left without anyone to hold his potty steady. It simply remained for William to take a deep breath and suppress the tantrum he could feel bubbling.

"Once dinner has settled, I intend to bathe," he said, dismissing them with a waft of his hand. "Remain out of my sight until then."

"Yes, sir," said all of them in unison, falling over each other to get out of William's sight.

Later, William dined with Cockburn, Ross, Lieutenant Scott, and, of course, the Ewell's themselves. Mrs Ewell was an attentive hostess. She smiled during every awkward silence and offered potatoes whenever anyone praised her cooking. With her smooth, auburn hair, freckled nose, and piercing blue eyes, she was also the best looking woman that Ross and Scott had seen in months. William was far from impressed by their obvious horn and mused to himself over the undercooked vegetables and knife resistant meat that she was likely the only woman, save for Kyra's fleeting appearance, they had seen since joining the army. Which would explain why Lieutenant Scott was only moments away from pushing the table aside and humping her leg.

"So are you staying in Washington long?" she asked, as if Cockburn and his thousands of troops had just stopped by to do some shopping. The question made even more bizarre by the blaze visible through the window behind them.

"No longer than it takes," replied Cockburn, politely.

"I couldn't help but admire the likenesses of your wife on the landing," said Scott, attempting to fork a potato. "The portraits are very proficient."

"My brother," replied the doctor, with a hint of disdain for Scott's obvious ardour.

"Why, he just loves to paint me," said Mrs Ewell, smiling at her husband. "Ain't that so my dear?"

"I'm not quite sure," replied the doctor. "I don't know whether it's the enjoyment of painting or the money he saves on getting us real presents." This caused a polite chuckle to spread about the table.

"Well," replied Scott, "I think he's captured your smile perfectly."

"Oh, do you?" replied the doctor, glancing with disapproval at his wife's blushes.

It was one of the most uncomfortable meals William had ever sat through. Worse than the time his parents entertained the Russian shaman, Vsevolod Adamian, who sat through an entire meal wearing a thick fur coat, carved face mask, and matching wooden hands. Vsevolod had thought, incorrectly, that the Peels wanted him to guide the pork loin into the spirit world. It was all very awkward when, five minutes into Vsevolod's shamanic chanting, the butler stepped forward with the gravy boat.

The Ewell's were, in effect, playing dutiful hosts to the very men responsible for the burning buildings outside their front door. This all made for very long breaks in the conversation.

"This really is a lovely meal, Mrs Ewell," said Ross.

"Why, thank you," she replied, politely. "More potatoes?" she enquired, offering Ross the bowl.

Later that evening, as Scott, Cockburn, and Ross were deep in discussion with the Ewell's about anything other than the delicate business of the invasion, William had the stable hands carry a tray of food to Volker in the back bedroom. On his way up to visit him, William glanced at the numerous paintings of Mrs Ewell on the landing. It's fair to say William was far from impressed by the likeness and mocked Scott's praise. '*I think he's captured your smile perfectly',* he parroted in a weak, weedy voice. "What a cock!"

The stable hands helped Volker into a seated position in the bed and plumped up the pillows behind him. He was bare from the waist up and wrapped with dressings that were blotted with blood marking every bayonet injury. His pain was dulled by the half-drunk bottle of rum in his big fist. His eyes traced the room drunkenly to the doorway where William appeared. Volker raised the bottle on seeing William and offered a salute. The stable hands moved the tray of food in front of him and wrapped the fingers of his free hand around the fork.

"I had dream of Carr," said Volker, managing a smile. "Ve vere younger men. Ve vere in za thick of it. Spain I zink." The gaunt stable hand took the fork from him and fed him some meat. "Ve thought ve vould live forever," he said, taking a mouthful of food. "Yet today I'm pizzing blood," he added, with a pained laugh. He clutched his side in a moment of pain. "How iz Zamuel?"

"Asleep," replied William. He cast a knowing glare at the stable hands. "Not the arsonist I believed," he added. "Still, that story can wait until you get your strength back."

As William turned to leave, Volker pushed the fork away from his mouth.

"I mizz my friend," he said, crestfallen. His gaze fell to the covers in front of him. "Zank you for zis care," he added, raising the bottle again. "I mizz my home."

William said nothing in reply but the smile he flashed and the nod he gave with it conveyed that Volker was welcome. As he pulled the door closed the stable hands went back to feeding him.

William went downstairs to find Scott in the living room doing his best to impress Mrs Ewell with stories of far away countries. Not being in the mood for Scott's waffle, William left in search of better company. The good doctor himself was on the veranda with a rather large whisky and an agitated manner. As William stepped through the screen door, he was met by a sigh from the doctor who was hoping it was his wife.

"Oh, it's you," said the doctor, gulping down his drink.

"Quite so," William replied. "She's in the living room."

"What?"

"Your wife," said William, clarifying. "I assumed you were hoping I was your good lady."

"She's with him," the doctor sneered, pointing with his glass to the house.

"Lieutenant Scott, you mean?" William enquired. "In

that case, yes. If that's the 'him' to whom you refer."

They looked out across the field in silence. Despite the sky being bright with flame, the field was partly shielded by the few large houses that surrounded it. The shadows created by the buildings, trees, and grazing cattle, gave the space a eerie, creepy feel.

"What a Goddamn mess!" said the doctor, stamping down his empty glass on the table and wiping his quivering lip. "This might be what you're used to but, by God, I am not."

"I don't follow."

"Sex mad men of war claiming womenfolk as a prize," he said, the neck of the bottle clattering the glass as he charged it. "Scott has desire for my wife and I'm powerless."

"Rot!" scoffed William. "Nothing of the sort. I don't think he would know what to do with her anyway."

"What?" questioned the doctor, angered.

"Lieutenant Scott," William clarified, "He's like one of Mother's Spaniel's. He knows there's a reason behind his urges but can't seem to get past mounting the soft furnishings or dragging his backside up and down the hall carpet for relief. Worry not dear doctor."

"You mean worms?" replied the doctor, quick to correct.

"Where?" enquired William, as he glanced about looking for them.

"Your spaniel dragging its backside on the carpet," said the doctor. "That's worms. It has nothing to do with fornication."

"Well, he seemed to really enjoy it," William chortled. "But I'm sure you're right. You being a medical what-not."

Suddenly, an ungodly scream echoed across the dark field. William and Dr Ewell moved to the end of the veranda and stared in the direction from which it came. They saw nothing. Moments later they heard the sound of hurried footsteps and breathless voices in the street outside. A second after that, they heard the front door to the house burst inwards and the same hurried footsteps cross the hall boards. Suddenly, the screen door on the veranda was rattling back into its frame and two Red Coats appeared trembling in fear.

"Doctor?" one enquired. "You must come quickly there's the most horrible sight, sir."

After a little more explanation, William, the doctor, and the two Red Coats headed out across the field. The doctor was poised behind his lantern as the two privates panted in fear with their eyes fixed down their musket sights.

"Do we have to walk so briskly?" snapped William with a slight limp.

"Shush," came a cry from someone.

"Don't shush me, blast you!"

Shadows flickered red, then orange, then black again as the lantern pointed in all directions. There was no sign of movement. There was no sign of anything untoward.

"There!" cried a Red Coat, and the lantern fixed on the direction of his aimed musket.

"What in the name of God!" said the doctor, as he rushed forwards.

It was the mutilated body of a militiaman going by the peasant farmer clothes. He had been torn to pieces. His legs were stripped to the bone and his chest was open to the ribs. Blood and offal were strewn about him on the blood soaked grass.

"What kind of sick butcher could do that to a man?" said one of the soldiers clutching his mouth.

"It's no way for a soldier to go," noted the other, wiping the sweat from his brow.

Suddenly, a noise to their right had the doctor turning with the lantern. "You hear that?" he said, his breath shallow. "There," he cried, as a shape moved in the shadows.

"It's the light," said William, dismissively.

"I sees it, sir, there," cried one Red Coat and let a shot fly.

"Oh, well done," said William, sarcastically. "You've probably shot some poor fellow relieving himself."

The doctor turned the lantern quickly but again found nothing but a shadow. "Let's try something," he said, and he flipped closed the lantern.

"Are you mad?" said one Red Coat.

"Let your other senses steer you," the doctor replied.

After a moment for their eyes to adjust, they scanned about them. They were all breathless with fear and anticipation. All except William, who pushed one of the Red Coats away for stepping back onto his boot.

"There!" cried someone with conviction.

As the lantern shutter opened, they came face to face with a cow. Its big eyes stared at them. As the lantern closed again, it fell into shadow and let out a moo. The group chuckled at their error.

"Never known a cow do that to a man before," said one Red Coat.

"One of those killer cows," chuckled the other.

Their merriment ended abruptly with the sound of ripping flesh and the cow's moo became a high-pitched scream. It was such a shock that the doctor dropped the lantern. As he bent to feel for it, there was the horrifying noise of cracking bone and tearing sinew. The beast then hit the ground with a heavy thud.

"Jesus Christ!" cried one Red Coat in fear.

"The lamp! The lamp!" shouted the other, with urgency.

"I can't," replied the doctor, his hands searching the ground in the darkness. "Wait, I have it!"

"Idiot!" snapped William, "Let's get a look at the quarry."

They could hear the doctor's hand tremble on the lantern and suddenly it flipped open. Light poured across the field. All screamed in unison as ahead of them, only ten feet away, was a large male lion with blood on its bared fangs. As it let out a roar, the lantern fell to the earth and closed. Everyone ran screaming back to the house. Everyone except William.

"You really are an ass, George," he said, picking up the lantern and flipping it open. George nuzzled his leg and licked his hand. "Just look at you," said William, ruffling George's mane, "more food about your mouth than in."

William bathed in a tin bath in the rear parlour of the Ewell's, waited on, as ever, by the stable hands. George, tired by his own adventure, slept a safe distance away from the splashes. The gaunt stable hand was busy washing William's hair as the fat one and cross-eyed one tended to cleaning William's hands and arms. The tall stable hand prepared William's razor and worked the shaving soap into a lather with a little brush.

"Best get those out," said William, glancing at Barker's stitches to his shoulder. The wound from Jennings' knife had healed nicely. He then glanced at the scab on his chest from Bowman's sword point and the fresh knife wound on his thigh from Eli. He sighed to himself at the many scars he had collected so quickly.

"Beats me, George, why the idiot Mandleson, or whatever his blasted name is, objects so strongly to the union of myself and Chloe. You would think he would be pleased she was marrying someone with thicker blood than some local ranine looking dullard. And why didn't she tell me there were other runners on the course? Doesn't seem very Quaker. Girls aren't the easiest of creatures to fathom. Ouch!" he cried. "Too much soap, you oaf!" he said, slapping the nearest stable hand he could reach. "Are you trying to blind me?" he demanded, then clicked his fingers for a mirror. "The whole affair with Chloe stinks like sour milk to me," he continued, checking each eye in turn. "Anyway, where was I? Oh, yes, Folsom. Well, he led me to believe it was a clear field. Oh, I don't know. If I could just find some way of getting a moment alone with her without the

Commander in Chief sticking his big fat head in. I can hardly go home without currency or a girl. Can I? I can picture Mother now, her arms tightly folded, her fingers drumming her taut bicep. Not to mention her disapproving stare." William let out a long sigh. "As for Chloe, George," he cooed, "you should see her. Ahh, such poise, such, such lovely woman-loveliness. Ahh, *amor vincit omnia,*" William added, picturing her pretty face. "Yes, love shall find a way to conquer all. Romance hath no barriers for W. E. Peel." He stopped talking and his eyes widened with urgency. "Quick! Potty time lads," he said, leaping out of the bath.

At approximately 10.30pm on the night of August 24, Admiral Cockburn and Major Ross assembled a small group of soldiers. It was a hunting party to track down the American President. Cockburn led the way through the streets and quizzed anyone they chanced upon. Despite the streets being bright as day from the many blazes, some of the soldiers carried burning torches. It was a menacing and forbidding sight.

"Where is your President?" Cockburn called out. "Where is Jemmy?" Most of the locals hurried off into the shadows without reply. One or two pointed Cockburn in the opposite direction with the hope of keeping their President safe. "I bet he is," Cockburn would reply, spotting a liar a mile away.

After twenty minutes of searching, Cockburn found

himself at the front doors of the National Intelligencer, the newspaper that had written some tough stories at his expense and printed the propaganda against him. It was payback time. Cockburn watched as the doors were kicked back off their hinges. He stepped inside and breathed in the smell of ink and oil. His men circled about him, their torches filling the room with light. The office was littered with dozens of composing frames. Each one of them with hundreds of tiny metal letters set in place that made up the words, sentences, articles, and pages of the paper. On the far wall was a row of drawers containing the individual metal letters themselves. Each drawer had the relevant letter denoted on the front.

"It will burn quickly," said Ross, holding up some previous editions.

"Let it stand," replied Cockburn, much to everyone's surprise. "But," he added, with a playful smile. "Remove all the letter C's. How will they print about me then?"

On their way up Pennsylvania Avenue towards The President's house, Cockburn's group were approached by a lone figure on horseback. He was galloping straight at them full pelt. The approaching beast's hooves kicked up huge plumes of dust in its wake. Accounts recorded that it was an appaloosa. The rider, who was said to be drunk, screamed a barrage of inaudible insults as he approached Cockburn and his men. Once in range, the man rose in the saddle and opened fire with the many pistols he had stuffed into his belt. Of the seven shots he fired, he hit no one. His shots had passed within inches of the Admiral without so much as clipping him. The drunken figure was John Lewis. He received a single musket shot to the chest and slumped forward in his saddle. It was the only direct challenge the British received whilst in the capital. Only one man made a stand.

By the time Cockburn arrived at The President's House it was deserted. Not a single soul stood guard nor watched on from the shadows. After a few moments of peppering the door hinges with shot, it took only Ross' burly shoulder to send the doors clattering onto the varnished timber boards of the hall.

"Knock, knock," called Cockburn, as he stepped inside. "Are you home, Jemmy?" he added, as a dozen men moved silently past him with their muskets poised.

As the soldiers met no resistance, the operation soon became more of a sightseeing expedition. Although much had been removed from the lower floors of the house, the upper floor, the private rooms at the very top, remained full of furniture and personal belongings. Cockburn took his time to look through Madison's writing desk. Although most official papers were gone, he found some old love letters between a young Madison and his Quaker wife.

Most of the men helped themselves to the silver or trophy weapons. Scott found The President's ornate silver pistols left on the dresser. They were still in their holsters.

Cockburn was reading the love letters in the study when a young officer appeared at the doorway with an excited glint in his eye.

"Sir?" said the young man, straightening his uniform.

"Major Ross says you best come look at this."

Cockburn was led to a dining room on the first floor where Major Ross was seated at the table. He was grinning like a Cheshire cat. About him, the scene was set for a feast. There were dinner plates, napkins, side plates, and crystal glasses on silver coasters. An array of vegetables were still steaming in their pots. Fruits were piled up in the middle of the table with fresh bread and butter. There were hot plates on a side cabinet with the meat and gravy ready to be served.

"We missed him by minutes," said Ross, resting his hand on a wine cooler next to him; the bottle was still chilling. "One last meal with his senior staff perhaps?"

Cockburn pulled out one of the Queen Anne chairs from under the highly polished table. "Until he saw our torches, you mean?" he suggested, taking a seat. He pulled in his chair and beckoned to the officers at the door to enter. "Let's not waste Jemmy's hospitality," he said, taking his napkin from its ring and placing it on his lap.

The meal was a jovial affair with tales of the battle at Bladensburg and the enemy who had judged the whole campaign so badly. For an invading army to eat in the house of its enemy's leader was indeed a moment in history. Cockburn and his men knew it. British supremacy was undeniably and indeed, indelibly marked. For word to reach home of their conquest would, no doubt, have the House of Commons in a rapture and see every public house in England run dry of ale. To see the end of Napoleon and the American capital fall in the same year would surely reignite the dwindling imperialistic fire.

All the officers cheered Cockburn and banged their palms on The President's table. Cockburn himself raised his glass and bowed his head in acceptance of their adoration.

"Gentlemen," he said, taking to his feet for a toast. "To the King!"

"The King!" came the reply, as everyone stood and raised their glasses with great enthusiasm.

Fresh from his bath, William arrived in the Ewell's living room to find Scott on the sofa polishing his musket with some vigour. There was no sign of the good doctor's wife.

"Mrs Ewell?" William enquired, helping himself to a brandy. "Retired has she?"

"What do you mean by that?" Scott replied, taking umbrage.

"Well, she's not here," William stated, making his drink a large measure. "And your vigorous buffing would indicate a certain frustration to the fact."

"She was…" Scott stopped talking the moment he saw George plod in. "Jesus! It's true," he said, gathering his feet under him for fear of having them bitten. George caught scent of some meat in the kitchen and vanished off in search of it.

"Oh, you mean George?" said William, over the sound of a kitchen bin toppling and George gnawing at some leftovers. "God knows how he got here, still, I missed him, of course. That's the thing with a pet his size. He's not like a quiet lapdog you can forget you have."

"It's not right!" Scott protested. "It's not natural to keep an animal like that as a pet."

William watched as Scott began pacing. He was getting increasingly agitated as he repeatedly checked on George in the kitchen.

"Mr Scott?" enquired William, his back stiffening. "Are you the type of fellow who can take criticism in the spirit in which it's intended?"

"No!" Scott replied, bluntly.

"What you suffer has but one cure," William proposed. Scott stopped in his tracks and began pointing a finger. William pre-empted the threat that was undoubtedly to follow. "You need a woman, Mr Scott," William continued, "and I don't mean the forced affections of another man's wife. I mean the tender attention of someone you love, or a whore, whichever."

Scott stepped forward with fire in his eyes and a torrid onslaught of insults poised in his throat. Although a couple of choice words slipped from his lips, they deflated in an instant. It was as if William's advice had struck some deep chord that even Scott himself could not deny.

"You are right, sir," he said, crestfallen. "I do want for myself the same love my mother had for my father. And he for her. And the type of enjoyment I witnessed in the summer house when I chanced upon him embracing the Austrian lady who embroidered his handkerchiefs."

"Then you must stop taking your frustration out on the

metalwork of your musket," William advised, pouring Scott a brandy.

"And you?" asked Scott, eagerly. "Have you such a love in your life?"

"Quite so," replied William, proudly. "The fair Chloe Hooper, except," he sighed, "she is at present being kept at arm's length from yours truly thanks to the dullard Mandylesson. He keeps her locked in his tower. If you're well read enough to see the simile."

"You don't mean President Madison?" asked Scott, with urgency, "and not at his house, surely?"

"Yes, his house. Probably locked in a cage like his foul beaked parrot."

"Dear God!" exclaimed Scott, with horror. "But the Admiral means to torch the place."

A moment later, William was away up the stairs and taking two at a time. "Which way is it?" he shouted, as he vanished into his room.

"I've no idea?" called Scott, from the foot of the stairs. "I thought you had been?" He listened as William banged on the doctor's bedroom door.

"Doctor!" went William's call, followed by another few bangs. "The President's House? You must direct me?"

"Leave me and my wife in peace," the doctor replied from behind his locked door. He sounded drunk and in no mood to help. "I'll offer no more quarter to you, your devil pet, nor the lecherous whoremonger, Scott."

William cursed at him through the keyhole then went back to his own room for the scarf Chloe had given him.

"George!" he shouted, as he ran down the stairs. "Come here!" George plodded into the hall causing Scott to shelter behind the banister. "Find her," said William, offering the scarf up in front of George.

"Why, you're joking, surely?" asked Scott, peering over the handrail.

"One of the most advanced hunter's on earth," boasted William, as George rubbed his nose in the silk.

A moment later, George was out of the front door of the house and off away down the street. William rushed after him doing up his sword belt as he ran. William was running but he didn't know where to. He recognised some buildings they passed but there was so much of the capital ablaze, and so much smoke, it was hard for him to fix his bearings. He passed locals who darted back into doorways and screamed when they saw George bounding down the street. Behind him in the distance came an almighty crash and William turned to see a large brick building collapse in on itself. Its timbers had burnt to ash.

Ahead, William could see George slowing to a trot. His feline nose was searching the air. Chloe was close, William thought, as he saw George stop and sit down. William approached with his chest thumping and lungs burning. He doubled over for a moment to catch his breath then raised his gaze to look for signs of the fair Chloe inside. William had considered the possibility that George, being George, would lead him to a butchers shop or a gardener with a sandwich in his pocket but he didn't expect what he found when he looked up.

"Oh Sparkling!" panted William, gazing at a hat and scarf shop with a perfect match for Chloe's scarf displayed in the window.

It took William another twenty minutes of searching before he eventually chanced upon The President's House. He was too late. Even from a distance, he could see the smoke pouring through the windows. The noise of shattering glass was peppered by explosions from inside.

"Chloe?" he called aloud, as he gathered his strength and pressed on towards the house. With George by his side, they leapt through the front doorway without a thought.

"Chloe!" he repeated, at the top of his lungs. Pulling his jacket above his head, he ducked the flames that leapt at him from all angles. He checked every room he could find calling her name as he moved.

As he burst through the doors into the state dining room, he was instantly knocked onto his back by the heat. Ahead of him was a huge pile of burning furniture. The heat from the flames turned his vision hazy and he buried his head in his jacket. George let out a roar by way of a warning as the entire ceiling collapsed above them. William looked up in horror as a grid of burning beams began raining down about him. His heels scratched at the floorboards for purchase as he scurried backwards out of the room only an instant from disaster.

A moment later, William and George were back out into the cross hall. William shielded his face as the pillars began falling and exploding about him. Shrapnel fired off in all directions as the ceiling cracked and splintered above them.

"Hello!" William cried, at the foot of the stairs. "Your William is coming. Be brave my love."

They had made it up the first flight of stairs when a pillar from the cross hall toppled and smashed through the steps below them. Their exit was cut off. The whole floor beneath them felt to shudder as William and George ran through each of the private rooms. They soon found themselves in Madison's bedroom. The four-poster bed itself was ablaze. It had been piled high with all the bedroom furniture and clothes the British could gather. There was still no sign of Chloe.

William ran back out into the corridor and was immediately hit by a wall of smoke that had him coughing and recoiling back against the wall. His lungs felt tight with smoke and each cough was agony. The smell burned his nostrils and throat. He spotted a vase of flowers on a side table and quickly poured the water over his blackened face and down his roasting back.

Following the wall with his shoulder, he found himself at a dead end and a large, arched window. Eyes stinging, he pulled his jacket tighter around his face and felt his way to a door. Throat raw, he called for Chloe and banged his palm on the panelling. In the thick smoke, his fingers found the handle and he pushed the door open. As the smoke dissipated about the untouched room, his heart suddenly sank. His worst fears were realised. He had walked in on a battery of unlit Congreve rockets that were poised at the ceiling above him. Sensing the precariousness of his situation, he nudged George out with his thigh and slowly pulled the door closed. Whether it was the sheer heat or a fuse William had not seen burning, we may never know, but at that moment the rockets ignited. The blast blew the door off its hinges and engulfed everything in an ever growing ball of flames. William and George were scooped up by the door and launched through the arched Window.

As the flames burned up, William could see the house getting further away as he flew through the night air. A volley of sparks and flames burst from all the shattering windows and grew outwards. It was followed by a rumbling groan as the whole roof collapsed through the middle of the house sending a plume of smoke and debris out of the lower ground floor windows. William was suddenly aware that they were quickly losing height. Next thing he knew, he could hear the rustle of leaves about him and could feel the gathering embrace of branches. With one almighty crack, he felt his vision drain to blackness. Like a dream, he was oblivious to the pain of the thumps as his body hit every branch. He never felt himself hit the ground.

William could feel the sun on his face through the cloudless sky above. He could hear branches creak in the gentle breeze and smell the warm grass of a Tornbridge summer. He was under the great oak back in the grounds of Peel Manor. It was a beautiful August day and he was far from the horror of war, bad hair, and bad food. There was a face peering down at him. It was a handsome, bearded face that was bathed in light. The figure was perfectly dressed in a white suit that shimmered from the heat haze about him.

"Hello William," said the stranger, with a strong, calming voice.

"Who the devil are you?" William could hear himself saying, although he wasn't in control of the words he said. "What, pray tell, are you doing on my property?"

"Our property, William," replied the voice.

William wracked his brain. He had seen the likeness before but couldn't place him. "Bainbridge?" he said, with a confident click of his fingers. "Yes, the tea merchant. But I heard you'd been trampled to death by a stampede of startled women."

"William!" said the voice, sternly. "You are an idiot! Look at my face. Do you not see anything which reminds you of your own?" It was the slightly hooked nose that eventually gave him away. The figure was none other than Mortimer Peel, the most famous adventurer of them all. The great man whose portraits hung on nearly every wall of Peel Manor.

"Good lord!" William exclaimed, suddenly realising. "But you're dead, surely?" he enquired, feeling himself gulp. "Wait, does this mean I'm dead? But, but what dark magic is it that gets your clothes to glow like that?"

"Oh, do be quiet, William," Mortimer demanded, drifting around him with a celestial glide. "The Peel line must not be broken. You must wake up."

"I say," said William, feeling a blackness drawing in about him like a lengthening shadow. "Do you smell that?"

he enquired, his nose twitching. "Why, it smells like smelling salts."

A Duel in Salona

William woke with a start to find Chloe holding a bottle of smelling salts under his nose. He sneezed violently and banged the back of his head on a tree root. It was then that he noticed the huge crowd huddled around him in the darkness. They cheered with joy that he was alive.

"What the blue blazes!" William exclaimed, rubbing his pained head. "This is a dream, surely? Some kind of peasant filled nightmare."

"You're in Salona," said Chloe, taking his hand. "You must rest. Settle yourself."

As the crowd slowly dispersed, William could hear them talking amongst themselves with some excitement.

"He nearly didn't make it," said one man.

"I thought he was a goner for sure," said someone else.

William was west of the Potomac in a settlement of farm buildings and cottages. The nearby fields were filled with tents and carts piled high with belongings. People were huddled in groups either consoling each other in grief or laughing off their troubles with the help of a restorative whisky. Washington was still ablaze across the river. It looked somehow worse from a distance as if every building was on fire. The night sky above it was red with flame and thick with smoke.

"There are many here," said Chloe, helping William stand. "There's nowhere else to go."

William stretched his aching back then yelped in pain when it cracked like a bundle of dry twigs. He cursed at the sight of his blackened clothes oblivious to his face being covered with soot.

"You look like a mole," Chloe giggled, as she wrung out a cloth from a bucket. "Are you injured?" she asked tenderly.

"It's nothing, I assure you," he said, modestly. "I fell from a tree." Chloe searched his expression, thinking he was teasing her. "I was in The President's House, you see," he continued, brushing her hair over her ear. "And it somehow blew up." Suddenly, a thought struck him and he glanced about, agitated. "George?" he asked, concerned. "Have you, by any chance, seen a lion? He's a large, fluffy, buff coloured thing. He's most likely eating."

Chloe's eyes lit up in a flash and she quickly led William off across the grass towards some distant farm buildings. She led him around a settlement of tightly packed bivouacs and then towards some old wooden gates in a high wall. The instant they neared the gates, William heard a noise he recognised. George was growling but it wasn't playful. He sounded in great distress and, what's more, each growl was accompanied by cheering.

Pushing open the gate, William found himself in a

lantern lit courtyard filled with people. To his left was an arched entrance with a well beyond it. As William stepped forward through the crowd, his eyes fell on a horrible sight. George was bound by the neck to a tree with a heavy rope and was being tormented by a group of young men who poked him with a stick. They jabbed George hard then ran out of range as he charged against the limit of his rope, snarling.

In a flash, William rushed them. Without a break in his stride, he backhanded the biggest lad across the face sending him straight into the dirt. As the others approached, fists poised, William grabbed his sword handle in readiness to draw.

"Drop that sword and you'll see a fair fight," said one of them, putting his fists up. "Unless you're afraid?"

"He ain't got the balls," said the lad on the floor.

"You misunderstand," said William, as George nuzzled his legs and licked his hand. "Now, gentlemen!" announced William, slowly drawing his trophy sword. "If it's a fair fight you want, well," he added, his eyes indicating to the tip of his sword as he rested it on George's tether. "You were saying something about balls?"

The men who were once so eager to fight tripped over themselves to run away. As they disappeared through the courtyard entrance, they passed a large group of armed militiamen entering. Chloe ran to William's side as hundreds of Americans encircled them. William peered at the blank faces that were lit orange from the lantern light. William was trapped. He cursed to himself as he remembered his banishment and the 'pain of death' condition that accompanied it. He was desperately trying to come up with a plausible reason for ignoring the order when the crowd parted and President Madison himself appeared. There was a moment of silence as William and the crowd waited for The President's words.

"You ignored my wishes, I see?" said Madison, approaching.

"Just leaving," William replied, quickly. "I forgot my lion, you see." William knew it was brave bluff but once again the automatic part of his brain leapt in without thinking. "We shall say our goodbyes and wish you a pleasant evening," he said, taking Chloe's arm and leading her a couple of steps.

"I saw how you searched my house for Chloe," said Madison, indicating that William should stay. "That's why you were brought here."

"Quite so," William replied, not sure whether that meant he was still in trouble or not.

"Lord Peel," continued Madison, graciously, "I won't weave my words into a cloth that would better suit your ears."

"Sparkling!" replied William, postulating over exactly what cloth would suit his ears.

"I have misjudged you." He paused, preparing to eat his own words. "To charge into a burning building without a thought, except for that of your woman, well, there can be no truer show of honour."

Mutters of agreement spread through the crowd and

Madison turned to address them all. "We have all lost something today," he yelled, rousing the crowd. "But it can be rebuilt. A lesson has been learned. But here," he bellowed, pointing to William and Chloe, "here is what good there is in all this madness." The mood of the onlookers warmed as their President's words fill them with hope. "Here is why we Americans will never be broken. Love of our family and our country will hold us true. The British have won this day, true enough," he shouted, brimming with passion, "but this dark day will soon end." The crowd erupted with applause and cheer.

Chloe's cheeks flushed as she ran to embrace him, knowing that in saying such words he was giving William the blessing she sought. William, not surprisingly, was somewhat baffled by the turn of events but equally happy that it seemed to mean that he wouldn't be shot.

"You mean it?" Chloe asked, squeezing The President's arm. "That I can return with Lord Peel to Tornbridge with your blessing?"

"Of course," replied Madison, kissing her forehead. "And Lord Peel," he said, beckoning William over, "I think we have business to conclude, don't you? May I call you William?"

"No," replied William, thinking it a step too far. "But just so I'm clear!" he said, stepping forward. "Are you saying William E. Peel is back in the presidential good books?"

"You bet," said Madison, letting out a laugh.

William had done it. After months of torture, imprisonment, bad food, worse company and a horrible collection of scars to show for his trouble, he had clinched the deal of a lifetime. True enough, the detail of the deal was yet to be hammered out but the fact that Madison was offering the hand of friendship instead of shooting him in the eye meant William would be returning home triumphant with a girl on his arm.

William was just taking a breath to speak when suddenly a commotion spread from the back of the crowd. There were gasps and muttering as people moved aside to reveal a figure stepping forward. He was a dishevelled and nervous man with a huge moustache and a month of stubble on his sunburned face. His clothes were weathered and warn. On his head was a rather tatty, feathered hat. When Chloe's eyes fell upon him, she covered her mouth with a gasp and fainted from the shock. The stranger rushed forwards and she collapsed into his arms.

"Oh, dear God!" said the figure, helping her lie down. "Help, someone please." An elderly physician rushed forward through the crowd.

Although William was dreadful at remembering names and faces, he never forgot a horrible moustache. He recognised it instantly and gulped. The dishevelled fellow was none other than Francis Loe, although William did not know him by name. He was the dandy American that William nearly had shot at Bowman's fort. By a strange twist of fate, he was also the idiot suitor that Folsom had said had gone on a mission to North Africa to buy slaves and prove his metal to Chloe. Folsom was wrong about him being dead though, he was very much alive. William knew that if Francis recognised him, the deal, and his courtship to the fair Chloe, would be deader than the branches of the famous Mongolian dead monkey tree. It was time for William to leave. Making the most of the commotion, William casually stepped back into the crowd humming some ditty as he went.

"By God, Francis, you're alive!" said Madison, with disbelief. "How can this be?"

"I have had the most horrible time!" Francis replied, breaking down. "I went to buy slaves as per the plan but bandits raided the auction." Sensing he too was about to pass out, people rushed forward to catch him. A moment later, a canteen emerged through the crowd and was thrust into his trembling hand. "I was robbed!" he cried, his mind fixing on the memory of it. "Left for dead!" He let out a scream of terror that made the crowd jump then he thrust his fist into his quivering mouth. "I was destitute. Without food. Without water. I was left at the mercy of the savages. All my thoughts were of Chloe and the country that I love. I feared I should never see either again."

William had managed to back away through the crowd without attracting attention when he suddenly felt a sharp point dig into his back. A hand then gripped his shoulder and he felt warm breath in his ear.

"You want to be careful who you back onto, Lord Peel," came a well spoken, English voice.

In the meantime, the local physician had revived Chloe and was helping her to her feet.

"They said you were dead, Francis?" she said, her voice quivering.

"A man took pity on me," he replied, trembling like a mad, broken wreck. "An English man," on hearing which the crowd gasped. "He gave me food, water, and a bed," suddenly he was stopped by an overwhelming thought that had him scream as if in fear of his very life. "Who?" he queried, barking at the silent crowd. "Who said I did that? Who?" he cried, madness in his eyes. "Who amongst you said I touched his cock for board and lodgings?"

The crowd backed away with fear. They shrugged and shook their heads somewhat confused by the unhinged man before them.

"Lord Peel here," said Madison, quick to change the subject, "is a financier. He's going to help turn our fortunes around." He stopped himself, conscious that William had vanished. Madison was about to call his name when Chloe rushed to him and urged him not to.

"Can't you see he is too much a gentlemen," she said, tears in her eyes. "He has too noble a heart to see Francis denied the love that has kept him alive. I must let him go," she said, clutching her breast, "knowing I shall never see his brave face again."

William suddenly felt a shove that propelled him out of the shadows and into clear view of everyone. It was as though he had appeared by magic and all eyes fell on him at once.

"Howdy," William said, with an awkward wave. "Which is 'how do you do' in proper English." He coughed, suddenly realising they might take offence. "Not that you care for English ways right now, of course. Especially with your capital burning."

"You!" shouted Francis, hardly believing his own eyes. "The devil himself has followed me here."

Chloe shook her head. "No!" she cried, assuming he must be mistaken. "You are wrong. This is Lord Peel of Tornbridge. He is a noble man with a brave heart and a large country house."

"He is a robber, my love, I would testify to it," said Francis, removing his hat and clutching it to his chest. "He is an assassin. A snatcher of men, and…"

"I'm sorry for this confusion, Lord Peel," Madison said, interrupting. "There's obviously some misunderstanding."

"No misunderstanding," urged Francis, with conviction. "This man is a scoundrel and beguiler of beautiful, naked women."

"What!" said Chloe, searching William's eyes for the truth. "Did you beguile a naked woman?"

"No, no, no, no, no!" William objected, strongly. "Which is to say, possibly." He quickly clarified. "But it turned out that she was my auntie, so," he rolled his eyes and tutted, "I'll pay for that mistake with a few awkward Christmases."

"SATAN!" shouted Francis. "See how he is unashamed." The crowd jostled and gasped at the revelation. It was all starting to go horribly wrong for William and it was soon to turn a whole lot worse.

"Did you steal from this man?" enquired Madison. "Because if you did, you stole from America."

"Er," William paused, the conflict plain for all to see on his face. "If I said 'yes' would you retract your blessing?"

"The truth!" Madison demanded.

William took a step closer to Chloe who he could sense was turning a degree chilly over this development. William wracked his brain for some clever words to mend it all but once again his brain let him down. Instead, he resorted to appealing to her rational side.

"Think of Tornbridge," he said, in his most convincing voice. "The rolling fields. The pretty lakes. The splendid parties. The delightful dresses."

"Did you?" she trembled, wiping a tear from her cheek, "did you leave this man, this good Quaker, to his death at the mercy of the savages whilst you beguiled your naked auntie?"

William was so conflicted over his answer that his face screwed up. He fought off a mixture of words that were desperate to leap from his grimacing mouth. "Errrrr. Well, it's all a bit complicated," he said, letting out a nervous laugh. "Did I mention we sailed into a Sicilian tavern?"

"Answer the goddam question!" barked Madison, impatiently.

"In which case, yes," William replied. "Yes, I did steal from America and eat one or two fruit salads off my auntie."

In the silence that followed, William thought that perhaps they all didn't really know Francis that well and, as such, they weren't too bothered by his months of malnourishment, probable torture, and his subtly inferred non-consensual sodomy. William was wrong, of course, and realised as much when the crowd erupted into an angry mob that began hurling things in his direction. He quickly shielded his face with his arm. A minute later, everyone fell silent again and the yard was littered with projectiles. There followed an awkward moment when a young man stepped gingerly through the crowd and picked up an apple. Wiping it clean, he indicated that it had been thrown in error and quickly stepped back into the crowd.

"The devil burned down The President's House!" came a cry from the shadows.

"He led the British to our doors!" shouted someone else.

"He's cursed us all!" came another shout.

"Hang on a bit," William protested, his head spinning from the extreme reaction. "I don't even know how to curse anyone."

Francis stepped forward, his eyes bulging with anger. He pointed an emaciated finger in William's direction and puffed out his cheeks. "You will be judged by this jury this night."

Silence fell.

"BURN HIM!" shouted everyone in unison, followed by cheers.

The crowd surged forward towards William then suddenly stopped in their tracks. Behind William stepped forward another figure, a man with a scimitar laid casually across his shoulders. He was a dandy man, wearing white linen trousers and matching jacket.

"Ladies and gentle American men," he said, with a camp, menacing tone. "My name is Captain Bowman."

The crowd was silent except for one solitary voice that

muttered. "Oh, shit!" Someone had obviously heard of Bowman's reputation.

"Who?" questioned Madison, surprised. "Are you a naval man?"

"A businessman," Bowman corrected. "Simply here to make a deal." The crowd took a step back as Bowman took a step forward. He then leaned on the handle of his scimitar as if it were a walking cane and he were Lord Byron himself. "Lord Peel of Tornbridge isn't a man to burn," he said, inspecting his nails. "Not without repercussions."

"You dare threaten us?" replied Madison.

"Warn you, sir."

"Speak plainly, damn you," demanded Madison. "I'm in no mood for English riddles."

"He is probably the richest man you will ever meet."

"His money's not welcome here," Madison replied, steadfast.

"Mr Loe's mission was to secure three hundred slaves," Bowman stated. "I will honour that contract in exchange for one, chubby young buffoon. It will be like you never met him."

Madison took a moment to consider it. "The slaves are here?" he asked, quick to clarify.

"They are," replied Bowman.

Madison pondered it again. It didn't take him long for him to make up his mind. "You have a deal, captain." The crowd erupted into a cheer.

"Rot!" cried William, with enough zeal to silence the crowd. "You're both fatheads! I've been kidnapped, shot at, half drowned, tortured, and hounded by savages. All in the name of the blasted silly deal you came to me for. I have no intention of simply trotting off with Mr Bowman to be once more in fear of my chastity."

Bowman took a step forward and placed the scimitar point on William's chest. "Enough!" he shouted, impatiently. "The deal is done."

"No, it bloody well, blasted well isn't!" said William, defiant.

"No?" exclaimed Bowman, with a chuckle of surprise for William's resolve. "So where is the crack shot, Carr, or the brute, Volker? Are they choosing their moment to spring you?" He pretended to glance about for them. "Ah, no, that's right. One is at death's door and the other one through it."

In one smooth action William stepped back, drew his sword, and slapped Bowman's blade aside. "I demand satisfaction," he said, with a full measure of Peel arrogance. "I challenge you, sir, and will accept no rebuttal!"

"You don't even have the wit to know when you're beaten," said Bowman.

"Yes, I do," William replied with confidence. A confidence that soon faltered. "Wait, what was the question? Was it one of those silly double-negative thingy's?"

"You will come back with me," said Bowman, raising his scimitar.

"You already have my answer," William replied, curtly.

"To the death then," said Bowman, launching at William so quickly that he barely had time to raise his guard and deflect Bowman's blade.

"To the death?" objected William, as he parried another cut. "A bit excessive isn't it?"

Bowman was at him with huge, clattering cuts. After one ferocious exchange, the blades locked at the hilt. Both yanked this way and that until they were only inches from each other's face.

"Lovely boots by the way," said William, his eyes indicating to Bowman's feet. "Are they Spanish?"

They pushed and shoved each other heedless of their surroundings until they eventually separated and took a minute to catch a breath.

"One last chance," said Bowman.

"And give Mother the satisfaction of paying the ransom?" William replied, breathless. "Go boil your legs!"

With that said, the duel was on and the pair set about each other in a blur of clattering steel that saw them weave through the crowd fighting as they went. At one point, they circled close to George who charged at Bowman pawing and growling against the limit of his rope. Bowman was agile and quick but William saw off every near cut and returned the pleasure. The crowd followed the fight out of the yard and onto the street. Bowman made a cut with such force that William was lucky to escape with his head and a shower of sparks exploded as his sword struck the entrance wall. Bowman leapt up onto the well and swept away William's attempts to slice his legs. Much to William's annoyance, he then goaded him by kicking away every one of William's cuts whilst adding some derogatory remark about Peel swordsmanship.

William had heard enough and kicked the bucket at him. Bowman leapt into a summersault to avoid it and the crowd cheered at such a gymnastic display.

Sharpened sword edges glittered in the faint lantern light as the pair crashed through a cottage door. Onlookers rushed to the windows and jostled for a better view. Inside, there was the sound of clattering pans and the sickening thud of William banging his head on a low beam. He cursed American joinery and slashed Bowman across his chest.

In a flash, the onlookers made a panicked retreat as William and Bowman went crashing through the window and landed in a tumbling mass of grunts on the road. As they leapt to their feet, Bowman took a lunge and stabbed William in the side. William cursed with the pain and backhanded him out of range.

There was a pause as both men charged their lungs and checked their wounds. The crowd paused with them and watched each man intently.

"Takes it out of you, doesn't it?" William gasped.

"Ready?" asked Bowman, wiping his brow.

"Not really," William replied, checking his bleeding side.

Bowman saw his chance and lunged at William. The fight was on again with a rapid exchange of slashes and parries. The pair moved down the street to the cheers of the crowd. As they neared another house, Bowman swept an arm full of plant pots off the sill and hurled them in William's direction. William ducked as they shattered across his shoulder.

"Bastard!" William exclaimed, as he pushed Bowman back against some barrels that toppled as he fell over them. "What kind of ass throws soil?"

It was then William saw Chloe. Her gaze was fixed on him. Her chest was heaving and her lips were quivering. William had taken a step in her direction when suddenly he found the urge to duck as Bowman's blade sliced the air only inches above his head. William turned and cut at him powerfully in reply. Sparks exploded along their blades. Each slashed at the other with all they could muster but with each swing they tired more.

The crowd watched with bated breath to see who would falter first. Then it happened, a moment that came with a gasp from the crowd. William's trophy sword was sent clattering from his grip and bounced on the baked dirt. William dropped to his knee, pained by his bleeding side.

"I will pay you fair compliment, Lord Peel," said Bowman, touching his own bleeding chest. "I have never been so much as scratched." He raised his blade for the killer strike.

"Do you know about the elusive Canadian snow baboon?" William enquired, wiping his neck with a handkerchief.

Bowman obviously hadn't heard of the creature and gazed down at William a little confused. "I don't follow?" he said, lowering his sword slightly.

William suddenly leapt forward and snatched his own sword from the dirt. Bowman made a cut but he was too late; William was already rolling to his feet. As Bowman turned and raised his sword again, William drove his blade through Bowman's ribs to the hilt.

"It's famed for its acrobatics during combat," said William, and he twisted the sword with an ungodly crack. Screams spread through the crowd and onlookers passed out at the horror of it.

For a moment the enemies were locked in a clinch. William's sword was skewered through Bowman's chest and he watched as the very life drained from his quarry. Chloe rushed forward a few steps then stopped, her face was filled with anger. All love was lost.

"I hate you!" she cried, repeatedly, before pushing her way back through the crowd and vanishing into the darkness.

"Girls!" William exclaimed, with a sigh.

Bowman's eyes faded, his grip on William was weakening. Suddenly, his eyes opened with a start and with the last beat of his heart, the last bit of spirit in him, he pulled William into a passionate kiss. William was powerless to stop him. A moment later, Bowman's arms fell limp and he slid off William's sword.

William retched and spat the taste from his lips. The crowd watched for a moment before dispersing. The shadows lengthened as the lanterns moved off in various directions. Only Madison remained. He watched for a couple of minutes as a panicked William rubbed his lips on a handkerchief. When William had finally regained some sense of calm, he straightened to find everyone had left. There wasn't a soul except for the desperate cries of the locals who had returned home to find their cottage windows shattered and the soft furnishings slashed.

William cursed as he contemplated his next move then rifled Bowman's pockets for anything of use.

No one, not even the fair Chloe, was there to wave goodbye when William and George left Salona. They walked along the dirt road in the general direction of the Potomac. It's fair to say William was far from happy and cursed to himself repeatedly as they crossed the causeway to Analostan Island (or Theodore Roosevelt Island as it was to become). He had lost any hope of a deal with Madison and any chance of returning home with the pretty Chloe Hooper on his arm.

The money he had lifted from Bowman's pockets bought some provisions and secured them a ferry east across river to the Washington shore. It was the first time the captain had ever taken a lion across and commented such, rigid with fear, as George jumped down from the jetty.

Once on the other side of the river, William found a spot he liked in a field and they both sat down for a meal. Using an old tree stump as a table, William opened out the napkin and placed their food on it. As he quaffed the wine, he looked up to the heavens and pictured Carr looking down at him. Perhaps he and his father had watched his duel, he noted to George.

"So it's back home to Mother empty handed," William

sighed, throwing George a lump of ham. "Can't say I'll miss this place," he added, checking the wound in his side. "Would have been nice to see that fathead, Mandyson, taken down a peg or two, of course." As William gently ruffled George's mane, he noticed something in his front, right paw. It was a brightly coloured macaw feather skewered on a claw. George licked his lips as if to indicate that it made a tasty treat.

"Good lad!" William praised, and gave George a big kiss on his nose. "An extra portion of meat for you, me thinks."

Farewell to America

The dawn light was barely over the horizon when distant lightning flashes lit up the sky. Thunder rumbled and brought with it a few gentle spots of rain. William and George had slept a few hours huddled up together at the edge of a field. They were rudely awoken by large raindrops splashing on their faces. A heavy shower soon followed.

It was noon by the time William had finally got within sight of Washington. The rain had turned much of the fire into smoke that had drifted across the sky for miles. It could be expected that the locals would have danced in the streets at the prospect of such a downpour but there was one cruel blow that still awaited them.

Within half an hour, the heavens were open with rain so intense, so violent, it bounced a foot high off the quickly saturated ground. The once clear sky soon darkened to black with lightning flashes cracking about it. The wind quickly gathered and whistled about the trees. Gusts became so vicious and powerful that they carried huge chunks of debris with it. On several occasions, William had to take shelter as God knew what flew by. Then, as if by magic, it suddenly blew itself out. Within minutes the sun was once again peering through the black clouds.

By the time William reached the capital, he couldn't believe his eyes. What he had witnessed hours earlier was little more than a light shower compared to what people had to endure in Washington itself. Almost all the buildings spared by the British a day earlier had been stripped of their roofs and their contents blown miles away. Pennsylvania Avenue was strewn with timbers, slates, clothes, and pieces of furniture. The Patent Office, ironically saved from burning by the British due to the international value of its contents, was obliterated in the storm. Its roof didn't have a single tile left on it and where the documents themselves ended up was a mystery. It must have appeared to the Americans as though God was on the side of the British with a conspiracy to eradicate all traces of the grand vision from the face of the earth. Fortunately for William, the Ewell's was one of the few houses that survived intact.

William reached the good doctor's by lunchtime and entered to find Cockburn and Scott seated at the table being waited on by the stable hands. William looked almost drowned and dripped from every seam onto the hall rug. So too George, whose proud mane was matted to his body.

"Good lord, William," said Cockburn, as the fat stable hand placed a napkin on his lap. "Is it still raining?"

"There's a moistness to the air, yes."

"Is that your blood?" asked Cockburn, looking William up and down.

"Some of it," William replied.

"Did you find her?" asked Scott, in his new, amenable

tone.

"No," William replied, smiling through the sadness. "No, I didn't." He paused for a moment then glanced at the stable hands. "Organise some fresh towels, quickly," he snapped, pointing to George, "the poor creature's already been sneezing."

A couple of the stable hands rushed off to make preparations.

William was on his way to the stairs when the good doctor appeared from the veranda looking somewhat worse for his evening's drinking.

"Rough night?" asked the doctor, covering a yawn with the back of his hand.

"Are you enquiring or confessing?" William questioned.

"Probably both. Sorry," he said, then indicated to William's side. "You want me to take a look at that?"

William shrugged, conveying it was probably a good idea.

Twenty minutes later, William's latest sword wound was stitched and dressed and he and the good doctor were on their way up the stairs.

"Oh, there was a man here last night," said the doctor, remembering. "A local man by the name of Loe. Looked in quite a state."

William made up some reason why it was all perfectly normal and quickly changed the subject. "And how's Samuel? Still repulsing the germs and making progress?"

"He finished his breakfast which is a good sign. I was

actually on my way to check in on him. The big fella, well, he's not so good." He paused for a moment and hushed his voice. "The infection is spreading, I'm afraid. He's very weak."

They had reached the landing when Mrs Ewell appeared carrying towels. "Why look at you," she said to William, with genuine concern. "You were never out in that frightful storm?" She was about to ask another polite and yet perfectly obvious question when she suddenly realised something. "My pictures?" she asked, pointing at the empty walls. "The portraits are gone!"

Both William and the doctor scanned the walls with puzzled faces. As the doctor rubbed his chin and replayed the night's events in his mind, a sudden thought hit William's frontal lobe with the force of a well aimed clog. The thought was a sudden recollection of Samuel's proclivity. It had not been simmering in William's brain long when Mrs Ewell spotted his expression.

"You have a theory?" she questioned.

"Err, no," William replied, passing it off with a chuckle.

"Really? 'Cos you looks like your mind is chewin' on somthin'."

"No, no," said William, quickly. "Gout pain! My big toe is throbbing like, like... Well, big toes do when you've had too much rich cheese and wine sediment."

The doctor suddenly broke into a laugh. "Well, you'll hear no complaints from me," he chuckled, reaching for the door handle. "With all that's been lost tonight, I can't say we've been dealt too harsh a hand." And with that said, he opened the door to Samuel's room. It all happened too quick for William to stop it. As all eyes focused, one by one expressions slid south with disbelief. Mrs Ewell, in particular, immediately turned pink about the neck and face. The portraits were on the bed facing Samuel who was naked from the waist down and making a vigorous assessment of the collected works. As Samuel became aware of Mrs Ewell and the others at the doorway, he turned his gormless, happy face towards them. His eyes were crossed and a foot of drool was hanging from the corner of his grinning mouth.

"Pretty lady," he said, concluding his appraisal all the quicker for her presence.

Mrs Ewell passed out and landed with a loud thud on the hall rug. The doctor, who was too much in shock to even notice her fall, was frozen, eyes wide in disbelief.

"He's certainly regained some mobility," said William, trying to pass the whole thing off as if perfectly normal. "I can see a journal article on this for sure. Minus the enormous privates, of course."

The stable hands arrived looking perplexed at Mrs Ewell laying face down on the floor. As they peered around the doorframe, the situation became all too clear.

"Yes, that's right," said William, casually. "Change of plan. We shall be leaving. If not, I imagine some spiteful medical procedure will befall us all once the good doctor's malaise has passed."

Admiral Cockburn had decided to retreat to his fleet. By the evening of the 25th, the British forces were marching back along the Washington Road towards Bladensburg. Cockburn had secured a number of horses and offered William safe escort back to *The Emily*. William, of course, accepted. The good doctor had been persuasive regarding his desire for William and the rest to leave his house. Cockburn had suggested that the reason for his own withdrawal from Washington was on account of American reinforcements heading their way from Baltimore but William suspected it had something to do with the meat cleaver Dr Ewell left in Cockburn's bedroom door. Cockburn and Scott never knew the actual reason behind the doctor's change in mood. Perhaps if they had, Cockburn wouldn't have organised a cart to carry Samuel and Scott wouldn't have bought one of the portraits of Mrs Ewell.

When they reached the scrubland on the outskirts of Bladensburg, William couldn't believe his eyes. The road and fields were still littered with the British dead, just as they had fallen, except they had been stripped naked.

As Ross and Cockburn stopped for discussions with a group of locals, William ordered the stable hands follow him with a shovel and he galloped across to the pile of logs in the field north of Tournecliffe's Bridge. It was the last place anyone had seen Carr alive and William wanted to make sure his body was not just left like the rest. Carr's body, however, was nowhere to be found. William dismounted for a closer look and discovered two steel canisters for his repeating musket in the grass. They were both empty and covered in dried blood.

The men Cockburn and Ross had discussions with were militia, still loyal to Barney, who was barely alive by all accounts. Ross had agreed to pay them to bury the bodies. Such is the complexity of war, William noted in his journal.

By the evening of the 26th they had, once again, reached Upper Marlboro and camped before making the trip back down the Patuxent in the boats.

The next morning, William was awoken early by some discussion outside his bivouac. There were raised voices then his tent flap opened and the stable hands crawled in.

"Surely it doesn't take all of you, damn it!" said William, rubbing his eyes as they all pushed their way into the cramped space.

As usual, the stable hands spoke as one:

"Beggin' your pardon sir."

"He's terribly ill, sir."

"Sorry to wake you, sir."

"It's Mr Volker, sir."

By the time William reached the medical tent, the young surgeon, Palmer, was stepping out. William walked past him on his way to the entrance but was stopped by Palmer's grip on his bicep.

"I'm sorry, sir," said Palmer, his eyes conveying what his words hadn't.

William's urgency was lost and he sighed. "They will take it hard," he said, indicating towards the stable hands who were helping Samuel walk to the tent.

"I'll organise a decent Christian burial, sir," said

Palmer. "The Admiral has expressed such are his wishes."

On hearing which the stable hands and Samuel rushed inside the tent to see Volker one last time.

"No," replied William, to Palmer. "He is a captain. We will take him to his ship, *The Emily*."

It was a long, quiet trip back down the Patuxent River. Volker's body had been wrapped in blankets and travelled with William, George, the stable hands and Samuel as far as Pig Point. After they recovered *The Emily*'s launch, *Little Fanny*, his body was placed in her and towed after them. That settled George, who appeared ill at ease with the human practice of keeping a body with them. Preferring a lion's practice, of course, of eating anything that couldn't run away.

The stable hands did their best to keep Samuel company and William couldn't help but remark in his journal how different things were than from the trip up. He wasn't exactly sure how to deal with the stable hands after their peculiar admission as to the true cause of the manor fire, however, as they appeared somewhat keener about their duties, he let sleeping dogs lie. William really couldn't see it causing Samuel's conviction being overturned anyway. Especially as the Magistrate, the thorough buffoon that he was, would most likely demand to see some evidence. William had visions of the onlookers in the gallery receiving singed eyebrows once Samuel's flatulence was unleashed and set to flame. There was also the risk of the Courthouse itself catching fire and William didn't want to see another burning building for as long as he lived.

The journey down river was boringly uneventful. William's mind wandered many times to the fair Chloe and the chance that could have been. His stomach also bubbled at the thought of facing Mother. She would most likely tear him to shreds about the cost of the adventure and the fact that there was nothing to show for it.

By noon of August 30th, Cockburn's little armada came into view of the British fleet and, of course, *The Pride of Emily*. She was a fine sight, William noted, as he signalled their return. Proud as her name, *The Emily* was riding her anchor with regal splendour. As the crew on board caught sight of the approaching launch, they waved and whistled. Moments later, young Daniel appeared at the stern rail with a huge smile across his face and a customary salute. William watched as Daniel took out his spyglass and sighted on them. William's heart sank as he saw Daniel's glass set on the launch behind them. There would be no mistaking the figure in the sheets. Alive or dead, Volker was not a man to be easily concealed.

Once they were alongside *The Emily*, William climbed the rope ladder up to the deck. He was met by Daniel and Barker and after a brief explanation regarding Volker's fate; the crew set to work winching him on board inside the launch. With great reverence and care, they lowered the little boat down onto its deck brackets. The crew then gathered around and removed their hats. They tugged their forelocks one last time for their captain.

"Alright," said Daniel to the men, "let's get him below. Lift him gently now."

That evening the senior staff dined in the great cabin. Barker, the surgeon, Daniel and William were to be waited on by the stable hands who had prepared a veritable feast. William had, of course, spent the entire afternoon bathing and preparing his outfit. Apart from some discomfort from his various wounds, he appeared restored to his former self.

"Tomorrow," he said, standing to make a toast, "we sail for home and the families that await us all. God help us!" He paused for a moment to choose his next words carefully. "Here's to an excellent captain and of course, his first rate, first mate." William was suddenly aware that Barker and Daniel had exchanged a look. He also noticed that they hadn't raised their glasses.

"That's not all entirely true, sir," Daniel confessed.

Daniel led William through the doors of the great cabin and into the aft companionway. They stopped at Carr's cabin and very quietly opened the door. As light poured inside, William squinted into the darkness where he could make out a figure asleep in the bed. It was Carr. William let out a yelp with surprise but was silenced by Barker. Daniel closed the door and indicated they head back into the great cabin.

"I'll be dammed," said William, "But he was at death's door and knocking pretty darn loudly when I saw him last."

"He was strong enough to make the walk," said Barker, taking to his seat. His ruse might have worked were it not for a nervous glance in Daniel's direction, which

William spotted.

"So this wound?" enquired William, playing along. "This hole, front to back in his guts. Not the sort of thing to stop one walking a great distance then?"

"Er, no," replied Barker, beads of sweat popping on his brow, "not if someone were determined."

"Really!" William acknowledged, with surprise. "How extraordinary."

"God moves in mysterious ways, sir," said Daniel, helping himself to vegetables.

William watched the pair for a while. Their little knowing glances indicating that there was much more to the story than they were ever going to let on. William was about to let it go when suddenly his gaze fell on George who was curled up in the corner, asleep, with his chin resting on his paws.

"Then there's the other two mysteries, of course," William continued with a superior smile dancing about his lips.

"Two, sir?" enquired Daniel, as he took a large gulp of wine.

"George getting off *The Emily*, for one," said William.

"A devoted creature," replied Daniel

"Famous for it," added Barker, dabbing his receding brow.

"And, of course, the mysterious figure following us," said William, "the one who rudely spied on my potty time."

"A dreadful invasion of privacy, sir," Daniel answered. "A mistake, I'm sure. Probably just a local trying to get home after the storm."

Nothing else needed saying. William knew in that instant that it was Daniel following them as, of course, William had never mentioned the actual time he observed someone. There was also the fact that Daniel was an expert tracker and able field physician. Both were qualities needed for the task to be carried out successfully. George was, no doubt, happy to follow Daniel as he had become fond of him earlier in the voyage, but once he caught the scent of his master, he must have had a change of plan. The unique aroma of Lord Byron's Wild Scabbard perfume would have been easily distinguishable and detectable for miles. William decided to let the matter go and simply stood to conclude his toast.

"To Peel adventures."

All raised their glasses and cheered their response.

The next morning, William stepped out onto the deck of The Emily to find the crew busy preparing for departure. The top men were high up the masts setting the rigging as the deck hands worked the windlass and capstan to raise her mighty sails. There was something strangely familiar about the whole thing that filled William with a feeling of being home. He sipped his tea and glanced at the various British warships anchored about them. Even at some distance, he could make out the calls of orders shouted on their decks. It was then William noticed the launch on a course towards The Emily. It had Lieutenant Scott at the helm and the unmistakable figure of Admiral Cockburn poised with authority at the bows.

"Permission to board?" cried Scott, with enthusiasm.

Moments later he had climbed the rope ladder and was jumping down onto *The Emily*'s deck.

"Beautiful day," William responded, with reference to the clear skies. "Gives my lion time to dry out," he added, pointing to George, who was sleeping by the helm.

Cockburn then appeared at the top of the ladder and climbed over the rail. "Lord Peel," he said, as if addressing a long lost friend. "Back to Tornbridge, I see," he added, removing his hat to smooth his hair.

"And yourself, Admiral?" replied William, passing his cup and saucer to the cross-eyed stable hand at his side. "Back to the bosom of Uncle George. I am talking about your King, of course."

"All in good time," said Cockburn, with a devilish smile.

"And how is Lieutenant Scott?" enquired William. "The Ewell's painting taking pride of place in your quarters?"

"A welcome addition, indeed," said Scott, enthusiastically. "Although it's more recently painted than I had imagined. The oil is still tacky in places."

"Really?" said William, somewhat repulsed. "Well, take care not to breathe the fumes."

Cockburn stepped forward and indicated he and William should find some privacy.

"Oh," said William, with a sigh. "I do hope it's not another hair-brained scheme."

They made their way to the stern rail where Cockburn's smile slipped. "Two nights ago, a unit of Navy scouts picked up a party of what they believed to be Spanish pirates looting a farm a few miles south. Turns out they were crew from a privateer gunship anchored near Mobjack Bay. It appears they are waiting for you."

"To what end?" William enquired, casually.

"To seize *The Emily* and Lord Peel himself," replied Cockburn. "She is heavily armed with an experienced crew. A Captain Banda. He is known to us."

"What of it?" dismissed William. "This Captain Banda will soon find trouble flying at him, will he not? Yes? His crew will feel what it's like to fall from the trouble tree and hit every branch."

"My Lord," said Cockburn, with concern, "they will have the advantage. You do not have a captain."

"Have no fear, Admiral," replied William, with resolve. "A mere trifle. I was schooled in the cut and thrust of naval warfare by Uncle Horatio, remember?"

"Indeed," said Cockburn, with a gracious nod, "but perhaps your crew would feel reassured by the offer of an escort?"

"Not necessary," said William, rocking on his heels with unshakable confidence. "My crew have absolute faith in my ability to keep them alive."

"In which case your crew have my prayers," said Cockburn, smiling. The veiled insult went completely over William's head and Cockburn quickly concluded that William's mind could not be swayed. Cockburn bowed and slipped his hat on. "Britain offers her appreciation for your efforts, Lord Peel."

"Pleasant voyage, Lord Peel," said Scott, with a smile

and a bow.

As Cockburn and Scott walked back to the rope ladder, young Daniel arrived at William's side curious about their presence.

"Should we be worried, sir?" he enquired.

"They wished to thank me personally for my contribution," replied William, his back straightening. "We Peels are often called upon when the rabbit of destiny gets stuck in the warren of providence." William was enjoying a moment of his own importance when suddenly he noticed Daniel's confused expression. It was obvious he had no idea what the heck William was talking about. "The Admiral was referring to Washington," said William, quick to clarify. "Oh, yes. Let's just say my expertise was called upon in putting flint to tinder."

"Oh," replied Daniel, somewhat unconvinced. "Only we saw the flames and initially thought of Samuel, sir."

"Yes, well," replied William, deflating slightly. "I can't deny he played his small part."

"So I hear, sir," said Daniel, with a cheeky wink. "A great lover of art if ever there was one."

"Quite so," William coughed. "It's fortunate for the Mona Lisa, however, that not every lover of art shares his proclivity." An awkward moment of silence followed. "Is there anything else you need of your captain?"

"Captain?" Daniel gulped.

"Quite so! De facto. The captain is dead, ergo long live the captain," said William, slapping his chest. "What?" he questioned, sensing Daniel's resistance to the idea. "Am I not the spiritual leader? Am I not the figurehead to which lesser men turn?" William sighed, unimpressed by Daniel's frosty demeanour. "Not to mention being the blasted owner of said boat."

"Ship, sir," Daniel corrected. "A boat has oars."

"Daniel!" replied William, sternly. "Join me in the great cabin. We must find Mobjack Bay."

Daniel unrolled the Chesapeake chart across the table of the great cabin as William stood at his shoulder. It was only when the chart was fully opened and corners weighted down that they could see the problem.

"Ah," William exclaimed, puzzling over the chart. "A somewhat peculiar twist. Do you suppose this Mobjack Bay is there-ish?" he said, pointing.

"Difficult to say, as the detail of that area is obscured by a large pair of breasts, sir."

What faced them was an oil painting of Kyra, reclining, naked in a hammock and covered in fruit. Although it had been painted on the reverse side of the chart, the colours had bled through the canvas to produce a perfect image on the map side as well. William had all but forgotten he had painted it.

"A handsome woman," he noted, his mind recalling the sitting.

"So, just to be clear, sir," Daniel summarised. "We have no idea where this warship is, do we?"

William, refusing to be beaten, studied the chart closely. "Not necessarily, young Daniel. We are both experienced men of the sea, are we not? We merely have to study what we can of the identifiable topography and select the most obvious place for ambush. Ah!" he cried, spotting a likely place. "See there, that cove?"

"That's not a cove, sir," said Daniel, blushing.

"It's not?" asked William, studying it closer.

"No, sir," replied Daniel.

"Then wha..." William stopped himself mid sentence as the reality dawned. "Ah, I see," he said, with a cough. "Yes, I rather enjoyed painting that bit. Although I don't recall it trimmed."

The Battle of Kyra's Cove

*T*he *Pride of Emily* cut through the sparkling water of the Patuxent and the ripples of her wash vanished into the undergrowth of its western shore. A field of purple heather swirled and danced to the rhythm of the gentle breeze. Crows argued in the high branches of a nearby tree. It was another blisteringly hot morning and *The Emily*'s crew were busy adjusting the sails and scrubbing the deck.

Whether the American ships had all been sunk or scuppered, like Barney's flotilla, William didn't know but as he gazed out of the stern windows of the great cabin, he couldn't see a single craft across the ten mile wide river.

William had an early breakfast. He expected an ambush from the mysterious ship at any moment and he didn't want to face it on an empty stomach. He was just enjoying a lovely spread of marmalade on toast when Daniel appeared urgently at the doorway clutching his spyglass.

"She's on us, sir!" he cried, pointing out the stern window. "She sprang from nowhere."

William followed Daniel's gaze out of the cabin window to see a large warship hot in pursuit. A blast of fire suddenly sprang from the ship's deck and moments later a cannon ball exploded in the water only forty yards from *The Emily's* stern. A huge plume of water lashed against the windows and a shockwave rattled the oak beneath their feet. George woke with a start as he slid a foot across the timbers.

"Bastard!" exclaimed William, as his breakfast dropped off the table.

"Oh, this isn't good, sir," said Daniel, rushing to the window. "They're using explosive charges!"

"What of a reprisal?" asked William, beckoning the stable hands to fetch his boots. "Well, man?"

"We have no stern cannon, sir," replied Daniel.

"This is no time to lose dexterity!" growled William, clipping the nearest stable hand around the ear for dawdling with his boot buttons.

Daniel was lost for ideas when suddenly a familiar voice came from the doorway. "It's a warning shot," said Carr, limping in using his trusty musket for support. "We risk being sunk if they think we're getting away."

He was naked from the waist up except for the clean dressings around his stomach. "They mean to disable us and to board us." He placed his musket down on the table and took Daniel's spyglass. Leaning back against the table, he sighted in the ship.

"Bowman has one last card to play it seems," said Carr, handing William the spyglass so he could take a look for himself.

"Tilly!" exclaimed William, as he spied him on the deck of the pursuing ship. "Why of all the ungrateful... I spared his smelly life!"

"That's twice he's pursued us," said Carr, taking back the spyglass and sliding it shut. "There won't be a third."

Suddenly, muzzle flare flashed again on the deck of Tilly's ship. Everyone watched as a trail of smoke blazed across the sky towards *The Emily* and exploded in the water only yards away from her starboard side. The violent impact shattered the windows of the great cabin and knocked everyone off their feet. Being closest to the window, Carr took the full force of the blast and was thrown back, hard against the oak panels.

Daniel was lucky enough to be able to dive for cover beneath the table. Flame and spray engulfed the cabin in seconds and the ship pitched violently to port. The oak floor boards of the cabin were covered with water that crashed against the port side then receded as *The Emily* righted herself. Although William was knocked over by the explosion, the impact was lessened by him landing on the fat stable hand. Carr staggered to his feet, dazed, wiping the blood from a deep cut on his forehead. George shook the water from his mane and growled loudly as William was helped to his feet by the stable hands. Above the ringing in all their ears, they could hear the topside cries of "Man overboard!" and the clatter of the alarm bell.

"We should turn!" shouted Daniel, as he picked himself up. "Open up a volley."

"As the ships passed each other we would only have time for a single exchange," Carr replied, supporting himself with the table. "And such a manoeuvre would put them between us and the Atlantic." He clutched his side in pain and took a moment to compose. It was then he noticed his trusty musket broken on the floor. The stock was smashed open revealing the intricate mechanism inside. Suddenly, his eyes flashed with an idea. "We use the sea brake!" he said, with conviction. "It's time we introduced Tilly to the self-repeating cannon."

Daniel stepped forward with concern. "We can't use the sea brake with the cannon balls loaded on the rails. The shock twists them. Charles was adamant about that."

"Then we unload the rails," replied Carr, limping to the doorway. "When that's done give the order to brace."

"But with the rails empty we would be unable to return fire," said Daniel, far from happy. "We'll take a hell of a pounding until the mechanism is primed." He paused, hopeful Carr would change his mind. "Volker wouldn't let his lady come to harm like this."

There was a moment between them. A pause to reflect on the loss of an old friend and a genius captain.

"He's not here, Daniel," said Carr, with sympathy. "It's up to us now." Carr was gone without another word.

"Sea brake?" asked William, catching Daniel before he too vanished out the door.

"One of your father's crazier ideas, sir," Daniel replied. "I suggest you quickly pack all that's breakable. May I also suggest you tie down your lion. Things are about to get exciting."

Tilly's sun-cracked lips broke into a smile and revealed the rotten teeth behind. He was standing at the bow rail with his spyglass fixed firmly on *The Emily*. He chuckled at the extent of damage to the stern.

"Just perfect!" he said, turning to the figure standing behind him. "A direct hit on his ladyship's wardrobe."

Captain Banda was a large, black man with a pitted face and a chest full of scars. His hair was platted with coloured cotton and a huge scimitar hung from his leather belt. Going by the chunks out of the blade edge, he had seen his share of trouble.

"What about Volker?" he said, folding his big arms. "Even at death's door, he'll have some tricks."

"Don't you worry none," said Tilly, weaselling forward. "He will have no time for tricks. He'll expect a boarding party not for us to open fire once we're along side."

"We had a deal!" said Banda, squaring up to him. "Bowman said her gold was mine. It's no good to me at the bottom of the river."

"Very true," said Tilly, recoiling. "But then…" he added, treachery oozing from his every word. "We don't even know if Bowman is alive." He waited to gauge if the captain was open to such talk. He seemingly was. "The true value of that ship be in one man. I says we change the plan."

As the stable hands were packing his precious clothes, William crossed the aft companionway singing a pleasing little ditty as he went. Much to his astonishment, he opened the door to the lower deck to discover the entire crew harnessed to the hull timbers. All eyes fell on him with great surprise, initially, then fear at the implication. What William didn't know, and they did, was that if William wasn't secured, his podgy body would likely do a lot of damage to the crew and the ship the instant the sea brake was engaged.

"Brace, sir!" came repeated cries.

William, somewhat confused by being addressed in a loud voice by common seamen, left to head up onto the deck. Still humming his little tune, he arrived topside to find the place deserted. After a moment of glancing around the masts and the launch, he eventually found Carr. He was strapped into a harness at the helm with his hand poised on one of the large levers that protruded through the deck. A lever which was already in its engaged position.

"What the hell!" cried Carr, as he looked up. "I gave the order to brace."

"Daniel said pack. I do wish you would make up your damn minds. Anyway," said William, lacking any sense of urgency. "I don't suppose you've seen my hair brush?"

"It's too late," said Carr, fighting against the lever, "RUN!" he shouted, his face filled with urgency. "Run for the bow and jump. NOW! Run for your very life!" he shouted again.

Looking over the stern rail, William could see the canvas of the sea brake drifting out under the water, ready to engage. It was the equivalent of the modern parachute except it was designed to suddenly catch water rather than air. It was only when William glanced once more at Carr's harness did the penny finally drop.

"Oh, sparkling!" he shouted, as he took to his heels towards the bows. Sensing that time was very soon to run out, he leapt with all the strength he had in his Peel legs.

At that instant, *The Emily* vanished below him and was replaced with a massive wall of angry water that hit him so fast it knocked him spinning. He plunged, head first, into the foaming river with no clue about which was up or down. After kicking and clawing against the blackness, his head finally broke the surface and he gasped in all the air his lungs could hold. He had just managed to get his bearings when he was hit by a high wave.

The Emily had stopped dead in the water a good hundred yards behind him. The force of the sea brake had almost upended her and her stern was still settling when William finally cleared the hair from his face. He could hear the groans from her timbers and the screams of pain from the men below her decks. Captain Banda's ship had suddenly found herself thirty yards away from *The Emily*'s stern and closing fast.

A powerful volley suddenly exploded from its cannon that pummelled *The Emily*. William swam back with all the speed he could muster as he saw *The Emily*'s rails and rigging shatter into splintering pieces before his eyes. It was so destructive, so violent, he could feel each impact shudder through the water. By the time he had reached her, the firing had ceased and the gun-ports of Captain Banda's ship were slamming closed. He could hear Banda barking orders at the powder monkeys, the young boys ferrying the charges to each of the cannon. William knew he didn't have long. An experienced crew could easily reload and be ready to fire in a matter of minutes. Using some rigging that was trailing over the side of *The Emily*, William managed to climb his sodden frame up onto her deck. He was immediately met with a barrage of musket fire from Banda's crew. Tilly himself sighted in a shot that ricocheted off the fore mast only inches from William's head. Diving to the deck for cover, William took shelter behind *Little Fanny*. He cursed the blaggard, Tilly. Ahead he could see Carr, he was still in his harness but looked in a bad way. The shock of the sea brake had opened his wound and the deck about him swilled with blood and water. He was barely conscious and his hand was hardly gripping the lever to engage the automatic guns.

Taking care to avoid the musket shot still peppering the deck about him, William peered down through the main hatch to see the crew passing cannon balls from man to man and loading *The Emily*'s automatic cannon rails as quick as they could.

"Daniel!" cried William, as he ducked to avoid a shot. "Are we set?"

"Wait!" came a reply, urging for patience.

"Daniel!" William snapped, as he saw Carr slump over in his harness and his hand slip from the lever. "We're out of time!" William was about to update Daniel on the turn of events when he spotted Samuel through the hatch; he was laden with powder charges. "What!" William shouted, doubting his eyes. "Samuel? Get your flammable backside away from those explosives. Samuel! Samuel!"

"He's fine, sir," replied Daniel, coming into view briefly. "We need all hands."

"Oh, my buttered crumpets!" William exclaimed, glancing back at Banda's ship as the gun-ports flipped open and the cannon suddenly appeared.

"This is my last word!" shouted Tilly, watching for William to show himself. "I promise safe passage to your crew," he added, cocking his musket. "No tricks."

"No tricks!" William shouted back, surprised by his effrontery. "Go brand yourself, you horse's cock!"

There was no time left, William knew it. In a matter of moments, Banda's gun crew would open fire with another wave that would surely finish them. In that instant, William found the Peel strength once more in his legs and sprinted towards the helm. Tilly and his crew let loose with a volley of shots that clipped everything but their target. William, sensing that his luck was about to end, dived and slid along the wet deck the rest of the way. He crashed, shoulder first, into the wheel and then scrambled for the lever. He clasped the gun trigger-release lever with both hands and drew it backwards until it clunked.

A moment passed. It had entered William's head, just for a moment, that there was some problem. He began cursing Samuel's backside, Samuel's massive privates, and his general ass-brained gormlessness, when suddenly cannon fire began shooting from *The Emily*'s side. He slumped back with relief as shot by shot the quarry was pounded with cannon after cannon. Banda's heavy windlass exploded into pulp, so too the helm, the foremast, the main mast, the aft mast. Tilly was hit square in the chest and vanished into vapour. It was relentless as one by one the ship's masts toppled as her crew jumped clear of the falling jibs. The upper deck of Banda's ship was literally disintegrating before William's very eyes.

After a few minutes of continuous fire the ship drifted past out of range and William pushed the lever forward again to cease the cannon mechanism. *The Emily* had taken a pounding but her masts were intact and so too her helm. Banda's ship was little more than splinters from the lower deck up. Her masts were floating on the water with the sails attached and her rigging was trailing behind in the water like a twisted spider's web. Smoke poured from every hole and crack. Suddenly, Banda's gunners came running out of the hatches coughing up their lungs. In less than a minute they all dived over the side and were swimming for the shore.

William turned to see Carr convulsing as he desperately tried to clutch the open wound on his side. Blood was pouring out of him and his eyes turned to William for help. William, conscious that the blood looked horribly messy, appeared initially hesitant and scanned the deck for anyone else that could help. There was no one. Carr's eyes eventually faded and his hand slipped from his wound.

For the second time in this adventure, Carr was dying.

With a sudden gasp of pain, Carr opened his eyes to find William pressing hard on his wound to stop the bleeding.

"This will never come out," said William, indicating to Carr's blood on his sleeves and britches.

"Take it out of my wages," Carr gasped, managing a smile despite the agony.

Barker rushed to them with his trusty medical bag and indicated that William should move aside. As William stood and inspected his ruined clothes, Daniel appeared at his elbow.

"You're going to want to see this, sir," he said, with an expression that conveyed a mixture of mystery, excitement and urgency.

The hold of Banda's ship was undamaged by the cannon fire. It was filled with terrified, malnourished slaves whose eyes blinked up at William and Daniel through what was left of the twisted iron deck hatch. They had been kept in even more cramped conditions than Jennings would have accepted. William covered his mouth and nose with revulsion as he peered down inside. The stench was too much for any creature to stand, perhaps, save for the flies that had settled on their cheeks.

"There's treasure too, sir," said Daniel, "more than I've ever seen."

Banda's ship was towed to shore and the crew of *The Emily* began unloading anything of value. All usable supplies were carried across a gangway and stowed in *The Emily*'s store. Enough rum to keep the crew happy and even a few choice wines from Bowman's cabin.

William was on the quarterdeck watching the fetching

and carrying from the comfort of a recliner with George sitting by his side. He was dressed in his finest jacket and ice-white britches. The stable hands prepared lunch on a table behind him. Barker had given William a cursory examination and concluded that William had retained all of his Peel parts.

"Less than half the slaves made it," noted Barker solemnly, "the rest are lucky. For now." At that moment, Daniel appeared for news of Carr. "He'll live," replied Barker, "thanks to Lord Peel's quick action." He suddenly remembered something and a smile found its way into his usually austere expression. "Southgate's hand is crushed," Barker advised William. "His cooking days are finally over."

"God has shown some mercy here today," replied William, somewhat forlorn. "Exactly how many of the slaves died, did you say?" he asked, gazing across at the other ship.

"A hundred and forty-seven on the voyage itself," replied Barker.

"Free the rest," replied William, casually.

Barker stood back, speechless. He had expected anything but that. His joy was like a wave rushing over him. He dropped his medical bag and had to stop himself from hugging William there and then. Instead, he thanked him repeatedly whilst clasping his hands in prayer and praising the events of this day.

As Barker hurried off to release the slaves, Daniel stood a moment watching William. Very few people have ever expressed warmth for a Peel but in that instant, Daniel believed he glimpsed a sliver that was decent in William after all.

"Is that it?" asked William, catching sight of him out of the corner of his eye.

"Aye, skipper."

It was then William saw Samuel. His gormless face was black from powder and his tunic stained with the blood from his wound. He was standing by the windlass, fidgeting, as he in turn watched William.

"He thinks you're upset with him, sir," said Daniel, spotting Samuel's eyes on William. "Because you shouted at him through the hatch."

"Tell me, Daniel," William asked, standing. "Did he ever save my father's life?"

"More than once, sir," said Daniel, with a smile.

William turned and gripped the rail with a sigh. He could feel Samuel's pathetic gaze still on him. He knew in that instance why his father had been so keen to employ him at Peel Manor. Why he had been so keen to keep him close. It was to help the pea-brained idiot out where he could. Even if the only job he could give him meant him shovelling dung. Samuel didn't care, of course, it wasn't as if he bothered with a shovel anyway.

"See to it he receives fresh clothes and dressings for his wound," said William. "Get what you need from Barker. I doubt the good doctor will object considering his present elation."

Daniel tugged his forelock and headed off with purpose.

William and George watched as the filthy, naked slaves abandoned Banda's ship as if it were on fire. They whooped and screamed as they leapt over the side and splashed into the river. Barker beamed with pride from the gangway as he helped some of the children disembark. The older men were already quickly scrambling up the banking. Their sodden loincloths hung off them as their hands grasped at the long grass and their feet pushed against mud.

"What to make of it all?" asked William, as George licked his hand. "Mother wouldn't approve." William smiled at the thought of her displeasure. He was very much looking forward to arriving home with Bowman's treasure. If for no other reason than to see the look on her face.

Within a matter of minutes, the slaves had dispersed into the distance. They presumably feared that William would change his mind. That never happened, of course, and for a few days at least they had their freedom. That was until Cockburn's scouts picked them up and 'enlisted' them in the fateful attack on Baltimore.

Captain Volker was buried at sea on September 1st 1814 with all the honours the crew could bestow. As for John Carr, he survived his injuries and retired on their return to Dover. Daniel was given his own ship to command and Barker set up a small medical practice in London with his young wife.

Major Ross was killed in action on September 12th 1814

during the siege of Baltimore.

Rear Admiral Cockburn became Admiral of the Fleet and lived to the ripe old age of eighty-one. True to his word, he ensured page one of the Treaty of Fontainebleau was replaced with a version that did not mention the Peel loan to Napoleon.

The second 'war of impudence' eventually came to an end in the summer of 1815 with President Madison having achieved nothing of his original objectives. It did, however, bring a wave of confidence throughout America. The so called 'era of good feelings' brought fundamental changes such as an end to the insistence that militia be the means to protect republican liberty. It also saw the country re-establish its national bank.

At the end of the war, the British promised to hand back all slaves that had been taken during the conflict and transported off to her territories. Despite the promise, and despite the slave trade being outlawed almost a decade earlier, the slaves were never returned. Instead, the two countries agreed on a sale price.

Commodore Joshua Barney survived Carr's shot but the bullet was so deep it could never be removed. He eventually died due to complications associated with the wound on December 10th 1818.

William's suggestion to President Madison that the song 'To

Anacreon in Heaven' would rouse people's spirits wasn't to fall completely on deaf ears. Francis Scott Key would later use the song as an accompaniment to his poem about the war, 'Defence of Fort McHenry', which later became known as The Star Spangled Banner and was adopted as the national anthem.

As for Napoleon Bonaparte, well, in the spring of 1815, he secured additional funds from the Peel coffers and used it to escape Elba and raise an army. His invasion of Britain was back on the cards and he promised to hand most of the country over to William as soon as the musket smoke had dispersed. Mother was opposed to the deal, of course. William, however, was so supremely confident of success that he decided to forgo the usual paperwork and percentage.

"You have little faith, Mother," William told her, on June 17th 1815. "Uncle Boney's in The Netherlands at a little place called Waterloo. I think you and Uncle Wellington will soon be feeling pretty sick after eating those extra portions of humble pie."

The End

Great care has been taken to ensure this novel is both factually accurate and without errors. We accept, however, that we're only human. If you think you have spotted something please drop us a line.

We would love to hear what you thought of

The Washington Adventure.

Please email any comments or questions.

info@clickimagination.com

For more Peel buffoonery, please visit

www.tornbridge.co.uk

Author's Note

Britain was responsible for over half of the world's Atlantic slavery traffic. According to slaverysite.com that traffic equated to 12,000 voyages transporting 2.6 million slaves. The 1790 US census reported a population of almost 4 million of which 18% (700,000) were slaves. In 1807 the British Slave Trade Act *supposedly* abolished the slave trade throughout the British Empire. America too, on paper at least, followed suit in 1808. By 1860 the US population had grown to 31.5 million of which almost 13% (4 million) were registered slaves. It would be a decade later before the slaves were eventually freed. Their suffering should never be forgotten. For more information about slavery and the War of 1812, the following titles are recommended reading:

Encyclopaedia of the War of 1812 edited by Heidler & Heidler, ISBN 1-59114-362-4

American Slavery 1619 - 1877 by Peter Kolchin, ISBN 0-8090-2568-X

A Short History of Slavery by James Walvin, ISBN 978-0-141-02798-2

The Scorching of Washington by Alan Lloyd

Napoleon on Elba by Sir Neil Campbell, ISBN 1-905043-00-7

The Dawn's Early Light by Walter Loyd

The Reign of George III, 1760 to 1815 by Steven Watson.

Acknowledgments

A huge and very special thanks to my family for their patience and support. Thanks to Cathie Bardell, The Tornbridge Museum, The Royal Naval Museum, Wikipedia and Google. Big thanks to Jack Treby, Pauline Scatterty, Heidi Etherington and Karen Naylor for their keen eyes and Jason Hewitt for support. Special thanks to all my fellow writers and readers on Harper Collins Authonomy, especially RJ Aitch, Lauren Grey, and Joe Kovacs.

Made in the USA
Charleston, SC
31 December 2015